Kidnapped Hope

Kidnapped Hope

Robin Newmann

iUniverse, Inc.

New York Lincoln Shanghai

Kidnapped Hope

iUniverse books may be ordered through booksellers or by contacting:

iUniverse
2021 Pine Lake Road, Suite 100
Lincoln, NE 68512
www.iuniverse.com
1-800-Authors (1-800-288-4677)

This is a work of fiction. All of the characters, names, incidents, organizations and dialogue in this novel are either the products of the author's imagination or are used fictitiously.

ISBN-13: 978-0-595-39277-3 (pbk)
ISBN-13: 978-0-595-67686-6 (cloth)
ISBN-13: 978-0-595-83672-7 (ebk)
ISBN-10: 0-595-39277-6 (pbk)
ISBN-10: 0-595-67686-3 (cloth)
ISBN-10: 0-595-83672-0 (ebk)

Printed in the United States of America

For

Brenda, my wife, whose devotion saw me through this project,

Adeline and Dominic, my children, who have always loved my storytelling,

and

Renée and Denys, my parents, who have always believed in me.

And if I had no other way,
I'd walk or crawl or run.
I'd search to the very ends of the earth,
For you my precious one.

—*I Promise I'll Find You*, Heather Patricia Ward

Acknowledgments

My sincere thanks to Glenn Cruz, Frank J. Patchett, and Dick Stevens for sharing their insight and technical knowledge with me; to Astrid Anderson, Peter Blattler, and Alex Zollinger for their help with the Swiss-German phrases; to Anne Roulet-Newmann for providing literary critique; and to members of my extended family for their encouragement and support.

Prologue

▼

July
Southern California

Her five-year-old body shuddered. Like a ripple in a pond, the quiver ran up her slender bare arm to her mother's hand.

"Ooh, Nicolette, a chill on a day like this?" Martine Zucker teased, looking down at her daughter as they walked through what felt like an oven. The air shimmered around them, and the tall date palms lining the walkway to the Snapdragon amusement park provided little respite from the fierce midsummer sun.

Nicolette drew toward her mother. But she also kept looking askance at something. Martine followed her gaze and saw a swarthy man in his thirties seated on a red bench, examining a map of the park. He smiled politely as their eyes met, but Martine felt her daughter's grip tighten. Nicolette suddenly spun around and buried her head in her mother's tan shorts.

"Hey, what's wrong, my little flower?" Martine's voice was warm and soothing. She caressed Nicolette's golden hair, neatly tied in the pink bows that had taken so long to perfect back at the hotel.

Motherhood had taught Martine that the most innocent of things easily frightened children at this age. Perhaps it was the man's pockmarked face? More likely the unfamiliarity of the area. It was the first time the family had vacationed outside Europe. And Martine mused that Nicolette and her brother must be finding Southern California's vast open spaces and dry golden-brown landscape quite different from their verdant, mountainous Switzerland.

They needed a moment's break from the frenzied excitement of a first trip to an amusement park. Martine called out to Peter, her husband, to stop for a moment. He constrained eight-year-old Mark, who kept pulling his father toward the park entrance like a dog on a leash.

"Oh, *Papi*, come on…" he urged, "they'll catch up with us!"

Martine drew Nicolette over to one of the well-tended flowerbeds and plucked a snapdragon stem laden with peach-colored flowers. There were snapdragons all over the place—the park was aptly named, she thought—and this one matched her daughter's sundress.

The girl's eyes softened as she clutched the stem. Martine crouched down and with two fingers lightly pinched the sides of a flower lobe, making it snap open into a pair of tiny jaws. Nicolette's eyes opened wide as she laughed in amazement. The flower became the child's sole preoccupation, and Martine was pleased. They moved on, quickly joining Peter and a restless Mark.

"Everything okay?" Peter asked.

"Yes, I think so…Something scared her, that's all. Why don't you help her get over it with your vacation cheerleading?"

"Sure thing!"

Martine stepped back to watch her husband work his magic on the children.

"One, two, three…Snapdragon! Snapdragon! Snap…drag…onnne…" he sang. Mark and Nicolette immediately picked up on the chant and were soon singing and stepping in rhythm on the hot pavement as they proceeded to the ticket booths.

Martine exchanged contented smiles with Peter. Their children were happy again. Peter was so good with them. She reminded herself how fortunate she was to have such a loving husband. *Life is great,* she thought.

"Was für a platz das isch…" As they chatted while waiting to enter, Martine noticed people glancing curiously at them—no doubt because they were speaking Schweizerdeutsch. It was only spoken in the Germanic cantons of Switzerland, and unless the Zuckers encountered another Swiss-German family, they would pass through the crowds without anyone understanding a word they were saying. Mark and Nicolette soon realized their advantage and made rude remarks about a couple of overweight tourists in gaudy clothes. Martine quickly rebuked them.

"Even though others don't understand us, you must always act as if they do—otherwise it's impolite, and your father and I won't be proud of you." Then, as an afterthought, Martine added, "And remember to stick close to us, especially to *Papi*, since he's the only one who speaks English. And don't wander off…"

"But if you do happen to get separated," their father broke in, "find someone in a red park uniform, like that woman over there," he said pointing, "and say *'Lost-lost-lost!'* and tell them your names. They'll help you find us."

Mark and Nicolette nodded obediently, mouthing the word *"lost."* Then they impatiently gestured to their parents to move on in line.

"What more can we do?" Martine said to her husband.

"Nothing—they'll be fine," Peter reassured her.

After nearly being jammed in the turnstile in their rush to get in, the children ran for the first ride in sight—the *Snapping Dragons*. Martine smiled after Peter translated the name for her. They followed the children in their frenzied dash to jump into one of the wildly painted suspended dragons, ready to be lifted into the air and tossed left and right.

Back on the ground, the children staggered dizzily and laughed. Then their eyes grew wide at the sight of the brightly colored cotton candy and the must-have metallic balloons glinting like beacons in the sun.

"That'll be for later," Martine told the children, reading their minds.

For three hours the family went from attraction to attraction, clambering into spaceships, roller coasters, rafts, or whatever else was the vehicle for the next exhilarating ride. Then, all of a sudden, elation faded into fatigue. *"Mammi, ech möcht öppis trinke..."* whined thirsty Nicolette.

Peter spotted an outdoor café. "Mark! Nicolette! A cool drink!" He led them to a table in the shade of a jacaranda tree.

"Now, children," Martine said, "sit quietly while *Papi* and I bring you something refreshing." She started toward the food counter, then stopped to look back and smile. How beautiful her children were, framed by the jacaranda's clustered lavender-blue flowers.

It took less than five minutes to buy hot dogs and ice-cold sodas and return. But when they did, laden cardboard trays in hand, all that remained at the table was Mark's crimson-and-black backpack.

The children were gone.

Part I

▼

To hell...

Chapter 1

▼

January
Trélex, Switzerland

The man was already screaming before the car hit him. In fact, he had been screaming from the time he ran out of his house.

Afternoon walkers along the wooded *route de St. Cergue* had stepped back to let the gesticulating runner go by, afraid of what this madman might do.

An elderly woman saw the spectacle from her living room window and called the police. "It's a *wild* man—running and yelling! He's obviously extremely dangerous—he's swinging his arms wildly, with clenched fists...and you should see the look on his face, it's—"

"Yes, but where exactly is he right now?" the officer on emergency-call duty asked in exasperation.

"Near my house—on the road near the new housing development! This is a respectable area," the woman went on. "A lot of children live in those new houses, you know, and—"

"Thank you, Madam," the officer cut in, as soon as he had the woman's location on his GPS screen. "Someone's on the way."

Unaware of what was happening lower down, Gerard Roulet drove his Alfa Romeo down the mountain road after a satisfying morning of skiing. The slushy surface didn't keep him from gunning the engine of his prized Alfa. Exhilarated by the exercise and fresh air, he was singing at the top of his lungs. He took a hairpin curve a little too fast—the Alfa's superb handling would save him from any misfortune. But he hadn't counted on this. He blasted the horn, swerved to the left and shouted obscenities at the oncoming runner, but to no avail. The man seemed intent on crashing into his moving car—and he succeeded.

The intensity of the dull thud surprised Gerard, but he quickly regained control and pulled up a few yards down the road. It wasn't just a bump; he had *hit* the man and sent the body rolling on the road behind him. Gerard nervously bit on his thumbnail as he sat in the car and looked around.

On the wooded section of the road and with no one else around, he thought fleetingly of driving on—making a getaway! He shook his head and took a deep breath. He must not *do* that! He glanced in the rearview mirror; the body was still there!

"God! What am I thinking?" he said aloud. He threw open the door and ran to the body. "God, let him be alive!" Bending over the man, Gerard panicked; they were in the middle of the road on a blind curve. "But if I move him," Gerard was sobbing now, "I'll kill him!" He fumbled with his cell phone, punching in the local emergency number. No service. "What the hell am I going to do?" he cried out.

The unexpected screeching of tires made him jump. But the sight of the white Opel police car pulling up near him brought such relief that he sobbed uncontrollably.

The two policemen in their red-trimmed, gray uniforms jumped out and waved frantically at the ambulance that had been following them.

Only after the ambulance had pulled away with the dazed runner inside was Gerard calm enough to give his account of the accident. "I don't understand…I really don't. I've got a clean record…He—he just collided with the car—I know you won't believe me but it was just as if he threw himself against it. I tried to avoid him…it was a blind corner…he ran out of nowhere and—"

"Calm down, sir," said the policeman taking notes. "We get the picture. I think we understand what happened."

Gerard was amazed; the policemen appeared to *believe* him; that the man had crashed into the car, and that Gerard had *not* run him down.

"Will you be okay to continue your drive?" one of the officers asked.

"I think so." Gerard still felt bewildered as he made his way back to the Alfa.

Once he had left, the two policemen exchanged glances. "The injured man's poor Peter Zucker, isn't it—the one who lost his kids on vacation in the States last summer?"

"Yup," the other agreed. "I think he was trying to kill himself."

"Looks like it. Whoever kidnapped Zucker's kids kidnapped his hope as well."

Chapter 2

▼

Peter Zucker drove into the parking lot of the Belvoir psychiatric clinic on the south shore of Lake Geneva and hesitated between two empty spaces. It was not indecision that made him pause, but his lack of courage to go on.

It had been less than a week since his run-in with the Alfa Romeo. "You're a lucky man—nothing's broken," they'd told him in the emergency room, and joked that he should stop running into moving vehicles. *It wasn't luck,* Peter thought bitterly. *I failed at suicide as I've failed at everything else.*

Peter stared emptily through the windshield out toward the snow-covered grounds. He barely noticed the ice-peppered horse chestnut trees or the crows picking at the few exposed grassy patches. His mind was drifting back to the ruinous events that had turned his life completely upside down. And the life of his wife...

He winced as he recalled the sickening dread that overcame him and Martine as they realized that their children hadn't simply gone astray in the crowded amusement park, but had been abducted. God! Their frenzied search of every possible corner of Snapdragon still made him sweat. Half demented, they had torn through the restrooms, the rides, the shops, the wooded gardens. They had run into the vast parking lot in the hope that Mark and Nicolette had somehow found their way back to the rental car. When this proved fruitless, they had run to the office for lost children near the park's entrance. Peter had stood outside scanning the exiting crowd for the bright little faces he knew so well, while inside Martine paced back and forth in front of a bank of security monitors, scouring the black-and-white images coming from all over the park. But it was all to no avail. Hours passed, and Mark and Nicolette were nowhere to be seen.

The police came and took a statement. The two patrolmen scolded park security for waiting so long before reporting the children missing.

"I know," a park security official said evasively, "but we're under orders to wait until closing—it's bad for business to have a squad car race in with blazing lights and wailing siren…"

Other squad cars soon arrived, and the police organized a methodical sweep of the park's now empty grounds. Peter described what Mark and Nicolette had been wearing and gave the police his wallet photograph of them. The photograph was about a year old and a little crumpled, but it showed their faces clearly. Then the squad cars left to check the surrounding area and question people who lived in the vicinity. When night fell, the returning patrolmen all discreetly shook their heads. One, who had assumed the job of intermediary with the despondent Zuckers, paused for a moment and took a deep breath. He assumed as kind and understanding a countenance as he could before striding over to where Peter and Martine sat.

"No need to worry—we've had cases like this before," he said more confidently than he felt. "Kids climb into something and get locked in by accident—it's happenin' all the time. We're checkin' but, as you can see, it's a big place, and it'll take time. Yeah, time…they'll turn up for sure," he tried to sound convincing. "Best you get along to your hotel and rest up. In any case, if they've gone somewhere and decide to come back, that's where they'll be lookin' to find you."

"But they won't have gone anywhere," Peter retorted. "We're *miles* from our hotel! They're only five and eight years old! We don't come from around here—there's no reason for them to go anywhere." He looked gaunt and afraid. "And if someone has taken them…?"

The patrolman hesitated. It was a question parents ask, but to frighten them with what his gut told him had likely happened…? Yet, he couldn't deny the possibility. He muted the radio on his equipment belt to stop the distracting chatter and dropped into the vacant chair beside them. He turned to face Peter directly.

"I'll level with you," he said. "We've had a few cases like this, you know, people takin' a likin' to a kid and givin' him or her a good time for a day. It's often people with no kids—they do it on the spur of the moment. Later they…um…realize their mistake and usually—most times—let the kids go. Everythin' turns out great in those cases—and there's no reason why it shouldn't here."

The blood visibly drained from Peter's face as he translated for Martine. She started weeping again.

"We have to remain upbeat," the patrolman said, getting back to his feet. "Now, it's best that you go and get some rest. I'm sure there'll be news by mornin'. Here, Officer Scott'll accompany you back to your hotel."

The next morning, the police came to their room and told Peter and Martine that the children still hadn't been found. An Amber Alert flashed on electronic road signs throughout California had produced nothing save a few crank calls and false sightings. The police had no leads. "Factual Missing" was how they termed it, which Peter felt was a bureaucratic and passionless explanation. It didn't bode well. A doctor put Martine under sedation.

Whenever Martine awoke after that, her first hazy words were: "Niki...Marky...my children...you've found my children?"

When the answer wasn't immediately "yes," she would break into interminable sobs. In the end, Martine sank into hopeless torpor, and Peter took her home to Switzerland.

The impatient sound of a horn put an end to Peter's reverie. Another car swung awkwardly around his to squeeze past, and Peter pulled into the first available spot. As he opened the car door, the *Bise*, the biting north wind that was part and parcel of winter in Geneva, swept through the exposed parking lot and smacked him squarely in the face. It brought Peter back to reality, as did the jab of pain from his bruised rib cage as he brushed against the steering wheel.

He gingerly eased himself out of the driver's seat and stood up into the full force of the weather. "God! The wind!" he exclaimed, turning up his coat collar.

Peter walked head down to the entrance of the clinic and through the glass doors into the reception area. It was too warm inside and the contrast stifled him. He hated this place. The subdued colors, the hushed sounds, the overly pleasant staff...it all made him want to scream at the top of his lungs and shatter this deceptive vision of calm.

The receptionist wasn't there, but that didn't matter. Peter was afraid of these visits and any delay, even for a few minutes, was welcome.

A mirror hung there in its gilded frame. Peter caught a glimpse of himself. O Lord! How far he had fallen! Pitiful, slightly hunched, like a war refugee, so unlike his former confident self. And he was only 32.

Peter unbuttoned the green loden coat that hung on him a size too big—he was thinner now than in the summer. He straightened out his wrinkled shirt, open at the collar, and tried to tuck it more neatly into his faded denim jeans. He nervously ran a hand through his wiry brown hair, now prematurely graying. He checked his reflection again—it was impossible to hide how dispirited he felt.

"Ah! Bonjour, Monsieur Zucker," a feminine voice said, breaking the silence. A smiling nurse clad in white was coming down the hall. Her cheerfulness was an act, Peter knew, to prepare visitors for the worst. He often wondered why the clinic's staff didn't just do the opposite and look grim; so that all patients, whatever their state of mental health, would appear in fine fettle in comparison.

"She's doing well," the nurse said as they walked down the corridor. Peter felt a spark of hope. "And, if you have time, Doctor Dubois needs to talk to you after the visit."

The nurse punched in a combination to unlock the double doors into the ward. The smell of antiseptic hung in the air. They proceeded down a corridor that Peter found far too wide. It was lined with white-painted metal doors, each with a round observation window. The light from these cast eerie beams that reflected off the polished floor.

They stopped in front of Room 217. Occasional cries and moans from other rooms punctured the stark quiet as the nurse slipped a key into the lock. Peter swallowed.

"She's a bit tired today," the nurse advised him. "Perhaps you should keep it to about ten minutes. And remember, steer clear of talking about the children."

Peter stepped in, and the door closed behind him. There, sitting in a chair by the picture window at the far end of the room, was Martine, dressed in a white hospital gown. She had her back to Peter, and he couldn't tell if she was staring at the blank wall or watching the mind-numbing video feed playing on the TV screen that was sunk into the corner behind safety glass. He glanced around, searching the Spartan room and the neatly made bed for inspiration.

"Hello, Martine," he said, finally approaching her. The warmth in his voice was genuine; he loved this woman profoundly. But it hid the deep sorrow that made his body tremble when he was in her presence. "How are you feeling today?"

It seemed the stupidest thing to say. But what else was there? Peter was not a doctor. He hadn't studied psychiatry. He had never been taught how to deal with a situation like this. *What a cruel joke,* he thought. *Peter Zucker, the great air traffic controller, who can help land a troubled 747 with 500 passengers on board but can't bring his dear wife back to earth and accept the reality that they have lost their children forever...*

He gently placed his hand on her shoulder and stifled a gasp. She had always been slim, but he could feel her bones now. Her hair, still the same golden color as the children's, was now straight and uncared for. At his touch, she looked up, obviously not having heard his greeting.

"Peter…Peter…*besch du's*…is it you?" Martine's voice was frail.

"*Ja*, it's me." Peter smiled down at her. The dark circles under her eyes and the droop of her jaw could not hide the youthful beauty of the face that Peter knew so well. He had cherished the hope that she might come home soon and help him pick up the pieces of their shattered life. But looking at her now, it was clear that the months of psychotherapy had done nothing to heal her wounds.

"Um—I've come to have a chat and tell you how things are going at ho—at work…" *I mustn't make her think of home or family.* His throat ached to say something positive. "Do you know, they said I might be allowed to handle landings again soon…the first time since—"

He cut himself off—everything always led back to the tragedy. The guilt of leaving his children unattended in a foreign land and the loss of Martine's sanity were emotionally too draining. What was he to do? He couldn't do his job anymore—there was too much at stake. His children were gone. And normal communication with his wife was impossible. Peter felt powerless to alter the course of his life and was buckling in the face of adversity. The inner strength that had kept him going for six long months was in shreds.

He scrunched up his face and choked back tears. He needed to leave. Martine was already weeping. His mere presence brought that on.

"God, why has all this happened?" Peter sighed. Everything had been going so well. They had been married only nine years, and Martine wasn't even thirty yet. They had been high school sweethearts; married as soon as he was out of air-traffic school and had a firm job. They had built their dream house in Trélex, a small village in the Swiss countryside, fifteen miles north of Geneva. The house was not large; quite small really. But it was theirs. They had planted bushes and trees in the compact garden, hoping to watch them grow year after year as Mark and Nicolette metamorphosed into young adults and eventually came back to visit from college. They had even found room in the garden for a swing-set. But now it stood there abandoned, a cruel reminder of what had been. Even the neighborhood children who used to play on it didn't come anymore. They shared the Zuckers' grief and expressed it in their own way.

Peter turned and pressed the buzzer on the wall. But as he did so, a sudden blow knocked him onto the bed. He turned and saw Martine's body at his feet, one of her hands still clutching his coat as if her life depended on it.

"Martine! Oh, Martine!" Peter uttered, falling to his knees beside her. She looked up at him intensely, desperately mouthing something…He cradled her head and shoulders and leaned closer to understand.

"*Gang zrugg*, Peter...*Go back*...find them...Nicolette-Mark—I implore...go ba—" She fainted. The effort of rushing to him had exhausted her.

"We'll have to inform Doctor Dubois," the nurse's stern voice said as she charged in. She looked more annoyed than perplexed.

As they retraced their steps down the aseptic corridor, Peter didn't hear much of what the nurse said. It sounded like a distant, irritating babble. Doctor Dubois' office didn't seem very real to Peter, either. He absentmindedly shook the doctor's outstretched hand, and, as if on autopilot, sank obediently into the offered chair opposite the imposing mahogany desk.

"Martine is in no condition to return home for the time being," Dubois said somberly. "She will probably have to remain with us for several more months, maybe longer."

Peter listened, expressionless, his eyes fixed on a point on the floor.

Dubois couldn't tell if Peter had taken in anything he had said. The doctor nervously passed a hand over the few remaining strands of gray hair on top of his head, then made a steeple of his fingers and waited for a reaction.

Peter finally looked up. He seemed at first to be studying something on the doctor's expectant face, but Dubois soon realized he was looking straight through him.

Peter cleared his throat. He would ask the question he had avoided for so long. "Doctor, please tell me the truth. Is this permanent?"

Now it was Dubois' turn to remain silent as he wondered how best to answer. He took off his glasses and turned them over in his hands.

"I don't know. I honestly can't say," he eventually replied. "In my forty-two years of practicing psychiatry, I've never dealt with a case quite like this. Emotional maladjustment is simple to diagnose but is probably the most difficult disorder to cure without attacking the source of the problem—and from what you've told me, there's nothing I or anyone else can do to help there."

Peter said nothing. He remained hunched in his chair, staring at the floor.

"You see," Dubois continued, "it's tremendously important for a mother of missing children to have definitive answers." He measured his words carefully. "She needs to know what happened to the children she brought into the world, even if the news is not pleasant. Your wife needs concrete information, not conjecture. Only then can she bury the matter and go on with her life. But until that happens, the pain cannot end."

Peter nodded as the doctor's words sank in.

"Most people hide their grief by maintaining an eternal hope that someday the children, who've never been found alive..." Dubois hesitated before deciding on his next words "…or dead, will appear again. Martine obviously hasn't got that hope…quite the opposite, in fact. For her, despair would be an improvement."

He paused for a few seconds before adding: "I can't be optimistic. I'm sorry."

A long, uncomfortable silence followed. Dubois wanted to say something to make Peter feel better, but decided against placebo statements. He knew Peter was still sane and intelligent—despite his appearance. He was amazed that Peter hadn't lost his mind as well.

Outwardly, Peter seemed to be only vaguely paying attention. Inwardly, however, he seethed. *He hasn't got the answers—the damn doctor hasn't got the answers! Doesn't he understand what's happening to Martine? The treatment's going nowhere. All that she can look forward to is more of the same.—My God! She could* die *like this!*

"Martine's right—I've got to go back," Peter suddenly blurted. It was an emphatic statement, not aimed at Dubois but at himself. He rose to his feet decisively as if remembering a forgotten appointment. "Thank you, doctor. There's only one solution and Martine gave it to me."

Peter started toward the door, leaving Dubois dumbfounded.

"*Monsieur* Zucker? Solution—what do you mean?"

"Martine and I are not giving up," Peter said firmly. "Look after her, doctor," he ordered, staring Dubois straight in the eye. "I'll be away for a while. Make her hang on as best as you can—I'm counting on you!"

Dubois stared, confounded, as Peter left the room.

Chapter 3

▼

Ambassador William Helm strode into the sixth-floor conference room of the U.S. diplomatic mission in Geneva, livid! He grunted as he sat down at the head of the long maple conference table.

The senior diplomats in the room abruptly stopped their early-morning chit-chat at the sight of Helm's leaden face under the neon lights, blood vessels seemingly ready to burst. Those who were not yet seated dropped into vacant chairs.

Nobody even dared a "Good morning, Mr. Ambassador."

"Jeez!" murmured Allison Cox. She folded her *International Herald Tribune* and looked at the ambassador, wondering whose head was on the chopping block this morning. Helm's agitation contrasted starkly with his perfectly-set black pomaded hair and wrinkle-free investment banker's suit, both intended to make up for the fact that he didn't come from a well-to-do family or have an Ivy League education. Standing only five foot six, he envied those who were tall and naturally imposing. But being chosen by the president of the United States as his representative made up for that. And during his two years in Geneva, Helm had never hesitated to wield the power of his office, especially over those he envied or despised. Allison Cox in particular knew this only too well.

"As you can all judge, I'm not very happy this morning," the ambassador spat out, disdainfully waving away a cup of coffee offered to him by his secretary. He looked intensely at Allison, an attractive woman in her late thirties, who was this morning wearing an Italian red wool suit and was seated halfway down the conference table. "And Allison can tell you why."

As everyone turned in her direction, Allison drew the paper cup of coffee away from her lips and racked her brain for what Helm was referring to. Something must have come up during the night. She hadn't accessed the overnight cable traffic yet, having come straight from her car to the conference room for the daily nine AM staff meeting. Most of her colleagues got in early and read through the numerous secure diplomatic cables that had come from the State Department in Washington and other U.S. diplomatic outposts around the world. As Head of Press and Information, Allison should have done the same. But as a single mother with two teenage boys to see off to school, she didn't want to give up any more of the time she felt she needed to spend with them. She nearly always worked late, and getting in only at nine was one small luxury she felt she deserved.

"Oops, here we go again," Allison murmured to those near her. She straightened up in her chair and, with a well-manicured hand, pushed aside the bangs of her short, light-brown hair. It was a seductive movement, although for Allison it was merely a nervous habit. But along with her athletic build and dimples that lit up her spunky face when she smiled, it made her a magnet to men—Helm included.

"I'm sorry, sir," Allison said, trying to look unperturbed. "I can't for the moment pick up your train of thought. In the interest of everybody's time, maybe you could come straight to the point."

Few officers dared be so direct with Helm, but then no one else was the constant target of his pointed and underhanded remarks. The ambassador objected to professional women and never missed an opportunity to catch her out. The fact that she had turned down Helm's amorous advances hadn't helped. But she was used to his digs and knew how to defend herself. She had, after all, spent three years in the U.S. Marine Corps.

"It's always the same," Helm growled. "What's the point of having a dog when you've got to bark yourself? Don't you ever read your cable traffic, woman?"

Allison wasn't going to give Helm the pleasure of admitting that she hadn't. She sat silently, ignoring the provocation.

Realizing he was beginning to look foolish, the ambassador came to the point. "It concerns '*baby-parts*,'" he said. When he spoke the words, he grimaced.

"'*Baby-parts*'..." Allison mouthed. The taste of bile rose in her mouth. Her day was ruined.

Helm put on his reading eyeglasses, picked up the top cable from the pile in front of him, and started reading it aloud.

> Geneva correspondent Maria Romero of *El Crónico* (Peruvian influential daily) writes: International traffic in 'baby-parts' for rich American families

continues despite U.S. denials. Two-column front-page story quotes non-governmental organization sources in Geneva as confirming that traffic to USA of parts from Latin American babies for transplants continues and says U.S. government pressuring to hide truth. Following is text of story headlined: "Peruvian Babies Shipped to USA for Parts."

"You can read the rest of the story for yourselves," Helm said, removing his spectacles and looking up at his audience. "The terrible thing is that there is nothing new here—"

"Then why are we worried?" interrupted Harvey Snyder, the economic affairs attaché, who loved to hear the sound of his own voice.

Helm glared at him: "*We* are not worried because *we* have been trained to protect U.S. interests abroad and *we* shall do so to our level best." The crescendo in his voice became more insistent. "However, *we* cannot help but be *concerned* about people in this very city we are meant to be keeping tabs on, who are repeating old lies about our country and giving renewed credence to them. It's obvious you are *ignorant* of the history of this matter."

Snyder, who normally liked to place himself close to the ambassador, moved uncomfortably in his seat.

"Will somebody please fill this officer in on the background of *baby-parts*?" Helm asked. He looked particularly exasperated.

There was a moment's silence in the room. Everyone had a vague recollection of the *baby-parts* episode, including the CIA station chief in Geneva, Eric Pimms. But neither he nor anyone else dared venture into these uncertain waters. Except…

"Yes, it's a very simple affair," said Allison confidently. She could see Helm's disappointment that she was the one providing the answer. "During the late 1980s, the last couple of years of the Cold War, the then-Soviet news agency Novosti put out a cleverly disguised piece of disinformation about the United States, channeling it through the Cuban news agency Prensa Latina. In whatever form the story appeared in the Latin American media—which picked it up from the Cubans—it contained the same basic allegations; namely, that private U.S. clinics were buying babies from South American countries, ostensibly for adoption by childless families, but in fact for obtaining organs for transplanting into U.S. patients—"

"Ooh…" Snyder said with distaste. "Would we *do* a thing like that?"

"Obviously, not!" Allison shot back, appalled that he would even consider there being any truth to the story. "The whole thing was a complete fabrication, cleverly aimed at discrediting the United States at a time when we were winning the Cold War."

"Of course," Snyder agreed, obviously embarrassed again. "I was just—"

"It took the information services of the U.S. government several years to successfully quash the allegations," Allison went on. "To my recollection, the story has not resurfaced since—until now, that is."

"There *were* reports of child kidnapping for slavery and body parts in Afghanistan after we toppled the Taliban," Pimms said knowingly. "And I'm not talking about classified CIA material."

"Yeah, I remember that *New York Times* story too, but you'll recall, Eric," Allison said, turning to look the CIA officer in the face, "that it didn't accuse the U.S. of being involved. It was an internal Afghan matter without a direct U.S. angle, and therefore the story went nowhere. As we all know, it's the alleged U.S. involvement in bad stuff, and not the bad stuff itself, that makes headlines."

She turned back toward Helm. "There has to be a political motivation for these things. That's why it's curious that *baby-parts* is coming up again now…and from Peru?" Allison felt perplexed.

Allison thought she knew all there was to know about *baby-parts* allegations, especially in South America. Her first assignment after entering the U.S. Foreign Service had been as a young information officer in the embassy in Lima. *Baby-parts* had been the priority concern of the post at that time, and she had been heavily involved in refuting the anti-American news stories that kept being fed by Prensa Latina.

"Well, I'm glad you seem to know all about it, Allison," Helm said sarcastically, "because you're the one who's going to find out why it's surfaced again and why here in Geneva."

"Might have guessed," Allison murmured.

"Allison, this is vital for our international reputation," Helm said. "We're still reeling from our prisoner abuse in Iraq, and we can't afford to have another attack on our integrity—especially on *my* watch here in Geneva. Get to it as an urgent priority and report back to me this afternoon before opening of business in Washington."

Jesus! Allison looked at her watch. Opening time for government departments in Washington was nine AM Eastern Standard Time, which meant three PM Geneva time. "Gosh, that leaves me a lot of time!" she whispered sarcastically to her neighbor.

As the meeting moved on to other business, Allison mentally cut herself off, and her mind wandered back to her time in Peru and the innocence of her first posting abroad. The *baby-parts* controversy had spoiled it and had introduced her to the reality of how other countries viewed the United States. She knew Americans would never knowingly be part of something as abhorrent as buying parts of babies, but she had seen how those who were virulently anti-American never missed an opportunity to slander and condemn her country. And now, like her most hideous recurring nightmare, the *baby-parts* matter was back again. *Oh, for a more carefree existence,* she sighed, thinking of her boys and home. But then she thought of her neighbor and his missing children—and *baby-parts*. The idea of a link made her shudder. Looking at the clock, she refocused, settled on a course of action, and prayed that it would work. The worst thing now was waiting for the staff meeting to end.

Chapter 4

▼

Freak torrential rains came in gusts off the Pacific Ocean, thrashing the houses and drenching the picturesque fishing port of Pimentel in northwest Peru. It was January, and the locals, used to these *El Niño* storms upsetting their Southern Hemisphere summer, knew that tomorrow's torrid sunshine would steam their town dry.

But the two children locked in the bedroom on the top floor of the grand Del Solar residence overlooking the beach did not know this. They sat huddled together on a bed across the room from the streaming windowpane that shuddered from the lashings of the ocean storm. Nicolette pulled closer to Mark and gripped his shirt as if her life depended on it. Their eyes were fixed on the glass, fearing that at any moment a massive wave would come crashing into the room and engulf them. Their gaunt faces expressed the terror and despondency that had been with them for the last six months.

Mark's arms were wrapped around his young sister. He tried to calm her, his hand stroking her dyed-black hair. "Shh…it'll be over soon. Shh…" It was easier to hide fear when someone else was more afraid, Mark thought. On his own, he would have been petrified.

Although only eight, Mark had become Nicolette's protector, her proxy mother. The role had been forced upon him, and since the summer he felt he had grown older. Nicolette had gone the other way—from an ebullient and impish sister who would stand up to him, to a trembling little creature, cowering and refusing food unless Mark spoon-fed her. Without him, her heart would have given way—simply stopped. He was sure of it.

The windowpane abruptly flexed and the crack made them jump from the bed and cower against the opposite wall. Neither uttered a word as the window shook again, but held in its frame. Life had become dull and hard, but they had borne it in silence. They lived in constant terror of any adult who came near them. In particular, they dreaded the mistress of the house.

Señora Del Solar was the young and beautiful "evil stepmother" who watched them and tried to mold them into something they were not. The look in this woman's eyes was more terrifying than anything that had befallen them—worse even than the horrible man who had brought them here. And her voice was like a coiled whip—ready to draw back and strike without warning.

Initially, she had tried to win them over with false tenderness and kindness. Mark and Nicolette had seen through this immediately, and at the children's refusal to succumb to her charms, her behavior changed to frustrated screams and bitter recriminations. Mark was often the target of vicious slaps to the side of the head, especially when her attempts at communication in Spanish or English failed. It was obvious she could not tolerate that they understood nothing. And Mark became increasingly defiant when he realized it was the only weapon he possessed to drive her from the room, even if it cost him an hysterical slapping.

"You'd better do something about those damn kids! And fast!" Señora Del Solar's commanding voice had no trouble reaching her husband's ears at the other end of the dinner table, despite the bellowing of the storm outside. She detested anybody and anything that refused to yield to her will. "Especially that boy—I will not tolerate it! If he talks back to me one more time in that fucking language of his, I'll…" She fidgeted in her chair, unable to think of a sufficiently horrible punishment. "Was that the best you could find?"

Gonzalo Del Solar, an affable man, hastily put a forkful of food into his mouth. Like the two children, he was afraid of her. Eight years of marriage had made him submissive and had turned his dark hair prematurely gray. He had once been in awe of her—of her movie-star looks and of what he had thought to be her breeding and culture. For a man of fifty-two, traditional in his ways, kindly and passive, the chance of having a beautiful woman half his age as his bride came only once in a lifetime. But how often he had regretted that fateful day when he had first met her and been seduced by her looks and attentive and flirtatious manner. At the time, he had been too blind to question why none of the more eligible young men had sought her hand. Rumors said she had *known* them all, but none wanted her for life. Don Gonzalo had assumed the reason was financial. Her family was near bankruptcy, which meant no dowry. But this did not worry him; he was among the wealthiest men in the region.

At their first formal meeting, Lucia had taken him by the arm and started to control his movements, even around the living room of *his* house. He had been seduced by her smile...Yes, the way it curved up toward her satin black hair, brushed back to the Spanish comb behind her head. She had appeared to be the traditional *señorita* he had been looking for. It all seemed so perfect...

Marry in haste, repent at leisure. Oh! How often he had repeated those words...Now he knew the truth. She had not been sought after by anyone else because she was in every way a *bitch*. Alone, he often muttered it under his breath, but he would never dare call her that to her face. He was not a courageous man in her presence. He couldn't refuse her anything, whether it was a new pearl-white Mercedes sports convertible or a pair of beautiful young children she didn't want to bother having herself. She never wanted to sleep with her husband anymore, but she required children. In her mind, they were a social necessity, and generously taking in two young orphans would be seen as a supreme act of praiseworthy behavior.

"They're good children," Don Gonzalo finally answered. "They were the best we could find. You'll have to be patient, my dear." He hesitated while the maid cleared the dinner plates. He did not want the servants knowing too much about the children. "They still feel a little uprooted," he continued as the maid left the room. "It's only natural at their age..." He could already judge from his wife's expression that she wasn't interested in such humane considerations. Don Gonzalo plucked up his courage and cut to the chase. "I've made some arrangements to—"

"*Mierda!* I've had enough of your *arrangements*," she interrupted, banging her fist on the oak table. "The *only* arrangement that will please me is for you to send those two miserable brats away and find me some kids who know how to appreciate becoming members of the Del Solar family! Who do they fucking well think they are—refusing *me!*"

Don Gonzalo hated his wife's vile mouth. He felt defenseless against it. As she shook her head and muttered on, he thought about the money the children had already cost him, and, above all, he thought of the man who had arranged it. Luis Chavez operated an import-export business—in fact, the only major one in this part of Peru. Everyone who had something to sell abroad had to use Chavez's network, especially if it concerned the U.S. market. And if you tried to circumvent it, then all of a sudden the labor you needed to harvest your crops didn't turn up. That had happened to Don Gonzalo just once. The police and the local authorities couldn't help him; they were all in Chavez's pocket. And nobody messed with the men in Chavez's pay. So Don Gonzalo had struck a deal with Chavez— a partnership allowing Don Gonzalo to sell his sugar cane crops at a premium through Chavez's network. The income let Don Gonzalo maintain his large estate near the regional capital, Chiclayo, and, above all, his prestigious residence in Pimentel. The latter was important to his wife since it was where the rich socialites flocked in the summer months. For Chavez, the partnership meant more power and influence and another family dependent on him.

During a particularly trying period at home, Don Gonzalo had mentioned over a drink with Chavez that his wife badly wanted children. He lied about the reason, merely saying that she couldn't have any herself. Sensing easy business, Chavez had smiled as he poured more Scotch into Don Gonzalo's glass. "I think that can be arranged. Tell me what Señora Del Solar has in mind…"

A month later, he had delivered the children and a bill for half a million dollars. "It's for a contribution to the orphanage," the deliveryman had said.

When the children had arrived, their hair had already been dyed black. Don Gonzalo had continued the practice to avoid attracting too many questions about their origin. He suspected they had not been adopted legally, and Chavez always sidestepped questions on the subject. Sure, Chavez would replace the children with another pair, if Don Gonzalo asked. But he shuddered to think how the Chavez network would dispose of the two upstairs.

"We can't give them back, my dear…" Don Gonzalo mumbled. "We can't afford another arrangement with Chavez—"

"Of course you can!" she retorted, getting up from the table. "We're the richest family in the region. I'm sure he'll give you a discount if *I* tell him you need one…" She stopped admiring herself in the ornate mirror above the mantelpiece and turned her piercing gaze on her husband. "How much *did* you pay him to bring those two brats here?"

For a fleeting second Don Gonzalo considered lying, but it would be no use. She always found out everything.

"Um—" he muttered, clearing his throat. "Just um—500,000—"

The room went strangely quiet. Don Gonzalo dared not look up from the table. He sensed the amazed look on his wife's face.

"Half a million…Half a million what?" she asked incredulously, already knowing the answer. "You don't mean *American dollars…?*"

"*Sí,*" he mouthed, his voice barely audible. "But, I was doing it for you, so that—"

She started laughing, her derisive, humiliating laughter which he had heard so often. "You pitiful little man."

But she was more annoyed at Chavez. She knew he had arranged for the kids to be brought there, but he had not told her about the half a million dollars. *It's about time he starts paying more generously for my favors.* She put the thought aside and focused on her husband. "Why did I ever agree to marry this inept man?" she mumbled loud enough for her husband to hear.

Don Gonzalo sighed and began to feel a little angry.

"Well, luckily for you, I have the solution," she resumed, picking up a newspaper from the sideboard. "Here, read this," she said, and threw that morning's copy of *El Crónico* onto the table in front of Don Gonzalo. It was folded around an article titled, "Peruvian Babies Shipped To USA For Parts?"

Don Gonzalo arched his eyebrows in shock. He hoped he had misunderstood what his wife was suggesting. He read the article carefully, wanting to find another reason for her interest in it. But a shiver went down his spine as he finished the last paragraph, comprehending his wife's thoughts. *How could she consider selling the children for parts?* He was horrified. *Oh my God! What have I done?*

The enormity of this brought him back to his senses. The solution he had been trying in vain to propose throughout dinner now had to work. Otherwise, he would live the rest of his life with the death of two innocent children on his conscience. He shuddered again at the thought of what his wife was capable of.

Don Gonzalo took a deep breath. "Let's not be too hasty. Look at this reasonably—"

"Reasonably!" Señora Del Solar interrupted. "You must think I—"

"Dammit!" Don Gonzalo shouted back, slamming his hand on the table.

She retreated a step, astonished that he dared talk back.

"Will you just listen to me for once without interrupting? I have been trying to tell you about the *arrangement* I have made to resolve this situation. Those kids are fine." He held up his hand, palm out, to quell another volcanic outburst. "They just don't understand anything of what is going on because they don't speak any known language. I haven't the slightest idea where Chavez got them, but that's all water under the bridge now. All we've got to do is to teach them Spanish and everything will be fine. It's as simple as *that*."

"Okay, *Mister Mastermind*, how do you propose doing that when they don't understand a single word of what anybody says?" Señora Del Solar felt spited at not being able to exorcise her hatred of the children by sending them away to be cut up.

"I've arranged for a special tutor to come here for a few months to teach them Spanish and anything else they will need in order to live with us."

"You're dreaming as usual," his wife said condescendingly. "You can try, but I guarantee you those kids won't come around." Getting rid of the children would take longer than she wanted, but if she gave her husband's idea a chance, and it didn't succeed, he would have to concur with her wishes. "Okay, who is this brilliant teacher then?"

"Her name is Romy Tincopa—"

"Ah! A *woman*!"

Don Gonzalo soldiered on. "She's Argentinean and an accomplished teacher and comes with the best references. In fact, she has worked with mentally handicapped children. I'm sure she'll do a fine job for us."

"And I *suppose* you've explained to her the precise nature of our problem and the circumstances under which the two upstairs came to be here," his wife said patronizingly. "I wonder how long it will take her to put two and two together and sell us out to the authorities. The chief of police hates us."

"Listen," Don Gonzalo responded confidently. "This Argentinean woman won't be a problem, I assure you. She's here illegally and needs the money. She'll keep quiet. And she knows that if she doesn't…" He drew his forefinger across his throat. He hoped it would help bolster his argument, even though he knew that he could never kill anyone—except perhaps his wife, one day.

Señora Del Solar paced back to the mirror and resumed fussing with her hair. "Does Chavez know about this plan of yours?" she asked in a calmer voice.

"It was Chavez who suggested her to me," Don Gonzalo replied.

Señora Del Solar smiled. *I might have guessed…* "Well, it had better work— and quickly." She began to think how to convince Chavez of the profit they could make from entering the *baby-parts* trade, starting with the two very saleable white children upstairs. Chavez was unscrupulous, and she couldn't resist that kind of man.

C h a p t e r   5

▼

Renée Hottinger always felt a bit furtive when she went into her neighbor's house while he wasn't there. Not that she intended to steal anything. She was as honest a Swiss citizen as they came. But she was also a young housewife whose husband was away a lot on business, and no doubt some of the neighbors had little else to do but peek through their blinds and fantasize as to why this attractive woman with bouncy auburn hair went to Peter Zucker's house so often. They could spot her easily in the new development of chalet-like houses; the hedges had not grown tall enough yet to mask people's comings and goings.

She went there less frequently now. Her husband, who knew about her visits, had grown tired of his wife spending time over there—especially when she had enough to do at home looking after their six-year-old daughter. He didn't work all hours servicing and flying airplanes just so his wife could clean and fix meals for their solitary neighbor. This had to stop, and one evening he had told his wife so.

"We can't just abandon him—not after what's he's been through," Renée protested.

"*Ja*, but it is about time he started fending more for himself," Bruno Hottinger said in annoyance, running a hand through his abundant chestnut hair.

She had dropped the subject. Her husband was tired after a long day flying three Swiss businessmen to Kiev and back. It wasn't just the flying that wore Bruno out—he was an excellent pilot who had been trained in the Swiss air force. He had come home at midnight after preparing the plane for the trip and left the house again for the pre-dawn takeoff. It wasn't an ideal situation and probably wouldn't have stood up to close scrutiny by the Swiss civil aviation authority. But

Geneva Business Jets was a small company with only three planes, and could not afford a large staff. If he wanted to stay employed there, he had to bend some rules. Renée knew that her husband was right about Peter Zucker, however sympathetic they were to his plight. Peter had to pull himself together, and she could not keep making him hot meals and clearing up the mess in his house forever.

Renée was thinking about all this as she turned the key in the lock of Peter's door and went in. Something was different about the mess in the house this time, but she couldn't immediately see what. Dirty plates and half-eaten TV dinners were piled up in the kitchen as usual. And a cursory glance around the house showed it to be as untidy as always. The difference, she surmised, was the papers scattered around the dining room. They had been torn up and flung in all directions—as if by a madman.

Deciding to deal with this particular disorder first, she knelt down to pick up the pieces. But as she did so, she couldn't stop herself from assembling some of the bigger scraps. It took her several minutes and several journeys across the room to piece together a rough picture of the papers' contents. Some were sheets of handwritten notes, but most were torn-up newspaper clippings showing photographs of the two lost Zucker children; she remembered that the Zuckers had paid for costly advertisements in the American press before finally giving up their search and returning home from California.

Renée shook her head in despair as she imagined Peter Zucker going over these past events again and falling deeper into depression. Other pieces of paper formed a map of the amusement park where the children had disappeared. A pad of lined paper with writing on it lay among the remains of a broken vase; it had obviously landed there after being slung across the room.

*Oh, the poor man…I wonder how all this will end…*She leafed through the pad. It was full of carefully written notes which she recognized as being in Peter's hand. She tried to read them, but they were in German. Renée was from the French-speaking part of Switzerland, and although she had learned some German in school, it wasn't enough to help her now. She wished Bruno were here. She glanced through a few more sheets but soon gave up. It struck her, though, that Peter had obviously spent time carefully writing these pages before flinging the pad away.

She put the pad on the table and noticed the computer was still on—in sleep mode. She shook the mouse to bring the screen to life and saw that Peter had been searching the Web. She clicked through sites he had visited: FBI, LAPD, and others that dealt with solving crimes. But what shocked her most was a question he had typed in the Google search box: "How to enter the USA illegally?"

Renée felt apprehensive and decided to just tidy up and leave. She quickly shut down the computer, flattened out the papers that she judged were not trash, and piled them onto the pad on the table. Then she went about putting the rest of the house in order. But her mind was churning.

Bruno Hottinger wiped the grease off his hands before closing the inspection panel on the cowling of the Gulfstream's number-two engine. The plane had to be spotless. The owner couldn't stand black finger-marks on the white fuselage— "Clean Service or Clean Out of Business" was his motto.

And he was right. The well-heeled businessmen and Arab sheiks who paid handsomely to be flown around the world wanted to feel as if they were being transported in their own private jet and not someone else's air-taxi service. Otherwise, they would fly first class on regular airlines. And Geneva Business Jets needed the cash flow to meet the lease payments on the expensive planes.

Bruno fumed; he would be late for dinner again. He had hoped to be home early for once and had told his wife so, much to her pleasure. But after a problem-free service of both engines, the last of the plane's fuel filters he checked was too dirty to leave as it was. In his frustration, Bruno felt like hurling the filter right across the hangar. But he maintained his self-control and began the time-consuming task of taking samples from access points in the fuel system to trace the source of the contamination. He eventually found it and proceeded to drain out jet fuel until his sampler showed there was only clear fluid left. He checked out a new filter from supplies and carefully placed it in its lodging in the engine compartment. With a sigh of relief, he closed the access panel, got down from the scaffolding and wheeled it away. He was spent and hoped this was the last problem of the day.

After taking off his overalls and locking up the hangar, he got into his twelve-year-old Toyota Corolla and headed north along Geneva's lakeside motorway toward Lausanne. It was past eight and the traffic was light, although he would gladly have joined the slow-moving snake of commuters going home earlier. He got off the motorway at the Nyon-St. Cergue exit, headed west toward the Jura Mountains, and after a couple of minutes was driving through the center of Trélex and up the Route du Soleil to his home.

Renée guessed her husband had been held up at work, but she wished that he had phoned to say so.

"I'm sorry," he said on entering the kitchen. "There was a problem with the new G5."

His wife understood the pressures he had at work, but was upset that he had not come home before their daughter had gone to bed. "I know…but it's always the same, Bruno…" she said in an exasperated voice. "And Irène—you should think of *her* a bit more…she stayed up especially waiting for you, but now she's asleep."

She turned her back on him and with unnecessary noise busied herself turning over his supper in the frying pan where it had been simmering for the previous hour. Bruno walked up behind her, put his hand on her shoulder, and kissed her through her hair. Apart from this, he didn't try to mollify her, for he knew she was right. It was pointless wasting time with an argument over a situation that would most likely reoccur.

"I'm sorry, *chéri*…" she said after a few seconds of silence. "I know you've had a hard day, but we were both looking forward to seeing you earlier…That's all. And…" she hesitated before continuing, wondering whether or not to mention it.

"And what?" Bruno asked, irritated that some other omission on his part apparently needed clearing up.

"Oh…I know you'll be mad but…well, it's about Peter. I'm concerned about him," she said, setting Bruno's dinner on the table.

Bruno sat down with a sigh. "Look, we've gone over all this…Peter's had an awful blow, and oh *God* how I sympathize with him! But he's got to stand on his own two feet. And the sooner he starts, the better it will be for him." Bruno adopted a more understanding tone. "It's the only way he'll get over it—or at least learn to live with the situation." He took a bite of the overcooked chicken breast that somehow Renée had kept appetizing and washed it down with a mouthful of white wine.

Renée sat down opposite him. "Yes, okay," she said. "I agree that he's got to take control of things, but he's going downhill again—"

"And, what can *we* do about it?" Bruno interrupted impatiently, his mouth full. He swallowed, and continued. "We're not doctors, and there's no way we can get his children back—it's heartbreaking, I know…"

"I realize that, but—when I was over there today…"

Bruno shook his head and tried to suppress a smile. "Honey, you are a good person. But you're not Peter Zucker's cleaning lady, for God's sake." He couldn't reproach his wife for her good nature, but he didn't want her permanently cleaning up for their neighbor.

"But you see," she pursued intently, "Peter was surfing police Web sites, searching for ways to enter the U.S. illegally, and—there were these papers all about the kids' disappearance that he had torn up...and..." She hesitated.

"And?" queried Bruno. He pushed his empty plate away and savored his wine.

Renée pulled something out of her apron pocket. "Please don't think me bad, but among the papers was this." She handed the pad with Peter's notes to her husband.

"And?" Bruno repeated impatiently. He glanced at the first page while waiting for the end of her explanation. Then he realized why she had shown the notes to him. "And, they're in German and you want me to tell you what they're all about? Renée, really! This is none of our business."

"I'm not prying," she protested. "We ought to make sure he's not going downhill again...It's for his own good—"

"Look, enough of this. I'm too tired," Bruno said, getting up from the kitchen table. "I haven't the energy this evening to deal with our own problems, let alone other people's—however deserving," he added. "I'm going up to bed, and it would do you good to get to bed early as well."

Bruno dropped the pad on the table and left the room.

Clearing up in the kitchen took Renée half an hour, and, once upstairs, she found Bruno already asleep. She put on her nightgown and quietly slipped into bed beside him. She leaned over and placed a loving kiss on his forehead. She gazed on his rough-hewn features, stroked his wavy hair, then turned on her side to go to sleep.

Thoughts of the Zucker family's horrible mishap melded with her concerns about their own existence. She and Bruno had been jubilant and carefree when they were first married. He had left the Swiss air force to become a pilot at the national airline, Swissair. But dreams of a prosperous career in the civilian airline sector were soon shattered when Swissair went bankrupt. It was a totally unexpected blow to their morale, especially with their first baby on the way and a mortgage on a new house. It had been a difficult time that had put their young marriage to the test and caused them to delay having a second child. The job with Geneva Business Jets was a lucky break for Bruno. The pay wasn't anything like Swissair's, and he was expected to do maintenance on the planes as well. But it was a job, and now Bruno was toiling harder than ever for a company whose fate was far from certain. Life was a constant struggle. Renée had given up her job as a flight attendant when she became pregnant, and now part-time work in her field was impossible to find. She wondered what the point of it all was.

No sooner had she drifted off than Bruno awoke from a fitful sleep. Restless, he went downstairs to get a warm drink.

Sitting in the silent kitchen, waiting for the mug of piping-hot milk to cool, he picked up the pad of paper Renée had brought from Peter Zucker's and glanced through it. He had to read some pages twice before he fully comprehended what it all meant.

"Oh my God!" he whispered as he put the pad down.

Chapter 6

▼

"*El Crónico.—Sí?*" Maria Romero's voice was tinged with irritation as she answered the phone. She was sitting idly at her desk in the international press center in the Palais des Nations, the UN's Geneva headquarters. She wedged the handset between her neck and slim shoulder, nearly smothering the mouthpiece with her curls of jet-black hair. This way, she could free her hands and resume the delicate manicure of her crimson-varnished nails that the ringing telephone had interrupted.

"Oh…Allison Cox…" she said hesitatingly, in accented English. "Yeah, I remember you." An impudent smile crept across Maria's face as she guessed the reason for the call from the U.S. press officer. "What can I do for you?" she asked innocently, putting down her nail file. She was more attentive now.

"Hey, look," Allison said, trying to sound cheery. "I'm coming down to the Palais later this morning, and I was wondering if you'd have time for coffee?"

Maria Romero was not one of Allison's regular contacts. The only other time Allison had met her—soon after Maria's arrival in Geneva some three months earlier—it had quickly become clear that this Peruvian journalist held definite anti-American views. Allison remembered that Maria had only set up in Geneva as a journalist because the man she was living with, a Peruvian diplomat, had been posted to his country's UN office here. Maria therefore didn't need to earn her keep, and she merely filed an occasional story for *El Crónico* in order to maintain her press credentials. At that time, Allison had decided that plenty of other correspondents needed to be cultivated before Maria. She realized now that this had been a mistake—had she reined in Maria earlier, Allison might have headed off the *baby-parts* article.

"Um—I don't know if—"

"It's been some time since we chatted," Allison said, pursuing her quarry. "Now that you've been working for a while, I thought it might be a good time to get together again. And there's no time like the present!"

Maria really didn't want to see any American diplomats today—unless they were going to tell her what a great story she had written—which obviously wasn't going to be the case. And the last thing she needed was to be criticized by the Americans—especially today, as she was basking in the glory of her article splashed across the front pages of nearly all of the South American dailies. She'd deliberately not asked U.S. officials for comment on the accusations in the story before sending it off to her newspaper. Any denial from the Americans would have weakened the story's punch, and *that* Maria wanted to avoid. "Oh…I'm a bit busy today…I'd love to though…" Maria feigned regret. "I'll give you a call in a couple of days."

"No!" Allison replied a little too desperately. She took a second to compose herself. "What I mean is, that today we could kill two birds with one stone—and by tomorrow it won't be as useful to you."

The word "useful" piqued Maria's curiosity. She liked *useful* things, especially if they fell into her lap. "How do you mean?"

"Well," Allison said more confidently, realizing she had gained the upper hand. "My ambassador's planning a press conference on the subject of *baby-parts* tomorrow, and, given your interest in the subject, he felt you might like to have an idea ahead of time of what he's going to say." Helm had no such plans, but any pretext would do to force a meeting with Maria. "But, if you're too busy…"

"No, it's not that," Maria replied quickly, suddenly not wanting to let this opportunity slip by. "When were you thinking of coming down here?"

"Oh, in about an hour. I have a couple of things to finish here first," Allison added nonchalantly.

"Sure, why not? Let's say eleven o'clock," Maria suggested. "I have half an hour between press conferences, and it'll be time for a cup of coffee by then."

"Okay," Allison said, trying to hide the relief in her voice. "We'll find each other—not in the press bar; it's too public," she added conspiratorially. "Let's go to the delegates' lounge on the third floor. It's more private there. Okay?"

"Perfect," Maria replied. "See you at eleven." She put down the receiver, now impatient to hear what Allison had to reveal away from indiscreet ears in the crowded press bar. She resumed her manicure.

Allison made sure she arrived in the delegates' lounge before Maria did. Luckily it wasn't very crowded, and she could easily pick the table she wanted. She strode over to one with a clear view of the entrance so that she would spot Maria when she arrived and have time to size her up.

Two leather-and-chrome easy chairs faced each other across the glass-topped coffee table. Allison sat down in the one with its back to the window, ensuring that her head would be silhouetted against the light, thus hiding her facial expressions. Maria's face, on the other hand, would be fully illuminated, making it easy for Allison to read.

Making Maria ill at ease was part of Allison's plan. Finding Allison already there would make Maria feel she was late—even if it weren't the case. Allison also ordered two cups of coffee. However rude such preparations might seem, they amounted to good tactics. This wasn't a friendly meeting—it was a business meeting that had to produce results. Maria was a tough cookie, and Allison had to take command from the outset.

Though eager to hear what Allison had to say, Maria abhorred waiting alone, and was purposely five minutes late. But she arrived to find Allison waiting and her coffee cold.

"Oh, let me order you another one," Allison said. "I assumed you were on your way."

Maria felt awkward and crossed her slim, designer-jeans-clad legs in an attempt to feel more comfortable. A man would have waited patiently for her for half an hour—or more—and still have acted stupid when she finally arrived! Maria wasn't used to dealing with professional women who didn't give a hoot about her looks. She began to wish she hadn't agreed to the meeting.

"Don't worry," Allison said, showing Maria that she sensed her predicament. "I can't stand cold coffee either." But she made no attempt to order a fresh cup.

When Allison saw Maria hastily light up a cigarette, she knew that she had started out well. Now was the moment to gain Maria's trust. Allison put on her most endearing smile. "We Americans," she said, "whether from the north or south continent, obviously have similar tastes—I liked your article."

"Oh—um…which one?" Maria said, taken aback.

"Why, the *baby-parts* one, of course," Allison replied, fixing her gaze on Maria.

"You *liked* it?" The surprise in her voice was clear. "I thought you might have been—"

"Annoyed?" Allison cut in.

"Well, yes…" Maria was totally flummoxed, and she knew that Allison had noticed. She squinted into the glare. *Damn,* she thought, *if I could read this bitch's expressions…*

"We at the U.S. Mission," Allison continued, "have been waiting for some time for an opportunity to put out a strong condemnation of the *baby-parts* issue. And your article was just what we needed. So we're really very grateful to you!"

"You mean…you're *pleased* about it?"

"Why, yes, of course," Allison said, still smiling pleasantly. "Oh…I know it probably wasn't your intention—you quite rightly assumed that we would be annoyed. You probably felt justified, given the horrible nature of the subject matter. *Baby-parts*…Yuck! I mean, you'd have to have a sick mind to believe in such stuff."

"It was a scoop and directly attacks the United States," Maria spat back. It irked her that her article hadn't struck the Mission like a thunderbolt.

"Oh, sure, it was anti-American," Allison replied nonchalantly. "We're used to this sort of thing. People like to criticize what they're envious of. It's just part of being the most powerful and democratic country in the world. I suppose that's why everyone wants to go to the U.S. By the way, how are things down in Peru?"

Maria was beside herself, but began to take control of her emotions. She reached into her bag for another cigarette. She was about to answer when Allison resumed.

"I can tell you, there's no *baby-parts* trade in the United States," Allison said in a way that made it difficult for Maria to counter. "*Baby-parts* is an old story. We successfully defused it when it first came out back in the 1980s. And the article you wrote contains nothing new."

Maria's fiery temperament would not allow that provocative remark to pass unnoticed. She pulled herself up in the chair to better challenge Allison. "What do you mean, 'nothing new'? My story ran front page all over Latin America."

Allison shifted a tiny bit in her chair, enough to move her shadow away from Maria's face and expose it fully to the sunlight again.

"Hey, calm down. Don't get me wrong," Allison shot back, enjoying the sight of Maria squinting. "It was a good article. You put it together very cleverly. But the NGO you cited, *Shield Children*—how it can honestly call itself an *impartial* non-governmental organization I don't know—has been peddling the *baby-parts* line for years. I've seen most of the quotes before."

Maria was clearly annoyed, but she couldn't stop Allison's onslaught.

"We were just wondering when someone would try to resuscitate the *baby-parts* story, and along you came."

Maria's mouth opened but no sound came out.

"Ambassador Helm has prepared a strong rebuttal on *baby-parts,* and he'll announce it at a press conference tomorrow. As you were the unfortunate journalist who swallowed the bait put out by *Shield Children,* the ambassador felt it would only be fair to give you a heads-up on the rebuttal and a chance to save your reputation."

"I didn't swallow any bait; the facts are there," Maria countered, finding her voice again. "You can't—"

"I understand you can't help but feel slighted by what I just said, but it happens to be the truth. Believe me, I know what I'm talking about. Wait…" Allison put up her hand to stop another interruption. "Let me finish, and you'll see that what I'm about to say will be to your advantage."

Maria held back, curiosity momentarily trumping anger. "What is it then?"

"I said I'd help you by giving you the text of the rebuttal ahead of tomorrow's press conference. In that way, you'll be able to prepare a follow-up piece and release it today—ahead of your colleagues in press corps. It'll give you a second scoop."

Allison bent down and pulled a single sheet of paper from the slim leather attaché case beside her chair. She handed it to Maria. "Here's Ambassador Helm's rebuttal. You can ignore the embargoed release time, and say in your story that you obtained it from…let's say…*sources close to the U.S. Mission.*"

Maria took the paper but made no attempt to read it. She was still too fired up with indignation at Allison's attack and wouldn't give her the pleasure of showing that she had anything but a passing interest in the statement.

"And—any other questions—you can reach me at the Mission."

So you think you're such a smooth operator, eh! Maria thought, folding the paper and putting it away in her bag. *You bitch.* But she could not let the conversation end in defeat and humiliation. An idea came to her as Allison rose to leave. *Let's see how your hallowed ambassador likes this!* "Yes, you're right. The story *is* the same."

Allison paused.

With a wily smile, Maria continued. "What you guys at the Mission don't realize is that the *baby-parts* trade has begun again. This time the traders don't fear media exposure since people will have the same reaction as you just did: *it's an old story, we've read it before.* You Americans will deny it, and then it'll drop from the front pages and probably from the inside pages too."

"You're joking, of course," Allison said, annoyed.

"No. You should know that news becomes old very quickly in your country. The traders know this and will continue their appalling business without consequences. I mean, they didn't start it—according to my sources, it's you Americans who are crying out for more babies to be cut up for parts to repair *your little kiddies*," Maria sneered.

"You surely can't believe that," Allison retorted. "You're making it all up. How can you be so callous? It wasn't in your article and—"

"Don't be so accusing. I love children as much as anybody else. Why do you think I'm trying to expose this dreadful trade?" She had Allison on the defensive. "Actually, that's going to be the subject of my next article; so I've given *you* some advance information as well. *And please inform your ambassador*," she said wryly as she stood and turned to leave the lounge.

What a mess, Allison thought. Maria was more of a loose cannon than she had expected. Allison needed to attack this problem from another angle. She sat down again and signaled to the waiter. She needed to think things through afresh, and black *ristretto* coffee always helped.

Chapter 7

▼

"You call yourself a 'press officer,' and you can't even convince a novice journalist to kill a story," Ambassador Helm barked at Allison. "I expected you to come back with a retraction, not promises of more dirt and lies—and who gave you permission to organize a press conference for me anyway?"

Allison thought the veins in his temples would burst. It was pointless arguing with Helm. He could never understand that the United States could not manipulate a free press, especially in a foreign country. Helm imagined he had presidential powers in Switzerland. In a sense, he did, but they were confined to the grounds of the U.S. Mission. Outside the compound, diplomacy, tactics, strategy, and patient work cultivating contacts were the rules of the game. In that respect, all countries with diplomatic missions in Geneva were equal players—and there were over one hundred of them.

"I never had any *intention* of organizing a press conference on *baby-parts*," Allison said calmly. "It was just a ploy to plant a U.S. denial with Maria."

"And did it work?" Helm demanded.

"No," Allison was forced to admit.

Helm snorted and began looking over some papers on his desk, ignoring Allison. That was the signal that the meeting was over. Allison let herself out of his office without a word. She returned to her own office on the first floor still mulling over her exchange with Maria.

A beep from her computer interrupted her thoughts. She turned to the screen. A response to her report had arrived from the State Department in Washington. It was marked *SECRET*. Washington wanted a more detailed transcript of her conversation with Maria, and urgently. Allison sighed. This would take time. She picked up the phone and tapped out her home number.

"Hello?" said a young man's voice. It was Steve, her older son.

"Hi, hon," Allison said. "Listen, I'm sorry, but something has come up, and I'm going to be late tonight." She heard a sigh at the other end of the line. "There's spaghetti sauce in the fridge, so—"

"So you're going to ask if me and Chris can make dinner for ourselves?" Steve finished her sentence ruefully. "Of course, Mom. It's not like we haven't done it before."

Allison ignored the sarcasm. "Thanks, honey. I'll be home as soon as I can. Say 'hi' to Chris for me."

"Sure, Mom." The line went dead.

Allison sighed. This type of thing happened often, and it had been happening for a long time. The boys' father had run out on them when they were just toddlers, preferring the company of a nubile secretary to Allison and her professional life. Divorce followed, and life as a single mother began. It had been tough, but she had survived. She worried about the boys, though.

It took Allison nearly two hours to reconstitute the interview with Maria, and another hour to answer the follow-up questions that popped up on her screen from Washington. Feeling tired and fed up, she decided to go home. If further questions needed an urgent answer, the communications center would see that she was logged off and would call her at home.

By the time Allison got home, all she wanted was to soak in a hot tub and fall into bed. She found a note on the kitchen table from the boys. They had gone over to a friend's house to watch a soccer match on TV and would be back by ten-thirty. She glanced at her watch; they would be home soon. There was also a P.S. on the note: *Mr. Hottinger called. Said it's urgent. PLS call back this evening, no matter what time.*

Allison looked at her watch again. In Switzerland people never called each other after eight PM. But the note did say "no matter what time."

"Oh, all right," Allison sighed, still dreaming of an inviting bath. She could hear the phone ringing at the other end and hoped nobody would answer. She was just about to hang up when Bruno Hottinger picked up.

"Oh, Allison, thank God it's you!" He sounded troubled. "I need to talk to you about Peter Zucker."

Allison wondered what this could be about. She hadn't known the Zuckers that well before their disastrous summer vacation, even though they lived only four houses apart. She had been busy at work, and her boys were too old to play with the Zucker children. But since she was American and worked at the Mission, the Zuckers had come to her for help after their children went missing. She had pulled all the strings she could, but to no avail. The children had simply disappeared without a trace. Investigations had uncovered nothing, and since the crime had no political motive or important overseas diplomatic connection, the case had been put on the back burner.

Allison remembered a particularly disturbing phone call with her long-time friend in the FBI, John Vandervelt. "We don't have anything to go on, and the local police have too many other crimes to deal with," he had said. "They're not focusing on it. I mean, look at it from their point of view. It's not a high priority case. Nobody's banging on the door for action. The Zuckers don't have any political clout. Frankly, unless there's a new lead of some sort, the case'll stay just where it is."

"You mean the case has been dropped because the Zuckers are political nobodies?" Allison asked, shocked.

"Listen Ally, this is political reality. Children have disappeared from amusement parks before. But we've also had much more gruesome stuff happening to young kids all over the country. Here we have two kids that disappeared just like that!" John snapped his fingers. "There's nothing, no rape, no bodies, no information, nothing. And the parents are foreigners who aren't savvy enough to arouse public sentiment, and who have no local platform. I'm not saying I agree with this," John added, "but you know that's the way things are over here. This is not a Charles Manson or O.J. Simpson type of case involving well-known personalities and bloody crime scenes that captivate public attention.

"I understand that you're close to these people. And I genuinely feel for them. Rest assured, if you ever get a new lead on this, I'll help in any way I can."

Allison had given a more diplomatic rendition to the Zuckers. But they weren't idiots, and they had understood. They had thanked her for intervening and then had withdrawn into their shell.

"So what is it, Bruno?" Allison asked a little too sharply. It had been a long day, and she needed sleep.

"Um, well, I have reason to believe that Peter is planning to go back to the States to find his children."

"Is that all? Can't we discuss this some other time?" she asked.

"Allison, this is serious—believe me!" Bruno was insistent. "He intends to involve you and me…I have to tell you *now*—it can't wait. We'll need to have an answer ready for him, otherwise—well, we can't let him go the same way as Martine…"

Sighing inwardly, she asked, "Why are you so worried now?"

"The important part is that we—you and I—are key elements in his plan. According to his notes, he's already assuming that we'll drop everything and go along with him."

"*According to his notes...* What do you mean?" Allison asked, more attentive now.

"Well, Renée was cleaning his place, as you know she does from time to time, and—she's not a busybody and wasn't prying into his affairs—but she was clearing up a bunch of his papers. Okay, we read them—but luckily so..."

"Please get to the point, Bruno."

"These notes are the plan he's devised, and it involves me flying him and you incognito to the U.S., going to the amusement park and investigating where the kids have gone—but without declaring our intentions to the police or to the park authorities."

Allison raised her eyebrows. "But how's he going to get into the States? He has to go through immigration at some point of entry."

"I haven't discovered all the details yet," Bruno said. "But he seems convinced that something illegal's going on over there and that there's some sort of cover-up."

Allison nodded knowingly. "And if he can discover what it is, it'll lead him to the kids?"

"Precisely. Then he would fly them out of the country—not telling the authorities. That's why he wants to get into the country without anybody realizing it. He's convinced that if the U.S. authorities find out he's back snooping around, they'll try to block his efforts."

"That's absurd. The U.S. isn't going to do that. It might be inefficient...or focusing on more high-profile crimes, but I think Peter's been watching too many movies." Allison breathed out heavily. "Thanks for telling me this, Bruno. Look, I've got to go to bed now."

"But what are we going to *do*?" Bruno asked.

Allison sighed. "I don't know. I'll give it some thought. We'll talk it over in the morning."

Bruno wasn't very happy with her response, Allison thought as she hung up the phone.

Now she had a second major problem to deal with, and she desperately needed sleep.

C h a p t e r   8

▼

Romy Tincopa had reached a stage in her life when she didn't question anything as long as she got paid for her work. She was not cynical by nature, but life had taught her that dreams were for the rich and influential and were a waste of time for people like her.

It was not that she had totally given up hoping that miracles might occur; her Catholic upbringing ensured that she was still a faithful believer. But at forty-three, she realized that her chances of having a normal family life, with a husband who honestly loved her and children of her own, were practically zero. She also refused the idea of being entrapped in a marriage of social convenience.

She paused momentarily on the gravel drive that led to the Del Solar residence, looking up at the house she was about to enter for the first time. It was certainly imposing. "You can't miss it," they had said when giving her directions. *This* was the kind of house Romy had dreamed about owning. But, she couldn't be further from fulfilling her dream. She admired the stone steps leading up to the front door on the raised ground floor. Two more stories towered above, and the windows of the top floor nestled in the massive roof.

Her admiring gaze took in the pale salmon façade and halted suddenly at the center window of the top floor. Two young faces were staring down at her. Romy waved and smiled. But to her surprise, she received no wave in return. Perhaps the children were staring out at the sea view. She was sure, though, that they had been watching her—children were always curious.

Romy had worked with enough children to know their habits. In many ways children were predictable. Usually, when waved at, children would either wave back or run away embarrassed and hide. These two did neither—they remained like statues. *Strange.*

She turned her attention to her ankle-length black dress, glancing over it to make sure it hadn't picked up any dirt on the walk up to the house. Satisfied that she looked clean and presentable, she mounted the steps to the front door and rang the bell.

Romy desperately wanted this job, even though it hadn't been clear in the job description exactly what she would be required to do other than teach Spanish. Romy's finances were in an appalling state; in fact, she needed this job if she were going to have money to live on for the next few months. Living illegally in Peru wasn't easy, and being at the mercy of corrupt local government officials meant that a sizeable part of her modest income went to greasing palms. She refused to consider offering her favors in settlement—she hadn't sunk that low yet. The result was that she lived from day to day on very little.

Romy was well educated and lucky enough to have come from a good family in Argentina. She had excelled in languages at school. Her mother was originally from Germany and had always spoken German to her. Romy had learned English from a tutor, and, of course, she spoke Spanish. Therefore, when it came to picking a profession, teaching languages seemed the most obvious. Less obvious was why Romy, smart and good-looking, had never married. But her parents' anachronistic ideas for her future had put an early end to marriage prospects—and eventually had driven her from her parents' home.

Romy had had no shortage of suitors. Her peach-blossom skin, steel-blue eyes, and raven tresses constantly turned men's heads. Having a German mother and Argentinean father had produced this effect, and had also made her tall for a Latin American woman.

Much to Romy's distress, however, her parents had not only turned potential suitors away, but had directed them toward her two elder sisters. Worse yet, Romy's mother had intended to *keep* her out of circulation and compel her to look after her parents in their declining years. When she had found this out, Romy had immediately left. As many Argentineans looking for work did at that time, she had made her way to Peru where she had found a position in an institute caring for mentally handicapped children. But that eventually had become too distressing.

The front door of the Del Solar residence opened, and a maid dressed in black and wearing a white starched apron inquired about Romy's business. Romy replied, and the maid hesitated as if uncertain whether to let her in at the front door or redirect her to a staff entrance. But Romy stood erect, clearly of a certain social stature, and the maid stepped back and opened the solid rosewood door.

Romy didn't have to wait long for Don Gonzalo to appear in the lavish vestibule and greet her. "I am Don Gonzalo Del Solar," he said pleasantly. "Everybody calls me Don Gonzalo." He seemed in a great hurry. *Perhaps he's going to tell me that the job has already been filled.*

But to the contrary, on seeing Romy, Don Gonzalo had been brought up short. This young woman was an extremely agreeable surprise. He had expected a matronly, middle-aged teacher, but seldom had he seen someone as naturally beautiful and serene as Romy. As she produced a smile for him, her striking features literally glowed. She did appear a little gaunt, but a simple and straightforward kindness shone from her—something Don Gonzalo had never seen in his wife. Such natural pleasantness caught him unawares. He was certain that *this* woman would succeed in bringing the children around.

"Bring us some tea in my study," Don Gonzalo ordered the maid—and he led Romy down the hall to meet with her in private before his wife could frighten her off. Lucia preferred to get rid of the children; what she had in mind still made him cringe.

Seated behind his desk, Don Gonzalo attempted to sound businesslike.

"Er—*Señora*—or is it *Señorita* Tincopa?" he asked.

"*Señorita* Tincopa," Romy answered.

The maid came in with a pot of tea and two cups on a silver tray. Don Gonzalo waited until she had poured the tea and left the room.

"Thank you so much for coming, Señorita Tincopa," Don Gonzalo resumed. "I have looked at your qualifications, and they seem excellent." He took a sip of tea, and the young woman did likewise. "Um, the reason we have called upon your services is to teach our children Spanish," Don Gonzalo said, a little nervously.

He saw that she was perplexed, but that she said nothing.

"You see, we—my wife and I, that is—recently adopted two young children…It's a difficult situation to explain…Even though they love it here—who wouldn't?—we are having difficulty communicating with them."

Romy kept looking at Don Gonzalo intently, not wanting to miss a word.

"You see," he continued, "we don't want to start off on the wrong foot. They can't understand us—and we can't comprehend a word they're saying either—and that makes it all rather difficult. The bottom line is that we urgently need for them to know Spanish." He smiled, satisfied that he had at last unburdened himself of his problem.

As Don Gonzalo spoke, Romy had pondered his words. "Where do they come from—what language do they speak, then?" she asked innocently.

An obvious question, and Don Gonzalo had prepared himself for it. Chavez had told him what to say. "They were in an orphanage in the United States but were not American," he explained.

His well-rehearsed manner struck Romy as quite different from his earlier nervousness.

"They" he said, "—a young boy and a little girl, presumably brother and sister—were in an orphanage for *abandoned* children. Very little is known about them, according to the U.S. authorities, apart from the fact that they were found apparently *abandoned*"—Don Gonzalo emphasized the word again as Chavez had instructed him to—"cold and hungry on the outskirts of Chicago. The little girl was suffering from hypothermia and had to be hospitalized, but she's fine now. Unfortunately, they speak no known language. They had no identification papers, and nobody turned up to claim them."

Don Gonzalo paused and looked at Romy keenly to assure himself that she believed the tale. She was still listening intently, obviously assuming he had more to say.

"We had been in the market—what I mean is, we had been searching for some time to adopt children so that we could have a family of our own..." Don Gonzalo continued. "You see, my wife unfortunately can't have any...and when we were told about these two, we simply jumped at the idea. We wanted to give them a good, loving home—all done legally, of course..." He immediately regretted the remark, but was relieved that Romy's expression didn't change. He resumed his story.

"But our inability to communicate with the children has made things extremely difficult, especially for my dear wife who put so much hope in having them here. It has been a costly adventure—what I mean is that it is costing us a lot in stress and anguish since we love the children so much."

"*Nobody* can make out what they are saying?" Romy asked incredulously. "Even the Americans in Chicago?"

"I suppose...They doubtless had the same—oh—experience we did," he replied, searching for words. "Well, the problem is that they don't say much at all. We thought at first that they couldn't speak, but then we overheard them whispering to each other in their bedroom."

Romy saw that Don Gonzalo was desperate. He wouldn't be going into such detail with her if the position were already promised to someone else. She felt more confident. "And you want me to teach them Spanish—that's the job?"

"Er—yes, that's it!" Don Gonzalo replied, relieved that the ordeal of telling his memorized story was now over. "Will you take it on? I assure you the conditions will be more than satisfactory—I mean…um…considering your current situation."

Romy hated living in this illegal vacuum—it hurt her pride that she had no choice but to accept what others offered. And it angered her that everybody, including this seemingly nice man, knew about her "situation" and felt the need to remind her of it. It was blackmail, of course, and she had no choice but to accept it. She chose not to comment and only nodded.

"You will reside in the house, naturally, so as to be in close touch with the children at all times. And…just one thing more, Señorita Tincopa," Don Gonzalo said. His voice was suddenly quieter and his tone more conspiratorial. "We must maintain the utmost discretion regarding this business. My wife's a little sensitive about the social implications of all this…you do understand?"

"Of course, yes," Romy said, not really understanding at all why anyone would be ashamed of having taken in lost orphans. It sparked her curiosity. "But how do you mean?"

"Well, my wife doesn't want to admit to her friends…they can be quite catty; you know these socialites…that she can't converse with her own children—"

"It is not that at all!" a sharp voice broke in from behind Romy and echoed all around the room. It quite startled her. Don Gonzalo's head jerked up, and he frowned as his wife entered the study.

Romy immediately rose from her chair and turned to face the person who could only be Don Gonzalo's wife. A servant would never be dressed so expensively in an embroidered turquoise silk dress, nor would a servant emit an air of such total command over all in her presence. Not a hair was out of place in her tightly wound bun. Nor was there a hint of a welcoming smile on her face. Romy sensed danger.

"I am Señora Del Solar," she said, without offering a hand or moving toward Romy. "Everybody knows how generous we have been in accepting the children into our family home. If we wanted to gain gratification from the *social implications*…" she looked disapprovingly at Don Gonzalo, "then we have done it already. Everyone is talking about our *generosity* for having offered a home to these poor children." She paused. "I assume you are the Spanish teacher?"

Romy felt uneasy; this woman scared her. She wanted to run from this house immediately. But she said, "Yes, I—"

"Let us be clear about this from the start," Señora Del Solar bellowed, glaring at Romy. "The children cannot participate fully in the social activities planned for them without knowing the local language. This is the reason why you are here. I trust you understand this?"

In an attempt to lighten the atmosphere, Don Gonzalo put on an excessively jovial voice. "Yes, I've explained the situation to Señorita Tincopa, dear. I was just about to take her up to meet the children. Why don't you come with us?"

"*I* will take her to see them. *You* stay here and look after the formalities," Señora Del Solar commanded. "Please follow me," she said to Romy in the same tone, making her way to the door to the hall.

Romy glanced back at Don Gonzalo for permission to follow Señora Del Solar. Don Gonzalo was smiling weakly, acquiescently. He nodded his head and motioned with his hands that she should follow his wife. *Poor man*, she thought as she walked away.

They mounted a grandiose staircase the likes of which Romy had seen only in American movies. The stairs were covered with patterned silk carpet that shone in the light from the huge window above the entrance door. The walls were lined with life-size portraits of what Romy assumed were members of the family lineage. It struck her as strange to see such a plush, old-European interior in a house in Pimentel where the hot climate lent itself to less-upholstered decoration.

Señora Del Solar moved along the landing past what Romy assumed were bedroom doors. The decoration was no different here except that the paintings were smaller and showed scenes from different countries. She followed Señora Del Solar up a narrow, less expensively carpeted set of stairs that led to the floor under the roof. In most houses of this size, these were the servants' quarters, *and the children are up here!* So the two faces she had seen at the window were the adopted children. She thought back to the number of doors she had passed on the floor below. *Why not give them a room down there?*

She was mollified somewhat when they entered the children's room. Despite the low attic ceiling, it was spacious and obviously newly decorated. But it felt cut off from the rest of the house. The two children were still standing near the window but now faced the door. Romy saw them draw back as Señora Del Solar entered. Their eyes shot toward Romy as they noticed her. But they quickly fixed back on Señora Del Solar. The children were obviously preoccupied—*or are they afraid?* thought Romy, perplexed. Both pairs of small eyes were wide open and now glancing back and forth between her and their adoptive mother. *It's as if they're waiting for an attack but don't know which one of us will strike first,* Romy thought.

Both children were dressed impeccably—*too* neatly, Romy thought. The boy, who looked about seven or eight years old, wore an English-style gray suit with short trousers and knee-length socks. The girl, who seemed about half his age, had on a pretty pink dress a couple of sizes too big for her, obviously purchased without the girl being present to try it on. Neither child smiled.

Their gaze abandoned Romy and concentrated on Señora Del Solar as she strode across the room and tightened, rather brutally it seemed to Romy, the loose knot of the boy's tie. He didn't make even the slightest attempt to resist, and he uttered no word of complaint—even in a foreign language. Romy thought she detected a look of defiance on his face. He glanced quickly at Romy again, this time with an expression that seemed to call for help. *No, I'm imagining things.* Romy dismissed the thought.

"This is Miguel and this is Alicia," Señora Del Solar said, turning to face Romy.

"I'm pleased to meet you both," Romy said, trying to sound pleasant and friendly in the hope that the children would understand her intent, if not her words. She approached them carefully and offered her hand; her smile must have touched something inside them, since, after a moment's hesitation, the boy advanced his hand and touched hers. But Alicia hung back and stuck close to her brother, gripping his clothes.

"Well, well, you're certainly *privileged!*" Señora Del Solar said with surprise. "I haven't had the slightest success from those little—" she cut herself off. "So," she said, "when can you start? I want results quickly."

"Right away, if you like," Romy answered without hesitation. It was the children—something inside compelled her to remain close to them.

C h a p t e r 9

▼

Peter knocked on Allison's door, then stood back and prayed she was home.

The door opened. "Peter, how nice to see you!" Allison exclaimed, though obviously taken aback by the late hour.

"I apologize for stopping by so late, but I've got to discuss something with you," he said urgently.

She beckoned him to come in and they sat down in the living room.

As Peter prepared to speak, he nervously picked at his fingernails. "Look Allison, I need your help. I'm going back to California to find Mark and Nicolette…"

My God! Bruno was right, Allison thought, casting her mind back to Bruno's call yesterday. Feigning surprise, she said, "That's great, Peter. Have you had some fresh news?"

"No, none. But here's what I plan to do…"

Allison listened as Peter, speaking non-stop and without emotion, laid his plan before her as if it were the most natural and logical approach in the world. She raised her eyebrows as he outlined her role and Bruno's. Feeling increasingly uneasy, she spoke.

"Do you realize what you're doing, Peter?" Allison said, cutting him off in mid-sentence. "You'd be committing a federal offense."

"But I'd use my own name, and they'd never know what I'd be bringing—"

Allison put her hands to her ears. "I don't want to know the details—anything that's not strictly honest will get you into deep trouble."

"That may be, but—"

"There's no *but* about it," Allison said. "Entering the United States under any kind of false pretense means that you could be deported on the spot and never allowed to return. And then what would be your chances of ever getting Mark and Nicolette back?"

"I've thought about all that," Peter said, confidently dismissing her objections. "That won't happen—not with my plan."

"Listen to me," Allison continued, lowering her voice so that her sons upstairs would not overhear. "I work for the U.S. government, and the mere fact that we're having this conversation is wrong. I am *bound* to report it—but I won't because of the special nature of the situation."

"I realize all that," Peter interrupted, "but please hear me out. I have more to tell you—"

"That's just what I can't do," Allison countered. "Let me explain my position. I could get into serious trouble for aiding and abetting any aspect of your illegal plan to enter the United States. And it wouldn't just be my *job* at stake—I could be sent to jail as well. What would Steve and Chris do then?" she said, pointing upstairs. "So, please don't ask me anything more on this subject."

Peter looked crestfallen. "Couldn't we just meet up in California? You don't have to know how I got there. And then we could work on the rest of my plan together. I'll need the help of an American on the ground there—someone I can trust!"

Allison stared at him; he *wasn't* giving up. "I'm obviously not getting through to you, Peter. I'll spell it out: I cannot aid you in any way in this mad scheme of yours."

Peter's expectant smile disappeared.

"It's not difficult to get into the United States," she said. "You have a passport. You don't need a visa. I can't understand why you have to hide your real purpose. You have every right to go and talk to the police and any other party who could help you pick up Mark and Nicolette's trail. It's a free country we're talking about—"

"Perhaps for you, but for me—a foreigner—I'm not so sure."

"What on earth do you mean?" Allison said.

"Okay. Here's what I think," Peter said. "I'm convinced the case has been dropped, essentially because we're foreigners living far away in Europe—"

"That's not true!" Allison was adamant.

"Why, then, has there been no follow-up? Nobody's contacted me even to say 'We haven't found Mark and Nicolette,' or 'You should assume they're dead,' or whatever. No, there's been absolutely nothing. I contacted your Mission, and they sent me to Bern where your consulate said it had no news. I'm not even convinced they sent off an e-mail to the States. But even if they did, they must have got nothing useful back, otherwise I would have been told about it. The Swiss consulate in Los Angeles wasn't any better. I got a polite letter from the consul saying he was sorry but there were no new developments. Try the police department myself, he suggested. And, of course, getting information from the Los Angeles Police Department is like getting blood out of a stone. They tell you nothing over the phone. I even wrote to them and the only answer I got was a pre-printed slip saying my letter had been forwarded to the proper department. And then nothing. Nothing at all. I'm a pariah—to be avoided at all costs. That's why I must go back and see what I can find before they discover who I really am and block my way."

"You've got it all wrong, Peter," Allison said. "Things don't happen that way in the States. Sure, you've hit bureaucratic brick walls—all Americans do. It's part of living in a large country and dealing with people who have too much to do. Yes, the squeaky wheel gets the grease. Maybe your case *is* on the back burner because you're not there to prod them. So go back. Demand answers. But do it openly."

He sighed. "It's different for you, Allison."

"Look, I've made some coffee," Allison said to break the tension. "Would you like some? Or a glass of wine maybe?" She got up to go into the kitchen.

"Nothing alcoholic," Peter replied. "I don't want to dull my senses. A cup of coffee would be nice, though."

Allison came back minutes later with two steaming mugs and handed one to Peter, who now seemed less combative. "You really mean to go through with this, don't you?"

"Yes," Peter replied in a clear voice. "And I'm not going to let anything stop me this time. I'm going to get Mark and Nicolette back, alive or dead. Martine will only get better if she knows what's become of them—and that goes for me too."

He paused and sipped the coffee. His look was blank, but Allison could see that his mind was working. They remained silent for a while.

"I'm sorry to put you in this position, Allison, especially after all you've already done for me," Peter finally said. "But, I wasn't the first to break the law. Martine and I went in all innocence with our family to see your country—this was our first trip to America. We went to see what everyone told us was a fine, welcoming and child-friendly country..." His voice was slightly sarcastic. "We abided by all the laws and rules; we paid all our bills, stole nothing, insulted nobody, and lost our two lovely chil—" Tears welled up in his eyes and he choked on his words.

"Don't do this to yourself, Peter."

"I don't know whether they were kidnapped, raped, murdered, or what—all illegal acts in the United States. And even if they just wandered off and got lost, nobody found them and nobody came to their aid. Surely non-assistance to minors is an offense in your country?"

"Peter—"

"Allison, I'll do anything to find them. Let's be clear on this. I swear by Almighty God that I'll let nothing get in my way anymore. I'll kill if need be. I know what I am doing is right. And frankly, I don't care what happens to me. If finding Mark and Nicolette means spending the rest of my days in a U.S. prison, so be it. It'll be worth it. But I'll get my children back first, of that I assure you…"

"Let's not get dramatic, Peter—"

"But the whole thing *is* dramatic! Don't you see? If you help me, it will make my task easier and get me to the children quicker. What would you do in my place if it were your two boys?"

The mention of her sons gave Allison an excuse not to answer Peter's question. "Excuse me a sec. I need to check on the boys upstairs."

Steve and Chris were in their bedrooms finishing their homework. For once she was glad to see that the television on the mezzanine had been left on—the noise made it difficult for them to hear the conversation downstairs. Allison proceeded to her bedroom and into the adjoining bathroom. The halogen spotlights over the large wall mirror were unflattering, laying bare the slightest blemish and line on her face. But she lingered there, looking blankly at herself and wondering what she should do. Although guilt-ridden by her refusal to help Peter, she knew she had no choice.

Ten minutes passed before she reappeared in the living room. Peter was seated, staring at the floor, deep in thought. He looked up at her expectantly.

"Peter…" Allison said, sounding unsure of herself. "It's difficult for me…in my situation. You must understand that my hands are tied—I *want* to help you, I really do. But…"

Peter dropped his gaze to the floor. Allison became angry at being put in this position. She couldn't stand this blackmail!

"Peter, you have to understand—"

"I do. Please forgive me for having asked," Peter replied politely. "Let's just forget this conversation ever took place." He wished her a pleasant night and took his leave.

From the window, Allison watched him return to his house. She didn't sleep that night—not at all.

Chapter 10

▼

El Crónico, Lima, lunes 22 de enero

EXCLUSEVE REPORT

U.S. CLINIC PAYS $2M FOR FOREIGN BABY-PARTS

A top American clinic has spent over $2 million on illicit children's organs to save the lives of young Americans in need of kidneys, livers, eyes, and bone marrow, according to a former employee of the New Life Clinic in Great Falls, Montana.

The body parts all came from illegal sources outside of the United States, with many originating from children butchered for the purpose in Peru, the employee revealed. He asked to remain anonymous, fearing for his life, notably from the U.S. authorities that "are turning a blind eye" to the illicit trade.

Among the recipients of the illegal organs are family members of prominent U.S. congressmen, the employee said.

"They come to Montana to be far away from the U.S. media and inquisitive eyes," he stated.

A Peruvian government statement expressed "outrage and disgust" at the trade, adding that it would lodge a formal complaint with Washington.

The U.S. State Department spokesman, Dean Finch, expressed strong doubts that Americans were involved in any such "abhorrent" trade, and promised that the matter would be investigated.

The U.S. ambassador in Geneva, where *El Crónico* first broke the story, was initially more categorical: "It is a total fabrication," William Helm said in a statement. However, he later canceled a planned press conference on the subject, no doubt afraid of probing questions from the international press.

Maria Romero smiled smugly as she put down the newspaper. She didn't need to read the rest of the story—she knew it by heart. But it gave her a thrill to see in print what she had helped put together. She imagined Allison Cox reading it as well. *See what comes from trying to push me around, you rich American bitch!* More than anything, she wanted to see Allison's dismay and to taunt her.

She would call Allison, ostensibly for an official reaction, but in reality to hear her annoyed voice. She dialed her direct line at the Mission. "I'll bet you're not as cocky now," she muttered.

The number rang several times before someone picked it up. "Public affairs," the female voice at the other end said.

"Hello Allison," Maria said slowly, relishing the moment. "I suppose you saw the *baby-parts* story this morning…"

"I'm sorry, but Mrs. Cox is away from her desk at the moment," the voice answered. "I'm her secretary. Can I help you or get her to call you back?" The woman's tone was polite but formal.

"Mierda!" Maria swore, then instantly regretted losing her cool. She hoped the secretary didn't understand Spanish. She would try another tack. "Do you happen to know if she's seen today's *El Crónico?*" she asked, trying to sound pleasant and innocent.

"I really can't tell you," the secretary replied. "Only Mrs. Cox can answer you. Give me your name and telephone number and I'll make sure she gets back to you as soon as she returns."

"Just tell her that Maria Romero called." It was all that Maria could muster, and she hung up.

At the Mission, the secretary knew that Allison was in the regular morning staff meeting, and it didn't take her long to decide that the message did not warrant disturbing her there. She stuck a note with the message on Allison's phone.

In the ambassador's conference room, the staff meeting was not going well for Allison. Ambassador Helm had disposed of regular business swiftly in order to focus on the latest *El Crónico* piece and to berate Allison in front of her colleagues.

"What kind of an incompetent sloth are you?" he barked. "You call yourself a 'public affairs officer' and you can't even contain a two-bit freelance journalist?"

Bob Peters, who headed up Humanitarian Affairs, came to Allison's defense. "I think you're overstepping a bit here, sir—with all due respect."

"How dare you interrupt me and use that tone of voice!" Helm shouted back, banging his fist on the table.

Allison, realizing it would serve no purpose and might prolong Helm's tirade, had said nothing. Now, however, grateful that someone was bothering to support her, she spoke.

"Thanks Bob, but I'm used to this kind of criticism from the ambassador. He's had it in for me ever since he hit on me and I turned him down."

"Why you little…!"

"You see," Allison said, motioning with her open palm toward Helm.

He was ready to explode. "This meeting is over," Helm shouted. "Except for you!" He directed his glare at Allison who was calmly finishing her coffee. "I want to see you in my office—*now!*" With that, he got to his feet and stormed out of the room.

"Watch out—maybe he's going to make another move on you," Bob joked to break the tension.

"Oh, yeah! I very much doubt that," she replied, allowing a tight smile to appear on her tired face. "He's probably going to have me shipped to some whorehouse in his home state!"

Deep down, Allison felt extremely nervous about her future. Over the last week, since the confounded *baby-parts* issue had resurfaced, nothing had gone well for her. And a difficult-to-destroy, explosive issue like this was just what Helm needed to rid himself of her. After this morning's outburst, Helm would have to find a way to save face—and she was obviously going to be the fall guy.

"Damn the man!" she swore once everyone had left the room. Since Helm had arrived two years ago, she had tried so hard to accommodate him. Now, she would most certainly be posted elsewhere and be forced to leave Geneva. The bad performance write-up from Helm would taint her personnel record and damage her promotion chances in the future. Her mind turned to her sons and all the problems of uprooting them again, changing schools. Then she put these thoughts aside and went back to her more immediate concern of the meeting with Helm.

The ambassador had requested his secretary to stay in the office, probably hoping that her presence would add to Allison's humiliation and allay suspicions as to what was going on. Although the secretary was seated when Allison entered the room, Allison was not invited to sit down. She remained standing in front of Helm's desk.

"The State Department," Helm said in a calmer voice, "has asked for your return to Washington for two weeks to help sort out this *baby-parts* business. I can't understand why they should want *you*—and I told them what I thought of your performance here at post—but they still insist it's you they want. That's their prerogative…"

Allison knew that a request from Washington could not be denied.

"But, before you leave, and to ensure that you don't come back," Helm added, "you won't be surprised to learn that I've put in an official request to Washington for your permanent recall from post. Among the reasons I've cited are ineptitude, inability to properly carry out your duties here, and my personal dissatisfaction with your performance as a foreign service officer."

Helm looked up at Allison with a self-satisfied smirk. Allison met his stare, expressionless.

"Here's the cable from State. Take it!" Helm said, nearly throwing the official government telegram across his desk. "I don't think we have any further business." His tone was dismissive.

"You don't, but *I* do," Allison said. She leaned toward him. "And it's for the record. You, *Mr. Ambassador*, are an asshole." She glanced pointedly at the secretary who was taking notes. "That's a-s-s-h-o-l-e—spelled as it sounds."

A shocked scowl replaced the contemptible smile on Helm's face. The secretary didn't dare look up.

"You might have the money to buy political appointments like this one," Allison said, pointing her finger at Helm. "But in no way do you command respect as a person or advance the interests of the United States of America. And one day, mark my words, that will be clear for everyone to see."

She turned and left the office, leaving Helm agape.

Part II

▼

...And back

Chapter 11

▼

"Please stop crying, Nicky," Mark begged his little sister. "They'll come up if they hear you—please, please!"

"I w-w-want *Mammi...*" Nicolette said more loudly through her sobs. "I want *Ma-mmi-iii*—"

"Nicky, shut up!" Mark clamped his hand over her mouth. He hated doing it, but it was the only way to prevent her waking up everyone in the house. Mark feared someone might come and silence Nicolette more viciously, or even take her away. He loathed all the adults in the house, and the possibility that they might separate his sister from him made him detest them all the more.

He cautiously released her mouth and took her by the shoulders. "You've got to pipe down—*now!*" He looked at her intently. "Listen, I'm working on an escape plan to get us home, and they mustn't suspect anything!"

Mark had been awake for several hours turning the plan over in his mind. Escaping from the house would be like running unseen from a playground jungle gym to the swings, and then—if his friends still hadn't spotted him—making a dash for the sandbox and over to the safety of the bushes behind the wooden bench. The idea excited him, and he had been thinking of finding his way through the house unseen to the front door and beyond when Nicolette had suddenly woken up in tears, screaming in Swiss German for her mother.

Mark's news had an immediate effect on Nicolette. The rhythm of the little girl's sobs decreased, and, through tears, she looked up to meet her brother's eyes. Curiosity about his escape plan momentarily overcame her distress. She sat up in bed to hear more; Mark's face was beaming with enthusiasm and expectation. But suddenly, they both froze...there was a noise outside the door.

The crying had also awakened Romy. It hadn't been very loud, but her room was directly beneath the children's. She was a light sleeper, and in the silence of the early morning hours, the sound had easily pierced the floor. She had hastily put on a bathrobe and crept along the hallway and up the staircase. She had stood for a moment outside their door, listening for the noise. But it had stopped. Romy thought about going back to her room. But no. She wanted to help them. That was now her job, and gaining their confidence was part of it. She turned the doorknob.

The door was locked. *But why?* Out of the corner of her eye, she spied a key hanging on a hook to the left of the doorframe. Without hesitating, Romy slipped it off and slid it into the keyhole, expecting it to work—and it did.

Stepping into the room, she was startled by the extreme fright on the children's faces. They were still traumatized by having been abandoned and moved down to Peru, but why were there tears on the little girl's face now? She approached them with a comforting smile.

"Oh…don't cry, my little one," she said to Nicolette. She gently dabbed the girl's cheeks with a tissue from a fancy dispenser near the beds.

Nicolette pulled away, her eyes wide open with alarm. She shot a *help me!* look over at Mark who sat frozen by her side.

"What ever is the matter?" Romy asked. "Your friend Romy is here." She wanted to take the girl into her arms and hug her tightly to comfort her. But she suppressed the urge, fearing it would break the tiny piece of trust she had established with the children, especially with the little girl, during the few days since she had moved into the house.

The situation increasingly puzzled her. Since her arrival, neither Mark nor Nicolette had uttered a single word—in *any* language. They had ignored her questions and attempts at conversation. But they seemed to have accepted her presence and now appeared more at ease around her than around the others. Once, they had walked around the garden with her and shown interest in the plants and other vegetation she pointed out. Miguel had been attentive that day, but then his concentration had moved to something beyond the garden. She had tried to make out the target of his interest. But when he noticed, he brought his gaze back.

Perhaps it was the starkness of the night that made the children wary of her, Romy thought. But now that she was up, she might as well use the moment to ease their fears about her.

"Hey, look, Alicia," Romy said, sitting down on the bed next to Nicolette and gently putting her arm around the girl's small shoulders. Nicolette looked away and wriggled uncomfortably. "No, look at me, Alicia...*Alicia, Alicia...*I know this is all very strange to you, but *please* try to understand that I am your friend—*friend*, try to understand the word *friend*. This will be a good word for us to start with."

Nicolette's disinterest increased, and she looked away again. Romy felt that she had to start insisting a tiny bit if she was to show the Del Solars some sign of progress.

"Alicia, *Alicia, please...*" She pointed at Nicolette and then to herself. "You are Alicia...I am Romy...Alicia...*Romy*—"

Miguel touched Romy's arm and wagged his finger in her face. "Nicolette, *ned* Alicia...*ned* Alicia...Nicolette, *Nicolette!*" Seeing that Romy still didn't understand, the boy thought hard: "Nicolette, *NICHT* Alicia!"

"German!" Romy exclaimed, bringing her hands up to her mouth in astonishment.

The children stared at her, motionless.

"*Wie heisst Du?*" Romy asked Nicolette, switching from Spanish to German. "What is your name—Is it Nicolette? *Nicolette?*"

The little girl looked at her, open-mouthed, as if about to utter something, but not daring to. Her eyes shot toward her brother again, and then a rapid stream of strange German-sounding words flowed from her mouth. Miguel instantly replied with a similar but shorter machine-gun burst of words. Then they both backed away, staring at Romy, wide-eyed.

Romy felt confused, but excited. She had made a breakthrough! She was certain of it. She wouldn't pursue it now; she needed time to think it all through. And she believed the children also needed time to digest this new possibility.

Romy smiled and got up to leave. She had left the door ajar, and had she turned toward it a second earlier, she would have made out Señora Del Solar moving silently away.

Chapter 12

▼

The three executives from Schwan Pharmaceuticals were making themselves comfortable in the wide and inviting fawn-colored leather seats. The single flight attendant on board the Gulfstream was carefully putting their suit jackets on hangers and stowing them away in the small wardrobe compartment at the forward end of the cabin. Two of the executives sat in adjacent seats on one side of the central table facing the company's chairman, who had been accorded, without having to ask, the pair of forward-facing seats. With its white linen tablecloth topped by a single yellow rose in a silver bud vase, the table held great promise. The base of the vase was weighted to prevent its toppling, so that even during extreme turbulence, it rarely tipped. And very little of that was predicted on the route to Los Angeles today.

The three had made this trip many times before. They knew that within minutes, the pretty flight attendant with the shoulder-length, fair hair and inviting smile would serve them drinks and take their breakfast order. These top decision-makers of Switzerland's mighty pharmaceuticals conglomerate enjoyed not only the luxury and convenience of private-jet travel, but also the seclusion that let them finalize strategy away from prying ears. They were heading to the monthly meeting of directors of the firm's twenty-three affiliates. This time, the chosen meeting place was their plant near Los Angeles—always a popular venue in wintertime because of guaranteed warm weather.

The jovial atmosphere on board instantly dissipated when a fourth passenger appeared in the cabin. Geneva Business Jets wasn't respecting its flight exclusivity agreement with Schwan!

"What nerve!" the chairman whispered to the others as he glared at the stranger. "He's even coming over here to introduce himself. Goddammit, this is a private flight!" Gesturing to the chief financial officer, the chairman said: "Walter, call the pilot!" But before he could get up out of his seat, the new arrival was already upon them.

"Good morning, gentlemen," the man said with assurance. He was in a plain dark-gray, slightly worn suit and was smiling affably. "Please don't get up on my account," he added, gesturing to the CFO. They looked at him coldly, unable to conceal their displeasure. But trapped in their seats, they were at the mercy of this stranger who was standing looking down at them. "I'll be traveling with you to LA—"

"But—"

"I know this is your flight, and I won't be interfering with you. I'm a Federal Flight Safety Inspector, and I'm obliged to make spot checks on privately chartered aircraft licensed to operate out of Switzerland." He put his right hand into his inside breast pocket and drew out a laminated card with his photograph and name on it. It had all the hallmarks of Swiss officialdom, including an ink stamp and the Swiss shield in the top left corner. The three executives stared at it, mesmerized by the authority that such a card always imposed on the citizens of a well-ordered country—even though they had never seen such a card before.

The three exchanged embarrassed glances and looked up at the stranger with polite smiles. They proffered their hands at nearly the same time in a clumsy race to greet the inspector and thus compensate for their initial impolite welcome.

"Um—yes, hello."

"As you can see, my name's Peter Zucker," the stranger said. He showed his card around again before pocketing it and shaking the hands awaiting his. During all this time, his left hand remained at his side clutching a black attaché case.

"I want to assure you that I will not be intruding in the slightest way during your flight—except for take-off and landing and in case of turbulence, when I will occupy a seat here in *your* cabin." With a slight chuckle, Peter added, "You see, even *I* must abide by safety regulations. And it isn't every day that you have a private safety control officer on your flight!"

"Yes, that's right," the chairman said unhesitatingly, laughing at the joke. Now that he felt in command again, his tone was back to one of extreme cordiality. "There are plenty of free seats here, and we can't sit in them all at once!" he added magnanimously. "So, please feel free to use one if you need to at any point in the flight…if you have to write up your report or whatever…"

"That's extremely gracious of you, sir," Peter said in gratitude. "I wish all private passengers were as understanding as you. Thank you again, and I wish you a smooth flight."

As soon as he was gone, the three agreed what an efficient country Switzerland was, constantly looking after the safety of its citizens, and how good it was to be Swiss.

The flight attendant returned with a small tray holding three tall-stemmed glasses of the best French champagne.

Peter quickly went into the tiny lavatory at the front of the plane opposite the small galley. He slid the aluminum bolt to the *LOCK DOOR* position and took several deep breaths. He had passed his first test. He had pretended to be someone else, and in a matter of seconds had quite artfully sold a stream of lies to three of the most powerful executives in Switzerland!

His satisfaction was fleeting, however. It was not easy to suddenly assume a different—and dishonest—existence after a life of normal, upright dealings with others. But in this case, the end justified the means. Even so, Peter fought an inner reticence that said: *Put it off. It'll be easier at another time.* He thought of his children, and the inner doubt vanished.

His mental preparedness was still far ahead of his body's physical reaction to what he was doing, however. In the mirror he saw beads of perspiration on his forehead. His shirt collar felt damp, especially in the air-conditioned cool of the jet. He looked pale and drained. Peter put down the attaché case for the first time since leaving home early that morning and mopped the sweat off his head and face. He dabbed his skin with paper towels soaked in cold water from the tap. He flushed the toilet to give the executives the impression that he had used it; they mustn't wonder what he was doing. Peter waited thirty seconds, and then, smiling confidently, stepped back into public view.

The flight attendant, who was in the galley busily securing loose objects before take-off, inquired kindly, "Everything okay?"

Peter was taken aback by the question, but quickly realized that she was referring more to the state of the lavatory than his composure. "Um—yes," he said, quickly thinking to add, "Very clean. But it's a bit difficult to turn around in there—I shall have to lose some weight!"

She smiled and continued with her tasks.

Peter glanced back down the passenger cabin and was relieved to see the executives relaxed and chatting over their drinks. *They suspect nothing!* he thought, and he immediately felt better.

He went into the cockpit where Bruno Hottinger was running through the pre-flight checks with the co-pilot. The two exchanged glances, and Peter nodded to indicate that things were going as planned. Bruno said nothing; the co-pilot was present and the cockpit voice recorder was on.

Peter and Bruno had gone over everything several times before today and one last time in Bruno's car as they drove together to the airport that morning. Bruno had dropped Peter off at the Intercontinental Hotel, and there Peter had caught a taxi to the far end of Geneva's Cointrin Airport where the private charter services were located. He had checked in with an official ticket that Bruno had given him and shown his normal red Swiss passport to the border police officer, who had given it only a cursory glance. His suitcase had disappeared through an opening behind the single check-in desk that Geneva Business Jets operated in the small, functional departure building. Through the window, he saw his suitcase disappearing into the back of a van to be driven out to the plane.

Because of the possibility that his luggage would be x-rayed, Peter had decided not to chance hiding his assault rifle in the suitcase. Instead, Bruno had agreed to take it disassembled among his tools straight onto the plane during one of his maintenance visits the day before; he would reverse the process in LA. Like all able-bodied Swiss males, Peter had to do a couple of weeks of military refresher training every year. And because Switzerland must be able to mobilize its civilian army at short notice, every soldier kept an assault rifle and several magazines of ammunition at home. Peter's 5.6 mm *Sturmgewehr 90* was an indispensable item for his trip. He knew how to use the weapon and was prepared for any contingency.

Bruno had assured Peter that getting onto the plane would be easy and that the other passengers would swallow any half-plausible excuse for his being there. He had been right. Everything had gone without a hitch. He was even a little disappointed that the *Schwan* executives hadn't scrutinized his identity card, especially after all the trouble that he and Bruno had taken to fabricate it. They had spent hours at Peter's desktop PC, scanning in his own air traffic controller's airport access card and Bruno's pilot's license in order to fashion an official-looking *Federal Flight Safety Inspectorate* identity card. According to Bruno, it wouldn't pass the scrutiny of a Swiss airport official, but would easily be accepted at airports abroad—especially outside Europe.

They had also made up business cards with a false name. These were in the black attaché case that Peter gripped so tightly. Also carefully hidden in a false lining were the children's passports, several recent photographs of them, and

37,000 dollars—all the money that Peter could pull together in cash from his life savings.

Peter felt a hand touch his shoulder. "You'd better take your seat, sir," the flight attendant said. "We're about to take off." She was always smiling. For the first time in a long while, Peter felt buoyant. He had begun his journey.

Allison's week had been hectic. In the days that followed her encounter with Helm and the request from Washington that she return as soon as possible to help investigate the *baby-parts* scandal, on top of everything else, she had been immersed in finding someone to look after her two sons during her absence. She had been lucky—finally. A middle-aged secretary at the Mission had heard of Allison's predicament and had offered her services. For her, the opportunity of living in a nice house and keeping an eye on a couple of well-mannered teenagers was not to be scoffed at. The alternative was the lonely life of a spinster who regularly worked late to avoid going back to long, uninteresting evenings in her tiny apartment.

Allison was overjoyed.

But on top of her other preoccupations, Allison couldn't get Peter Zucker out of her mind. She thought of him leaving her house that evening, determined to undertake his trip and disappointed at her unwillingness to help him. *Why am I feeling so guilty about it?* she kept asking herself. Zucker's trip was interrupting her concentration. And when she thought of Peter, an image of Martine in the clinic also flashed through her mind. And then there were the Zuckers' children…it pained her to imagine what they might be going through.

Allison knew, though, that however hopeless Peter's task seemed, she could never have dissuaded him. Maybe an earnest attempt at finding his children was what he needed to finally move on with his life. The chances of success were extremely slim, though, in a vast country like America where people went missing every day. For all anybody knew, the children were dead and their bodies disposed of. But—if they were *her* children, she would do the same as Peter, moving heaven and earth for the rest of her days to search for them. *Dammit! When he came to me for help, all I gave him was a bureaucrat's answer.*

Allison finished packing for her early-morning flight. It was nearly seven o'clock in the evening; she would go and say goodbye to Peter. She couldn't help him in his venture, but it would make her feel a little less guilty if she saw him again.

She was surprised that there was no light showing in Peter's house, and that he didn't answer the doorbell. He might be ill, and she berated herself for not getting in touch with him sooner. She went next door to Bruno Hottinger's house; he would know if Peter were okay and possibly give her an update on Peter's travel plans. In any case, she would say goodbye to the Hottingers.

At first there was no response at their house either. But plenty of lights were visible. She rang the bell again, more insistently. Finally, Renée Hottinger asked through the front door who was there.

"It's me, Allison...Allison Cox."

The door opened and Renée beckoned Allison to come in.

"I'm sorry to disturb you so late—"

"No, no...please come in," Renée insisted, her voice ragged. She looked tired and upset. It was evident that she had been crying.

"Are you all right?" Allison's tone was anxious.

"*Oh, ça va.* Come into the living room. Please sit down. Can I get you a drink?"

Something was seriously wrong. Renée was usually bright and bubbly. Allison agreed to some tea; perhaps in the relaxed atmosphere that sipping a hot drink creates, Renee would unload her troubles. In fact, Renée started sobbing even before the water had come to a boil. Allison ran into the kitchen to comfort her and take over the preparation of the tea.

"There's something very wrong, isn't there?" she asked. "Why don't you just sit down and tell me all about it."

Renée nodded acquiescently and walked like a zombie into the living room. By the time Allison had brought in the teapot and cups, Renée was already sitting on the sofa, looking miserable and clutching a very wet tissue.

"Here, take a sip of this," Allison beckoned. "You don't want Bruno to find you in such a state when he comes home."

"Well, *he's* the one who's *put* me in this state," Renée replied harshly.

Allison said nothing. It would be better to wait for Renée to pour forth her problems at her own pace. After a few seconds, Renée continued, this time in a more conciliatory tone.

"It's like this, you see...Bruno and I had a big argument over Peter—I don't know whether you knew or not, but Bruno decided to help Peter with his harebrained scheme to find Mark and Nicolette..."

At the mention of Peter Zucker, Allison's interest in the Hottingers' family squabbles grew.

"Well, he flew Peter to Los Angeles this morning on one of the company jets. God, what a fool! He'll lose his job if he's found out...and I'm expecting another baby. What's worse, Allison, I've a feeling he'll keep helping Peter and get into even deeper trouble. He wouldn't listen to me…"

"I'm sure it's not that bad—"

"Oh, why did we have to get involved? *Why?* Why did they have to take the children? It's all your stupid country's fault," Renée said, looking directly at Allison for the first time.

This last comment struck Allison like a blow to the stomach. *Why is everything always America's fault? Bad things also happen elsewhere!* She let the comment slide. She was more concerned right now that Peter Zucker had already left for the U.S.

"So they left this morning for Los Angeles?"

Renée nodded. "But I don't know when Bruno is coming back—you see, we didn't part on very good terms."

"Oh, now…Nothing's as bad as it seems, *not even in the States*," Allison said with a reassuring smile.

"I'm sorry Allison," Renée said. "But *every*one around here has been affected by what happened to Peter and Martine. And I feel as if our lives are heading into a tailspin."

Yeah, I know the feeling, Allison thought. "How long does Bruno normally stay in LA?"

"Usually he spends just one night there and flies straight back. He prefers not to hang around. But this time…"

"I'm sure it'll be no different this time. You've called the company to see when he's due back?" Allison asked.

"Um—no."

"Well, that's the first thing to do. Give 'em a quick call in the morning, and then you can go and meet him when he lands." She brightened. "Hey, it's great news about the baby," Allison said, changing the subject. "Bruno must be thrilled."

"Well, he seemed more interested in Peter's travel plans," Renée said. She sounded despondent again.

Allison swallowed another mouthful of tea, wishing it were something stronger. Bruno was obviously sticking his neck out for Peter, while she'd refused to help him. *Damn government rules!*

"A lot of what's happened may be my fault," Allison said, meeting Renée's surprised glance. "Peter came to me for advice, and I told him I couldn't help him since I work for the U.S. government. You see, I couldn't even discuss it with him because of the illegal aspects of his plan. I feel so stupid about it now. If only I had insisted that he go about his search more openly," Allison sighed. "I could have headed a lot of this off…and yeah, Peter told me that Bruno was taking him to the States, but I assumed Bruno had cleared it with his company."

It was Renée's turn to say nothing. She looked totally forlorn.

Allison put her hand on Renée's. "It's time for us to put everything back on a better track and give Peter—and Bruno—all the help we can," Allison said. "We both know what Peter's gone through. I'm sure you're the same as me—I hate to think about what's happened to the children. If they were ours, we'd do the same as Peter."

Allison guessed by Renée's expression that she agreed. But it was obvious she was desperately worried for her husband.

"Why don't we be positive and have more faith in these two men?" Allison said, trying to buoy up Renée. "Let's assume everything went smoothly and that Bruno delivered Peter safely to the U.S., and that Bruno will be back soon with no one in Geneva Business Jets the wiser. I mean, it's extremely possible that everything went without a hitch."

Renée's expression betrayed the fact that she had not considered the possibility.

"Bruno has shown great courage and support that'll give Peter the start he needs," Allison said. "And if he finds Mark and Nicolette, it'll all have been worthwhile. And, by the way, tomorrow I'm also flying to the United States."

"To help Peter?" Renée queried.

"No. I've been recalled to help sort out a problem in Washington—it concerns children as well, strangely enough, but is unconnected with Peter's problem." The thought of a link between the two flashed through her mind again. "Look, I'll try and locate Peter and see what help he needs. You can tell that to Bruno when he comes back, but please don't tell anyone else." *I'm already in enough trouble with my job*, Allison thought.

"You mean you're leaving tomorrow *morning* already—for how long?" Renée sounded concerned.

"I'm not sure when I'll be back, and when I am, for how long I'll be here. It's all up in the air for now."

It was obvious that her answer did little to comfort Renée, and Allison guessed it left her feeling even more alone.

Allison pulled out a card and scribbled a number on it. "Renée, here's a number where I can be reached in Washington," she said, trying to sound more upbeat. "It's what we call the Operations Center, and it's open twenty-four hours a day. So you can leave a message anytime. I'll keep in touch as well. Okay?"

"Yes." Renée's voice was a whisper.

Allison squeezed Renée's hand again. "And remember, there are two things that we have to do together. One is to help Peter get his children back, and two is to make sure we don't get into trouble ourselves. Do we agree?"

Renée nodded and managed a small smile.

"Good. Your first job is to make up with Bruno when he gets back, okay?"

Renée nodded enthusiastically.

Allison suddenly thought of something else to occupy Renée's mind. "One more thing, it would really help me if you keep an eye on the boys while I'm gone. I've arranged to have someone live in, but knowing that a friendly neighbor is also looking out for them would give me more peace of mind. Would you do that for me?"

"I'd love to; that's really no problem," Renée said, sounding more like her old self.

Allison left without having the slightest idea how to go about finding Peter. It reminded her of going behind enemy lines as a Marine—yet she was going to her home country.

For Peter Zucker, everything continued to go well right up to his arrival in Los Angeles. The flight was uneventful and nobody questioned his being on the plane. Actually, he had carried out his role so convincingly that the *Schwan Pharmaceuticals* executives had insisted that he join them for lunch. Peter would have preferred a box lunch in the galley to a captive business lunch washed down with wine. But no eyebrows were raised during the social chitchat that accompanied the lobster, and Peter detected no probing questions. Indeed, the lunch helped him relax and to realize that when people have no cause for suspicion, they blindly accept whatever's told to them. It was a ploy Peter that would use again later.

Peter's nervousness returned as the Gulfstream touched down at Los Angeles International Airport, "LAX." The omnipresent palm trees and hazy sunshine confirmed that he was back in California. He felt his stomach tighten as the plane taxied to the customs ramp, obediently trailing the "FOLLOW-ME" vehicle. He moved uncomfortably in his seat. There was no going back now.

The noise wound down as Bruno shut off the engines. The flight attendant opened the outer door and waited patiently for the disembarkation stairs and the customs agent to arrive. The *Schwan* executives got out of their seats and stretched, and Peter did the same.

"Hi, there," the agent said as he came on board—a general greeting to everyone.

Bruno emerged from the cockpit with a black plastic file containing the aircraft's papers and proof of insurance. He handed it to the agent along with all the passports and customs declarations. The agent quickly entered the numbers into his tablet computer and asked the standard questions about who was aboard, the purpose of the trip, where the businessmen were going and staying, and when they would be leaving U.S. territory again. He seemed satisfied.

It was all going precisely as Bruno had told Peter it would. He had also said it was unlikely that the luggage would be checked, especially since they were coming from Switzerland, with its reputation for honesty and orderliness, and not from a drug-exporting country in South America. The agent was just about to give them permission to disembark when he turned to Peter, whose presence on board seemed to intrigue him.

"So, you're a 'flight safety inspector,' eh?" the agent read from Peter's immigration card. Peter tensed up as he prepared to act out his part again, but he said nothing in reply to the agent's rhetorical question. "Yup, this is a first for me," the agent continued. "I can't say I've come across one of you guys on a Swiss flight before. How can you explain that to me?" The agent looked Peter squarely in the eyes.

Peter felt the blood drain from his face. He met the agent's stare to avoid the temptation of looking aside and seeming flustered, and held it there for what seemed an inordinate amount of time. An eerie silence invaded the cabin as all eyes were suddenly riveted on Peter.

"It's quite simple, officer," Peter eventually responded with as much assurance as he could muster. He was smiling generously but deferentially. "New regulations," he said, launching into his well-rehearsed explanation, "calling for tighter safety standards following the crashes of several foreign-leased airliners with Swiss citizens on board. I'm the first officer to be assigned to this task—after several months of rigorous training. That's why you haven't come across us before."

The agent glanced at the *Schwan* executives who were enthusiastically nodding obvious agreement with this new policy. He looked down at the identification card again. It was Swiss and stamped. He glanced at the tablet screen which was hooked wirelessly to the main immigration databank. *There are no flags on the guy's passport.* There was still something, though, that rankled him about this new element on a corporate flight. But he couldn't put his finger on it.

"How long are you planning to stay in the States?" he asked Peter in a final attempt to heed his instincts.

"Oh, just overnight," Peter answered. "I'm flying back with the plane tomorrow. And," he said, anticipating the next question, "here's the name and address of the hotel I'll be staying at with the rest of the flight crew." He showed the agent the faxed hotel confirmation.

The agent finally seemed satisfied, stamped the passports and handed them all back. "You can now deplane and go about your business," he said, adding the usual, "Have a nice day."

Of course Peter wouldn't be returning to Europe the next day. But it was improbable the customs agent would follow up on that. And if he did, Bruno would say that the "flight safety inspector" had decided to take a few days' vacation before returning. In any case, by then, Peter would have moved on from the hotel and lost himself in the wilderness of America's constantly moving population.

Chapter 13

▼

Romy was giving the children a Spanish lesson, using the house as her classroom. She was describing the house's main features, first in German and then in Spanish. She used simple vocabulary and short phrases to describe a door, the carpet, a vase—whatever they came across while roaming around the house. They were in the hallway on the main bedroom level looking at the etchings and watercolors that lined the walls. The pictures here depicted famous European cities. Romy was reciting the names of the cities in the pictures—London, Paris, Rome, Geneva, Madrid—when out of the corner of her eye, she noticed the children anxiously whispering to each other. She repeated the names, carefully observing to see what had sparked their interest.

"Is this the one you like...you like this...yes?" Romy pointed at one. However, this time, her question provoked no visible reaction from either Mark or Nicolette. Romy looked at them suspiciously, inquiring with a smile what they were up to. Mark looked purposefully back down the hall at other pictures, but Nicolette stole a glance at the one just next to Romy. It was of a city at the end of a large lake with a distinctive water fountain rising high into the sky. *Clearly, this little girl has seen the Swiss city of Geneva!*

Romy crouched down until her face was level with Nicolette's and took the girl by the shoulders. She tried not to be rough with her, but she needed to prevent Nicolette from running back down the hall. "Geneva, you know Geneva, *Genf, Ginebra...*" Romy said in all the languages she knew. "You've been there, haven't you?"

Nicolette looked frightened and pulled away.

"You can tell me. It's okay...you've been there...you've been there before, haven't you...*haven't you?*" Romy demanded more loudly.

Tears welled up in the girl's eyes. She looked truly afraid now and pulled harder to free herself from Romy's increasingly tight grip.

"Oh my God! What am I doing?" Romy chided herself and instantly released her hold. Then, before the girl had time to run away, Romy drew her to her bosom and embraced her tightly. "Oh, I'm sorry," she said. "Please forgive me. I didn't mean to hurt you. I was just trying to—oh, Alicia...I wish you could understand what I mean..."

Mark pulled his sister away from Romy and quietly led her back to their room. Romy remained there in the middle of the hall, on her knees, fearful that all the progress she had made with the children might have just been lost. *Oh Lord, why is it all so difficult...?*

That evening in bed, Romy turned the incident over and over in her mind. It was clear that the picture of Geneva had set something off in the children. But what? Her emotions were clouding her thoughts. She drifted in and out of sleep. When at last it came to her, she sat up in bed. How obvious it was! She would tell Don Gonzalo about her discovery first thing in the morning.

Peter Zucker drove past the large, white, shoebox-shaped office building without realizing that it was the headquarters of the Los Angeles Police Department. He had left the congested freeway—the most direct route out to the San Fernando Valley and Snapdragon—opting instead for surface streets through downtown LA. He was on North Los Angeles Street, faring little better and wondering whether he should have stuck to the freeway.

A sign, *Parker Center LAPD*, caught his eye as he inched along in his red Hyundai Accent. Peter didn't pay much attention to the building at first, except to notice the homeless people draped on the public benches around it, obviously unperturbed by the possibility of arrest for vagrancy so close to a police building. He concluded that this must be an important police center, given the black-and-white squad cars sitting idle in the vast open-sided parking garage. *Why weren't they out patrolling the streets and keeping down crime?* His thoughts reflected his negative state of mind about a police force that had failed to locate his children.

He drove on past, thinking he would have preferred a less conspicuous color car than bright red, but this was the only economy model the rental company had left on its lot. He scrutinized the street signs again, and, trying to find a match, glanced down at the map spread out on the passenger seat. He began to seriously regret straying from the freeway into this maze of one-way streets. Time, Peter knew, was not on his side. Every moment wasted meant more time for Martine to languish in the clinic and less time for him to find Mark and Nicolette.

He finally spotted a sign to the freeway—101 North—took the ramp and headed out to the LAPD's area bureau that housed the West Valley Detective Division.

Romy went to Don Gonzalo's study as soon as she had finished her breakfast. Don Gonzalo spent most mornings here, much of the time on the telephone dealing with matters of his estate in Chiclayo. She knocked timidly on the door and waited for him to answer. But instead of his voice, Romy heard a woman's.

"Who is it?" asked Señora Del Solar. Her tone was a mixture of surprise and annoyance; she never liked being disturbed.

Like everyone else, Romy was afraid of Señora Del Solar. She thought of turning around and leaving, but she turned the handle apprehensively and pushed the door until it was a quarter open, showing her face.

Señora Del Solar looked up from her husband's desk. "What is it—what do you want?" she asked irritably.

"I'm sorry, ma'am," Romy said meekly, "I was looking for Don Gonzalo."

"Well, he's not here—you can see that perfectly well," she barked. Romy began closing the door.

"Wait!" Señora Del Solar said quickly. "*Why* did you want to see him?"

"It was about the children—" Romy blurted.

"Well, what about them?" she asked dryly.

"Um—I think I might have found out where they're from," Romy said, unable to hide her excitement despite Señora Del Solar's frown.

The muscles suddenly tightened in Señora Del Solar's chest and throat. She immediately forgot what she was doing, got up from the desk, and beckoned to Romy. "Come on in and sit down," she said more affably. "And close the door."

Romy needed no further prompting. "You see, I was with them in the upstairs hall yesterday...We were looking at—admiring the pictures on the wall—and it was evident from Alicia's reaction to the view of Lake Geneva and its famous *Jet d'eau* water fountain that she knows the place."

Señora Del Solar walked up and down in front of Romy like a school mistress meditating over the punishment to hand out to an unruly pupil. *What is this teacher getting at? Blackmail?* "And?" Señora Del Solar urged, impatiently.

"I've been thinking about it," Romy went on. "The children speak a kind of German, and a German dialect is spoken in much of Switzerland. Perhaps they come from there."

"*German*...Hmm. And if they did...what are you suggesting?"

"That perhaps we could find their parents."

"They are *orphans!*" Señora Del Solar said without feeling. "They have no parents and—"

"But Don Gonzalo did say they were found abandoned in Chicago," Romy persisted. "Perhaps they got separated from their Swiss parents while on a trip to the United States? I don't know, but it's possible..."

"Improbable."

Romy frowned. She couldn't understand her employer's attitude.

Señora Del Solar looked at her suspiciously. "Are you implying that they're not happy here?"

"No—well—*yes!*" Romy said, plucking up her courage. "They're not at home here—they obviously miss their real home, wherever that is..."

Señora Del Solar quickly pulled her thoughts together. Romy didn't know the truth and was naively trying to be a good woman. *How I hate simple people*, she thought. She wanted to be rid of the children, but she could not let Romy find out that they were indeed *procured*.

Señora Del Solar put on a grateful smile. "Thank you, Romy, for telling me this. I don't agree with you that the children are unhappy here. It *is* the language that's bothering them—so the sooner you make progress, the happier they will be. As to the matter of their possible Swiss origin, we will look into it—you mustn't bother yourself with it anymore."

"Oh, thank you," Romy said with relief. She was agreeably surprised that Señora Del Solar hadn't treated her ideas as completely foolish.

As soon as Romy left the study, Señora Del Solar picked up the telephone and called Chavez. "It's me," she said when he came on the line. "We need to talk—urgently."

Chapter 14

▼

"Good heavens, Allison. You actually look *sassy* for once!" His voice was uncommonly jocular for someone usually sober and pensive. "Don't tell me you've finally stowed away that serious, businesslike look of yours!"

"Oh, be quiet, John!" said Allison, looking at him askance. He was well into his fifties with salt-and-pepper hair, and still an attractive man. Daily workouts had kept him fit—there wasn't an ounce of excess fat on him, even now. But it was his nature, gentle and honest, that had always attracted her to him. Now, after all the years she had known him, Allison realized she liked him immensely.

"There's no way any self-respecting woman could look anything *other* than sassy—after last night. Let's just call it *embarrassment*." She smiled inwardly as she took another sip from her mug of freshly brewed coffee. The mug was white with "The Morning After" in gold letters on the side. The same words were embroidered on the front of the white terrycloth bathrobe that Allison was wearing. John Vandervelt wore a matching one, but his bore the inscription "Thanks!" on the pocket. Neither wore anything underneath, and both looked as relaxed and satisfied as they felt.

"Tell me you weren't a willing participant last night, and I'll charge myself with sexual harassment!" he quipped. "Really, you government people!"

"By the look of these robes, I wouldn't have much trouble getting a conviction..." Allison added.

"Hey, if that's the case," John said, pretending to get up from the small kitchen table and lunge at Allison, "I've got nothing to lose! And the robes I won in an office raffle—it's the first time I've used them."

"Oh, sit down, John!" Allison said with a girlish laugh. "I thought they taught you to control your emotions in the FBI. How long since you last did this?"

"Probably the same as you."

"I'd be ashamed to admit how long ago that was…"

"Oh, come now," John countered, looking surprised. "A good-looking gal like you—"

"You'd be amazed how few and far between the good offers are in my line of business." Allison thought of Helm and the distasteful way he had tried to seduce her when he had first arrived in Geneva. John was so different in every possible way. Over dinner the previous evening, she had explained why she was back in the United States. She was relieved to let her hair down with an old and trusted friend. She had not been so open with anyone for years.

Allison had known John for longer than she had known her former husband. A golfing partner of her father's in the Bethesda suburb of D.C., John had often been at her parents' house for social gatherings. Allison had always enjoyed talking with him—had felt at ease in his company. But she had stupidly overlooked the possibility that John was in love with her, and had taken the plunge and married someone else after a whirlwind relationship. She had met her husband in the Marines where the forced confinement of the training camp and its isolation from the outside world had thrown them together. When they had moved on to jobs in the U.S. Foreign Service and more open social surroundings, the mistake became clear and he had soon abandoned her and their two young boys.

Once Allison had been married, in his typical gentlemanly way, John had discreetly drawn away from her and concentrated on his work. Their paths had rarely crossed, and when they had, it merely served as a reminder of what could have been and wasn't.

"A penny for them," John said.

"For what?" Allison looked startled.

"Why, your thoughts, of course." He was smiling kindly. "You were miles away."

"Oh, I'm sorry…It's true. I have a lot on my mind at the moment."

"You're not still worrying about that *baby-parts* nonsense, are you?"

"No, it's not that," Allison said, sounding removed. She had told John she was part of the State Department team investigating the *baby-parts* story, piecing together evidence to discredit it. The team had flown to the clinic in Montana that had been cited in the *El Crónico* article. The clinic was entirely open; it specialized in organ transplants and produced proof that all the organs used came from well-documented, voluntary donors. Clinic officials had categorically denied that any had come from abroad. Moreover, the former employee cited in the article was merely a disgruntled orderly who had been fired for stealing from patients. The team concluded that he had lied, probably for money, but also to seek revenge. They still needed more evidence though, and Allison guessed that she would be heading off to Peru sometime soon to find it.

"…It's something else that's bothering me," Allison continued. "Remember that guy I asked you about late last summer—the one who lost his kids at Snapdragon—you know, that amusement park near LA?"

"Yeah, I remember. Weren't he and his family Swiss…and lived near you in Geneva?" He added, "I said then that there was nothing the Bureau could do about it, or something like that…"

"Yes, the—John, I need to talk to you about this off the record," Allison blurted.

"My dear," he said, throwing open his arms and looking down at himself and then at Allison, "nothing could be less official than this!" He smiled broadly. "I assure you, I don't carry out FBI business in this attire!"

"I'm serious, John," Allison said. "You're a good friend—one of the few I can trust—but I don't want to compromise you vis-à-vis the Bureau. So, if we can talk about this freely, and then forget this discussion ever took place, it would help me greatly. But if you feel you can't, then I understand—I as well as you have taken an oath of allegiance to the government. And," she added with her previous impish smile, "it won't change our—um—friendship."

John sensed that Allison needed to unburden herself, and he stopped joking. He placed his hand on her forearm. "Sure, there's no problem," he said thoughtfully. "This is a private conversation between friends, and we both know it won't go any further. Tell me what's troubling you—it would give me much pleasure to help in any way I can."

Hearing these words, Allison felt a sensation of relief. Tears formed in her eyes and her throat constricted.

John remained silent, waiting until Allison was ready to continue. Although he thought he knew her well—she was tough, and she had proven that in her foreign service career—he had overlooked the fact that she was used to hiding her emotions.

A couple of minutes passed. John quietly refilled her coffee mug. Finally, Allison managed to speak: "I'm sorry; I don't know what came over me."

John squeezed her hand. "Why don't you just start from the beginning?"

"It's difficult to know where to begin, actually," Allison said, wiping her eyes. "It's stupid really, because, objectively speaking, it's all quite simple—"

"You want me to see if there's anything new in our case files?" John interrupted.

"No—well, okay, yes, if there is something...The thing is that the kids' father, Peter Zucker, has come back here to find them—"

"That seems a perfectly normal thing to do."

"Yes, but there's more to it than that," Allison said. "First, he was planning to enter the country illegally—or not entirely honestly; second, he told me he'll kill anyone who gets in his way—and I believe him; third, he asked me for help, and I turned him down."

"I'm not surprised, if he's about to commit a felony!"

"But for all I know, he just wanted general information about procedures over here—you know, how the police operate, that kind of thing. But I refused to listen."

"Hmm...I see your point," John said. "Now you feel you were being unjust and unhelpful, because he was merely trying to get his kids back, and you feel guilty. Is that it?"

"Yes, exactly, John. I knew you would understand."

"Look, cheer up and don't feel bad about it. You've already helped him by not reporting his intentions. But why did he want to enter illegally? Surely he can just come back in as a tourist?"

"True, but he's convinced the authorities are hiding something from him...that there's some kind of cover-up—"

"That's kinda dramatic, isn't it?"

"That's what I thought too, but look at it from his point of view," Allison continued. "Ever since he went to California on vacation last summer, his life has been one big Greek tragedy. His children were taken away from him, and only God knows where they are and even whether they're still alive. His wife is in a mental hospital where she lives under sedation. He finally comes to the realization that he might as well do his damnedest to find his children, even if it means killing somebody. From his point of view, the worst that can happen is that he goes to jail for the rest of his life." She paused, and then looked up at him. "Didn't you tell me last year that the FBI had dropped the case?"

"Yes," John conceded. "But we often receive orders to lower the priority on cases that lack viable leads. I'll look into it again for you."

It would be relatively simple, since he was special assistant to the Director of the FBI. He had risen to this level in just eighteen years—a time period that coincided with Allison's departure from his life. He hadn't summoned up the courage to attend her wedding, and for weeks after had often stomped around his apartment cursing her and wishing she had never come into his life. He had thrown himself into his work and received accolades and promotions for his devotion to duty. There was nothing about the Bureau that he didn't know, and no classified information to which he was barred access.

"Allison," John said, getting to his feet and putting his arm affectionately around her shoulders, "I understand your distress and what your friend Zucker is going through—more than you might appreciate. You have to do what your heart dictates—trust in that gut feeling of what's right and act on it, win or lose. Without that, you can't look back and say *I tried.*" He looked down into Allison's glistening eyes and smiled warmly. "From what I can judge, you are now committed to helping Zucker—your heart's in it, where it wasn't in Geneva. You had other things on your mind there. Stop agonizing over what's past and let's see what we can do to help him succeed."

John's mention of "what *we* can do" was the most heartening thing Allison had heard for some time. She looked up at him again; he was a true friend indeed.

"I'll tell you what," John said, pulling away and beginning to pace with his hands thrust into the pockets of his bathrobe. "I'll find out what I can as soon as I get to the office today. I don't know how long it'll be before I have anything concrete for you, but you're reachable at the State Department Ops Center if I can't find you at your hotel?"

Allison nodded, feeling that a great load had been lifted from her.

John, on the other hand, remained pensive. His mind, a well-oiled investigative machine, was already searching for sources of information that could be relevant to the Peter Zucker case.

The note was extremely cordial and clearly an invitation that was not to be turned down. A uniformed chauffeur had delivered it to the front door of the Del Solar residence without saying a word or waiting for a reply. The maid who had answered the door had not needed to ask who the note came from, for she had immediately recognized the livery as that of an envoy from Luis Chavez.

Since everything that happened in the house had to pass by Señora Del Solar, Romy received the sealed envelope directly from her. She carefully slit it open and read the note—handwritten in black ink on cream-colored, embossed paper.

Estimada Señorita Tincopa

It would give me much pleasure if you would meet with me at my residence this coming Wednesday at eleven AM. A car will be sent to pick you up at ten-forty AM precisely.

Cordially
Señor Luis Chavez

Romy could not imagine why Chavez, the most powerful man in the region, would want to see her.

She was unaware that Chavez had been instrumental in her obtaining the position in the Del Solar household—just as she did not realize that Señora Del Solar already knew the contents of the note.

Since Señora Del Solar was standing there, erect and expectant, Romy handed her the note after reading it. In any case, Romy needed her permission to leave the house at a time when she would normally be working with the children.

Señora Del Solar looked at the note, feigned surprise, and then granted her permission. "You can go," she said, "given Señor Chavez's important position."

The note intrigued Romy. For several days before the appointment she ran over possible reasons for the invitation. She hoped Chavez wasn't going to give her trouble about her irregular situation, but she assumed that if that were the case, he wouldn't be sending a car and driver for her. Perhaps he wanted to take stock of progress with the children? It was no secret that the Del Solars had adopted two children who spoke no Spanish.

When Wednesday arrived, she dressed conservatively but smartly for the appointment. Chavez's reputation dictated deference and respect; Romy had heard rumors about what happened to those who crossed him.

The white limousine pulled up at exactly ten-forty. Romy, not daring to be late, was already waiting. When the chauffeur opened the rear door of the limousine with extreme courtesy and helped her in, she forgot her apprehension. She had never been inside such a car before; so spacious and luxurious. She sank into the red-leather seat and *Oh! Good heavens!* There was a television screen in the partition that separated the driver from the rear-seat passengers. She couldn't believe her eyes. She felt hardly any motion when the car pulled away. *Chavez must need something from me to treat me like this.* She wondered what it was. His attentiveness flattered her. Her opinion of him went up, and she started dismissing the disagreeable rumors she had heard about him. *People are just envious,* she concluded.

As foreseen in Chavez's invitation, it took just under twenty minutes to drive to his main residence a few miles outside Chiclayo. Romy would never have thought it possible, but it was even more grandiose than the Del Solar residence. *How can people amass the kind of money needed to own something like this?* Romy contemplated, as the car drove through the tall wrought-iron gates that had opened as they approached. The limousine crunched on the gravel drive and swept to a stop at the front door. The chauffeur handed Romy over to a maid who, with all the attention given to a guest of honor, accompanied her inside and into a spacious living room.

"Ah, *Maestra* Tincopa!" The voice came from a man seated in a red chintz-covered chair next to an expansive bay window that offered a breathtaking view of the surrounding countryside and the ocean in the distance. He put down the book he was reading and stood up to greet her. He was not a tall man—in fact, several inches shorter than Romy. But he was slim, wore a dark suit with a long-cut jacket, and stood erect in expensive kangaroo-leather boots with sizeable heels.

"We haven't met, but I am Señor Luis Chavez." He moved his lean, pointed face closer to hers and maintained a welcoming smile. "Thank you so much for accepting my invitation." He beckoned her to sit down, pointing to the matching chintz chair. Chavez's every action made Romy feel pampered and a member of the local élite.

They had hardly sat down when the maid placed a silver platter with tea and small cakes on the inlaid pedestal table between them. "Tea?" Chavez asked.

Something in Chavez's voice made it impossible to say anything but yes to even such a mundane question. This is what diplomacy must be all about, Romy thought, admiring her host's suavity. Chavez was in charge of the situation and had accomplished this merely with polite words. She wondered again why she was there, but she would not think about it anymore, preferring to sit back and fully absorb this momentary opportunity to be part of a highly dignified way of life.

"Yes, thank you," Romy answered, although Chavez was already pouring her a cup.

"You are a handsome woman, *Maestra*," Chavez said after a short pause. He saw the sudden change in Romy's expression. "Oh! Please don't misunderstand me," Chavez immediately added. "I assure you, I have no dishonorable intentions."

Romy visibly relaxed again.

"…It's just that I very rarely have the opportunity to receive such educated people as yourself here, and those that I do, if I may say so, are rarely as young or attractive!"

Romy felt herself blush and tried to cover it up by bringing her teacup to her lips and sipping.

Chavez noticed her embarrassment. "Please excuse my frankness and take it as a compliment—nothing more. Now, tell me about yourself—what brought you here, how you became interested in teaching…"

Romy felt flattered by his interest and gave him a capsule description of her life. In the back of her mind, she still questioned why this important man was spending his valuable time with her. But the relaxed atmosphere made the questioning seem less significant.

"I understand you are settling in the household admirably," Chavez said when she had finished. "Señora Del Solar has spoken highly of you—so I assume you are happy there and that there are, of course, no problems…?"

"No," Romy answered automatically.

"And how are things going with the Del Solar children?" Chavez asked cautiously. "They must certainly be making progress under your excellent guidance…"

"Yes, yes they are," Romy replied eagerly. "But it's not easy when you see where they come from," she said with no forethought.

"How do you mean?" Chavez said innocently.

"Neither knew any Spanish when I started with them," Romy went on. "They obviously felt very uprooted and afraid of their new surroundings. However, now they can understand some words and basic phrases in Spanish and say a few things as well. Their absorption of the language can only accelerate from now on." This was an exaggeration, but Romy guessed that it was what Chavez wanted to hear. She didn't want to admit that they still only understood her when she repeated the phrases in German. "However, it will obviously still take some time before they get through the transition between their past life and their present one."

"An interesting analysis," Chavez said. "You have evidently studied the children, which is good." He paused to offer Romy a cake. "Your experience in child psychology was one of the reasons you were chosen by the Del Solars for this position. Mmm…" He swallowed a small cake with apparent appreciation before resuming. "And Señora Del Solar has confirmed to me that you have been successful in getting through to the children—which is, of course, really excellent, and I tip my hat to you."

"Why, thank you," Romy said politely, grateful for the recognition and eager to acknowledge Chavez's flattering remarks. "I do my best…but there's one thing—"

"Yes?" Chavez said in a tone that encouraged her to continue.

"I don't know whether I should mention it to you…but I have already spoken of it to Señora Del Solar."

"Please feel free to go on. Señora Del Solar and I are old friends," Chavez said. His voice sounded reassuring.

"Well, I may have stumbled onto where the children come from."

"Oh, really?" Chavez said, feigning surprise.

"Yes, I think they are Swiss-German and might have lived in Geneva."

"That's *very* interesting. How did you come to that conclusion?"

Chavez watched Romy closely as she enthusiastically went through her explanation about the pictures of European scenes, trying to look interested, though he had already heard it all from Señora Del Solar.

"How very impressive, and, may I say, perspicacious of you," Chavez said when Romy finished. "And you have some ideas about what to do next?"

"Actually, I have already been trying to get them to tell me their real family name," Romy said, ebullient over his interest in her investigative efforts. "But all they come up with is something like *sugar*."

"Sugar?" queried Chavez.

"Yes, the German word for sugar; *Zucker*. And that's what I keep hearing."

This revelation took Chavez by surprise. His agents in the United States had informed him about the photographs in the U.S. media following the seizure of the two children, and he vaguely remembered the name resembled *Zucker*. However, by the time those photographs appeared, the children were already safely out of the country. He pondered, weighing carefully what Romy had told him. *The situation with this woman is worse than I thought. But I have dealt effectively with much tougher problems than this.*

"I do commend you for your interest and diligence in the children's *welfare*," Chavez told Romy, smiling convincingly. "And I can assure you that *everyone* concerned, the Del Solars and myself as a very close family friend, shares your concern—by the way, have you told anyone else about this, apart from the Del Solars?"

"No, no one," Romy replied innocently. "Only you."

"Good, and we must leave it that way."

Romy noticed the sudden hardening in Chavez's voice, and a hint of anxiety came over her again. His benevolent smile was gone.

"Now, *Maestra,* as a skilled teacher, you'll know that welfare means well-being, health and prosperity—"

"And happiness," Romy added.

"Yes, happiness as well—I was coming to that..." Chavez tried to hide his annoyance at being interrupted. "The Del Solars and I have invested a lot in giving these poor *orphans* a home when they had none, a home where they will be prosperous, healthy *and happy.* Exposing them to a doubtful past will *not* attain this well-being."

"I know, but we shouldn't just let it drop," Romy said, anxiety creeping into her voice. "Someone should look into this and—"

"No one—I repeat *no one*—will look into this. *We will just drop it,*" Chavez insisted.

"But you can't—"

"I *can* and I *will.*" Chavez placed his teacup harshly back on the table and stared at Romy.

She tried to avoid his frightening expression.

"*I* will not stand by," he said, "and let the Del Solars be hurt by losing their children. Let me make myself absolutely clear. I am a powerful man, and what I say goes. It's as simple as that."

Romy could hardly control the trembling that came over her. She was unable to speak.

"I'm even interested in *your* well-being, *Maestra* Tincopa," Chavez continued. "And I would hate to see any misfortune come your way. There are those who would wish harm to a *Che,*" he said, using pejorative slang for an Argentinean, "working in Peru illegally and against the interests of her employers."

Certain that Romy had felt the full effect of his message, Chavez got up and pulled a bell-cord by the window. "It was a pleasure talking with you, *Maestra,*" Chavez said, returning to his former effusive self. "And I will be profoundly grateful if you continue to keep me personally informed of any development that could have an effect on the children's welfare."

Romy nodded obediently.

"My chauffeur will, of course, drive you back to the Del Solar residence where I'm sure you're eager to resume your excellent work with the children—and *only* the work you're trained for."

Romy could barely utter "goodbye." Contrary to the ride over, she remembered nothing of the limousine ride back.

"Bruno wanted in office! Bruno wanted in office! Urgent!" The shrill tones of the loudspeaker cracked sharply throughout the hangar.

Bruno heard the summons with trepidation. *Had someone found out about Peter?* He put down his wrench, wiped the black grease off his hands, and set off in the direction of the glassed-in office in the far corner of the hangar.

"Morning Bruno," the managing partner, Erik Uhl, greeted him. Bruno, in his one-piece gray overalls, was clutching a greasy rag. "Here, sit down for a second," Uhl said in his usual businesslike voice.

He's giving nothing away, Bruno thought, always dreading the possibility that he was going to be fired.

"Bruno, you're doing a great job."

Bruno was relieved. Uhl always started out this way when he needed to squeeze some extra work out of pilots.

"I've a favor to ask."

"Sure—whatever," Bruno replied, glad that his secret was still safe.

"Great!" Uhl looked pleased. "And this is far from a hardship assignment. I need you to make a flight to the Bahamas and stay there a few days."

Bruno smiled at the thought of flying to the Caribbean instead of to another wintry European destination. Then he frowned. *There must be a catch…*

"There's just one thing…this is a new customer for us—he wants us to fly him and some colleagues out to a conference in the Bahamas—but I can't find a flight attendant. It'll be from this Thursday through the weekend, and everyone decent is taken. I can't take the chance of using an inexperienced girl—this could be a very lucrative contract, and I don't have to tell you that we need it!"

Bruno wondered where all this was leading.

"I understand that Renée used to be a flight attendant, and by all accounts, an excellent one. I need her for this flight."

"But Renee's expecting a baby—"

"But it's very early on isn't it?"

"Yes…" Bruno replied, searching for another excuse. "We've also got a young daughter—"

"Yes, I know that—can't you leave her with grandparents?" Uhl sounded exasperated. "Look, Bruno! I need a favor. It's not as if I'm asking you to fly to the moon and stay there! I'm really offering you—and your wife—a vacation in the Bahamas! All you have to do is fly a plane out there and three days later fly it back. I'm going to give you the best plane. And all your wife has to do is serve the passengers food and drinks and so forth during the flight and make sure they're content! *Dammit*, man!"

Uhl leaned back in his chair, annoyed. "You can call your wife and discuss it with her if you like, but I need to know one way or the other in the next few minutes." Changing his tone to a plea: "Bruno, we can't afford to turn this business away..."

"Okay, we'll do it." Bruno said quietly. He didn't like the idea of Renée working again, especially now. But he had no choice.

"Are you sure you don't want to speak to her first—I'm certain she'll jump at it!"

"No, it's okay," Bruno said a little more assertively. "Go ahead and plan for the flight."

Uhl looked at him dubiously. "You okay, Bruno?"

"Yes...I'm sorry. I'm a bit tired...we've been under a lot of pressure lately. The flight'll go fine. Don't worry about it—we'll make sure they come back for more business."

"That's what I like to hear!" Uhl sounded relieved. "I understand the weather's terrific out there this time of year."

"You're right; it'll do us both good to get away from this gray Geneva February and into the sun," Bruno said.

Chapter 15

▼

"Doctor, doctor, please come quickly—room 217, Madame Zucker." The nurse's voice over the intercom was desperate. Dubois leaped up from his computer and hurried to 217 without asking for details.

He arrived in less than a minute, out of breath, but no more so than the nurse and the two white-jacketed male orderlies who were resting after the struggle. Martine Zucker was lying on the bed, rocking violently and trying desperately to escape from the straitjacket that the three had finally succeeded in putting on her. The formerly quiet and unimposing Swiss mother and housewife had snapped. Dubois had never seen her in such a state. And yet, he thought, she had shown signs of improving.

"Get fifty milligrams of *Trazine*," he ordered the nurse as he approached the tossing bundle. When Martine caught sight of Dubois, she stopped rocking and lifted her head as far as she could off the bed in the doctor's direction.

"I'm a failure...a *failure!*" she shouted. "I've failed my family...I couldn't protect my children...Oh...Nicolette, Mark where are you? Forgive me...Even God can't help me—*me*, who was such a good Christian...Oh, what a fool I was to believe! I hope you're not a believer, doctor—it's a total waste...and I can't even die...How could hell be worse?" Her head dropped like a stone back onto the pillow; she was exhausted from the strain. She didn't even flinch as Dubois stuck in the needle.

"It's hopeless, hope...*hope-e-les-ss-*..." Her voice trailed off as the tranquilizer sent her into a deep sleep. Dubois withdrew the needle and dropped the syringe into the disposal bag that the nurse held out to him.

"What happened?" he asked brusquely, as a sudden calm hit the room.

"I don't know exactly," the nurse replied. "She was in the cafeteria eating quietly and sobbing—which she does a lot of the time. And then, all of a sudden, she started screaming at the top of her voice—'I'm a failure,' like what we've just heard—and throwing things around and kicking tables and chairs. You can ask the guys how difficult it was to restrain her. And then we carried her straight here, out of sight of the other patients."

The doctor's next question was immediate. "What was on the cafeteria TV?"

The nurse thought for an instant. "Oh yes, some harmless travel program about vacation spots in the sun—oh, no—it was on a vacation that they lost their children!"

"Merde," Dubois swore. He looked at Martine and her damp and matted hair. She was soaked in perspiration. "Now that she's out, take off the jacket and give her a sponge bath. When you've done that, just secure her wrists to the bed. You won't need the jacket. And call me as soon as she comes around."

Dubois returned to his office at a more measured pace. He was disappointed; Martine had seemed to be making progress since her husband had stopped visiting and reminding her of the past. *But the human mind will not let go, and there is no way to change that*, he sighed. Briefly, he wondered what had become of Peter Zucker. Then he reached his office, made a couple of annotations in Martine's file, put the incident out of his mind, and returned to his research.

Forty-five minutes after leaving the congestion of downtown LA, Peter drove into the parking lot of the West Valley Detective Division. He needed no time to prepare himself for the visit; he knew what he was going to do and had thoroughly rehearsed it all. And he was familiar with the layout of the building. He and Martine had spent endless days there last summer during the initial investigation. Without hesitation, he walked inside and up to the reception window.

"Gute morning," Peter said. His tone was formal and the young uniformed policeman appeared unfazed by Peter's accent. "My name is Knoblauch, Wilhelm *Knoblauch*," Peter added in a heavy German accent. "Here is meine—my karte," he said, proffering a visiting card.

The policeman took the card, looking at Peter quizzically. He peered down at the black German script, trying to make out the name. "Mister Noo…um—?"

"K'now-blough—K'now-blough…" Peter said. "It is very easy to pronounciate in Zurich where I come from, but not so common here."

The officer looked Peter up and down, taking in his charcoal gray suit and black felt hat, quite out of place in the sun-filled reception area. Everyone else had come in that morning in shirtsleeves.

Peter saw that the officer was suppressing a grin; *good, my disguise is working.*

"I verk for zee *Zürcher Lebensversicherung*—you understand German, yes?"

"Um, no…" The officer looked embarrassed.

"Vell, it is zee largest life insurance company in Zurich, in Svitzerland. Vee do not have much business outside of Svitzerland. Zat is vhy my cards are only in German." Peter chuckled, and the young officer feigned a polite laugh, but obviously did not get the joke.

"How can I help you, sir?" the officer asked impatiently.

"My company has received an insurance claim concerning a case of missing children zat occurred here last summer," Peter said, getting to the nub of his presentation. "Yes, vee have a claim of two millions of Swiss francs from a Mister Peter Zucker whose two children disappeared here—zat is one million each child…to make two millions total, or more than one million of your dollars. Zat is a lot, no?"

"Phew, you ain't kiddin'!"

"You see, young man, because of zee size of zee sum, my company has sent me here to investigate—or perhaps a better word is *check* to make sure zat zee facts are correct before vee *pay up*, as you Americans vould say." Peter chuckled again. He sensed that the officer was still wondering whether he was for real.

Peter pulled a typewritten sheet out of his attaché case and pretended to translate from German. "According to zee insurance policy Mister Zucker contracted vith us, zee money vould have to be paid either on death or if zee children disappear without trace, vich Mister Zucker says is zee case." Peter turned to the officer. "All I have to do is confirm dis. And since dis police station was zee one zat dealt vith zee investigation, here I have come. You have understood?"

"Sure," the officer replied unconvincingly. "Let me just run this past you again, and you correct me. Okay?"

Peter nodded.

"You're looking for information about a case of missing children that occurred here last summer, one investigated by this bureau, to see if your company needs to pay up an insurance claim—is that it?"

"*Ja,*" assented Peter, nodding his head enthusiastically for effect.

"That's great," the officer said, sounding relieved. "There's just one thing, though…the connection with this guy Zucker?"

"He's zee vater of zee children," Peter replied. He felt a sudden tightness in his throat, thinking of them.

"And what is it exactly that you want me to do for you?" the officer inquired again.

Peter took a deep breath before answering, to keep up his act. "First, I vant to confirm zat zee children disappeared. Second, I vant to go over zee investigation vith you—vee are very thorough in Svitzerland, you know—quality, quality…and third, take a copy of zee investigation report back vith me for my company's files."

"Okay, sure…I'll have to ask about this," the officer said, looking down a list of internal telephone numbers. He found the right extension and picked up the receiver. "Sir," he asked Peter before punching in a number, "write the name of the father on this piece of paper and the date when it happened, and then please take a seat over there while I find out what we can do for you."

Peter wrote down the information and walked over to a row of seats by the window where he sat wondering what would happen next. He thought back to the previous time he had been in this building and the long, fruitless sessions he had had with the investigating detectives. The possibility that he might be recognized by one of them concerned him, but before that happened, he hoped he would get the case file in his own hands.

The officer hung up the phone and shouted across to Peter, "They're gonna call back—shouldn't be too long."

During the fifty minutes that Peter patiently waited, the officer made and answered several other telephone calls. Two people came in with complaints to lodge. They both left quickly and neither had to wait around. And now the officer was reading *Sports Illustrated!*

"Excuse me…vhy is it taking zo long?" Peter's sudden appearance at the window surprised the officer, who hastily closed the magazine and pushed it aside.

"Um—well…they haven't called back yet."

"I have not got all day, and I must fly back to Zurich dis evening. Zo please, can you find me someone I can consult vith."

"Oh, sure—um—I'll call again."

He punched in a number, which Peter assumed was the same one as earlier, and asked if someone could speak to *this guy* about the Zucker case. The officer listened intently to the answer, repeating it aloud to confirm that he had understood: "Case's been sent downtown…and even if it was here, only a family member can have access to the file…Is that it? Okay, thanks." He glanced up at Peter to see if he had been listening, then hung up the phone.

"Did you get that? We can't help you here. The case's been sent downtown." The policeman could see that Peter was visibly worried by what he had heard.

"You mean zat only members of zee family can see zee file?"

"Uh-huh."

"But vhy? I need information on dis case…two millions of francs…"

"That's the rule. I'm sorry, bud."

"But vat am I to do now…? I have come all dis vay from Svitzerland," Peter said, sounding genuinely frustrated. He became more insistent. "I must see some-one—dis is very important."

"Why not try the Parker Center directly," the officer suggested. "That's where the file is."

"The *Parker Center?*" Peter repeated, in his surprise momentarily forgetting his accent. "You mean that big police building in the center of Los Angeles…ver all doze police cars are?" he added quickly as the officer looked at him strangely.

"Yeah…150 North Los Angeles Street—you want me to write it down for you?"

"No, I know ver it is."

"I'm sure you'll have better luck there. That's where unsolved cases are sent."

"Danks," Peter said. "I vill go dere."

So the case is officially unsolved and was sent to police headquarters, Peter mused as he walked back outside. But he was troubled too. *Only a family member can have access to the file.* He quickly got into the Hyundai and headed back to Los Angeles.

Nicolette stumbled at nearly every step as Mark all but dragged her across the stony beach. She still wore her nightdress under her jacket.

"Stop it—stop it!" she cried out. Her staunch protector had all of a sudden turned back into a bullying older brother.

"Don't make any noise, and hurry up!" Mark commanded, giving her wrist a jerk. "We've got to get as far away as we can from the house before they find out we're gone!"

Even Nicolette's panting seemed to pierce the early morning mist and dark-ness like a siren. And although they had run quite a ways, they were still within sight of the house.

A dog barked in the distance.

Mark chided Nicolette for the *ouches* she let out as she stubbed her toes against the scattered rocks on the beach. Her shiny black patent leather shoes gave her lit-tle protection from the jagged rocks embedded in the damp sand.

Suddenly Nicolette uttered a shriek of terror. Mark stopped in his tracks, instantly swung around and put his hand over her mouth. Then he saw. She was gazing up at the old wood and ironwork pier that loomed ominously out of the mist. The moonlight played eerie tricks on the water flapping around its pylons.

And the jagged holes in the rotting boardwalk above looked like rows of broken teeth.

"A monster!" Nicolette shrieked.

"No, it's just the pier—it's our friend tonight," Mark reassured her. For him, the sight was a relief. When he had first spotted the pier from their bedroom window, running out to sea, he had thought it was the key to their escape. It was old and dilapidated, and the only people he observed around it were fishermen tranquilly casting their lines over the side by day, but never by night.

The rowboats tied to the pier's iron struts had caught Mark's attention. Every day, he had focused his young, sharp eyes as hard as he could to see if one was always moored at the pier, and he never counted fewer than two. He had found their escape route; it was now just a question of getting out of the house. Mark had noticed that their teacher sometimes forgot to lock their bedroom door. Was this a simple oversight or a secret signal that they should try to escape? Whichever it was, it was the opportunity they needed. Tonight, when she did not turn the key in the lock, Mark had rushed over to the window and peered through the fading twilight to make sure the two boats were still there. They were!

Nicolette had wondered what Mark was doing in his pajamas, his back to her, huddled over something. "Just go to sleep—I'll tell you in the morning," Mark had said, fearful she would ask questions in a loud and excited voice. But she was tired, and Mark, relieved to hear her deep breathing, quickly prepared.

He was too excited to sleep, but he was also afraid. He had tiptoed to the window seat and had sat there staring into the moonlit night as he waited. How long had it been since anyone stirred in the house? When it seemed like ages, he had dressed in silence, then woken Nicolette and commanded her in whispers to put on her jacket and shoes. At her first complaints, he had hushed her with dire warnings. Frightened, Nicolette had done as he said.

They had crept down the carpeted stairs to the main hallway by the front door and nearly jumped out of their skins when the grandfather clock struck three AM. Mark had put his hand viciously over Nicolette's mouth to muffle her shriek. He felt her trembling and then noticed that he was shaking too. When they heard no other sound, they had gone to the front door and quietly let themselves out.

Within seconds, the two small figures had been racing down toward the beach. It had not been not long before they were out of breath, but Mark had refused to stop and rest.

Now by the pier, he held Nicolette tightly. She was terrified by its monstrous appearance, and he couldn't bear to see her in such distress. He released her mouth and looked her straight in the eye. "We're escaping—yes, escaping back home! We're going home, and the pier will help us…"

His words completely captured her attention and brought a gleam of joy and excitement to her eyes. "*Mammi…Papi…*" Her utterance was barely audible.

The dog barked again, reminding Mark of the dangers of dallying. "Yes, but we've got to keep going." He pointed to the base of the pier. "You see that boat over there; we're going to take it and escape to sea. And then a big ship will pick us up and take us home. Doesn't that sound great?" He didn't wait for an answer. "Come on," he urged as he picked up his bundle, and they waded hand-in-hand out to the boat.

The water was cold as it came up to their waists, but neither seemed to notice. With difficulty Mark lifted Nicolette into the old wooden rowboat and then clambered in. The unexpected sway made him lose his balance, and he fell into the boat's bottom. But there he found the oars. He had rowed a boat only once before—on a lake in Switzerland. He struggled to lift the oars—heavier than those he had used then—and carefully slid them into the oarlocks on either side of the boat. He sat and pulled hard, but the mooring rope jerked up out of the water and held. Mark had forgotten to untie the boat from the pier. He stood, steadied himself, and scrambled past Nicolette to the front. The rope was tied around one of the pier struts high above his head—too high for him to reach. Suddenly this seemed an impossible task!

"Why don't you cut it?" Nicolette said, uttering her first complete sentence since waking.

Mark lost no time clambering back to his bundle. From it he took a knife stolen from the kitchen weeks ago—to stab Señora Del Solar with if she ever tried to beat him again. It took his trembling hands an eternity to cut through the inch-thick rope, and when at last it parted, he was breathing heavily. He again took up his position in the center of the boat and grabbed the oars.

Never had he felt so small, his arms aching as he strained against the sea as it rocked and tossed the boat. Suddenly, he was terrified to see they were circling around back under the pier. But then he found the secret; an even, smooth sweep of the oars made the little boat move swiftly forward. The outgoing tide and approaching dawn spurred him on, and by daybreak the pier was but a speck on the distant shore.

Chapter 16

▼

Peter was in a quandary. *Only a family member can have access to the file.* This had thrown a wrench into his plans.

The obvious solution was difficult to accept. Who was better suited than the father of the missing children to inquire about progress? But he was loathe to reveal his identity. He couldn't put aside his hunch that the police had something to hide, and that that was why the case had come to a dead end. They would be more on their guard if he, the father, rather than a Swiss insurance agent, started asking questions. But now it was obvious that Knoblauch would keep running into the same administrative brick wall.

Half an hour later, Peter arrived back at the Parker Center and pulled into a parking spot masked from the building by the broad leaves of the ficus trees along the sidewalk. He sat in the car thinking, and suddenly sensed he was being observed. A "street person" sitting on a nearby bench was eyeing him distrustfully. Was this man with unkempt beard and dirty, baggy clothing really a police spy keeping an eye out for suspicious cars parked around headquarters? *Perhaps he's part of the homeland security system to thwart terrorist attacks.*

The last thing Peter wanted was to attract undue attention. So he pulled some papers out of the glove compartment and leafed through them—to give the impression that he was merely checking a brief before going to a meeting.

It was clear that if he wanted to get any information out of the police, he would have to be Peter Zucker again. *What choice do I have?* He recalled what Allison had told him. *Perhaps honesty is the best way.* He got out of the car, locked it, and walked away, still eyeing his unkempt observer. *Maybe he's just a simple car thief.* He tightened his grip on his black attaché case and proceeded around the corner to the front entrance. Without hesitating, he walked inside.

Good heavens! Peter thought, coming in from the bright sunshine, *it's dark in here!* He had expected to find a well-lit, bustling police facility, not the calm, discreetly lit area that greeted him.

"Howya doing, sir—can I help you?" A voice from nowhere reached Peter's ears, its tone pleasant but correct—and commanding.

Peter waited while his eyes got used to the dimness—dimness made worse by the black composite tile floor and the lowered blinds.

"Sir?"

Peter peered in the direction of the voice and saw a long reception counter at the far end of the entrance lobby. A face peered above it. He turned back to regain his bearings and was nearly blinded by the white block of light coming in through the entrance doorway.

"Over here!" the voice beckoned. The man in his dark police uniform stood up, and Peter advanced toward him, trying to seem as meek as possible. "Ah, yes! Hello, officer. Um—I've come to get some information on a case. Yes, that's it."

"What kind of information would that be, sir?" the officer asked in a way that made Peter feel as if he were after something he had no right to. His discomfort increased.

Peter, unsure how to proceed, hesitated for a moment. The officer looked at him skeptically. *It's now or never,* Peter thought.

"I've come to find out if you have any new information about my two children who went missing here last July." Peter made the statement as impassively as he could; it was the only way to control the emotion he felt whenever he spoke of his family.

The officer's tone instantly turned sympathetic. "Your kids disappeared and you haven't had any information on their whereabouts?"

Peter nodded.

"Okay…could I have your name please, sir?"

"Peter Zucker." He felt instant relief at not having to act a part anymore. He wrote out his name on the slip of paper the officer slid across the counter. "My children's names are Mark and Nicolette—Mark and Nicolette Zucker, and I miss them terribly. Since they disappeared, their mother's gone into a—please help me find them…" Peter's breaking voice betrayed his pent-up feelings.

"And where and when did the disappearance occur?"

"At the Snapdragon amusement park last July."

"But that's out in the San Fernando Valley," the officer murmured. "It'd be under the West Valley's jurisdiction—"

"It was," Peter broke in. "But I was just down there, and they told me the case had been sent here."

"Hey, that narrows it down some," the officer said, lightening his tone. "You wouldn't happen to know the name of the lead investigator?"

"Yes," Peter said without hesitation. "Sergeant Mayo."

"*M* for Mayo…Mayo…Mayo…" the officer mumbled as he scrolled down a list on his computer terminal. "Hmm…" he said pensively.

Peter sensed that something about the name had rung a bell in the officer's mind.

"Mr. Zucker," the officer said abruptly, "why don't you take a seat over there while I see what we can do for you."

The reception lobby seemed less dim now, and Peter's task less daunting. The officer motioned to a row of seats near the entry doors, and Peter went over and sat down. From here he could see the top of the officer's head behind the reception counter. He was speaking on the phone.

After what seemed like hours, but was only fifteen minutes, a feeling of utter frustration came over Peter. Again, others had come into the building, talked to the officer or his partner and left. He sat preparing himself for answers full of platitudes designed to make him go away and leave the investigation to them. To say the least, Peter's faith in the American system of justice was small. And now he had given away his true identity as well…*Siech!* he swore under his breath.

"Sir?"

Everything was fraught with complications…the search too difficult to accomplish…and on his own, impossible! He didn't know what to do next. *Where else can I go? What else is there to look into? Oh, Martine—*

"Sir? Mr. Zucker…*Mr. Zucker?*" The voice echoed through the lobby. A strong hand shook his shoulder. "Are you okay, sir?"

Peter looked up. It was the officer from behind the counter. He'd had to walk over to where Peter was sitting to get his attention. He looked concerned. "You all right?"

"Er—yes, fine." Peter felt dazed.

"If you would come with me, there's someone who'll talk to you about your case. But first, I need some ID so that I can prepare your visitor's badge. Just step back over to the counter and we'll set you up."

Peter felt a mixture of relief and disbelief—*are they actually going to help me? Thank you, Lord,* he thought, breaking his promise never to believe in God again.

Chief of Police Bill Hunt answered his phone. "Hunt here," he said.

"Pardon me for disturbing you, sir. This is Detective Lucas in Missing Persons. You did ask to be alerted if there were movements in a Mayo case?"

At the name *Mayo,* Hunt put down his pen. "Yeah, that's right. Go on, detective."

Lucas quickly told him about Peter Zucker's presence and outlined the case that he had skimmed through before calling the top man in the Parker Center.

"Um…that's real interesting, son—look, treat the guy nice and see what he wants. And find out if the detective now in charge of the case is around. He'll remember the details. Okay? Keep me posted."

The chief put down the receiver and made a mental note—*Detective Lucas…bright kid to remember that!* He pressed the intercom button and spoke to his secretary. "Lynn? I asked you to pull together all the recent Mayo cases. Get me the one dealing with the Zucker family. That begins with a *zee.* Thanks."

He thought for a moment about Mayo, picturing in his mind the overweight retired cop. *I'll get that fat sonofabitch yet!*

"Hi. Take a seat. My name's Lucas." Lucas shook Peter Zucker's hand genially. "I'm a detective here in Missing Persons. How can I help you?"

Peter sat down on an uncomfortable metal chair in front of Lucas's desk in the unpartitioned second floor of the police building. He quickly sized up Lucas; young for a detective, mid-twenties, average build, clean-shaven, a nondescript face. He wore a crisp white shirt and plain blue tie. Peter thought he could be a young manager in any profession—except for the small brown leather holster at his side. The detective leaned back in his chair waiting for Peter to start.

"I'll come straight to the point," Peter said. "My two children disappeared here last summer—without a trace. I've heard nothing for months, despite the telephone calls I've made and the letters I've sent. All my efforts have yielded nothing about their fate—they were *so* young, and my wife's lost her mind…the despair…she couldn't get over it. So, here I am in person to see what progress has been made—if any! And, if none has been made, I want to know why."

Wow! Lucas thought. He righted himself in his chair in order to look more businesslike. "Sure…I read you." His tone was now more understanding. "I'm sorry, but I wasn't on the case—and I know nothing about your letters or calls; so, I'll try and pick it up from here the best I can…"

Peter bit his lower lip. At these thoughts about his family, he hardly heard the detective. "While you were waiting downstairs, I quickly reread the file on your children—a very tough case, for sure. All I can tell you at this stage is that we've worked this case very hard—and it's still open, very much so. But, we've gotten no new leads. I'd be lying to you if I tried to be more upbeat."

Peter sat deep in thought, his outstretched fingers forming a triangle over his closed mouth. He felt sullen and annoyed. He had not come all this way to hear the obvious—that the investigation had come to a dead end.

Peter's silence and stern expression made Lucas feel uneasy. "You know, we've had a lot of cases like this. They command the attention of the highest levels of the police and—"

"Bullshit!"

Lucas was startled by the obscenity.

"That's a load of bullshit—and you know it," Peter said. He slammed his hands down on the desk and rose to his feet. "My wife is in an insane asylum—in such mental torment that she can't live a normal life. She's under constant sedation…and all you can tell me is some shit about commanding high levels of attention."

Lucas drew back in his chair, and Peter loomed over him.

"My life has been ruined—do you understand? *Ruined!*" Peter shouted down at him. "Have you got children?"

"Er, no…"

"That's too bad, because if you did, you would understand my feelings and not let a moment go without trying to find them. My hope coming here was to find help. And all you can tell me is that you've—what were your words? 'Worked the case?' *Siech*—you've closed the case! You couldn't give a damn…"

"Hey! Wait one—"

"Don't you *get* it? They could be tortured, molested—killed—and all you can come up with is—"

Peter suddenly stopped. Everyone in the office was looking his way.

"Please calm down, sir," came a voice behind him—unruffled, deep and commanding. "Let's see what we can find out about your kids."

Peter turned to find a graying, heavyset officer in uniform towering over him. He was well into his fifties and a good six foot five, and his expression reminded Peter of a doctor telling a difficult patient to get back into bed.

"Everyone back to work," the new arrival ordered. He motioned to the chair, encouraging Peter to use it. He beckoned to Lucas, who had quickly stood up, to sit back down. He drew up a spare chair and lowered his hefty body into it.

"I'm Bill Hunt, Chief of Police. I'm in charge of everybody here. I guess you're the kids' father?"

"Yes..." replied Peter, astonished that this new man knew about his case.

"Pleased to meet you, Mr. Zucker. What Detective Lucas told you is true—the LAPD never drops a case until it's solved. You may or may not believe it, but I can assure you of that. And what's more, I'm personally very interested in *this* case. That's why I'm down here."

The chief turned to Lucas. "Did you get hold of the investigator currently assigned to this?"

"No, sir. Not yet. He's out of the office."

"Figures." He turned to face Peter. "One of the daily problems our detectives have to contend with is the little downtime they have for administrative work like writing up reports. Because of the level of crime in LA, they're constantly on the move and," he emphasized, "they have to give priority to the cases where there are clear leads."

Peter understood that he was being gently admonished. But before he could say anything, the chief pressed on.

"I think it might be useful if I explain how we deal with cases here. It'll help you understand what we're up against. After that, we'll go through your case in detail to see if anything's been left out, and maybe, you never know, find something—maybe a new lead. You have a moment to do this?"

Peter couldn't decide whether he liked Hunt or not, nor did he understand the sudden high-level interest in his case. He did feel suddenly excited and hopeful, but didn't want to show it.

Hunt took Peter's silence as acquiescence and continued. "Let's start at the beginning—I know this will bring back some painful memories for you, Mr. Zucker, but that can't be helped. As you might guess, we aren't in a happy business here."

"Don't worry," Peter said. "Pain has become part of my life—you have no idea how much."

"Yeah, and I'm sorry about your wife. Okay, let's look at the facts. Your two kids disappeared, apparently without a trace, last July out at Snapdragon. You left them alone for a few minutes at an outdoor café while getting them some food. You shouldn't have done that, but still...You contacted the park authorities who called us when the kids didn't turn up at the end of the day—"

"Late enough to let whoever took my children get away," Peter interrupted.

"Be that as it may, let's just stick to the facts for now, please, Mr. Zucker. Okay?"

Admonished again.

"Even though," the chief muttered, as he leafed through Lucas's copy of the case file, "you would have thought the park authorities would've wanted to call the police in real quick to avoid liability…We'll come back to that one later."

"Yes," Peter agreed sarcastically. "One would have thought…"

"Okay, let's move on. They've dialed 911, and a patrol car turns up to check on these reported missing persons. As soon as the patroller realizes that the kids have gone missing—you know, that it's not just a prank—and that it involved foreign kids who obviously don't know their way around, he radios his watch command, which assigns other cars to patrol the area around the park. They search the area, ask questions, check out the local hospitals, interview park employees and so forth."

The chief peered at a page in the file. "They sent out an Amber Alert…but no results there either.

"When all that produces nothing—as it apparently did—then a couple of investigators from the local LAPD division are assigned to work the case. That would be West Valley."

Peter listened attentively, glancing from Hunt to Lucas to catch signals between them.

"The captain in charge of the detective unit out in the Valley reviews what the investigators did, and when he sees that they came to a dead end, he notifies his boss, the deputy chief of police out there. The deputy chief makes the determination to send the case downtown, meaning here to the Parker Center—and that was done."

Hunt turned to another page. "Now, to make sure no stone is left unturned, we go through the whole thing again here with a fine-tooth comb. And, according to this file, it seems that nothing was overlooked…Ah, yes," Hunt added as if in afterthought, reading from the file, "we notified the FBI—"

"The FBI?" Peter jumped at the name. This had never come up before. "Why?" Peter demanded.

Hunt took off his glasses and leaned back in his chair. "It's just routine when visiting aliens—foreigners like yourself—are involved."

"Yes, but there must be a reason—"

"Sure—well, I can't answer for the Bureau, of course—you'd have to ask them directly, but in cases where a foreigner is involved, it is routine to notify the FBI."

Peter felt dissatisfied by this explanation, and Hunt noticed.

"The FBI is always involved if there's a ransom demand or some indication the victim's being taken across state lines or out of the country," Hunt added. "Then they check at airports and are involved that way. But there's nothing directly pertaining to that in the file, and I understand that you haven't received a ransom demand of any kind. Is that still correct?"

"Yes," Peter replied pensively. "We've received nothing—no indication at all as to what's happened to them."

But Hunt, Peter thought, wasn't listening; he seemed distracted. He leafed through the file twice in short succession, obviously searching for something.

"What's the matter?" Peter demanded.

The chief looked surprised that Peter had noticed. "Oh, nothing," he replied.

"Hey, there must be something!" Peter insisted. "You're looking for something, and my children are at stake here—what is it?"

"Oh, it's nothing to do directly with your case—"

"But you were looking at my file!" Peter insisted.

"Yes—no…"

The chief looked suddenly uncomfortable, and Peter wondered if he was on to something.

"I'm telling you, Mr. Zucker," Hunt declared a little too firmly, "this has *nothing* to do with your case—"

"What is '*this*'?" Peter demanded.

"Just an administrative slip-up." Hunt's voice had an edge to it. "I'm annoyed because the detective who wrote up a part of this report was a little slipshod—"

"Slipshod? What does *that* mean?"

"Careless—" the chief countered. He shifted uncomfortably in his seat. "Look. I'm not going to be drawn into a discussion with you on an internal police matter—"

"What is this '*internal police matter*'?" Peter refused to be bullied. Cold tinges ran down his spine. Peter *was* on to something.

"Now slow down, Mr. Zucker," Hunt said in a calmer voice. "This is a *purely* administrative matter."

"If it's so minor, why don't you tell me what it *is*?"

Hunt saw that Peter wouldn't let go.

"Okay, you win!" Hunt conceded, glancing over at Lucas. He had to appease Peter's concerns. "But I'm only telling you this in order to demonstrate how open we want to be with you on this case. Okay?"

Peter smiled inwardly but remained stony-faced.

"We have been having some minor administrative—and let me stress the word 'administrative'—problems with one of our detectives. The way he wrote up reports—you know, bad grammar, incomplete sentences; he was incorrigible." Hunt feigned a laugh. "And we had to go over his stuff again and again. He was a…um…good detective, but when it came to writing reports, he was a pain in the ass."

"Did he work on my case?"

"Yes, in the early stages," Hunt conceded. "But as I told you, your case has been gone over several times by other detectives since—so nothing's been overlooked." Hunt smiled warmly at Peter to regain his confidence.

"Who was this detective?" Peter asked matter-of-factly.

"I'm not at liberty to—"

"Was it Sergeant Mayo?"

The chief's face flushed slightly. "I've just said I can't name names."

"Tell me it wasn't *Mayo!*" Peter was adamant. He felt he was getting somewhere. "He *was* the one in charge of the initial investigation, wasn't he? If he slipped up, then it *is* of serious importance, and I have a right to know."

"I'm not talking about Mayo—Sergeant Mayo," the chief said, looking away from Peter.

Hunt's lying, Peter thought, *but he'll never admit it.* What mattered was *how had Mayo slipped up?* And *why?* Peter resolved to find out, but he wasn't going to find out *here.*

"Okay," Peter said, "now that we've gone through the process, how about the looking-for-new-leads part you promised? When do we start that?"

"Now," Hunt said, relieved that Peter had dropped the Mayo element. "I'm a busy man, but I'll prove to you how much the LAPD wants to solve your case by personally combing through it with you and Detective Lucas. How d'ya feel about that?"

Chapter 17

▼

Raoul Moreno was a loner and an idealist. Rosa had told him as much the last time they spent the weekend together—before she had broken up with him—again. But he could not change what he was—a dreamer with unrealistic expectations about life. All his visions of an exhilarating existence were constantly dashed by the simple fact that he was a poor fisherman's son.

Raoul had been brought up to take over the family fishing boat—if one could call it that. In reality, it was an old, rusty shell. It had witnessed more glorious days when his grandfather first owned it. But now his father could barely make a living with it, let alone help Raoul pursue his dream of becoming a journalist. But that did not stop the seventeen-year-old from fantasizing—imagining himself as a *Bob Woodward* writing a story that had repercussions the world over. It wasn't the fame he was after, but the opportunity to change things—make his simple existence worthwhile and even useful. Journalism meant daring and courage, and Raoul wanted a piece of it.

These thoughts filled Raoul's mind as he sat on the concrete ledge that jutted out over the water in the small harbor of Puerto Eten down the coast from Pimentel. He gazed out at the ocean, his pimple-scarred chin resting on his knees. The afternoon sun was already low on the horizon, and he closed his eyes against its blinding glare off the water. He clutched his folded legs against his chest and rocked back and forth, daydreaming. Behind him was the wooden railing that kept passers-by from the sheer drop to the water. He knew that he was barely noticeable from the landside, but that from the sea, he stuck out like a solitary spectator in the front row of a theater.

Raoul basked in his fantasies in the sun's late afternoon warmth. Neither the harbor activity behind him nor the familiar sounds of fishing boats chugging back to port disturbed him. In his imagination, he was in a newsroom, surrounded by frenzied activity. He was putting the finishing touches to an article that would be splashed across the front page—

A sound disturbed his concentration—a sturdy throbbing noise. *Leave me alone! I'm trying to finish my article!* But the sound wasn't in the newsroom…

Raoul opened his eyes to search out the source. It was an engine, smoother and more powerful than those of the ordinary fishing boats he knew. He squinted through the sun's glare and saw a sleek boat steadily approaching the harbor; a police launch.

As it drew nearer, Raoul noticed it was towing an old wooden rowboat. They must have found it out at sea, he thought. His eye turned to two uniformed men standing guard over a heap of cloth on the exposed poop deck behind the pilot's cabin. *What have they found?* Raoul wondered, focusing harder.

He got to his feet as the launch passed the breakwater and headed for the mooring berths. He scrambled over the wooden railing and broke into a slow jog along the wharf to keep pace with the vessel. He could see everything clearly now. There were two heads sticking out of the large cloth bundle—two children wrapped up in a gray blanket.

"Hey! Looks like a rescue," Raoul shouted to the harbormaster who was standing idly in the doorway of the harbor office and who turned his head to look at Raoul running past, but otherwise didn't move.

The youngsters looked wet and cold—and sad, Raoul thought. Breathing hard, he reached the mooring dock where several other onlookers already stood. He maneuvered himself to the front and waited as the police launch tied up. As the two children rose, he saw they were a boy and a girl, both quite young. Their police guards herded them—a little roughly, thought Raoul—up onto the dockside and toward a white limousine that had pulled up a few yards away.

Raoul moved closer. "What happened to you two?" he asked, falling in step with the children. His voice caught the attention of the young boy who then turned his head and locked Raoul in a stare. Seeing this, Raoul followed up: "Your rowboat got caught in the tide?"

"Lost-lost-lost!" the boy suddenly blurted out in English. "Lost—*Aidez-nous s'il vous plaît? Aidez…*"

But before he could finish, the policeman following behind whisked the boy off and shoved him and the little girl into the back of the limousine.

Raoul understood nothing of the boy's plea, except that it wasn't in Spanish. This piqued his curiosity even more, and he decided to intercept the two policemen as they returned to the launch.

"What did the kid say? What happened?"

The first policeman stopped abruptly in his tracks. He turned his head and looked at Raoul with a mixture of annoyance and amazement. No one dared ask the all-powerful and aloof *Policía Nacional del Perú* to explain its actions. He glared for a moment at Raoul and then turned away, resuming his steady pace back to the launch.

"I'm a journalist," Raoul shouted, setting off after him. It wasn't a complete lie since he had offered several stories to the local paper, although none had ever been published. "I need to know—for my paper," he quickly added.

When the policeman heard this, he knew he could not afford to dismiss this young man entirely. It *was* possible that *El Crónico* had sent someone down to cover the event. But how did the paper find out? He glanced back at the departing limousine. Perhaps Chavez had ordered it. But this youth?—He was hardly more than a boy! He considered the situation as he walked. "They were adrift—at sea in a small boat—and we rescued them," he told Raoul without turning his head.

"Who are they?" Raoul pursued.

"That's none of your business," the policeman replied gruffly.

"And whose car was that?"

The policeman came to a halt. He looked at Raoul with a contemptuous smile. "You don't know whose car that is! Well, boy, I'll tell you for your own good—it belongs to *Señor* Luis Chavez." With that, he stepped off the dock onto the launch, leaving Raoul standing open-mouthed.

"This is a story!" Raoul uttered in excitement. "This *is* a story!"

"Huh!" murmured Chief Hunt.

They had been going over the case file page by page for more than an hour, and this was the first sign of anything untoward. Peter felt a spark of hope that there might be a new lead in the investigation.

For Hunt, however, the utterance carried an entirely different meaning. He had discovered a cleverly disguised flaw in the investigation that confirmed his long-held belief that Sergeant Mayo was a crook. That this might help Peter Zucker was not in the forefront of Hunt's mind at that moment. His thoughts were on Internal Affairs, which had investigated Mayo's suspected dishonesty but had failed to pin anything on him. Mayo had always been artful in covering his tracks. He was suspected of being on the take. His lifestyle was too rich for a police sergeant, even though he claimed the money was his wife's. Mayo was arrogant and had challenged his detractors to put up or shut up. He had eventually agreed to take early retirement from the LAPD—on full pension. Chief Hunt had remained determined, nevertheless, to unearth something that would put Mayo behind bars and uphold the integrity of the police force.

"Huh!" he said again, wondering whether this could be it.

"What's the 'huh' about?" Peter demanded. He leaned forward, as did Detective Lucas, to see where on the page Hunt had stopped.

"Um—oh!" Hunt said, faltering. His preoccupation with Mayo had made him forget Peter's presence. "Um…I don't know…Gimme a moment—I need to check something…"

"Can I help, sir?" Lucas asked eagerly.

"No—stay here with Mr. Zucker." Hunt grabbed the sheet that had caught his attention and strode off toward the elevators. Before entering his private office on the sixth floor, he went to the filing cabinets next to where his secretary was sitting.

"Oh! There you are, sir," Lynn said. "Several people have been looking for you. Can—"

"Are those Mayo case files in here?" Hunt demanded, gesturing impatiently toward the cabinets and ignoring what she was saying.

"Yes, but sir, the—"

"Well, get 'em out for me, will ya!"

Surprised by his tone, she pulled open one of the heavy metal drawers and pointed to a series of files marked "Mayo." Hunt put his hand in, grabbed a half-dozen at random, hurried into his office, and closed the door behind him.

Hunt knew that all crooks had habits and routines that ended up being their downfall. He hoped he had discovered Mayo's…

He sat down at his desk and rapidly leafed through the files, stopping at a similar place in each. "Gotcha!" he exclaimed. He grinned with satisfaction.

Hunt couldn't believe it. It had been so simple that everyone had overlooked it. Mayo had removed from the files the statements of potential key witnesses and substituted false testimony that said they had seen nothing, thus reducing their status from essential witnesses to mere extras at the scene of the crime. As such, they were unlikely to be contacted again during later re-examinations. This is what Hunt had discovered in the Zucker file. There was a clear inconsistency in it; one part said that a particular security guard in the Snapdragon parking lot had been questioned by telephone following the children's disappearance, and that he had stated he had seen nothing out of the ordinary. However, in another part, which Mayo must have overlooked, investigators had reported being unsuccessful in contacting the guard at all. *How could the guard have said he saw nothing if he never actually spoke with investigators?* Hunt concluded that the security guard knew something critical to the case, and that Mayo had tried to cover it up. But what? And why? Hunt was determined to find out.

Hunt realized this new lead could also help Peter Zucker. Yet, he couldn't let Zucker know the investigation was flawed. He thought for a few moments before going back down to Missing Persons.

"I'm sorry to have kept you waiting," Hunt said affably to Peter. "But I had to check something out." He spoke positively in order to forestall embarrassing questions.

Peter eyed him suspiciously but said nothing.

"You'll be pleased to know that I've found what might be a possible—and let me stress the word 'possible'—new lead in the case. But, before you get too excited, I have to warn you that it may also be a wild goose chase."

"You mean—"

"Yes, Mr. Zucker. If this—let's call it, um…possible new element—just leads us up a blind alley, then I'm afraid there's nothing more we can do."

"But there must—" Peter interjected.

"I understand how much this means to you, Mr. Zucker. And I feel for you and your wife, of course—and if something new comes out of the blue, then that's another matter…but for now, all we have to work with is this possible new lead. And we'll follow that up right away."

"Okay," Peter said. He did not want to waste any more time. "What is this 'new element'?"

The chief turned to Lucas. "Listen carefully, detective, and then put all your other work aside and immediately do what I say. Is that understood?"

"Yes, sir." Lucas opened his notebook and leaned forward with pen in hand.

Hunt commenced. "All amusement parks in California have security guards who patrol the parking lots to ensure that cars aren't tampered with, that people drive in a considerate manner, and so forth. If people felt their cars weren't safe while they were spending the day at an amusement park, or felt insecure going to and from their cars with their children, then they wouldn't patronize those parks anymore—and that's bad for business."

Hunt glanced at Peter to make sure he was following. "These security guards don't receive any special police training. They're just minimum wage or contract employees in uniform who serve as a deterrent to car thieves, muggers, and other unsavory characters, and who are told to call in the police if anything gets out of hand."

Peter pictured in his mind the vast parking lot at Snapdragon.

"Well, part of the investigation of your case, Mr. Zucker, involved interviewing all park employees. And if our detectives couldn't speak to them in person—you know, if they had gone off duty by the time we got around to them—well then, we conducted telephone interviews. That's standard procedure. It works fine and actually saves us a lot of time. Well, one of the parking lot security guards who was on duty at the time of your kids' disappearance was never reached by detectives—so we don't know whether he saw something suspicious or not. That was the 'huh' in the file, if you like. The parking lot is the only way in or out of the amusement park, and it seemed odd to me that the only park employee who was never contacted worked there. So, there it is. It's thin gruel, I'll grant you that—but it's worth following up. And Lucas, I want you to find this guy, get his story, and get right back to me—today, if possible, or sooner!"

"Now, sir?"

"Yup, right away! Mr. Zucker here hasn't come all this way to sit around and admire the view at LAPD headquarters!" The chief grinned at his own joke as Lucas grabbed the phone and dialed the security office at Snapdragon. Hunt got up to leave. "So, Mr. Zucker, we'll be in touch with you as soon as we've found something. I'll accompany you back downstairs."

"*Why* was such a basic piece of investigating overlooked?" Peter said. He remained in his chair, indicating to the chief that he wasn't budging until he got an answer. "Both you and Lucas insisted that the LAPD went over the case file several times before putting it away—"

"It wasn't *put away*—"

"Yes, it *was*," Peter insisted. "I've been without news for months. My children, if they're still alive, have been living God only knows where for all this time, and only now, because I bothered coming here, is a new lead found—"

"Hey, Mr. Zucker, that's unfair—"

"Don't interrupt me," Peter said aggressively. "If it's *unfair*, it's *unfair* to me, my wife, and, above all, to my children…And it's sloppy work on the part of the LAPD—"

"That's going too far—"

"Didn't anybody ever ask this man Mayo why he didn't check on the security guy in the parking lot? Dammit, it seems obvious to me—the main way in and out of the park! I mean, he was in charge of the initial investigation—was he this sloppy in all his cases? Or was it because we're foreigners and weren't that important?"

The chief looked uneasy, and Peter realized that he had touched a nerve. But the time was over for polite, diplomatic talk. *These people can* share *my hell,* Peter thought.

"Sir, I know it's hard for you to believe, but I do understand your feelings," Hunt replied sympathetically. "I disagree with a lot of what you've said, but I do admit that this omission in the case should not have occurred…"

An omission that cost me six months! Peter clenched his teeth and dug his nails into the attaché case on his lap. He could have punched Hunt.

Hunt continued. "I have been on the force for thirty-two years, and I would be the first to admit that mistakes have been made. We're all human. But I do reject the idea that cases concerning foreigners are treated differently. So please do not insult me by repeating that kind of accusation."

Peter still seethed and the chief could see it.

Hunt's face grew weary. "I'll remind you, Mr. Zucker, that I'm chief of police here, and that I've spent the better part of the last hour on your case. Very few people get this kind of personal attention. I am also a father and a grandfather, and I do feel the pain you and your wife are going through. One thing I'll do here and now is give you my personal guarantee that the LAPD'll do its utmost to find out what happened to your kids. Time may have been lost because Mayo was a—um…fell short on the investigation. But that's in the past. Now we're moving ahead."

Peter stood up and faced Hunt. "Because Mayo was a *what?*"

The chief thought quickly. "I'll tell you *for your information only,* Mr. Zucker, that Mayo was not the best cop on the force. He made mistakes on other cases as well, and that's why we retired him early. So, accept things as they are and give us a chance to work this new lead—you never know where it might take us."

Peter was satisfied that he had made his point. It would at least keep the chief on his toes. He had also learned something useful that he intended to follow up by himself. "What's the next step then?" Peter asked, impatiently.

"Make sure you leave us your contact information, and we'll get back to you as soon as we have news from Lucas."

"When will that be?"

"I can't say for sure, but you did hear me ordering him to drop everything and find this parking lot security guy. *Please,* Mr. Zucker," Hunt insisted, "bear with us for a couple of days. I've given you my word—what else can I do?"

"Okay," Peter replied. "But I'll be a pain in your ass until I find my children."

"Here's your ticket for Lima, Mrs. Cox, and also your travel orders." The young secretary passed them over the desk to Allison who was seated in front of her computer screen.

"Thanks," Allison said, not even glancing up. She was busy finishing her report on her visit to the New Life Clinic in Montana.

"You're lucky traveling to all those cool places," Jen commented, still standing in Allison's temporary office in Washington. Allison wanted to continue working on her report, but felt it would be rude not to chat for a couple of minutes with this girl who was still full of illusions about life.

"Yes, it does seem so," Allison said, swiveling in her chair and smiling at the girl. "Not everything is always as it seems, though," she added. "It seemed glamorous to me as well when I was your age. But nobody told me about the other part—constantly living out of a suitcase and spending hours in airports…Actually, I'm only going to be away for three nights, and I probably won't even have time to call any of my old friends from the time I was posted down there."

The secretary looked unconvinced. *Why ruin her illusions,* Allison thought. "Okay, Jen, I see that I can't pull the wool over your eyes. Sure, I am looking forward to my trip to Lima; it'll be fun being there again and perhaps I'll make time to link up with some friends. But don't go telling anyone otherwise, or they'll make it my last trip!"

Jen smiled. The telephone on Allison's desk rang. Jen's reflexes were good and she picked the receiver up before it rang a second time. "Mrs. Cox's office. Yes, let me see if she can speak to you now. Who's calling please?…Okay, just one moment, Mr. Vandervelt…"

Pressing the mute button, she asked Allison if she wanted to take the call.

"Sure…" Allison tried to conceal her enthusiasm, "…and that'll be all for now, thanks Jen." Allison took the receiver and waited for the secretary to leave the room and close the door before releasing the mute button.

"Hi there! How are things?" Allison's voice was effervescent.

"Absolutely great, thanks," John said in his distinctive voice. "I need to see you."

"Same here," Allison replied. "When and where? I'll cancel all my appointments!"

"If only life were that simple," John said, regret in his voice. "How about tomorrow for lunch?" he suggested more brightly.

"Oh, damn! I can't," Allison said. "I'll be on a plane to Peru, but how about this evening?"

"I'd love to, but I have to work."

Allison felt a pang of disappointment and momentarily wondered if she could delay her trip.

John interrupted her thoughts. "When are you coming back?"

"Only at the weekend—can you wait that long?" Allison asked, teasing him.

"No…but for other reasons…I have something for your friend—it could be urgent." John's voice was serious, and Allison knew better than to ask him for details over the phone.

"Hey, I've got it," Allison said, glancing down at her ticket. "I'm flying out of Dulles at eleven thirty-five tomorrow morning. Why don't we meet there for coffee beforehand—um…let's say at ten. I'll check in early so we can have time to chat."

"That sounds…fine," John replied, double-checking his PDA. "I'll find you in the check-in area. Which airline?"

"Continental."

"Okay. Bye." He hung up abruptly.

Allison wondered what he might have found. But then, seeing the time, she quickly put it out of her mind and went back to her report.

Chapter 18

▼

Peter Zucker peered through the windshield at the elegant house, then looked back down at the map spread out on the front passenger seat of his rental car. He was certain he had noted down the Coldwater Canyon Drive address of Sergeant Mayo correctly, but he hadn't expected such a well-to-do neighborhood.

It seemed inconceivable that Mayo could afford such a place on a police pension. The best way to check would be to go to the front door and ring the bell. It was six fifteen AM, however, and still too early to attempt a visit. Peter had been up for three hours, his biological clock still operating on European time. He had eaten breakfast—ham and eggs and terrible coffee—at an all-night diner near his motel, all the while flipping through notes that he had scribbled right after leaving the Parker Center yesterday.

Now he was parked two houses up and across the street from what he presumed was Sergeant Mayo's house. This offered him a clear view of the house from an unobtrusive vantage point. The two-story mansion seemed large enough to accommodate a family of four plus guests. Its driveway curved up from the main road through the mature, well-tended front garden, past a triple-car garage, to the front door. Ivy-covered walls and leaded windows gave the house an old-English look.

Peter fiddled with the radio to find something to help pass the time. Apart from Spanish-language programs, the only clear stations were broadcasting traffic reports and rock music, neither of which interested him. He switched off the radio and went back to admiring the surrounding properties.

A sour feeling of envy crept over him. How could all these people live here in quiet luxury while he had to fight every minute of the day to maintain his sanity?

The stress of the last half-year made him feel that his life had been a failure. Any hope of finding Mark and Nicolette and resurrecting some sort of normal family life was constantly dampened by the certitude that grief was not far away. He banged the steering wheel with his fist.

Peter's thoughts drifted to Martine in her stark hospital room; it would be mid-afternoon in Geneva, and she would be quietly dozing. It gave him comfort to imagine her at peace, even if it was only because of sleeping pills. He also thought about the children, but the agony was too great, and he had to stop.

The digital clock on the dashboard changed to six forty-five. Peter shifted nervously in his seat. He had met Mayo at the time of the children's disappearance, but he was counting on Mayo not to remember. Posing as an insurance agent would present him in an entirely different light and complete the deception. He had to believe in that; otherwise, he might as well give up.

Peter looked at the clock again—six fifty-eight. He decided not to wait any longer and risk missing Mayo if he left for an early appointment. Peter pulled a photograph from his wallet, and his throat constricted as he saw his family's happy faces in a former time. He slid the picture forcefully back in place, stuffed the wallet into his inside pocket, and got out of the car. With a measured pace he crossed the road to the house, determined to get what he wanted.

Peter rang the doorbell. Nothing stirred. He pushed the button several times before he heard muttering from inside. In the door, a panel the size of a paperback novel slid open at face level, and a middle-aged woman peered out. "What do you want?" she snapped.

"My name ist Wilhelm Knoblauch, madam—of Zurich Life Insurance." Peter knew this would mean nothing to the woman, who he assumed was Mayo's wife, and quickly continued in order to pique her curiosity. "It concerns zee one million dollar reward your husband, Mr. Mayo, might be entitled to for a case he verked on." He passed his business card through the opening. She didn't seem convinced, so Peter added, "I got your address from Chief Hunt at zee Parker Center…"

"Wait a minute—I'll be right back," she replied curtly and abruptly slid the little door shut. A few minutes later the front door swung open and a heavyset man in a bathrobe appeared. Peter immediately recognized him as the detective who'd worked on his case.

"I'm Mayo—this is a fine time to be disturbing law-abiding folks like us," he said gruffly. "You'd better come in."

Mayo's wife had evidently understood his message, Peter mused as he was led into the front room. It was neat and tidy and seemed rarely used.

"What was it exactly that you have for us?" Mayo said impatiently but with obvious interest.

"I apologize for coming here zo early, but, you zee, I vill be flying back to Svitzerland shortly, and I need to check some facts about a case you ver involved in."

"Okay," Mayo said hurriedly. "But you told my wife something about a reward?"

"Ah, *ja!* Zat is zo. But I need some information first."

"Who are you?" Mayo asked suspiciously, furrowing his brow. "Haven't I seen you somewhere before? And what's with the music case?" he said, pointing down to the black viola case Peter was carrying.

"As I said," Peter explained again. "My name is Knoblauch. I verk for a Sviss life insurance company, and I need to certify zee disappearance of two children here last summer at zee Snapdragon amusement park." Peter was talking quickly to avoid interruption and get to the point. "If I can attest it to be true zat dey disappeared vithout a trace, den zee parents vill get two million Swiss francs insurance money. If not, zee persons who can give me information zat vill point me toward ver I might find zee children—zat is, let's say, if dey ver kidnapped and are still alive—vill receive part of zee one million dollar reward money."

"Ya mean a million bucks just for helping with inquiries?" Mayo asked eagerly, his eyes sparkling.

"*Ja,* but zee information has to be good," Peter stressed.

"What do you want to know?" Mayo asked, obviously impatient to move along.

"It vas zee case last summer zat you dealt vith out in zee Valley," Peter said. "It concerned two children called Zucker...Mark and Nicolette," he added with difficulty. "According to zee police file, you closed zee case on September 5 last year due to no leads—"

"Yeah, yeah—somethin' like that..."

"Of course, if you maintain zat as zee detective in charge of zee investigation at zat stage zat zee two children disappeared vithout trace, and you *still* have no idea vot happened to dem, den zat vill be sufficient for me, and I'll leave and disturb you no longer—"

"No, no!" Mayo interjected. "Sit down—please. You want some coffee?"

"Thank you, zat vill be very nice," Peter said, satisfied.

Mayo shouted the order to his wife who was in the kitchen. Then, leaning forward in his chair as if to avoid someone's overhearing them, he asked quietly: "Um...how confidential is all this?"

Peter disliked this man and had difficulty hiding it as the round shaved head and beady eyes came closer to him. "Completely, of course," Peter replied, as if insulted by the insinuation of impropriety. "Do you have new information?"

Mayo was pensive. He stared at Peter, examining him up and down and making Peter feel uneasy. "There's something that doesn't jibe here," Mayo said after a few seconds. He looked perplexed. "There were other people involved in that case—why do you come to me?"

Peter's heart started pounding. *Why did Mayo recall the case so easily?*

"It's quite simple," Peter replied. "I've been to zee Parker Center; I've discussed zee case vith Chief Hunt. Dey have no new leads but suggested I come down to see you as you ver involved in zee early stages of zee investigation. You are zee last person I'm seeing before I go back and close zee case."

This seemed to satisfy Mayo, but he still looked a little dubious. Peter forged ahead.

"Look, I can understand your concern, Mr. Mayo. I come to you out of nowhere—out of zee blue, I fink you say over here—asking you about a case you dealt vith six months ago, and you correctly vonder how genuine I am. I vould do zee same in your position—anyone vould. However, my company is up against an extremely tight deadline because dere is a time clause in zee insurance policy zat stipulates zat zee money, zee full two million francs, vill have to be paid out to zee family if I find no new information on zee case. And zat deadline is very fast approaching, Mr. Mayo. Zo, for my company, dere is some urgency in settling."

Peter bent down and picked up the viola case from the floor beside his chair. "Zat is vhy dey have sent me out here *fully equipped*," he stressed, "to avoid bureaucratic delays and pay for zee information on zee spot."

He placed the case on his knees with the opening side toward Mayo, and carefully undid the metal spring clips. Peter opened the lid a little way, enough for Mayo's eyes to widen as he caught sight of the piles of dollar bills inside. "Vee are in a hurry, Mr. Mayo, and vee are villing to pay cash for any information that vee find useful. Can you help us, Mr. Mayo?"

Peter paused to let the full force of what he had said sink in. Mayo's eyes were riveted on the money.

"If not, I vill leave and not take up any more of your time," Peter said, abruptly closing the case and placing it back on the floor beside him. He leaned back. Now it was his turn to sit and examine Mayo.

"This is a strange way of doing business, Mr. Knock…"

"Knoblauch," Peter added helpfully.

"But I might be able to help you."

"Ah, zat vould be great," Peter said.

"Now, it's not new, but there was a lead we didn't follow up at the time," Mayo said. Peter felt his heart pounding again. "There had been a series of kidnappings at parks around here—how much information do you need for the million dollars?" Mayo suddenly asked.

"All zee truth, naturally," Peter responded, shocked not only at the callousness of this man but also at the fact that no one had talked before about *a series of kidnappings.*

"And how would I get the money?"

"If zee information leads to zee children, den you vould get a large part of zee one million dollars—perhaps zee whole sum, if you ver zee only one giving us good information. Obviously, I haven't got a million dollars vith me," Peter added, "but enough to show my company's good faith." He tapped the case beside him. "I am empowered to make a substantial down payment in cash. Zee remainder is sitting in my company's bank account in Svitzerland and can be transferred anywhere once zee information turns out to be OK. For now, can you please elaborate on dis kidnap aspect?"

Mayo was pensive again and seemed to be fighting within himself. At that moment his wife brought in the coffee and Mayo appeared relieved at the interruption. But he soon picked up the conversation again.

"The thing is, there had been a spate of kidnappings, and we suspected the children were being taken by a ring—"

"A ring?" Peter asked, confused by the term and not wanting to misunderstand a single word of what Mayo was saying.

"Yeah…" Mayo fell silent as he caught a warning glance from his wife. Peter looked at her and saw it too. *Damn,* he thought.

"You ver saying," Peter prompted.

Mayo glanced up again at his wife who was shaking her head. "I think I'm going to have to check with someone first—I'm not really sure about what I'm saying…"

Peter saw the new lead slipping out of his grasp. "Look, this whole conversation is confidential, I assure you," he said more desperately. "You'll get no money if I get no information." In his excitement, Peter dropped his heavy German accent and spoke in his normal, nearly perfect English.

"Hey, who are you?" Mayo asked.

Peter realized the ruse was collapsing. He picked up the viola case again and placed it on his lap. Opening it toward himself, he pulled out a sheaf of large-denomination bills and laid it on the coffee table in front of Mayo. "I have authority to pay cash," Peter stated forcefully.

While Mayo and his wife stared at the money, Peter carefully reached inside the viola case again. As he pulled out his *Sturmgewehr 90*, more money fell onto the carpet. He pointed the assault rifle at Mayo and deftly cocked it, placing a 5.6 mm round into the firing chamber. "As you can see, I have other authority as well."

Mayo froze. The muzzle was so close that he could see the rifling in the barrel. It looked like bared teeth.

"What I need is information, and I need it *now!*" Peter said harshly to the astonished couple.

After a few seconds, Mayo smiled ruefully. "You're fucking Zucker, aren't you? The kids' father. I remember you now…Why you fucking—!"

"Stay seated!" Peter barked as Mayo started rising from his chair. "And you stay put, too," he told Mayo's wife. "Yes, I'm their father, and I'm prepared to use this to find my children."

Mayo laughed. "You poor sucker. Just give 'em up for lost—that ring I was telling you about works only in one direction. Once they're on it, there's no comin' back."

"How do you know that?" Peter asked, stunned.

Mayo saw the change. If he could distract Peter, he might wrestle the weapon away from him.

"'Cause I worked for this ring! Ya think I can afford a place like this on a cop's lousy pay?" Mayo laughed derisively. "You stupid, naïve bastard—your fuckin' kids are down in South America somewhere, and, believe me, you'll never see them again."

As Peter absorbed Mayo's words, he didn't notice Mayo's wife reaching back onto the shelf behind her.

The glass paperweight struck him a glancing blow just above the left ear, and he grunted in pain and surprise. At the same instant, Mayo jumped up from his chair and grabbed for the gun. Instinctively, Peter pulled it away to his left, causing Mayo to stumble over the coffee table and fall, knocking his head hard. Peter pulled the gun free as he saw Mayo's wife heading for the door. He had no time to think. The gun's report resounded throughout house as the bullet blew a hole in her bathrobe. She collapsed and rolled over, blood spurting from a gaping hole in her chest.

Peter stood momentarily stunned. A movement near his feet brought him back to the reality of what Mayo had just told him. His eyes flashing with fury, he thrust the still-smoking barrel deep into Mayo's mouth, making him choke and wince in pain.

"So where are my kids?"

"I dunno—I swear, I dunno!" Mayo spluttered, and his wide eyes darted back and forth with fear.

Peter thought quickly. He couldn't kill Mayo or he'd never get what he wanted. And he couldn't waste time arguing; the whole neighborhood must have heard the gunshot. Peter's eyes darted over Mayo's body, contorted on the floor, and picked the spot. He pulled the barrel out of Mayo's mouth, aimed it at his elbow and pulled the trigger. Mayo screamed in pain. Peter rapidly moved the gun back toward Mayo's head, this time ramming it against Mayo's throat just above his Adam's apple.

"Where are my kids?" Peter demanded.

When Mayo didn't answer immediately, Peter aimed at Mayo's shoulder.

"No, please no...Jesus...have pity—"

"Okay, *where are my children?*" Peter snarled.

"They went to a child prostitution ring...sold...I'll repay you—"

"Where?"

"In South America...I dunno where exactly—it operates all over...please—"

"How do you contact it? You'd better give me a name—"

"I...I haven't...they contact me—"

"I need a name," Peter insisted, his teeth clenched tightly and his hands shaking. "I need a *name!*"

"Pedro...*Pedro!*—It's the only one I know..." Mayo was screaming now.

"Who's Pedro?—Pedro *what?*" Peter jabbed Mayo's throat with the barrel.

"I dunno...I swear I dunno—he contacted me...he's the only one...They just sent me the money..." Mayo gagged.

"I need more," Peter yelled, seething with hatred and utter disgust. His muscles were taut to the point of snapping. At the horror of Mayo's words, Peter involuntarily gripped the gun tighter, and it discharged another round. The bullet went through Mayo's chin and took off most of his head, leaving the man an unrecognizable, bloody mess.

Peter stood there motionless. He felt violently sick and threw up. Wiping his mouth on his sleeve, he looked back at Mayo on the floor.

"Oh my God!" Peter uttered, "what have I done? Christ Almighty!" Killing Mayo wasn't as upsetting as the fact that he had eliminated the best clue to where his children were..."*Huere Siech!* How stupid...how stupid!"

The phone suddenly rang, bringing Peter to his senses. He urgently placed the gun back in the viola case and stuffed in as many of the wads of bills as he could gather, some sticky with blood and tiny pieces of bone. *God! It's all over the place,* he thought, and abandoned the rest. He clicked the clasps of the case closed and heard the distant wailing of a siren; it was different from the barking sirens of Swiss police cars, but he recognized the sound. Terrified and panicky, he ran from the room, nearly tripping over the body of Mayo's wife. He hastened out the front door and walked briskly down the driveway, grateful for the tall hedges and large yards that separated the mansions in this neighborhood. It took great resolve to not break into a run. He was soon across the road and in his car, driving down the nearest side street.

Chapter 19

▼

John was already waiting at Dulles airport when Allison hurried into the departure terminal pulling her suitcase on its well-worn wheels. He rushed forward and took over her load. They embraced quickly, bringing their cheeks together before leaning back and admiring each other's smiling faces.

"You look great…but rushed," John told Allison. He didn't mention the bags under her eyes.

"It's good to see you," she replied a little anxiously.

Together they walked to the airline counter where John waited while Allison checked in. He was pleased to see her face relax as her suitcase lumbered down the rubber beltway and she pocketed her boarding pass.

"How about that coffee you promised me?" she said with a smile, and took him by the arm.

While sipping frothy lattés they exchanged pleasantries and laughed together—a sharp contrast to the other travelers in the airport coffee shop, all of whom appeared lifeless. Then Allison spied the time on the wall clock.

"All right, let's get down to business. What good news do you have for me?"

"Whether it's good or not is for you to judge, my dear," John replied, pulling a folded sheet of lined paper out of the inner breast pocket of his crisply pressed gray suit. He unfolded it and rubbed his thumb along the crease so it would lie flat on the cafeteria table in front of him. "These are just notes, but I can't give them to you," he said as an aside.

She understood that he would probably put the sheet through the shredder in his office soon after their conversation.

"Simply put, there are two things I have found that might help your friend, but they are far from being conclusive—and I know I don't need to tell you this, but please keep the source of this information strictly to yourself."

"Sure, John, I understand."

"Well, first of all—and, let me say again, this is pretty tenuous—there was a child-prostitution ring several years back that operated, we think, out of Peru and provided young kids and teenagers for select clients throughout Latin America. I use the word 'select' because it wasn't a large ring, and its clients were generally well-to-do and influential people in these countries. That, of course, made it difficult to pin down the ring and close it. We suspected that some of our kids—I mean U.S. citizens—were being taken for the ring, although it seems that the majority came from various South American countries…"

Allison listened intently, keeping an eye on the clock.

"Don't worry, I'm coming to the point," John said. "Well, we contacted the Peruvian government about this, expressing our deep concern, and of course they denied that U.S. kids were involved. We also discreetly mentioned that Congress would look unfavorably on further aid for Peru if this continued. They took the hint and made a big show about cracking down on the ring. Unfortunately, it seems the prostitution ring is back in operation, *but* with no U.S. kids involved—so overt moral concern on our part has waned."

"Hmm…" Allison murmured.

"Yes, I agree," John added, acknowledging Allison's thoughts. "It's morally indefensible, but our leaders have more pressing problems on their minds."

"But if the ring hasn't operated in the States for several years, where's the connection with my friend's kids?"

"Well, that's the question. It doesn't operate here; no U.S. kids, at least none living in this country, are involved. Here's the point though: there's some suspicion that foreign kids have been plucked from here by the ring. These slimy perverts pay large sums of money for variety—they get tired of dark-haired Latinos—they want nice pale-skinned blondes as well. God, they should all be sent to the chair, they make me sick…"

"So what you're saying is that Peter's—my friend's—kids might have been victims of the ring?"

"Sure, it's a possibility. It'd be easy. These hoods go to the amusement park and target good-looking kids speaking a foreign language. Europeans are also distinctive in other ways—their dress, their mannerisms—and we're dealing with professional criminals with vast amounts of money at their disposal and no scruples," John added. "It's shocking."

"But it's still a pretty slim lead, John."

"Yes, but when you put it together with something else I found, it becomes a tad more solid—at least worth following up." John pulled another sheet of paper from his pocket. It was a photocopy of a short news article. "Here, look at this," he said, handing it to Allison. It was in Spanish, and it read:

> Puerto Eten—On Friday, a police patrol launch rescued two unidentified young children whose rowboat had drifted out to sea. They were brought into port and taken back to their home through the generous intervention of Señor Luis Chavez.

"Do you think…?"

"I don't know," John said. "It might be them, but then again it could be anybody. There's no way of telling."

"Was this all there was—one short paragraph?" Allison asked.

"Uh-huh. It was tucked away in the 'Briefs' section of *El Crónico*; probably a last-minute addition to fill space before going to press." John glanced around to make sure nobody was eavesdropping. Satisfied, he went on. "Our embassy in Lima wouldn't normally have given it much thought and certainly wouldn't have included it in the media roundups it sends back to Washington—you know that from your time down there. But a friend of mine in the CIA ran a discreet search of all the newspapers in South America to see what might come up. And this did."

"How old is this?" Allison asked.

"Less than a week—February 5," he said, looking down at the date scribbled next to the article.

"Yeah," Allison said after a few moments' thought. "But it's very little to go on." She sounded disappointed.

"At first sight, yes," John answered. "But I've been mulling it over, and it raises some interesting coincidences. First, and most obvious, is the possible connection with the child-prostitution ring. I mean, what were *young children* doing out at sea in a rowboat? Had they been set adrift by a ship that was transporting them illegally and was about to be searched? Were the kids trying to escape by themselves from…I don't know what? And if the event wasn't out of the ordinary, why did it make the papers? Then there's the reference to Luis Chavez—if it's the same Luis Chavez I'm thinking of, then we're talking about a very powerful man in Peru who, by the way, owns—"

"*El Crónico*," Allison answered pensively.

"That's right, my dear."

"But then," Allison said, "if the kids were illegal, surely the last thing Chavez would want is for the incident to receive publicity in the papers, least of all in his own newspaper."

"Yes, that occurred to me as well…but what if the people putting together the paper didn't realize what was going on? And seeing the reference to the 'generous intervention of Señor Luis Chavez,' they would be afraid not to run the story. I mean, it's only two sentences—what harm could it do?"

"And if Chavez saw it?" Allison asked.

"Oh Chavez—he's pretty full of himself. He'd probably focus more on the mention of his name in doing good than the extreme possibility that anyone would link it to two children who went missing six months ago—I mean, we only noticed it ourselves because I asked for a special search."

Both Allison and John remained quiet for a moment, pondering the implications of the article. Allison broke the silence. "Did you say there were more coincidences?"

"That's right," John replied. "When we were having problems with this child-prostitution ring, guess whose name kept cropping up?"

"Don't tell me. Chavez?" Allison said, incredulously.

"Uh-huh. But I can't be sure that it's the same Chavez. As you know, it's a pretty common name in those parts. However, coincidences do occur."

They sat in silence. Allison was mulling over the information.

John, however, was contemplating whether or not to share with her yet another coincidence that he had uncovered. For the first time in his professional life, he hadn't shared it with his colleagues at the Bureau—as he ought to have done—and was still caught up in a moral dilemma over whether or not to give the information to Allison first. She meant a lot to him, and through her he could understand Peter Zucker's horrible predicament…

"Hey! They're calling my flight—I'd better get moving!"

"Yes," John said absentmindedly. He was still deep in thought.

"Are you all right?" Allison asked him. "I'm flattered if you're worrying about my welfare. But I'll be okay. I'm a big girl, and I'll be back before you know it!"

"No…It's not that—look, there's something else you ought to know—"

"Is it about Peter? Otherwise—"

"Yes. He could be in big trouble. You heard about the retired cop and his wife who were shot to death in their home in LA yesterday?"

"Sure, it was all over the news."

"Well, I think your friend could be involved in it."

"What! You're kidding—how?" asked Allison incredulously.

"It's just another coincidence that's difficult to explain," John said. "The slugs found in the house were 5.6 millimeter, shot from an assault rifle—"

"How does that implicate Peter Zucker?" Allison broke in.

"Simply, 5.6 millimeter is a standard Swiss army cartridge. Everyone else—meaning the U.S. and all other NATO countries—uses 5.56 millimeter."

"Yeah, but that proves nothing," Allison said. "Tons of people collect fancy guns in this country, and millions of assault rifles are in circulation—"

"Yes, but the 5.56 millimeter NATO cartridge, which you can find everywhere, is accurate in Swiss 5.6 millimeter barrels, but not vice versa. So why should a collector or some mad gunman in this country use a cartridge that is not normally imported? And, if he were going to kill someone, he'd surely use the anonymous 5.56 round he can buy almost anywhere. No, this points to a weapon that came into this country with its own ammunition."

Allison went pale, recalling Peter's words that he would kill to get his children back. "And all Swiss men keep an army rifle and box of cartridges at home because they're in the reserves…"

"There's more," John continued. "The cop who was killed was suspected of dishonesty and corruption—and, get this, he was in charge of the initial investigation of the disappearance of Zucker's kids."

"Oh my God!" Allison's look of shock deepened. Her whole body slumped. "Do the police know about this?"

"Sure, they know the facts, but I don't think they've put it all together yet. I doubt they know as much about Peter Zucker as I do, and I haven't heard his name mentioned. But they'll get there eventually, especially since it's about a murdered cop."

"And…you haven't told them what you—"

"What I know? No. All that we've discussed was in confidence—as this is. But I can't keep this to myself for long, not when it concerns a homicide."

"What are you going to do, John?"

"Give you a little time to investigate the leads I've given you—with Zucker. Allison, convince him to leave the country and join you in Lima to follow up the leads. What I am saying is, give him a last chance to find his kids, or at least a chance to find out once and for all what's happened to them. Then it's up to him to sort out with his conscience what to do about this business."

"Thank you, John. Thank you so much." Fatigue hung on every word. "I wish all this were over, and I were getting onto a flight back to Geneva—I really miss the boys."

"Just do what you have to in Lima and don't worry about anything—you're a capable gal. I'll see you this weekend."

"Can't wait—but…" Allison said as an afterthought.

"Don't worry," John said, handing her a small card. "Here's a couple of contact numbers you might need. Mine's a direct line in case of a real emergency; the other's for your friend Zucker. He's holed up in a cheap motel outside LA. He wasn't difficult to find. You'd better get going!"

Allison squeezed John's arm, kissed him quickly on the cheek, and hurried off. John felt his throat tighten. He prayed she would be okay as he watched her attractive form disappear into the flow of people heading for the departure gates.

It was cruel, worse than heartless. And Romy was powerless to stop it. If she went upstairs to intervene, she would just make things worse for the children. Even with all the mental torment and anguish it gave her, she had to endure it quietly in the hope it would soon be over.

Romy had risked losing her job by refusing to be the instrument of punishment. But she could not bring herself to raise a hand against the children. She had grown attached to them, and sometimes she felt that they even regarded her as a friend. She prayed that her refusal to punish them would not cause her to be sent away—especially now that it was obvious the children were not only unhappy in the Del Solar household but were also being kept there against their will. She had to stay in order to help them. Romy was determined to find out once and for all where they really belonged.

But…oh God! It was utter torture to sit meekly downstairs and listen to the screams.

Miguel, defiant at first, had bravely absorbed the initial whipping that Don Gonzalo administered. But that hadn't been vicious enough for Señora Del Solar.

"Give me that!" she shouted, snatching the riding crop from her husband. She pushed him aside and laid into the boy without the slightest mercy. She was angry and humiliated over the children's attempted escape, and they had to pay for it.

This more intense rain of blows was too much for Mark, who started to yell. He rolled across the floor, attempting to get away from the stabs of pain. When he was striped and bloody and looked like a terrified rabbit, panting and weeping and staring through wide, wild eyes, Señora Del Solar finally seemed satisfied. A sadistic smile appeared on her face as she turned to the boy's sister who was cowering in the corner. One slash on her tender arm with the cutting whip was enough to send a heart-rending shriek throughout the house. It was clear to all that it came from the little girl, and sent a cold tremor down the spines of everyone in the household.

It made Romy's heart miss a beat. She put a hand on her chest in horror. "Alicia! Oh my God! I can't bear it!" It was too much. Romy rushed to the door, intent upon running upstairs to stop this awful punishment. But before she had gone two steps, the screaming was replaced by the sound of adult voices arguing.

"That's enough—what's got into you!" Don Gonzalo shouted at his wife. He was shaking as he twisted the riding crop from her grasp.

At first taken aback by his reaction, she soon recovered. "You've gone soft, you pathetic little man," she spat. "I didn't realize you were so thin-skinned—anyway, I was getting tired; I'll resume later." Haughty as ever, she left the room.

Don Gonzalo bent over Mark and saw the terror in the boy's eyes. "Miguel...Perdón...Perdón..." he said, with sorrow on his face. He looked at the gash on the young cheek and saw a tear mixed with blood running down it.

Mark looked at him with hate in his eyes and viciously swatted away the hand that Don Gonzalo was extending toward him.

The nominal head of the household got up and left the children's room, crestfallen and angry.

Chapter 20

▼

Insistent ringing tore apart the wonderful imagery of Peter's dream. His subconscious mind tried to hold on to the smiling faces of his wife and children, but they faded out.

"No!" he groaned, still drowsing. Peter tried to recapture the image of his family, but each ring pulled them farther away from him. "No, no…" Deeply agitated, he tossed and turned in bed. "*No!*"

He forced open his eyes. He was groggy and felt sick. The persistent ringing now caused a different pain—a purely physical one throbbing inside his skull. *That ringing—God! It's irritating…* Then it stopped.

Peter looked around, not knowing where he was in the penumbra of his awakening. A terrible fear of the unknown took hold of him while his brain adjusted to his surroundings. With relief, he finally recognized the yellowed popcorn ceiling, the worn wallpaper and the cheap furnishings of the dingy motel room that had been his home since landing in the United States two weeks earlier.

But the comfort of awareness was soon spoiled by the remembrance of the day before. He had killed two people. Peter had never harmed anyone before in his life. And even though he knew the Mayos had deserved it, he was traumatized by the deed. It was not so much the fear of getting caught, but rather the nagging thought that he had eliminated his best source of information. *Thou shalt not kill* was a commandment in the Bible, and Peter now feared the consequences of his act in the next life—if there were one. And he had no one to confide in. The garrote of despair began tightening around his throat again…

"*Focus!* Focus on the facts!" he chided himself. He was sure now that Mark and Nicolette had indeed been kidnapped. Mayo had said as much, and, if what he had said was true, they were in South America somewhere. But where? Peter needed a better lead. He doubted Chief Hunt's parking-lot-security-guard theory would lead anywhere. And Peter had already spent days at Snapdragon trying to figure out how his children had been spirited away. Every time, Peter had left the park empty-handed. And now Mayo had not only confirmed that the children had been abducted, but had added the nauseating tidbit that they had been taken by a child-prostitution ring!

After fleeing Mayo's house, Peter had bought a flask of Korbel brandy and chugged a generous shot of it. Once back in his motel room, he had finished it off in the hope it would numb his brain and kill his grief. It had knocked him out and sent him into a deep but troubled sleep that had endured even when the sun came up and shone squarely on his face through the still-open blinds.

The ringing started again…

In Peru, Allison Cox calculated that it was now seven o'clock in the morning in LA. *Surely Peter would not go out that early?* The motel desk clerk had assured her that he had not checked out. She had not asked for Peter by name, in case he was using a false one, only referring to him as a "German-sounding guy."

Allison was about to hang up a second time when the ringing gave way to empty airwave noise. A groggy voice came on the line, "Um…*Ja?*"

"Peter, is that you? This is Allison—Allison Cox…"

"Al—lison?" Peter repeated in disbelief. He sat up quickly to clear his head. "Allison Cox…from Geneva?"

"Yes, Peter. It's me! I'm so glad I reached you."

"But…how did you find me?" Peter asked. He was more focused now.

"That doesn't matter, Peter." Allison shrugged off the question. "I'll tell you later. What's important is that we get together."

"Where are you?"

"I'm in Lima—Peru—"

"Peru!" Peter repeated incredulously. "What are you doing in *Peru?*"

"Look, Peter. It's too complicated to explain over the phone," Allison said. "But you need to join me here—"

"Join you in Peru?"

"Yes," Allison confirmed. "Listen, Peter. I have a lead on that business you're looking into, and it's down here in Peru." She would keep the conversation vague.

"You mean—"

"Yes," Allison interrupted to ensure Peter didn't say too much over the open phone line. "That business you asked me about at my house in Geneva—"

"Mark and Nicolette?"

"Yes, yes! But let's not talk about it over the *phone!*" Allison said, annoyed that Peter wasn't catching on. He was usually quicker than this—what was *wrong* with him?

"But I haven't finished here yet," Peter said, his befuddled brain still not making the connection between South America and Peru.

Peter's voice sounded strange. "Are you okay?" Allison asked.

"Yes, I'm fine," was Peter's tired response. "I just woke up."

"Peter?"

"Uh-huh—"

"You've *got* to get on a plane and join me down here."

"Why?" Peter queried again.

Allison was exasperated. "For crying out loud, Peter—*trust* me! I have a good *lead.*" She paused, suddenly at a loss for words to convince him. "Peter, here's what we'll do…Are you listening?" There was silence at the other end of the line. "Peter—Peter! Are you still there?"

Peter was mulling over all that Allison had said and blending it in with what Mayo had told him. *Peru—South America—child-prostitution ring.*

"*Peter!* Are you still there?"

"Um—*Ja*—yes!" Peter replied with more enthusiasm. "Yes, I am!"

"Good. Now listen carefully, Peter—you'll need to note this down. I'm staying at the Miraflores Park Plaza Hotel in Lima—*Miraflores Park!* Here's the telephone number." She read it off to him from the small, headed notepad on the bedside table in her hotel room and made him repeat it back to her. "My cell phone doesn't work down here—so it's the only way to contact me. I'm not going to be out here for long—just until the end of the week. Please, if you want to follow up this lead, get on the next plane out here—there are other reasons for you to leave, Peter…"

Peter scribbled the information on the corner of a newspaper. "I'll try to make it out there tomorrow, perhaps—"

"For Christ's sake, Peter, *today!*—There are planes leaving all the time from LAX…Just call the airport and book a seat over the phone! Promise me you'll do that? *Today! It's extremely important that you do it today, Peter!*"

"Okay, okay!" Peter consented.

"Good. I'll reserve you a room. I'm looking forward to seeing you. Just get here as fast as possible. I've got to go now. Bye."

Peter was left with the receiver buzzing in his ear. He clumsily replaced it in its cradle and stood up. Pain shot through his head. *I've got to find some aspirin.* He shielded his eyes from the harsh sunlight that filled the room. He felt awful. His body was telling him to stay in bed, and his mind was refusing to focus on what would probably be another wild-goose chase.

There are other reasons for you to leave, Peter! Allison's urgent words stuck in his mind. What had she meant by that? Peter should have asked her. *It couldn't be anything to do with Mayo,* he told himself. *How would she know about that?* He suddenly felt insecure.

What he needed most was a jolt of caffeine to help him come to. But he couldn't go outside and find coffee—not looking like this. He forced himself into the shower.

"So, what did ya find out, detective? We got anything on this poor guy's kids?"

"Well, something, chief, but I don't know how useful it'll be." Detective Lucas was sitting in Chief Hunt's office flipping over the pages of his notebook to make sure he hadn't forgotten anything. "What I mean is, I tracked down the parking lot security guy who worked at Snapdragon at the time of the kids' disappearance—you know the one we didn't interview before—"

"Yeah, yeah," Hunt said impatiently, annoyed at the suggestion he'd forgotten the details.

"Uh—sorry, sir—well, he was difficult to find because he stopped working at the park soon after. He had a disagreement with the management over damage done to his ATV."

"*ATV*—what's that and what's it have to do with the case?" Hunt's uncustomary impatience was due purely and simply to the Mayo homicide. The chief was deeply frustrated over what he saw as the ex-policeman's escape from the earthly consequences of his sins. It was unjust. Hunt needed physical proof that sinners got their just deserts; otherwise, what was the point of the law? He couldn't share the general feelings of regret and sympathy that were prevalent at the Parker Center over the killing of a fellow police officer. Any other cop? Yes. But Mayo? No. Hunt knew Mayo's background; he just hadn't been able to pin anything on him. In Hunt's mind, Mayo didn't deserve to be called a *police officer*—no corrupt member of the force did.

"Please, sir," Lucas said, irritated by the chief's interruptions. "Let me just run through it from beginning till end, and I think you'll see where I'm headed."

"Okay, go on," Hunt grunted.

"Now, the incident with the ATV—that's one of those all-terrain, four-wheeled vehicles—is key to it all," Lucas said. "You see, this parking lot guy was fired for damaging his ATV, which was park property. He had a reputation for popping wheelies—that's accelerating hard and riding with the front wheels in the air, sir—and doing other reckless stunts in the Snapdragon car park. The vehicle got damaged and he was fired for it. He claims the damage was caused by someone who clipped him with a car leaving the parking lot in a hurry."

"And?" Hunt added, more attentive now.

"The security guard chased the car and got the license number. He was concerned, and rightly so, that he would be held responsible for the damage to the ATV unless he could prove that it was someone else's fault."

"Why did he give up the chase then?"

"Because the ATV had no license plates, and its use was restricted to park property. Once he got the other vehicle's number, he felt that would be enough. And he didn't want to get into trouble for driving illegally on the freeway."

"But he still lost his job?" the chief said.

"Yup. They didn't believe him."

"And you reckon this speeding car has something to do with the Zucker kids?"

"There's a good chance, sir," Lucas affirmed. "It occurred at about the same time of day that the kids were first reported missing and on the same date—"

"You're sure of that?"

"Yes. The date the security guard was fired—I got it from him and independently from the park's personnel office—was the same day the Zucker kids disappeared," Lucas said confidently. "As soon as he reported the incident to his boss and showed him the damaged ATV, he was told to leave on the spot."

"But, he had the car's license…"

"They didn't believe him. Like I told you, he had a bad reputation. And the park authorities assumed he made up the number or that he just took it off some parked car that already had body damage. You see," Lucas explained, "the one thing the park is paranoid about is its reputation. Anything that might create bad publicity, anything that runs counter to its image of being a safe and family-friendly amusement park, is put down—they don't want any incident to sour good client relations."

"You ran a check on the plate?"

"Yes, sir. The car was a rental. It was rented out to a *Carlos Gonzales*."

"Anyone we know?"

"Not by that name, sir. I ran a check of his photo through our records, though—"

"Photo?" Hunt asked.

"Yes." Lucas passed the chief a piece of paper. "The rental car agency had a photocopy of his driver's license—they regularly do this when a foreigner rents a car. Since Gonzales returned the car at the express drop-off, he didn't get the photocopy back."

Hunt scrutinized the poor-quality photocopy. He examined the man's face, thinking that he looked like just about any other Latino with a moustache and dark hair.

"So you ran a check on the photo?" he asked Lucas.

"Uh-huh, and it seems that someone who strongly resembles this guy has been in and out of this country under several different aliases. But always using the same nationality, Peruvian."

"What have we got on this guy?"

"Nothing so far. But why use a false identity unless you're up to no good?" Lucas suggested.

"Hmm…" Hunt murmured. "But that doesn't really get us very far, does it?"

"'Fraid not, sir," Lucas agreed. "It's possible this is the guy who took the kids. But he might have absolutely nothing to do with it. It's all very circumstantial, and apart from the probability that he's Peruvian, we've really got nothing more to go on—until he strikes again. And no other kids have been reported missing from Snapdragon since."

Hunt sighed. Lucas sat in silence while the chief turned in his swivel chair and stared out the window, deep in thought.

"Let's do the following," Hunt said after a minute, turning back to face Lucas. His tone was more businesslike now. "Run what you've got by the FBI and check with Immigration in case they've got anything new on this guy—whatever his name is. You never know; he might be a regular visitor, and we could pick him up next time he comes in. And when you've done that, let's get Zucker back in here and talk to him about it. Maybe he has some connection with this Peruvian guy or something."

"Will do, sir."

"Those kids have got to go!" Her utterance was neither a question nor a request. And the venom that accompanied it made it more than a mere statement of fact. It was an order. And there was no doubt in Señora Del Solar's mind that Luis Chavez would carry it out—effectively.

She slipped out of bed and quickly covered her naked form with the silk Yves St. Laurent robe that had draped lazily on the chintz-upholstered chair nearby.

Chavez, his head still on the pillow, found that false modesty; he knew every inch and contour of her body from the many times they had been together in his Louis XV double bed. They regularly serviced each other—not out of love but out of convenience. At thirty-three, Señora Del Solar had an exciting shape. And despite her sharp tongue and commanding manner, she had a way of arousing Chavez that no other woman possessed.

From her voracious appetite for sex whenever her husband was in Lima on business, Chavez assumed that her marriage had degenerated into nothing more than a social front. And although he was a man of few scruples, Chavez felt better knowing he wasn't merely filling in for Don Gonzalo. He played second fiddle to no one.

"What would you have me do with them?" Chavez asked lazily, still relaxed from his exertions, and then as an afterthought, "It's unlike you to give up so quickly."

"I don't care what you do with those damn kids—just get them out of my sight!" She spat out the words. "And I'm not giving up—if you'd only brought me some children who could at least speak a normal language, I'd be well ahead by now. But, oh no! *You*—with all your power and *extensive* contacts—all you can find me are a couple of ill-mannered brats who talk back to me…and in a fucking language that I can't even understand! The whole thing's a mockery— I'm the laughingstock of all my friends. *'So when are we going to meet the children?'* they ask me with a sneer, knowing full well I'm having problems. No, you can fucking well get them out of this house and *this time* find me some that know how to behave and express gratitude for what I'm doing for them."

"Hmm…" Chavez murmured, leaning over to fondle her thigh and tempt her back into bed. "You're really set on this, aren't you?"

Señora Del Solar didn't reply. She had made herself perfectly clear already. She twisted out of his grasp, walked over to the window, and stared out at the sea.

"I mean what I say," she said calmly. But there was determination in her voice. "You're a big boy. You can sort it out…and in a way that will make me feel and look good. You know what my needs are. But—"

She paused for effect and turned to face him. "If you can't ful*fill* my needs, then…well…I'll have to turn elsewhere!"

"Now, don't get dramatic," Chavez said, trying to regain control. "I brought the kids here; I can take them away. I was just considering what to do with them."

"You can hang them up by their ears and let them starve to death for all I care!" Señora Del Solar shouted, throwing up her arms demonstratively. "Why the hell didn't you just let them drown at sea instead of rescuing them…another missed opportunity!"

"They were rescued by the *Coast Guard*," Chavez corrected her. "And we are very lucky that the Coast Guard contacted me so I could whisk them away before anyone started asking embarrassing questions. These kids are still a bit hot, you know, and you don't want anyone talking about them in the press!"

"And now he tells me the kids are *hot* too!" She threw up her arms, and her gaze shot to the ceiling in amazement.

Chavez lay back on the bed and sighed.

After a long pause, Señora Del Solar appeared calmer. She had her hand to her chin and was obviously engrossed in thought. Finally, she spoke.

"Wait…didn't you have an article in your paper about…what was it called? Um…'baby trade,' or something like that—"

"*Baby-parts*," Chavez corrected her.

"Yes, yes, that was it," she proclaimed enthusiastically. "Cut them up for *baby-parts*. What a great idea!"

"Wow…these kids have really gotten to you," Chavez said. "We can't do that."

"Why ever not?" Señora Del Solar protested, relishing the idea and annoyed at Chavez's refusal. "There would never be the *slightest* trace of them again!" She laughed.

"Look Lucia," Chavez said in a voice intended to calm her down. "That *baby-parts* stuff is not true—"

"It was in your paper!"

"Yes, but I own the paper and can write whatever I like!"

Señora Del Solar was thunderstruck. "You mean—"

"It was a complete fabrication."

"But why?" she asked.

"You haven't got to worry about *why*. It's of no concern—"

"Don't tell me it's of no concern to me—I'm not one of your brainless floozies," she snapped. "And what other lies have you been telling me? I will not be *used*, not by anyone, even *you!*"

"Calm down," Chavez implored. He got up from the bed, walked over, and placed his arm reassuringly around her waist. "If you really need to know, I'll tell you—but it's to go no further. Okay?" She neither nodded nor shook her head, but merely looked at him, waiting. He took that as acquiescence. "Look, the American government has been poking its nose into my business, into my trading business with them. I didn't like it, so I fought back by putting out that story. They hate it because it tarnishes their public image. They'll leave me alone now."

"But how will they know it's you who started this lie?" Señora Del Solar asked.

"They'll put two and two together soon enough and start bullying somebody else. Look, nobody messes with me—not even the U.S. government."

Seeing his explanation satisfied her, Chavez gently nudged her back toward the bed.

"Now, let's make a deal," he proposed reassuringly. "I'll dispose of those kids for you in a way that you'll never see or hear of them again—trust me. All you have to do is…well…just lie down again, and while we're enjoying ourselves, you can be thinking of a way to explain to your friends the unexpected departure of the children."

Chapter 21

▼

"Sheraton Gateway Hotel Los Angeles Airport," the clerk at the reception desk answered. "How can I help you?"

"Can you put me through to a Mr. Peter Zucker, Z-U-C-K-E-R, please?"

"Sure, just one moment," the clerk said, typing the name into his computer terminal. *UNKNOWN* flashed up. But during hectic arrival times, guests' names were often typed in incorrectly. He manually scrolled down the guest list, searching under both "Z" and "S," but the result was the same. There was no name close to *Zucker*. Probably got the wrong hotel, the clerk thought. It happened all the time. "Sorry to keep you waiting, but no one under that name is registered here."

Detective Lucas wasn't that surprised. People changed hotels in California all the time, often for reasons as minor as the quality of the coffee served at breakfast. But he thought that Zucker would have informed him of any change. "When did he check out?" Lucas asked.

"I don't have any record of someone of that name staying here," the clerk replied.

"But he said he was staying at your hotel. Is there another Sheraton near the airport?"

"Nope. This is the only one."

But Zucker had given Lucas *this* telephone number. *Odd*, he thought, but it did not set off any alarm bells.

"Can you check again?" Lucas persisted. "I'm sure he must be in your computer somewhere—and check the registration cards. He's not American and would have had to fill one out."

"I'm sorry, sir, but he's not in our system—you've got the wrong hotel," the clerk said impatiently. "I have a lot of people waiting—I'll have to put you on hold—"

"No, wait," Lucas demanded. "I'm with the LAPD and I need this information urgently."

"You'll have to speak to my manager," the clerk said, eager to rid himself of this caller.

"Okay, put me through to him," Lucas snapped, irritated.

"Have a nice day," the clerk added automatically, his voice suddenly cheerful. The line went momentarily dead and then Lucas heard ringing. But nobody answered.

"Damn!" Lucas swore, slamming the phone back into its cradle. He hated it when people gave him the runaround. No sooner had he let go of the receiver, than the phone began ringing again. He picked it up in a huff, ready to vent on whoever was at the other end.

"Yeah, what is it?" he asked irritably.

"Lucas?" The voice sounded surprised at the junior officer's tone. The young detective instantly recognized the deep voice of his superior.

"Um, yes, lieutenant," Lucas responded with sudden deference. "Yes, sir!"

"Lucas, there's a gang fight going on in the Hollywood Hills, and we've been asked to send all available officers. Are you working on anything urgent?"

"Um…no, sir."

"Okay. Team up with Perkins and get over there pronto."

Lucas obeyed, exhilarated at getting out from behind his desk and seeing some action. As he checked the 9 mm semi-automatic pistol holstered at his side, thoughts of Peter Zucker disappeared completely from his mind.

The cold shower brought Peter to his senses. Things that Allison had told him started falling into place, and with knowledge came suppositions and ominous conclusions. Panic set in, and Peter worried that the police might already be on to him for the Mayo slayings. The specter of being arrested right here in his room loomed large.

With a damp towel wrapped around his waist, he peeked furtively past the bathroom door to make sure no one was already waiting for him in the bedroom. Satisfied that he was alone, Peter quickly stepped to the window and peered out. No police car and no unusual activity—but he still felt unsafe.

Grabbing the first clothes that came to hand, he dressed, then literally threw his other belongings into his single suitcase and forced it shut. Although normally a tidy man, Peter now focused on one thing only—getting as far as possible from the *Quick Sleepin' Stop* motel. And, he wouldn't waste a second doing it. He was glad now that he hadn't given Lucas his real address.

Peter placed the suitcase by the door next to the viola case. He swiftly made one last check of the closet and chest of drawers, glanced under the bed, and stepped back into the bathroom; he had left nothing behind. He threw the contents of the waste bins into a plastic laundry bag to dump it somewhere away from the motel. His gut told him he must leave absolutely no trace.

The red Hyundai was parked conveniently near his door. With his black attaché case containing passport, papers, and sheaves of bank notes, he walked briskly but watchfully to the reception area to check out.

There was nobody behind the desk; the place seemed deserted. He impatiently banged the old brass bell on the counter, but the piercing jangle brought no one. Peter attempted a final, "Is anybody here?" His panic grew. He opened his attaché case and pulled out seven $100 bills—more than enough to cover his stay. He put the money in an envelope, sealed it, wrote the number of his room on the outside, and placed it on the desk along with his room key.

Peter hurried back to the car and drove off. He was perspiring. The hairs on the back of his neck were standing on end. As he pulled onto the freeway at the first entrance ramp, not caring about direction, his eyes searched in the rear-view mirror for signs of a police car following him. He saw none—his luck was holding.

After about twenty miles of anxious driving at the speed limit—but no faster—Peter felt a bit safer and began to unwind. As he relaxed, he became aware of his empty stomach—he hadn't eaten anything that morning. Satisfied that he had put sufficient distance between himself and the motel, he pulled into the parking lot of a diner that advertised breakfast specials.

He selected a table by the window on the parking lot side with a good view of his car and ordered coffee, pancakes and bacon, plus a side order of fried eggs—a hearty breakfast in case he didn't have time to eat again today. When the food arrived, he wolfed it down nearly as quickly as it was served. After downing a second mug of watery coffee, he felt full and satisfied.

He glanced around but no one showed any particular interest in him. The day-old stubble on his chin and his generally untidy appearance helped him blend in with the other early morning diners.

Peter paid the bill and wasted no time in getting back to his car. He grabbed the laundry bag of garbage from the trunk and dropped it into a nearby dumpster. Back inside the car, he locked the doors and pulled out his map of Los Angeles and Southern California. Finding his location wasn't easy; in his flight from the motel, he hadn't paid any attention to where he was going. He made a couple of quick assumptions, marked the most direct route to the airport, started the engine, and set off.

Having made several wrong turns, it took him an hour to reach LAX, where he left the Hyundai in the parking garage nearest the departure buildings and found a baggage cart.

He tensed up as he passed among the taxis and cars that were dropping off travelers in front of the terminal, alert to anyone watching for him. But, given the number of people scurrying to catch peak mid-morning flights, Peter felt secure, and he melded into the anonymity of the crowd.

He made his way to the first counter he saw, Delta Airlines, and his turn finally came. The blasé brunette behind the counter entered his destination requirements into her terminal, and between bursts of typing, examined the flight information that came up on her screen. "The earliest flight I can get you on leaves this evening at nine-twenty. It stops in San Jose, Costa Rica, to refuel and then flies on to Lima, arriving at twelve-twenty local time tomorrow afternoon. Everything else's full," she said. With the demand for Delta flights that morning, she hadn't the time to be polite.

"Are you sure there's nothing earlier?" Peter asked, disappointed.

The woman sighed but then typed furiously again. "Nothing. Even the waiting lists are closed on earlier flights—do I book you on the nine-twenty or not?" she asked impatiently eyeing the long line behind Peter.

"How about other airlines?"

"You can check them if you like, but I can't guarantee this reservation will be available when you come back." Seeing Peter's hesitation, she added: "I'd advise you to take it—you won't do any better."

"Um…Okay," said Peter reluctantly. "I'm sorry, I just need urgently to get down there…" He handed her his credit card.

Perhaps it was his crestfallen look, or just that she suddenly felt sorry for this polite foreigner. "Here's a voucher for free refreshments while you're waiting— and, if you want, I can check your luggage now to save you carrying it around all day," she said pleasantly. "But you'd better hand-carry that one," she added, pointing to the viola case. "Musical instruments and baggage handlers don't mix."

Peter froze. The gun! What the *hell* was he going to do with the *gun?* It would never get through the hand luggage screening. If he checked the case into the plane's luggage hold, there was no guarantee it wouldn't be x-rayed. *Siech!*

He looked around, nervously searching for inspiration. All he saw was the line of impatient travelers that had accumulated behind him. "Oh! Um…thanks," he said, turning back to the Delta woman. "Yes, I'll only check in the suitcase—busy day, isn't it?" Peter stammered, attempting to sound self-assured.

She just smiled and expertly wrapped a destination tag around the handle of his suitcase, then sent it down a conveyor belt.

Peter thanked her and turned away. He walked to a secluded spot near a bank of telephones and stood there with the viola case in one hand and his attaché case in the other. How *stupid* not having anticipated the problem with the gun. He thought of abandoning it; but the gun had already proven useful and might well do so again.

Peter looked around the terminal again, not knowing what he was searching for, until his eyes fell on a large, red neon sign, "*PARCELS ETC.—DELIVER ANYTHING ANYWHERE.*"

Peter eagerly approached the counter. "Can you mail this to a hotel in Peru?" he asked, proffering the case.

"Sure thing, bud…like the sign says, *anything anywhere.*"

"Um…it's delicate—and it's urgent," Peter added.

"As I said, no problem, bud—you tell me when you want it there, and I'll give you a price…you'll need to wrap it—we have bubble paper. We can do it for you, but that'll cost extra."

When Peter hesitated, the man said, "Here, put it on the scale and I'll tell you what it'll set you back." He was keen on reeling in business. "Hey, it sure is heavy for a musical instrument," he added, taking the case. The electronic digits on the scale spun as he consulted his computer screen. "When do you want it there?" he asked.

"As soon as possible," Peter replied. "You see…my friend has a concert there tomorrow night, and he needs it…"

"Tomorrow," the man murmured. "Hmm…Peru, you said—whereabouts?"

"Lima," answered Peter, eager to hear if it was really possible.

"It'll cost ya…um…two hundred and thirteen even—that's door-to-door guaranteed overnight delivery. But you can save five bucks wrapping it yourself."

It was his only option. "Okay—you said there was special paper for wrapping it?"

"Yeah…" He turned to a gigantic roll of brown paper hanging from the wall behind him and tore off a large piece. It was padded on one side with plastic bubble paper. The man handed it across the counter along with a roll of brown adhesive tape. To the man's surprise, Peter took it and walked away into the crowd.

"Jesus!" the man said under his breath, "that was a new roll of tape!"

Peter headed for the men's room, found an unoccupied stall, and squeezed into it with his two cases and an armful of wrapping paper. He locked the door behind him, placed the viola case across the toilet seat and opened it. Quickly, but careful not to let any greenbacks fall into the toilet, he transferred money to his attaché case, and when he had crammed it full, hung it on the jacket hook behind him.

The spare rolls of toilet paper stacked in a locked container on the wall gave him an idea. He taped the viola case closed, yanked open the wall container, grabbed a couple of rolls and taped them on either side of the case's neck. This altered the shape to look less like a mobster's tommy gun case. He tightly wrapped it in the padded brown paper and taped it. He started to address it to himself, but paused, hurriedly crossed out the letters, and wrote Allison's name instead, then added, "Care of Miraflores Park Plaza Hotel," and the address. He finished, briefly admired his work, and—as an afterthought—flushed the toilet.

The man at PARCELS ETC. seemed surprised to see Peter again and thanked him for returning the roll of tape. He passed Peter a "sender information" slip and a customs declaration.

"Here, bud," he said, "fill this out."

Peter was taken aback; he hadn't expected to do anything more than give the man the package and the money. He didn't like leaving traces of his whereabouts or what he had been doing. But he kept calm and started filling out the forms. For the contents, Peter wrote, "Musical Instrument." And for sender…"Do I need to fill this part out?" Peter asked the man.

"Yup, otherwise it won't go!"

Peter thought quickly and wrote his own name followed by his Swiss address. If the package went astray, it would end up back in Trélex, far from a possible ballistics test in the United States.

The man slapped on a large sticker marked *"FRAGILE—HANDLE WITH CARE,"* and the stamp coupon that his computer had printed, plus a copy of the forms Peter had filled out, and then tossed the parcel into a cart heaped with other packages.

Peter paid in cash, then turned around and merged into the crowd.

Now he had the day before him. He looked at his watch. The thought of cooling his heels at the airport for ten hours didn't appeal to him. If the police were looking, he'd be a sitting duck as the airport emptied between peak traveling times. Instead, he'd lose himself in a crowd somewhere else, and only one place came to mind.

One final trip to Snapdragon...

As Allison, wearing her form-fitting mauve body suit, stepped out of the elevator and walked through the luxurious lobby of the Miraflores Park Plaza Hotel, she was aware that the admiring stares of the male staff at the reception desk and guests lounging on the leather sofas were following her.

She made her way through glass revolving doors past the uniformed doorman, and then broke into a jog down the hotel's tree-lined access road. Allison needed her daily thirty-minute run to drive away stress and maintain her athletic form. It was a habit she had kept up since leaving the Marines, and she had never regretted it.

The dank smell of vegetation in the early morning and the panoramic view of the Pacific Ocean beyond were a welcome change from the closeness and recycled air of yesterday's flight down.

"Ahhh..." she sighed in relief as she drew in lungfuls of crisp morning air. Soon into her running rhythm, she closed her eyes, turned her face up to the sun and absorbed its delectable warmth. Her thoughts went back to her days as a junior U.S. information officer stationed in Lima. She had often been in the Miraflores Hotel back then, but not as a guest—only as a working member of the embassy's staff organizing accommodations for visiting U.S. dignitaries.

She smiled in recollection of her secret yearning all those years back to be a distinguished guest herself. And now she *was* one, on a special mission for the State Department. The embassy's political officer had met her at the airport and whisked her through customs and immigration straight into a waiting limousine. During the drive to the hotel, he had handed her a sealed envelope containing classified cables and other briefing materials she had requested. "*And if there's anything else—anything at all—just call me at the embassy,*" he had told her before leaving. She found it all wonderful—a dream fulfilled!

Allison's pace slowed to a trot as she came to the bottom of the hill and hit level ground. The carefully tended grounds of the luxury hotel gave way to dusty dry roadsides covered with gray-green vegetation and strewn with litter. She rounded a corner and became the object of attention of a group of barefoot kids who looked as if they hadn't washed in weeks.

"*Hola!*" she said with a smile as she waved, regretting that she hadn't brought any coins to give them. But they looked as if they didn't care, and timidly waved back while tossing rocks at discarded soda cans.

The sight of the kids brought her mind back to her current mission: how to tackle the *baby-parts* problem? It wasn't going to be easy. And then there was

Peter Zucker. He kept creeping into her thoughts. Was she bringing him down here on a fool's errand? The lead that John had given her about children found adrift in a boat was meager to say the least. Was she just trying to appease her own conscience after refusing to help Peter in Geneva? And helping a possible felon? Putting her whole career at risk? But then, might Mark and Nicolette be living like the children she had just seen? Were they somewhere close? Or miles away—or *dead?* Allison felt confused and filled with self-doubt. She quickened her pace until the pain of running took these thoughts away.

The embassy had made an appointment for her this morning with the owner of *El Crónico.* It hadn't been easy. Luis Chavez was rarely in Lima, and he usually refused to meet with anyone below ambassadorial rank. But the embassy had impressed upon him that refusing to receive this distinguished visitor from Washington could have adverse effects on his commercial business with the United States—a business already under scrutiny because of suspected involvement in the illegal drug trade. Chavez's staff had passed this message on to him, and he had agreed to meet the U.S. envoy.

Allison decided she would ask Chavez if he knew anything about the rescued children who had been written up in his newspaper. It was highly unlikely that those were Peter's children, but maybe Chavez, through his connections, could actually find Mark and Nicolette. But she would only get into this subject once she had tackled Chavez on the *baby-parts* articles. Resolution of the *baby-parts* problem—an issue of U.S. national importance—had to take precedence over the fate of Peter's children. That she knew—however wretched it was.

She calculated that the best way to quash the *baby-parts* issue was to quietly convince *El Crónico,* through its owner, to stop publishing libelous stories about the United States. The issue would then become stale and gradually be forgotten. It would also help the paper save face. But her superiors back in the State Department were hungry for an actual published retraction. In Allison's opinion such a hard-line approach might backfire and worsen the problem by generating even more *baby-parts* articles.

She had authorization to quash the *baby-parts* issue by whatever means she thought best, and she intended to do so. "*Baby-parts*" was the instrument Ambassador Helm had unjustly used to bring her down in Geneva. For her own self-confidence and for her future in the U.S. Foreign Service, she was determined to come up with a professional success.

Chapter 22

▼

Peter drove to Snapdragon, had the last tab punched off his ten-visit pass, and once again sat down at the table where he had last seen Mark and Nicolette. He would allow himself one hour to sit here and nurse his lemonade. After that, he would move around the park. Peter was determined to make full use of this visit to Snapdragon—possibly his last—to gather any piece of relevant information he could find, however insignificant it might seem.

His task was made more poignant by the sight of children enjoying the park's thrills. He smiled ruefully at parents whose strained faces revealed their weariness at their children's incessant demands, or who glanced at their watches to count the hours before they could go home. *If only they knew,* Peter thought, *how insignificant their weariness is compared to the pain of losing their children forever.*

The family at the table next to his rose to leave. The children tugged at their parents who were loaded down with camera bags, sweatshirts in case the weather changed, and gifts the children had begged them to buy now instead of when they were leaving the park, because *"they might run out of them."* Peter's freedom from such shackles did not give him joy.

Then he spied a small, pink backpack suspended on one of the chairs at the table where the family had been sitting.

"Hey!" Peter cried out, trying to get the family's attention. But they were already out of earshot. He grabbed the bag and ran to them. "Is this yours? You left it at the table."

Instead of thanking him, the parents started scolding their daughter for her forgetfulness. "Thanks," the father finally said as an afterthought when Peter walked away.

But Peter, suddenly absorbed in thought, was not listening. "Mark's back-pack..." he mumbled. "What happened to *Mark's* backpack? *That damn back-pack!*"

Dummkopf! How could he have forgotten about that backpack? Mark had made such a fuss over it. He had needed a new one for school, and he was ada-mant about getting that particular one—crimson and black!—and taking it along on vacation. He wouldn't settle for one of a different color that was half the price, because it wasn't "*cool.*" Peter had objected to paying extra for the brand-name, but Martine had intervened: "It's just for once, dear..." And he had relented. But none of that mattered now. *What had become of that damn bag?*

Peter thought hard. After all that fuss, Mark hadn't even worn it much at the park; he was always too tired, pleading for someone else to carry it—and that someone usually turned out to be Peter. It had been left at the table—just like that family's. Panicked over their children's sudden disappearance, Peter and Martine had forgotten totally about the backpack. They hadn't picked it up, so it must have been left there!

Peter broke into a run, heading for the lost-and-found office next to the park's exit. It was deserted except for a college student behind the counter.

"Hi there!" he said as Peter, out of breath, stepped into the office. "Lost some-thin' already!" The young man's glibness annoyed Peter.

"A backpack...a child's backpack...crimson and black—with French writing on it!"

The young man looked at Peter quizzically. "If ya lost it this morning, it won't turn up 'til later in the day."

"No...not this morning," Peter said urgently. "Last summer...in July!"

"You're kiddin' me! Come on, when did you lose it?"

"No, I'm serious," Peter said adamantly. "It's a backpack that my son lost when we were here last July—please look to see if you have it!"

"We don't normally keep things that long," the young man said.

Peter found his tone unconvincing; it was obvious he didn't want the bother of looking.

"Where's your supervisor?" Peter asked. "And what's your name?"

The young man looked at Peter to see if he was serious and decided he was.

"Okay, okay...! I'll have a look but it'll take time—there's a ton of junk back there—why don't you come back later."

"No! I can give you a hand," Peter proposed.

"That's not permitted."

"I'll wait then," Peter said, sitting down at a nearby chair.

"Fuckin' hell," the young man murmured under his breath. He disappeared into a back room and returned less than a minute later. "Sorry, but nothin' of that description there—okay?"

"No, it's *not* okay!" Peter said between clenched teeth. He knew the young man hadn't searched. He started toward the back room himself.

"Hey! You can't go back there—I'm going to get security!"

Peter grabbed him roughly by the arm. "You're going nowhere except to help me search back there," Peter snapped, pushing him toward the back room. "And if you don't cooperate, I'll break your arm…!"

The young man winced, turned white, and walked hurriedly with Peter to the back room.

There were lost items everywhere. A lot of bags, pieces of clothing, and other everyday items were set out neatly on long wooden shelves down one side of the room. Peter glanced quickly over these, but the backpack wasn't there. On the opposite side were large plastic bins piled high with the same paraphernalia.

"And you looked through all these? Get over there and empty them on the ground and I'll search," Peter ordered, propelling him in that direction. As the young man tipped over the huge bins one by one, Peter dug through the smelly, dusty leftovers of people's trips to the park, slinging the items he wasn't interested in behind him like a dog digging for a bone. Near the bottom of the third bin, he stopped abruptly. The crimson caught his eye, then the black. Reaching in, he gingerly pulled out a wrinkled backpack. Peter turned it around slowly in his hands until he came to the brand-name markings that he and Mark had argued about.

"This is it!" Peter shouted. "This is *it!*"

Scowling, the young man surveyed the mess on the floor. Peter put a hand in his pocket.

"Thanks a lot for your help," Peter told him. "Here's something to make up for the mess." He stuffed a $100 bill into the young man's hand. "And it's also for you to keep your mouth shut—is that clear?"

"Yeah," the young man replied uncertainly, looking down at the note in disbelief. "Sure thing!"

Peter walked to the other side of the park as briskly as he could without attracting suspicion. He found an empty bench in a secluded grassy area and, without wasting a second, searched through the bag's contents. He knew what he was looking for and soon found it—in between Mark's teddy bear and a half-empty box of candy—the disposable camera that Peter had purchased for Mark the day the children had disappeared.

Camera in hand, Peter set off in search of the One-Hour Photo place he had seen next to the roller coaster.

The next sixty minutes seemed an eternity. Peter re-entered the shop exactly one hour after dropping off the camera, and the packet of photos was waiting for him. He fought a burning desire to look at the photographs there and then, but decided to find somewhere more private.

Peter returned to the grassy area, sat down on the ground, hesitated a moment, and then flipped open the envelope. His hand shaking, he pulled out the glossy prints. As his eyes focused on the top one—Martine posing with Mark and Nicolette on either side of her in front of the artificial lake—his throat tightened. A flood of tears burst from his eyes and streamed down his face, forcing him to place the pile of photographs down to one side to avoid them getting wet. He yanked off his sunglasses and held his head in his hands. His whole body shook uncontrollably as he let flow the pain and anguish he had bottled up for so long.

After several minutes, Peter looked up and saw that a little boy was staring at him. Peter sighed and pulled himself together. His eyes felt puffy, and he knew they must look red. He wiped his cheeks, put his sunglasses back on and took several deep breaths. A feeling of relief crept over him—he had exorcised the worst of the pain, and now he could tackle the photographs.

He picked up the pile with care—these, the most recent images of his lost family, held an inestimable value. With warmth in his heart, he gazed at the smiling faces looking up at him. Peter took the first photo by the edges to avoid smudging the surface and gently slid it to the bottom of the pile. The second picture was identical to the first. *How wonderful!* Peter said to himself joyfully; they had printed two copies of each picture.

He relished the others as he had the first. They were all very similar: the children with Martine, then with Peter; Peter and Martine with Nicolette and then with Mark, taken by Nicolette—that one wasn't very straight, but then she was only five. Peter laid them all out on the grass in front of him to survey them all together. They were incredibly clear, he thought, for a disposable camera. His eyes ran over them again; he wanted to savor the images fully.

Then something caught Peter's eye. He examined two of the photos more carefully. *All* the pictures had people in the background; the amusement park had been crowded that day. But *two* pictures—taken at different times and at different ends of the park—showed the same man. It seemed too great a coincidence to find the same man in both photographs. What's more, the man's attention was focused on Mark and Nicolette! *That son of a bitch wasn't merely passing by!*

The man had a mop of brownish-black curly hair and a matching thick moustache. The photograph clearly revealed his pockmarked skin. He was dressed casually in an open-neck tennis shirt and jeans, and carried a beige sports jacket over his arm. He was of medium build, but it was hard to judge his height. Peter couldn't explain why, but in his gut, he did not like this man.

Could he have seen what happened? Peter wondered. *Perhaps he's the ONE!* Peter couldn't contain his excitement. But where was he going to go from here? He could take the photos to the police—they could check their criminal files. But Peter had killed Mayo; he couldn't go to the police. And there wasn't time before catching his plane for Lima.

Peter thought hard, then found a store where he bought envelopes and paper. He wrote a note to Chief Hunt, pointing out his discovery and saying he would check with him in a few days. He folded the note around the two photos, sealed it all carefully inside an envelope addressed to the Chief of Police at the Parker Center, and marked it *"Urgent and Personal."*

Peter mailed it from the post office at Snapdragon and left the park much more satisfied than when he had arrived.

Back in Peru, Romy sat in the kitchen with Miguel and Alicia, where the children were eating absentmindedly, looking downcast and lifeless. Romy's concern was increasing day by day. Neither Miguel nor Alicia talked to her now, and their sudden coldness pierced her to the core.

Romy had grown to care for them deeply. She had found them lost and devoid of motherly love, but had won over a little part of their hearts. She was sure of it—she'd seen it in their eyes. But now the warmth and trust were gone, and Romy was faced with the indifference once reserved only for Señora Del Solar.

Why didn't I intervene and stop the whipping? she chided herself, convinced it was that episode that turned the children against her. She had been making *so* much progress with them. They had learned a few words and phrases in Spanish. She had surprised them with some words in German—and this, she was sure, had drawn them closer to her. Romy was convinced Miguel and Alicia spoke a Swiss-German dialect. From language school in Buenos Aires, she remembered that French, Italian, and German were official Swiss languages, but that the German spoken there was a dialect that varied from one region to another. She was *sure* that the children spoke one of these dialects.

Romy didn't dare tell Señora Del Solar; it would set her off on another rampage. She was at a loss as to what to do. But events were about to overtake her concern.

"There you are!" Señora Del Solar stood in the kitchen doorway, hands on hips, looking at Romy. The children shuddered and hunched over their food. "Come with me, if you please," Señora Del Solar barked. "I have something to discuss with you."

Romy stood up and followed her—but only after placing a reassuring hand on the children's shoulders.

Señora Del Solar preceded Romy into her husband's study. "Sit down," she said, pointing to a European wheelback chair in front of the massive desk. Señora Del Solar took the chair behind the desk. Even seated, she sat straight and dominant.

"I'll get straight to the point," she said. "The children are leaving."

Señora Del Solar gazed at Romy, thinking how she had *never* liked this woman. She allowed herself a moment to gloat. Not only did she despise Romy, she *relished* the fate Chavez had planned for the children! She had no intention of telling Romy the truth. Chavez had suggested a story to account for the children's departure. Señora Del Solar liked it; it would, enhance her social prestige. Don Gonzalo didn't like it at all, but he no longer had any say in the matter. His role was to acquiesce in silence, and Señora Del Solar would use Romy to practice telling her cover-up story. *How convenient!*

"Romy," she said pleasantly, but with a grave undertone to her voice. "Unfortunately for you, but fortunately for the children, we have found their real parents."

Romy's eyes grew large. "Really?" she said incredulously.

"Yes, *really*," Señora Del Solar repeated. "After months of searching—and at great expense—their parents have been found. They are Polish, and the children got separated from them during a visit to Chicago. That's why you had such a hard time communicating with them—I assume you don't know Polish?" Señora Del Solar asked as an afterthought.

"No," replied Romy, now growing uneasy. "No, none at all," she added more naturally.

"Well," Señora Del Solar continued, sounding relieved, "their parents are being brought to the United States, and next week we will fly the children there to reunite them. Isn't that nice?"

"Um…yes!" Romy replied. "I'll be sorry to see them go! What day are they leaving?"

"Probably Wednesday. That still gives you…what…nearly a week to say your good-byes—that is, if you can get through to them." Señora Del Solar then added, "We, of course, take it that you'll remain here until then, to minimize disruption for the children. Afterward, my husband will round off your stipend—generously, as you would expect from him—and he'll give you a good reference letter so you can find another position without difficulty."

Romy nodded acceptance. But her head was spinning. *What had she just been told?*

"Of course," Señora Del Solar went on, "in return we expect you to be completely discreet about this entire episode. We are closing a sad chapter here. We are a very private family, and it would not be well for you to tarnish our reputation with stories of what you *think* you have seen. I hope I have made myself clear?"

"Um…yes, madam."

"Good," replied Señora Del Solar, pleased with herself. She had carried out the explanation masterfully, and Romy had swallowed it all.

Had she been less conceited and taken a few seconds to examine the tutor's face, she would have realized that Romy did not believe a word of what she had been told.

Pedro Delgado put down the phone. He had received his orders for the day from Chavez, and he would carry them out faultlessly. That was why Pedro was Chavez's most trusted employee.

Chavez had picked him up when Pedro was fifteen and operating as a small-time criminal in the seedier parts of Lima. Nicknamed *"The Dragon"* because of his fiery temper and the tattoo on his shoulder, Pedro's *efficiency* had caught Chavez's eye. He'd made the investment and turned the boy into a suave, professional henchman he could rely on—whatever the task.

Pedro stroked his ample dark-brown moustache in satisfaction. Chavez's order wasn't going to be difficult to carry out. In any case, it was Pedro who had put the idea into his employer's head in the first place. And since Pedro hated Americans nearly as much as Chavez did, he looked forward to his mission with relish. Yes, he would have fun with this *Cox woman* sent by Uncle Sam to bug his boss.

There were still some things about the American psyche that puzzled Pedro. Perhaps if they'd granted him a visa to study in the United States, things would have been different. But the authorities had refused, not liking his association with Luis Chavez, whose criminal pastimes were well known. Pedro would never forget that rejection, and he had vowed to get back at the mighty United States.

Since then, he had carried out several successful illicit operations on U.S. soil for Chavez, easily bypassing the immigration authorities and running circles around American law enforcement.

The last operation had been the abduction of the Swiss boy and girl. Chavez had called Pedro's work "*masterful.*" Pedro, happy his mentor was pleased with him, had accepted the praise without comment. Now Chavez wanted him to get rid of the children—a much easier task than grabbing them had been. *Ningún problema, jefe!* had been his unhesitating reply. Yes, it would certainly be no problem for him. His child-prostitution ring always needed nourishment.

Chapter 23

▼

"Señora!" the desk clerk called to Allison as she walked back through the hotel lobby after her run. "I have a message for you…!"

Glistening with sweat and still slightly out of breath, Allison went to the desk. The young clerk seemed proud to be the chosen messenger for this good-looking American guest. Allison recognized the signs and smiled agreeably as she took the folded note he handed her.

"Thanks. Is this the only message?"

"Sí, Señora," the young man replied, his pimply cheeks coloring slightly.

Poor kid, Allison thought. *I'm old enough to be his mother!*

As soon as she was alone in the elevator, she opened the note and read it. "Damn!" Peter Zucker had telephoned late the previous evening and they'd only given her the message now! She instantly regretted being pleasant to the desk clerk. Well, at least the hotel had written down Peter's flight arrival details clearly. She hoped they were correct. His plane was to land soon after midday—today! She glanced at her watch. Luckily her appointment with Chavez was early enough that she could meet Peter at the airport afterward.

Allison suddenly realized that she was running late. She still had to shower and get ready for her meeting with Chavez; the embassy car was coming at nine o'clock to take her to the offices of *El Crónico*.

Peter stepped off the plane.

There, at the bottom of the gangway steps stood Mark and Nicolette, with Martine between them, her hands on their shoulders. She looked pale and slightly haggard—not surprising after being holed up for months in a mental hospital. But she was smiling radiantly. She looked great.

Peter couldn't believe it! He put down his black attaché case and rubbed his eyes with both hands. Was the bright sunshine playing tricks on him? He focused again through the shimmering heat haze. It was them—there was no doubt about it. They were there, waiting for him, smiling and waving. He opened his mouth but no sound emerged...

So the children had been in Lima after all. Mayo hadn't lied. Peter started down the steps, and in his haste, tripped and went tumbling, banging his head against the hard aluminum stairway. He came to rest on the tarmac, holding his throbbing head. He looked up to where Martine and the children had stood. But all he saw in his hazy focus was a woman in uniform. The sun wasn't shining anymore and someone was leaning down, reaching for a metal box on his lap—

"I'm terribly sorry, sir," the flight attendant said. "It fell from the overhead bin as I was pulling out a blanket. Are you okay?" She sounded genuinely concerned. She quickly examined Peter's head.

"Ow!" Peter exclaimed as her fingers found the spot where the box had hit him.

"I'm sorry," she said again as she opened the box and withdrew a band-aid. "I'll just put a small bandage on it...at least I didn't have to search for the first aid box!"

Peter was too groggy to be amused. The plane was still in the air, and he was still in his seat. He'd been in a deep sleep, and felt cheated and disappointed at having been brought back to reality so harshly. He looked around and saw that the other passengers had already had their evening meal; the trays were being cleared away. He must have fallen asleep soon after takeoff. He'd been exhausted. Now he wished he were already in Lima with Allison's shoulder to cry on. He looked at the video-animation of their flight-path; the plane wasn't even halfway through its eleven-hour flight.

Uncomfortable and claustrophobic in the crowded cabin, Peter turned awkwardly in the narrow seat to find a new position. Then the cabin lights dimmed and the first in-flight movie started. *Good*, he thought. The darkness would help him lose himself again, and perhaps...just perhaps...he would recapture his joyous dream.

Polish parents? No, Romy thought, it wasn't true. Any other nationality and she would have swallowed the story. But Polish! No. She was sure of that.

Romy had never studied Polish but, as fate would have it, she had known a family of Polish immigrants who lived near her home back in Argentina. Their children hadn't spoken much Spanish, and when they had babbled among themselves, it hadn't sounded like Miguel and Alicia's chatter.

Perhaps it was just her imagination, or a natural suspicion of Señora Del Solar. Was Romy merely searching for a reason to prevent the children from leaving? She would certainly be heartbroken to see them go…but not if it were to their real home. Her innermost feelings told her they were *not* going home, but to an even more dubious fate than their present one.

Reka—yes! *Reka*—the Polish word for *hand!* The Polish family's four children used it often while playing a favorite game. Romy had never understood the game, but she had seen them engrossed in it nearly every time she'd gone to their house. *Reka* was definitely the word for hand, and definitely *not* the word she'd heard Miguel and Alicia use. *Hand* was both German *and* English, and *reka* was Polish. They were too different to be confused!

Miguel and Alicia were not going back to Polish parents—of that she was sure.

But what could she do? They'd leave in a few days. And she had been asked to break the news to them—to *lie* to them. *No*, she couldn't do that. She sensed that they would see through it, at least Miguel would.

She could run away with them! But where to? Romy was a foreigner in Peru; she wouldn't get far traveling without papers with two young children. She remembered Chavez's warning about interfering in the children's fate; Chavez, he controlled everything that went on…everything, that is, except for the local head of police, who, she had heard, despised him. The thought gave her an idea…

"Sure chief, I'm on my way up!" Lucas put down the receiver to the inquiring stares of the other detectives at their desks close by. The chief of police rarely summoned a junior detective without going through his Detective 3 supervisor. Before starting for Hunt's office, Lucas had the presence of mind to hurriedly search through his desk for the file on the Zucker case, which he presumed was the reason for this "convocation." It was a good thing the chief had called; Lucas had something new that he was sure Hunt would find interesting.

Hunt motioned him in. "Sit down, detective," he said, "and tell me what you think of these." He tossed a couple of photographs onto the desk in front of Lucas.

Lucas put his Zucker file to one side, picked up the photos, and carefully studied each pose. "Zucker!" he said, "and his kids—and the woman?"

"His wife," Hunt said. "They were taken out at Snapdragon last summer—the day the kids went missing. But there's something else in those shots."

Lucas examined the pictures again, hoping to light on what the chief expected him to find. He didn't have to search for long. "Hey! It's the guy in the driver's license…!" he said excitedly, looking up at Hunt for confirmation. "The *Peruvian* guy who clipped the Snapdragon parking lot attendant! Where did these *come* from?"

"Zucker sent them. He found them in one of the kids' backpacks that had been *sitting* in Snapdragon's lost and found *since last summer*—and naturally, our great LAPD never thought of looking there!" Enraged, Hunt tried to calm himself. "I'm sorry, son," he said, "it's not your fault—you weren't assigned to the case. It was that goddam Mayo—"

Lucas shook his head, and with all the sarcasm he could muster, said slowly, "Dear departed Mayo."

"Yeah…*that* one." Hunt fell silent, still calming himself. "Mayo should have found that bag. We'd have uncovered the photo of this Peruvian Carlos guy, or whatever his name is, and had a chance of picking him up at the border—possibly with those kids…*Damn* the man!"

"Carlos—?"

"No, *Mayo!*" Hunt said. "If Mayo had done *his* job, we wouldn't have had to wait for those kids' poor father to come and show us how to do *our* job."

"Our one lead…" Lucas said, still looking at the photos.

"Yeah," Hunt growled, "and damned *cold!*" He paused. "This Carlos guy's a pro and out of the country by now. All we can do is wait for him to come back and hope the next time we'll be smart enough to put cuffs on him!"

Lucas remained silent, wondering.

Hunt continued, "Lucas, get the lab to blow up one of these and have it circulated. It'd be stupid if Carlos returned and nobody spots him because they don't know what he looks like. Hell!" he said. "What a *screw*-up!" Shaking his head, Hunt picked up a sheaf of papers. "Thanks for coming up."

Lucas knew he had been dismissed, but he made no effort to get up from his chair.

"Sir…" Lucas said, still unsure whether now was the time.

Hunt lifted his gaze, surprised to see Lucas still sitting there.

"Yeah, what is it?"

"Zucker, sir—you asked me to get him in for another meeting…"

"And?"

"Well," Lucas hesitated, "I can't *find* him."

Hunt stared. "What do you mean—you can't *find* him?"

"Just *that*, sir…He's disappeared and, um…" Lucas wondered if he should venture any further, "…well…I'm afraid he might be connected with the Mayo murder."

Hunt's jaw dropped. "The *Mayo* case? Detective, what are you saying?"

"I'm saying Zucker rented a red Hyundai Accent on his visit here, and witnesses said an identical car was seen driving away from near the Mayo residence the morning of the shooting."

"Are you *sure* of this?" Hunt demanded. "Do the license plates match?"

"Nobody got the number of the car—but don't you think that's rather coincidental, sir?"

Hunt said: "Yes, totally. But you need something more than that to link an innocent man with the death of a crooked LAPD cop—"

"Yes," Lucas said, "but this cop was the lead investigator in his kids' case and, as you've already said, Mayo fell down on his duty—"

Hunt was about to interrupt, but Lucas stopped him.

"Please, sir—there's more. First, our ballistics guys believe that Mayo and his wife were shot with a Swiss-issue army weapon. Second, Zucker's red Hyundai was found in the long-term parking at LAX. I checked with the airlines, and he left the country on a flight to Lima, *Peru*—where this guy Carlos is from. That was day before yesterday. And third, immigration records show that Zucker entered the country posing as a Swiss aviation inspector, whereas in the case file he said he was an air-traffic controller. I'm sorry, sir, but this character sounds fishy to me." Lucas paused, relieved that he finally had everything out.

Hunt was still staring. "Very interesting Lucas," he said, "…and you have a theory about all this?"

"Well, sir, I do. I think we can conclude that Zucker got some kind of information from Mayo—about his kids—and he's off to Peru to follow it up. He obviously came here to find out what happened, and as you've just shown with the backpack photos, he's good at finding things out."

"But why kill Mayo?" Hunt queried.

Lucas shrugged. "Maybe he was pissed off that Mayo hadn't done his job—I mean, his kids are gone and his wife's lost her mind because of it." He raised his brows. "Or maybe Mayo just said something that set him off."

Hunt took a long, slow breath through his nose and exhaled loudly. "You may be onto something, detective. We'd better add Zucker's photo to the general circulation order, and the next time he shows his face, pick him up for questioning." Hunt felt infinitely tired. "Thank you, Lucas," he said. "You've done good work."

As soon as the young detective had left his office, Hunt leaned back in his swivel chair and turned to stare out of the large plate-glass window overlooking downtown LA. "You son of a gun, Zucker—you *did* it! You took Mayo out. I just hope that bastard gave you what you needed to find your kids."

Chapter 24

▼

Allison Cox was disappointed that the embassy's political officer had decided at the last minute not to accompany her to the meeting with Luis Chavez. As political officer, his job involved maintaining good relations with higher-ups who had political clout in the country—and Chavez was certainly one of those. He knew Chavez personally, and his insight would have been useful. If nothing else, Allison would have appreciated his moral support in what she expected to be a difficult encounter with this powerful and, according to some reports, dangerous man.

The black U.S. embassy limousine was standing outside the hotel waiting to chauffeur Allison to her appointment. What irked her most was that the limousine driver had broken the news that she'd be going alone. The political officer could at least have given her the courtesy of phoning her himself. Her annoyance showed.

"He asked me to give you his apologies," the driver said in what sounded to Allison like a well-rehearsed tone. "He'll contact you after your appointment."

"Yes, I'm sure he will!" Allison replied, irritated that, while the political officer didn't want to sit in on the meeting, he wanted a briefing from her afterward.

Dressed in a well-cut, beige silk matka suit, Allison stepped into the back of the roomy limousine. Experience with these kinds of interviews had taught her that being conservatively but smartly dressed not only boosted her self-confidence but also gave her an edge. Allison used the disarming effect of her good looks to gain an initial advantage over her adversary. And she had no qualms about it. It had worked in the past, and she was sure that it would help today. Allison quickly did a discreet visual check of her attire, noting approvingly that the short European cut of her skirt showed off her legs to advantage. Satisfied, she turned her attention to the upcoming meeting, running through the points she was going to make and the answers she needed to obtain. *This is not going to be easy,* she mused.

In the back of her mind was also the nagging thought of the *El Crónico* article that John had given her, about the rescue of two youngsters adrift in a boat. She couldn't decide if it would be appropriate to raise it during this official meeting with Chavez. She would see how the meeting progressed and decide on the spot.

"Express package for an Allison Cox—please sign!" the deliveryman said, slamming the sizeable parcel down on the reception desk. He paid no attention to the other people already waiting their turn for the sole hotel receptionist on duty. The uniformed PARCELS ETC. man was known at the Miraflores as an impatient type, and this kind of interruption was routine. Not really surprising; speed was of the essence in the highly competitive world of private mail-delivery companies.

"Uh—sure, okay…thanks," the flustered receptionist said as he stretched over and scribbled his initials on the form on the deliveryman's clipboard.

The package was still sitting there occupying a large part of the marble counter space when the desk manager returned. He abhorred clutter, and the instant he spied this infringement on the clear counter, he barked at the receptionist who had just finished dealing with the last of the waiting guests.

"What is *this* doing here?" Without even trying to explain, the receptionist lifted the object from the counter and placed it on the floor beneath the wall of message pigeonholes. He glanced at the name again and started to write a note to Allison.

"Who's it for?" the desk manager bellowed again.

"Señora Cox, sir," the receptionist replied.

"Señora Cox!" the manager exclaimed, recalling the shapely American that his eyes had feasted upon as she had crossed the lobby that very morning. "Have it taken to her room as soon as she gets back."

As the receptionist wrote instructions for the bellboy, the desk manager thought again. He was trying to remember something about Allison Cox. "Didn't she ask for an adjoining room for a friend who's arriving today?"

The receptionist nodded, not daring to admit he couldn't remember the request.

"I want you to personally make sure the room is ready; and leave my card in both rooms in case they have any special requests." The desk manager puffed out his chest and stood like a rooster surveying his territory. He liked being in charge, especially when it meant he could lavish extra attention on guests who caught his eye.

El Crónico's main office was on the Avenida del Golf in Lima's fashionable San Isidro quarter. It was the garden district of Lima, known for its fine restaurants and centuries-old olive grove. Allison had occasionally dined there many years previously, but now hardly recognized the area because of the many modern office blocks that had shot up. The embassy car pulled up outside an older, aristocratic-looking building with a large sign over the entrance door: EL CRONICO— *El Periódico de Hoy.*

El Crónico—Today's Newspaper, Allison mentally translated, and then added, *but peddling yesterday's baby-parts news.* She felt nervous as she stepped from the car and walked up to the glass entrance door, but she didn't let it show. She glanced at the Patek Philippe watch on her left wrist to make sure she was not late. It had been foolish to bring such an expensive Swiss watch to crime-ridden Latin America. But living in secure Switzerland had dulled some of her instincts. Allison felt increasingly uncomfortable with the way the day was progressing.

Preoccupied with these thoughts, she placed her hand on the brass handle of the hefty glass-paneled, polished wood door, expecting it to be heavy. It opened far too easily, swinging inward to reveal an elegant, smiling man who had courteously pulled the door open just as she had touched the handle. Allison nearly fell headlong into the lobby, but swiftly regained her balance.

Despite the clear glass panels, she had not spotted the man before entering; the strong daylight outside had reflected on the glass and made it difficult to see through to the darker interior. For his part, Pedro Delgado had the advantage of the opposite effect; from the lobby he had seen Allison's arrival quite clearly, and he had taken full advantage and literally thrown her off balance with a seemingly courteous gesture.

"Mrs. Allison Cox, I presume?" he said, showing off his English. "Welcome to *El Crónico!*" Allison was taken aback that someone had been waiting for her at the door. She had assumed she would have to announce herself at the front desk and wait for someone to escort her to Chavez's office. *This is one weird appointment,* she thought.

"Why, thank you," she replied, forcing herself to sound confident. "How did you know?"

"Ah!" the man said, stroking his ample dark-brown moustache. "I could say I figured it out from your overall demeanor, and thereby impress you with my powers of deduction—but that would be a lie," he said smiling. "Actually, I saw the U.S. diplomatic license plate on the car that brought you here!" He laughed, as did Allison. "I'm too honest—I wouldn't make a good diplomat!"

Allison was not sure how to interpret the man's last remark. *Was it meant as a serious insult or as a joke?* She put on a radiant smile and proffered her hand. "You're absolutely right; it's a pleasure to meet you—Señor?"

"Pedro Delgado at your service, Señora. I am the assistant of Señor Chavez. He asked me to meet you and show you around *El Crónico*—that is, of course, if you have the time? Then I'll take you to meet him."

"That would be nice," Allison replied. Peter's arrival time flashed through her mind, and she hoped the tour wouldn't take too long. In any case, she thought, it could be interesting to look behind the scenes of the paper. Allison supposed Chavez had been held up, and the tour was an impromptu way to cover up his late arrival.

Pedro led her through offices where employees were busy at their desks, through the photo-editing shop with its banks of digital equipment, and then down through the basement where huge presses were rolling out the evening edition. Finally, they emerged in the quietude of the editorial office. Here everyone was dressed casually—except for one bespectacled man well into his fifties, the oldest in the room and the only person other than Pedro wearing a suit. He had removed his jacket—it hung on the back of his desk chair—and his shirtsleeves were rolled to his elbows. He was sweating and looked uneasy as they approached. Oddly, Allison sensed that this overweight, balding professional was fearful in the presence of Pedro Delgado.

"Ah! Marco," Pedro said affably. "Let me introduce you to Allison Cox—she has come all the way from Washington to see our famous newspaper!" Marco visibly cringed, his forehead produced even more beads of perspiration, and as Allison shook his hand, she was revolted to feel it clammy with sweat.

"Allison—if I may call you that?" Pedro said.

"Sure, *Pedro*," Allison conceded nonchalantly, emphasizing his name.

"…This is Marco, our day editor. He's been with the paper for an extremely long time—too long maybe…he deserves retirement." Pedro smiled coldly at the trembling editor. "He's in charge of putting the paper together and sending it to print. He reads everything that our journalists write and ensures the continuing quality of the paper—don't you Marco?" Pedro added, urging the man to say something.

"*Sí*, Señora, that's right!" Marco replied too enthusiastically, keeping one eye on Chavez's right-hand man. "I read everything—"

"Everything?" Allison queried.

"Oh, yes, everything that is written, even the ads!" Marco said, encouraged by Allison's interest in his work. His relief at giving what he thought was the right answer to this important visitor was short-lived, however. Allison's brain was working fast.

"Well, you might be able to help me then—actually, help a friend of mine who's writing a research paper on the influence of the press," Allison said very naturally. Both the poised, smiling Pedro and the damp, worried Marco now hung on her every word. "Knowing that I was coming down here, my friend passed me...um..." Allison paused while leafing through some papers in her slim attaché case. "Yes, here it is...this!" she exclaimed, pulling out the photocopied *El Crónico* article John had given her at the airport in Washington. She handed it to Marco. He took it without thinking and read it, and then his face went white.

"I—I—d—dd—don't know," Marco stammered.

He seemed to be looking to Allison's escort for help.

Pedro swiftly intervened. "Of course, Marco reads everything, but naturally he can't be expected to remember all that passes by him!" Pedro snatched the sheet of paper from Marco and rapidly scanned it. "Yes, it is one of our articles." He turned toward Allison. "Curious that your friend should be interested in this—a mere rescue at sea of two children..."

As he gazed at Allison, Marco Bustamente was reliving all of his worst nightmares. More than a week had gone by since the paper had run the article, and he had hoped the incident was closed! But now, this woman from Washington...! Where had he gone wrong? He avoided eye contact with Pedro, who days ago had stormed into his office and severely castigated him for printing these few lines. "They were sent in by a stringer...someone on the coast, a Raoul Moreno, I think was his name," Marco had explained to Pedro. "I thought Señor Chavez would be happy to see his name in the paper—it was *me* who added the words *generous intervention of Señor Luis Chavez!*" Marco could not find out why printing these few lines had been such a *blunder*. But with blood in his eye, Pedro had warned him not to print any follow-up stories and never to address questions on this article without consulting him first.

Luckily for Marco, since then nobody had shown any interest in the article. In the fast-paced newspaper business, where news becomes old and uninteresting after only a few days, Marco had assumed the subject was closed. But now, suddenly, here it was again—and from a totally unexpected quarter.

Though as surprised as Marco, Pedro hid his astonishment from Allison. The *last* thing he had expected this emissary from Washington to ask about was those *damned kids* at Don Gonzalo's. Pedro couldn't work out whether this was merely a coincidence, or whether Allison was actually on to him for the kidnapping. She *was*, after all, an agent of the U.S. government. He could not allow this. Pedro's mind raced, and the outlines of a plan soon came to him. He would first run it by Chavez, but it was only an extension of what they had already planned for Allison. In the meantime, he would continue to handle her with the utmost care and diplomacy.

"What aspect of this short article might your friend be interested in?" Pedro asked, casually taking Allison by the arm and leading her out of the room. She glanced back at the receding form of Marco, intrigued. *Why had her question caused him so much unease?* She had assumed he would not remember such a minor piece. But it seemed uppermost in Marco's mind—and Pedro knew about it too...or was she reading too much into this?

Allison maintained her innocent smile. "Well, quite simply, he's interested in freedom of the press around the world, and he's curious as to why there was no follow-up story in any paper on the rescued children," Allison said matter-of-factly. "I'm referring to the obvious questions, such as 'What were they doing adrift in a small boat?' and 'Where are they now?' It seems to him—and to me—that these are the kinds of questions the average reader would like to see answered."

"Oh, I'm certain it's because of space limitations or the need to cover a more burning story that we dropped it," Pedro replied. "I'm afraid I don't know anything about this story—I don't read the paper as closely and diligently as I ought," he confessed coyly. "But rest assured, we'll find the answer for you. Now, we'd better finish off our tour, otherwise you'll be late for your meeting. And that will not do!"

"Maybe I could go directly to meet with Señor Chavez," she said. "I have another appointment afterward..."

"But, of course, Allison," Pedro said brimming with charm. "Let's proceed to his office immediately!"

Pedro discreetly glanced at a clock on the corridor wall. *Why hasn't Chavez's pilot called to confirm that the plane is fueled and ready to go? Has Chavez made a last-minute change in plans?* But he quickly discounted that possibility; he would have been the first to be informed. He led Allison up two flights and into a plush waiting room across the hall from the office suite Chavez used when in Lima. "I'll be back in just a minute," Pedro said.

As he stepped back into the hall and closed the door behind him, the cell phone in Pedro's breast pocket suddenly vibrated. *Finally!* Pedro extracted the phone, flipped it open, and swiftly brought it to his ear. Pedro rarely let calls go into voicemail; a timely call might save him from one of the many enemies he had made. The phone was as important to his life as the custom Tanfoglio 9 mm pistol that he kept in the holster under his left arm.

"*Sí?*" He listened impatiently, attentively. "*Sí—Sí*—but you should have been ready sooner," he added. "I'll call when we're about to leave." He slapped the phone closed and slipped it back into his pocket. Then, without knocking, he hurriedly opened the door to Chavez's office suite. He wasn't looking for his boss; Chavez wouldn't be there. What Pedro needed was the secure phone.

In fact, Chavez wasn't even in Lima; he had remained at his home in Chiclayo 400 miles up the coast. At that very moment, he was relaxing by his guitar-shaped swimming pool, studying a detailed file that he had obtained from a contact in Washington—a file on Allison Cox.

The more Chavez read, the more impatient he grew to start this game of mental agility with her. He was not worried—he loved a challenge. The *baby-parts* stories were bogus, but he relished the opportunity to make people believe what he wanted them to believe. Hitler's infamous minister of propaganda, Josef Goebbels, had shown the world how manipulating information could alter the "truth" in people's minds. The Americans had fine-tuned the art, calling it public relations or PR, and made it part of everyday life. Chavez used it even more effectively by lacing it with personal charm. He would run circles around Allison Cox until she didn't know *what* to believe.

His thoughts were interrupted by his manservant bringing him an aluminum briefcase at the end of a long cord—his secure phone. He didn't trust cordless or cell phones; they were far too easy to tap, and this particular phone had a scrambling device. The servant guessed Chavez's question before he asked it. "It's Señor Pedro, sir!"

Chavez said nothing until the man was out of earshot. He glanced at the caller-ID screen and knew it must be important for Pedro to use the secure line in Lima. "What is it, Pedro?"

"We have a problem, sir. It's the Cox woman—she's asking about the Del Solar kids—"

"*The Del Solar kids?*" Chavez repeated, astonished.

"*Sí*, Señor—she has the article about the rescue and is asking for details."

Chavez was thinking quickly. "What did you tell her?"

"Nothing, Señor, except that I would look into it for her."

"Hmm…"

"I have a bad feeling about this woman—I think she's trouble," Pedro added.

"What do you suggest?" Chavez asked.

"Bring her up as planned, see how much she knows, and if she knows too much, silence her."

"I hope we won't have to go that far," Chavez said. He sighed. He had hoped he might show Allison a good time and charm her into forgetting about *baby-parts*. His idea had been to get her to report back to Washington that *El Crónico* had done nothing wrong. But *this* added a whole new dimension!

He glanced down at the file on his lap. "We'll have to tread carefully with this one—she is an American agent, and we don't want to attract further interference from her government. Fend off her questions until she gets here—but make sure she comes today. We cannot let her do any more snooping. And there's another problem you'll have to take care of when you get down here, this Tincopa woman—the teacher. She's meddling. You'll find instructions on the plane."

"*Sí*, Señor," Pedro said, knowing not to solicit other details from Chavez until he offered them.

"Be careful with this American, Pedro!" Chavez warned. "I don't want any slip-ups." With that cautionary note, he hung up with the same disregard for polite good-byes as Pedro.

Chapter 25

▼

A feeling of guilt swept over Romy as she stepped back into the Del Solar house, a feeling that she could not shake off. She felt as if the words "I've been to the police" were tattooed across her forehead; anyone who stared at her for even a moment would see her guilt. And yet, Romy knew she had done the right thing. She just had to keep thinking of what might happen to the children if she remained silent.

But she was troubled and disappointed that the district chief of police had been unable to meet with her. At the mention of the *Del Solar* name, young Lieutenant Rodriguez had stepped in and whisked Romy away to the privacy of the interview room. "There's no need to inform the chief," he had said. "He asked me to deal with all matters and not disturb him under any circumstances."

Romy hadn't argued; she had heard that no one ever crossed swords with Rodriguez. Everyone knew that the chief left the implementation of his orders to this Lieutenant Rodriguez—a man who had an uncanny knack for getting things done. Especially when the chief came up against Luis Chavez; as soon as Rodriguez intervened, the problem was solved. What the chief did not realize was that Rodriguez was in the pay of Chavez, the chief's sworn enemy.

The chief particularly hated the Del Solars' complicity with Chavez. He had once held them in high esteem, but no longer. They were money-grabbers who constantly undermined the chief's efforts to weed out corruption. Given the chance, he would have welcomed Romy with open arms.

Romy had no reason to suspect Lieutenant Rodriguez of being anything but an honest upholder of the law. He appeared well-disciplined and efficient. Unlike his barrel-chested colleagues who verged on obesity, he was slim and solid.

Well-groomed black hair framed his clean-shaven, tanned face. The brass buttons on his uniform shone, and his black leather belt and shoulder strap were polished as if ready for inspection. Romy should have been suspicious, though, of the ivory-handled silver pistol in his holster; it looked expensive and playboyish, but she was preoccupied with other things.

"The chief apologizes sincerely for not being able to meet with you, especially since it concerns the Del Solars," the lieutenant told her convincingly. He was sitting casually on the edge of the table, smiling down at Romy. "He assigned me to act on his behalf and help you out with whatever problem you have." His voice was still calm but more eager when he asked, "And what exactly is the problem you have with the Del Solars, Señorita Tincopa?"

Romy had no time for lengthy explanations. She had left the house on a pretext and should have been back by now. But this had taken longer than she'd expected. She had to be brief and precise. "I suspect that Don Gonzalo and his wife, in league with Luis Chavez, are arranging to do away with the two foreign children they adopted."

Rodriguez instantly knew what this meant. *Thank God I caught this in time!* Not that he was in the least concerned for the children; the only thing that interested Rodriguez was his status with Chavez—and his own bank balance. Rodriguez knew about the children; how could he not know about two small children picked up at sea? Chavez had told him to keep an eye out for anyone asking suspicious questions. And here was someone.

In his mind, Rodriguez rubbed his hands in triumph, but outwardly he remained poker-faced. "Please tell me more, Señorita..."

"There's so much to tell and I have little time..."

"Just start at the beginning and calmly run through all of your suspicions," Rodriguez said understandingly. He wanted every detail. "It won't take long," he assured her. "And I'm here to help you."

Romy willingly unburdened herself of her problem. She told Rodriguez that the children were there against their will; they were Swiss-German, not Polish; they would *not* be returned to their parents. "You have to stop them somehow...Seize the children and put them in police custody before it's too late!"

"Yes, we certainly need to do something..." Rodriguez reassured her. "But we must do it lawfully and according to procedu—"

"But this is urgent!" Romy interrupted. "They'll take them away and—"

"Please trust me," Rodriguez assured her, getting to his feet. "When Señor Chavez's name is mentioned, we always give the case top priority." This was the truth; he would contact Chavez as soon as she left.

Romy understood it differently—as she was meant to: she had done her duty, and help was on the way. "Thank you—I must get back now before they suspect something," Romy said with much gratitude.

Yes, and I am grateful to you, señorita!

Pedro put on his most apologetic face as he re-entered the room where he had left Allison.

"Oh, Allison! I don't know what you are going to think of me, but I have made a most monumental blunder!" he said a little too dramatically. "I have made a mistake over your appointment with Señor Chavez—what am I to do?"

Allison looked at him with suspicion. She didn't trust this man, and yet she felt sorry for him; he looked so distraught. Her feelings quickly turned to annoyance; her meeting with Chavez was slipping away. She tried hard to remain unfazed.

"What's the problem?" she simply asked, trying to hide the mild anger in her voice.

"I just don't know where to start…and Señor Chavez is most annoyed with me—I just this minute got off the phone with him…"

This man is exasperating! Allison thought. *He takes forever to come to the point.*

"…he'll probably fire me for such a mix-up—"

"Please tell me what's happened," Allison interrupted. "The appointment's off—canceled—is that it?"

"No, no…not at all," Pedro reassured her. "Señor Chavez wants above everything—especially now—to keep the appointment. It's just that—"

"What?—Please spit it out!"

"—that we'll have to fly out to his country residence to see him," Pedro said.

"You mean he's not in Lima—why did you invite me here then?"

"I thought he was," Pedro lied. "Señor Chavez told me he wouldn't be in town today and I just forgot. I would never have invited you here under false pretenses—why would I do that?" Pedro pleaded.

"I have no idea, but we could have saved each other a lot of time."

"But please do not be cross with me! Señor Chavez is sending his private plane to pick you up—it should be here within the hour—and you'll have the pleasure of meeting him at his beautiful country home. It's only an hour away!"

Allison thought before responding. She saw Pedro looking at her expectantly, and, thinking about Peter, she glanced at her watch. "How long will this take?"

"For as long as you desire," Pedro replied. "To make up for the inconvenience I have caused you, Señor Chavez would like to offer you extended hospitality. He invites you to his home for a couple of days to see northern Peru." Pedro noticed a slightly worried expression on Allison's face. "But, of course, you can stay for less time—if you prefer, the plane can bring you straight back here after your appointment. But I would get into less trouble if you allowed my boss to make up for my mistake…" His voice trailed off for effect.

Indeed, Allison did not want to go; it was not what she had planned. *This man knew Chavez wasn't in Lima.* It irked her to be lied to, but she put on her best dimpled smile. "It's a great invitation!" She saw Pedro was pleased. "But I have to be back here by midday to pick up a friend at the airport. And I doubt that we could do the return journey in that short a time!"

"Oh! But that is no problem," Pedro shot back. "I can arrange to have someone pick up this friend of yours."

"No, that won't do," Allison said, trying to think how she could still meet Peter at the airport without sacrificing her meeting with Chavez. Chavez was the main reason for her travel to Peru, and she couldn't run the risk of not meeting him. But she didn't want to let Peter down again. Pedro interrupted her thoughts.

"May I ask if this friend is, um…special?"

"Yes," said Allison automatically. "But it's not what you are thinking," she added, annoyed at the innuendo.

"Oh no! I understand," Pedro said knowingly.

"Could I go tomorrow instead?" Allison asked brightly.

"Of course…yes, normally, but Señor Chavez will not be there tomorrow."

"But you just said he wanted to invite me down for a couple of days." Allison felt suspicious again.

"But he does, Allison, and he means it. He has told me to look after you and show you the sights after he leaves," Pedro said enigmatically.

"I don't understand," Allison said. She was growing more exasperated by the minute.

"It's quite simple," Pedro said, thinking quickly. "You see, my boss is leaving for some extended travels tonight, and the only time left for you to see him is today. Could your friend not accompany us?"

This seemed simple and straightforward enough, and it would be a solution to Allison's dilemma. She couldn't abandon Peter in Lima after persuading him to fly down. "I suppose he could," she replied. "But would Mr. Chavez not mind?"

"Of course not—he would wholeheartedly approve," Pedro replied confidently. "He always likes showing our beautiful country to foreigners, especially the region where he lives."

"And where is that?" Allison asked. She wanted to know where she was headed.

"Less than one hour north of here by plane, near the town of Chiclayo. It's on the *ocean!*" Pedro said with much encouragement. This American fish seemed to be biting, but he must reel her in without delay.

"I think I know how we can arrange all of this to meet everyone's needs—that is, if I might venture a plan…" Pedro feigned servility.

"Sure, go ahead," Allison said.

"With Señor Chavez's private plane, we have much flexibility," Pedro said. "You can go and meet your friend at the airport, which you said was at midday…"

"Yes, that's right."

"I assume he is also staying at the Miraflores?"

"Yes, of course," Allison said.

"Perfect. You can meet him at the airport, take him back to the hotel, quickly pack for a couple of days—let's say you decide to stay—"

Allison stared at him neutrally.

"And I'll pick you up at the hotel at two PM. We'll drive straight to the airport and fly to Chiclayo. What do you think of that?" Pedro seemed quite pleased with himself.

"All right, Pedro," Allison said. "How can I object when you make it seem so easy?"

"Wonderful," said Pedro. "Let me escort you to the front entrance."

Allison left not knowing what was in store, but Pedro was too smooth to be honest. She would be on her guard.

C h a p t e r 26

▼

It was a strange reunion—for both of them.

"Peter! Peter!" he heard Allison call out. "Over here!"

Peter was relieved to find Allison's face in the waiting crowd—though, strangely, he had had the surrealistic hope of finding Martine there instead. A melding of reality with wishful thinking, but dreams seemed the only hope left to him now.

At the sound of her familiar voice, Peter realized how desperately he needed to unburden his confused thoughts—he could have done it so easily with Martine, especially the terrible thing he had done in killing two people. She would have been like a caring mother who sorts out her little boy's problems, accepting without blame what he had done and telling him what to do now—however difficult it might be. But this was Allison, not Martine.

Having been afraid she'd miss Peter at the airport, Allison was nervous. She had forgotten how bad the lunchtime traffic could be and arrived after the aircraft landed. After running through the building, she had made it to the arrivals gate just seconds before he appeared. The moment she spotted him, relief replaced tension, and her heart stopped pounding. She waved enthusiastically.

"Allison...Allison! I'm...mm..." Peter's throat constricted as he rushed forward. The words stopped coming, and he broke down, overwhelmed at the sight of Allison's face—the first familiar face he had seen since he left Switzerland. He collapsed to his knees by his suitcase, head in hands, and sobbed deliriously.

Allison's heart went out to this quiet and kind neighbor who now lived in his own emotional hell. She ran to him, knelt before him, saw his tears of desperation and grief, and with her hand, gently touched his face. "Peter! Oh, Peter!" she said tenderly. And then in an urgent whisper, "Peter, listen to me! Please listen. I may have a lead on the children. Can you pull yourself together? I'm so sorry I refused to help you. Come with me now! Come with me, and perhaps..."

As Peter slowly looked up and his eyes met hers, she saw that her words had pierced the fog of his mind..."

"We can work together," Allison assured him. From the haggard and crazy look in his eyes, she saw that he was desperate and at the very end of his tether. She had to help him! Screw everything else!

They exchanged few words in the taxi as they rode back to the hotel. To assure him, Allison held Peter's hand.

At her touch, Peter relaxed, put his head back, and closed his eyes.

Allison looked at him. His two-day growth of beard could not hide his gaunt and sickly complexion; he had been through a *hideous* time. First she must clean him up and give him a good meal. Then they could exchange information and prepare for the trip up to Chiclayo.

She prayed that Peter and Martine would soon have their answer.

The meal was the same as Romy had often eaten at Don Gonzalo's house. The cook was not very imaginative in preparing the staff's meals, but they were always wholesome and tasty. Tasty, that is, if you liked spicy food! Chilies were the old cook's favorite ingredient; she threw them into everything. Luckily, Romy liked hot food—but the cook always encouraged her to eat more than she wanted.

This evening, it was chili con carne. Whew! Romy thought, as she tasted her first spoonful. The cook must've dropped the whole bunch into the pot! But Romy was hungrier than usual. Perhaps it was the tension of going to the police station. For whatever reason, she dug into the chili with unusual gusto. But, oh God! Was it hot! And it left a bitter aftertaste. Strange. With her bowl empty, Romy put down her spoon. She had terrible heartburn and felt faint.

Romy was alone at the refectory table, with nobody to witness the agonized look on her face or see her lose consciousness and slip off the bench. The dull thud when she hit the floor brought Señora Del Solar to the kitchen doorway. It was music to her ears, and it brought a wicked smile to her face.

Allison listened enthralled to Peter's tale. They were seated at a small table by the window in the ground-floor cafeteria of the Miraflores Hotel. The tables around them were vacant, so their privacy was ensured. Their view of the huge orange birds of paradise and white and pink hibiscus blossoms provided the calm setting Peter needed to unburden himself.

Allison had explained the possible lead in the *El Crónico* article—the two children adrift at sea. At this, his eyes glimmered with a faint hope.

He confessed that it was indeed he who had gunned down the retired detective and his wife. Confessed it so matter-of-factly that Allison was shocked.

"They deserved what they got," he said. "I only have to picture Martine in the hospital to realize that," Peter said. "Still," he added wistfully, "I killed them...and it haunts me."

"What's done is done," she said solemnly. "And you got the information that you needed from Mayo, information that coincides with what I found."

"Yes, Allison, but like all that's gone before, it's going to lead to *nothing*...! An utter waste of effort, and now I'm a killer. It's only a matter of time before they pick me up and throw me into prison. How will that help Martine?"

"Christ!" Allison said. "We've got *good* leads—please don't give up now!"

"But there's no hope—"

"Look, Peter," Allison said, raising her voice. "I'm sorry I didn't help you back in Geneva, but *Jesus!* I've done a lot to help you now...! *And* I'm going to go with you—Don't throw my help back in my face...! Dammit, snap *out* of it! Or else you'll end up like Martine..."

Peter looked as if she had struck him in the face.

"I'm sorry Peter—I truly am. I shouldn't have said that. But you've got to give this your best shot. I have a strong feeling about those kids set adrift. There's a chance they might be *yours*! And if they aren't, well, they might lead us to the ring that abducted Mark and Nicolette."

Peter still looked dubious.

"And even if this is a complete wild-goose chase—what else have you got to do with your time? Sitting and moping won't get Mark and Nicolette back. And you obviously can't go back to the States!"

Peter appeared calmer; he was obviously thinking things through. Perhaps she was reaching him.

"Look, I need your help, too," she went on. "This meeting with Chavez over the *baby-parts* issue isn't going to be easy. I need your moral support and advice once we get down there. Maybe we'll kill two birds with one stone! I don't know..." She felt exasperated. "Are you with me, Peter? Are you going to give it a try—at least for *Martine's* sake?"

Peter nodded his head like a little boy who had been reprimanded. He felt ashamed and for the moment forgot his despair. Then he suddenly brightened. "Let me show you the photographs!" he said.

"I'd love to see them, but it'll have to be later," Allison said, looking at her watch. "We'll have time on the plane." She got up from the table. "We'd better get upstairs and pack what we need for the trip—they're coming to pick us up in fifteen minutes." Looking down at her short skirt and dress shoes, she added: "I think I'd better put on some sneakers and more practical clothes for the plane ride!"

C h a p t e r 27

▼

Pedro watched the car pull away from the Miraflores with Peter and Allison inside. When it was out of sight, he got out of his black BMW parked inconspicuously in the shade of a palm tree at the far end of the hotel's parking lot. He carried a large, empty suitcase and a master cardkey that he had *borrowed* from a hotel maid—in exchange for $100—no questions asked. As agreed, he would drop it in the flower vase in the hall on the fourth floor once he had finished.

Pedro took the service stairs up to the fourth floor, scaling them confidently. He expected no problems, and he knew how to handle any that might arise.

He found room 401, and, after glancing discreetly up and down the hall, slid the cardkey into the lock. It clicked open and he disappeared into the room. He hung the *Do Not Disturb* sign on the outside doorknob, and quickly went to work. Allison had taken only a small overnight bag for her trip to Chiclayo and left her main suitcase in the room. In it, Pedro packed all her remaining things. First he emptied the wardrobe and then all the drawers; finally, he threw the few toiletries that Allison hadn't taken into the case.

A knock froze Pedro in his tracks. He crept to the door and looked through the peephole. A bellboy was standing there holding a large package.

"What is it?" Pedro shouted in English through the door.

"Package for Mrs. Cox," the boy answered.

"Leave it outside the door," Pedro ordered. The boy seemed not to understand. "On the floor—outside the door!" Pedro repeated in Spanish. He pulled a ten-dollar bill from his pocket and slid it under the door. He heard the package dropped carelessly onto the floor and saw the bill snatched away. As soon as the bellboy left, Pedro opened the door, grabbed the package, and set it inside. He had no time to examine it now.

He repeated the clean-up operation in Peter's room next door. This was much easier; this friend of Allison Cox's had hardly unpacked anything.

Within fifteen minutes of entering the hotel, Pedro was throwing the suitcases and the package into the back of his BMW. Then he slipped into the driver's seat and sped away. Later he would phone the hotel to say that Allison Cox and her friend—he would have to find out his name first—had left the hotel and hadn't had time to check out. *Would the hotel please charge their room expenses to Mrs. Cox's credit card?* Pedro knew this would be no problem; guests did it all the time.

"Where's Pedro?" Allison asked the steward on board Chavez's plane. Her question was polite but edged with a hint of irritation. "I assume he's coming with us?"

"Oh, yes, of course," the steward replied. "He'll be here—we have strict orders not to leave without him!" The man smiled, but Allison didn't find him likable at all. His rough-and-ready manner didn't jibe with the role of a white-jacketed steward. She also had the distinct impression he knew something important that she didn't. It irked her.

"Can I get you some refreshment while we're waiting?" he asked in what Allison thought was an overly servile manner.

Both she and Peter declined. Allison examined her surroundings, admiring the plush comfort of the small business jet; a kind she had never been on before. Peter was searching in his bag for the photographs.

"Here they are!" he exclaimed. "And that's the man who appears in two of them," Peter pointed as he passed the pile to Allison.

She took one look and clamped her hand over her mouth to stifle a gasp.

"Oh—my *GOD!*" she exclaimed under her breath.

Perplexed, Peter saw that her face had turned white as a sheet. Allison hurriedly took the photographs and flicked through the rest, stopping and staring at those that contained the man.

"Christ *ALMIGHTY!*—What are we going to *do?*" she uttered in a whisper. "We've got to get off this—"

"Get off this plane? No, I'm afraid it is too late for that now," a voice that Allison instantly recognized said from above her. Pedro reached down and snatched the deck of photographs and proceeded to sift through them.

"So that's why you're here…Interesting. I thought there was something more to your interest in that article in the paper," Pedro said sardonically. "I can smell a phony—"

Pedro's sentence was abruptly cut short as Peter lunged out of his seat and grabbed for Pedro. It was an awkward maneuver, and Peter never had a chance. Pedro stepped back, and Peter stumbled over Allison's legs. At the same instant, the steward appeared, and, with one expert blow from the butt of a pistol, sent Peter to the floor, blood oozing from the back of his head.

Allison, stunned, bent down over him. She searched for a pulse and found it. She felt sick to her stomach. Pedro was the man in the photographs. He was the man who had abducted Peter's children!

She looked up. "You *god damned son of a bitch!*"

"Perhaps," he said with a wry smile. Then, changing his tone, he sneered, "Now sit down and *shut up!*"

Allison hesitated. Her instinct as a Marine was to fight back, but Pedro clearly had the upper hand. Her momentary indecision was resolved as the steward jabbed her shoulder and knocked her back into her seat. He held the pistol in his other hand ready to quash any further reaction.

"Put him in the seat over there and tie him up," Pedro ordered, pointing to Peter's body. "And stick something on his head, or he'll get blood all over the plane."

"And her, sir?" the steward asked Pedro, looking at Allison.

Pedro gazed down at her with disdain.

But Allison thought she saw alarm in his eyes.

"Tie her to the seat, and we'll deal with them in Chiclayo."

A chill ran through her. She was frightened—more frightened than she had ever felt in her life. Thoughts of her two sons at home in Trélex flashed through her mind. *If I'd only looked at those damn photos back at the hotel!*

Pedro was smiling at her discomfort. Enraged, she refocused. "So," she said matter-of-factly, "what did you do with the kids?"

"He's the father, isn't he?" Pedro nodded toward Peter's crumpled body. "Yes, I remember him now."

"Where *are* they?" Allison asked, not knowing whether she wanted to hear the answer. "What have you done with them?"

"Ha!" was all that Pedro replied.

The steward passed a white nylon tie under the seat arm and up around Peter's wrist and yanked the loop tight. Then he came to Allison and did the same.

She saw now he was using those small industrial cable ties that ratchet closed and lock in place; there would be no wriggling free. The steward yanked the tie harshly, catching her skin in the ratchet.

"Ow—*ow!*" she shrieked in pain. "Please! Please *loosen it!*" She fought back tears. The tie had cut her wrist and now it was her turn to bleed.

"I told you to shut up! Any more noise and he'll put one on the other wrist too," Pedro warned. He then stormed off down the aisle and disappeared into the cockpit. The steward followed, leaving her and Peter alone.

Allison moved her wrist, but the motion produced searing pain; she was securely attached.

"Dammit!" she swore. *"Dammit!"*

"Five hundred thousand each or the deal's off," Chavez said. He produced two more large color photographs of Mark and Nicolette from a stiff envelope and slid them across the table until they were under his interlocutor's eyes. The children were blond once again. Chavez had had the black dye bleached out of their hair, knowing that they would be eminently more marketable that way. And they were naked. "This is unique merchandise, and there's no more on the market."

"Hmm…" the fat, greasy man murmured, digesting the photographs. He liked what he saw—he clearly did! But he must temper his enthusiasm. Besides, Chavez's sales pitch seemed uncharacteristically desperate.

"Well?"

"Hmm…" the potential buyer said again, "but there's the question of them bein'—shall we say—*hot* merchandise?" He removed his ugly black plastic-framed glasses and looked Chavez squarely in the eye. "I would be taking a risk…"

"There's no risk involved," Chavez snapped back. "None whatsoever, and you know it—you've never had any complaints about the others I've provided you with."

"Um…no…but—"

"No buts about it—take it or leave it," Chavez said.

The buyer examined the photographs again through his smeary lenses. He shook his head, feigning doubt and indecision.

Chavez knew the man wanted the kids, but he had no more time to play these trading games. He had to move the kids quickly and get back and meet with this U.S. emissary, Allison Cox.

"Leandro wants these kids, and he wants them badly," Chavez said. "His clients pay top whack for pale-skinned youngsters like these. But you and I have been doing business for years, and I felt you should have first choice. But if you're not interested…" Chavez began gathering up the photographs.

"Leandro! Ha! His clients don't care what they screw! Come on, gimme a break on the price? I mean a million dollars—it's difficult to come by…these are tough times…"

"Bullshit!" Chavez shot back. "The price is right, and you know it." He thought for a moment. "Look, I'll give you time to pay. When can you take the kids?"

"Oh,…my friend, Chavez!…You push me too hard. I haven't said that I'll take them!"

"Okay—nine hundred thousand, or I leave," Chavez said, exasperated. "Put up or shut up!"

"You must be desperate, my friend," the man said, waving his hand to stifle the objections Chavez was about to utter. "Okay, I'll take them—but only to help you out. When can you deliver?"

"You have to pick them up."

"You drive a hard bargain, my friend, and then you tell me delivery's not included! Okay—okay…when will they be ready?"

"They're ready now."

"Hmm…Today's Monday…They're the ones at Don Gonzalo's—right?"

This old fox knows everything, Chavez thought.

"I suppose I could get over there tomorrow. Will that be soon enough for you?"

"No! You come tonight," Chavez replied harshly. "After dark. I want full discretion on this one—I don't want anyone seeing you. Come after nine—you take the kids and disappear. I never want to see a trace of them again. Is that clear?" Chavez barked.

"Clear and simple," the man replied. "Tonight it'll be."

Chapter 28

▼

It was not like Pedro to feel fear or panic. But both spooked him now. He was a hood who had done innumerable horrible deeds in the past—and done them with impunity. Nobody had ever come looking for him, and no one at U.S. Immigration had ever as much as batted an eyelid when he cruised back and forth across the border to carry out Chavez's orders. But this time he was afraid—probably more afraid than Allison Cox was. A U.S. agent was on his tail, and so was the father of the kids he had abducted, carrying photographic evidence linking him to the crime. He had to act—and without delay.

An envelope that the steward had passed him contained orders from Chavez on another matter, and it gave him an idea. He could kill two birds with one stone and get rid of this problem today. *Yes, today...*he mused with satisfaction. As the plane droned on toward Chiclayo airport, Pedro sat quietly in the jump seat putting together his plan.

"Easy!" he exclaimed.

The pilot turned his head at this, the first sound from Pedro in twenty minutes. Pedro was now smiling like a Cheshire cat.

"We're approaching Chiclayo," the pilot said, "getting ready to land."

"Good," Pedro replied. "The sooner the better."

As the plane bounced upon touchdown, and the narrow nylon strap dug into Allison's wrist, she winced and clenched her teeth. She slammed her free hand down on the attached wrist to steady it until the plane was solidly down on the runway.

Peter was still out cold, and that worried Allison.

The plane came to a halt away from the terminal, near two waiting vehicles—a shiny black Cadillac Escalade SUV and an aging off-white Ford sedan. Pedro reappeared in the cabin.

"He needs a doctor," Allison said. "You don't want to be responsible for his death, do you?"

Pedro seemed unperturbed. He leaned down and checked Peter's pulse. "Don't worry, he's still alive," he smirked.

"You're a bastard—do you know that?" Allison said with contempt.

"Actually, it happens to be true!" Pedro replied. "But I don't think you were referring to the legality of my birth." He chuckled at his own joke.

By then, the steward had stepped up and extracted a vicious-looking knife from his sleeve. He deftly sliced through the nylon tie that secured Peter, then roughly pulled Peter's body from the seat, and, walking backward, dragged it through the fuselage and out the front door of the plane.

Allison knew it was pointless to ask what was happening; she would find out soon enough.

The steward reappeared a couple of minutes later, straightening his white jacket. He drew out the knife again with such speed that the tip flew within an inch of Allison's nose. She gasped, and the steward found this amusing. He cut through her tie and left. She gingerly moved her sore wrist before looking up and seeing the gun. And Pedro standing there pointing it at her.

"It's time to get up now—and please don't force me to use this."

Allison rose slowly and made her way toward the exit with Pedro right behind her. She had no doubt that he would use the gun, and even a minor wound would jeopardize an escape attempt. She walked down the steps of the plane and over to the waiting cars where two other dubious-looking men stood. Peter had been thrown like a sack of grain onto the rear seat of the old sedan, and he was slumped against what looked like her suitcase. It *was* her suitcase! She recognized the labels, but she hadn't brought it with her…She looked up at Pedro in confusion.

"Just in case you needed to stay a little longer than planned!" His smile disappeared. "Now get in!"

Allison was trembling as she sat down on the front passenger seat. The steward placed a tie around both her wrists this time, binding her hands together in her lap, before walking around and getting behind the wheel. Pedro and the two other men got in the SUV and sped away. The steward started their car and followed—terrifyingly close—behind it.

The convoy sped across the tarmac. The guard at the gate in the wire fence waved them through, and they proceeded directly out onto a main road. They had landed at a small regional airport on the outskirts of Chiclayo, and if there were administrative formalities, Pedro obviously didn't need to go through them.

Allison couldn't work out where they were going. She had never been this far north in Peru before and didn't recognize any of the place names she had seen so far. All she knew was that they were heading west—that is, if the old compass stuck to the dashboard was accurate. From her recollection of the map she had consulted back at the hotel, Chiclayo was slightly inland. This meant they were bound for the coast.

After a couple of miles, they passed a sign that said it was 17 kilometers to Pimentel and that the road also led to Puerto Eten.

Puerto Eten? She had seen that name somewhere before...but where? She couldn't place it. Maybe it would come to her.

Gazing out the window, she asked the steward as nonchalantly as possible, "Where are we going?"

"Señora, you ask too many questions," he grunted in reply.

It was getting hot in the un-air conditioned car. Outside, the dry vegetation was yellow against the pink-brown landscape. *It must be in the 90s,* she thought. February was summer down here south of the Equator, and it became hotter as they traveled north. Allison was getting a headache. She wanted a glass of water but asking would be a waste of time.

Allison thought about locking her arms around the steward's neck and strangling him with her tied wrists as she had been taught in the Marines. But it wouldn't work; there was still Pedro's SUV in front of them, whose passengers would certainly notice their car careering off the road out of control. And the steward had a knife and a gun...

Something stirred behind her. She looked around and saw that Peter was slowly coming to.

"Ouch—*Ow!*" he said, touching the sore spot on the back of his head.

Peter was in a daze. He felt dreadful, with a ghastly sick and stale taste in his mouth. He didn't know where he was. And the blinding sunshine on his face added to his confusion. A familiar voice was beckoning to him, but he didn't recognize it.

"Peter? Are you all right...are you okay? Peter, can you hear me?"

No, he didn't feel okay—not at all. *Oh, God! My head!* He looked up and squinted at the blurred shapes in front of him. Eventually he recognized Allison's face; she looked pale and anxious as she peered over at him from the front seat.

"Allison…ooh!" he groaned again. "What the hell's *happening?*" Peter's voice was suddenly strident. "Where *am* I?"

A voice answered in Spanish: "Tell your friend to calm down and shut up—or else I'll put a hole in both of you." The steward waved his gun in the air above the seatback to demonstrate his point. Allison quickly summed up the situation in English.

"Peter! Don't make any foolish moves—he's got a gun, and I'm sure he'll use it. They knocked you out on the plane, and now they're taking us somewhere—I don't know where…They're the ones who took Mark and Nicolette—but we'd better stay calm—*very* calm!"

Peter began to remember what had happened. And with the recollection and the pain in his head came anger. Allison saw it boiling up inside him.

"Peter—calm down!" she said in French. "He's got a gun. We've got to stay calm—it's the only way to find out what happened to Mark and Nicolette. They took them. You've got to stay calm! Please believe me—this *is* the best we can do…"

The steward's expression remained unaltered when Allison switched from English to French. She hoped this was because he didn't understand either language, a thing that could be useful to them. Or else he was being particularly shrewd. Whatever, she thought; *we need every break we can get.*

Once Peter had completely come to his senses, it wasn't too difficult for him to overcome his urge to attack the driver; the throbbing bump on his head was sufficient reminder of his folly on board the plane. What helped as well was the package on the seat beside him. It contained his gun! It *must,* for it hadn't been opened. He looked the package over while the driver's attention was focused on the road. He had wrapped it and was certain it hadn't been tampered with since he had sent it from LAX! But why was it here in the car with them? He didn't recall seeing it at the hotel, and Allison hadn't mentioned anything about receiving it. And, with everything else he had to tell her in the short time they were at the hotel together, he had not had time to ask her about it.

He noticed the driver looking at him in the rear-view mirror. Peter met his stare and turned to look nonchalantly out the side window.

Could it be that I'm the only one who knows what's in here? Peter felt uplifted. He tried to recall if he'd left the gun loaded or had taken out the cartridges for safety. Not being able to remember dampened this fleeting optimism, as did the thought that he had packed the weapon so well that it would take several minutes to tear apart the package, open the case inside, assemble the gun, snap in the magazine, and shoot the driver. *Perhaps Allison could distract him long enough…*

Peter's thoughts were interrupted by a sudden bounce as the car ground to a halt in an unpaved area at the side of the road. The road curved sharply here, overlooking the ocean; they had pulled off onto the side nearest to it, and there was a straight drop to the water below. The only warning of this danger was a ridge of dirt and gravel along the edge, about a foot high. If not for their predicament, Peter would have found the view beautiful and awe-inspiring.

"He wants you to get out, Peter," Allison said, translating for the steward who now stood by Peter's door.

Peter obeyed, although he was hesitant to get far from the package on the seat. No sooner was he on his feet than the steward prodded him with the barrel of his pistol toward the driver's seat.

"He wants you to get behind the wheel," Allison translated again.

"Yes, I can see that," Peter answered, recoiling from the gun's muzzle.

Peter suddenly wondered whether they were going to be freed and given the old car to drive away in. He slid somewhat hopefully into the driver's seat. He saw that Pedro had joined the steward and had his own gun pointed at them. In one clean movement, the steward holstered his own gun and extracted a new white nylon tie from his pocket and snapped it expertly around Peter's left wrist and the steering wheel. He did it so swiftly that Peter had no time to protest. He tried to try to pull his hand free, but all that did was to confirm how securely he was attached. The steward walked around to the other side of the car, leaned across Allison, pulled Peter's free wrist over to Allison's tied hands and bound them all together with the same dexterity as before.

Allison and Peter exchanged horrified glances.

"What are you going to do with us?" Allison asked Pedro, her frightened voice full of contempt. "What are you going to do?"

"I see you're losing your confident air!" Pedro sneered. "Why, quite simply, you're going to take a little joyride over the edge into the sea. I wish we could have gotten to know each other better!" He laughed and slammed her door shut.

"Oh my God!" Allison said. "They're going to *kill* us! This can't be happening—"

"—and I never found Mark and Nicolette…" Peter sounded resigned. "Oh—Martine!" he suddenly shouted.

Outside, the hood had been thrown open. It blocked their view and reinforced their feeling of being trapped. In seconds, the engine sprang to life and roared to full throttle. Peter felt the accelerator pedal sag under his foot; someone had pulled the cable from inside the engine compartment and fixed it so that the engine kept turning at full power. The hood was slammed shut and the deafening roar of the engine filled the car. Peter and Allison watched, mesmerized—everything was happening too fast for it even to be unnerving. Almost immediately, the steward's arm came in through the open side window and shifted the gear lever from PARK to NEUTRAL. Then, he and the two other men pushed the car backward up the road for about twenty yards. As soon as they let go, the steward leaned inside and slapped the automatic transmission shift lever sharply into DRIVE. He barely had time to pull his arm free as the car surged forward, tires screeching…!

"God—No!" Peter cried out.

Allison screamed with terror as the car picked up speed and shot back down the road. At the curve, it left the road, flew across the ground and struck the ridge at the edge of the precipice. The impact threw Allison and Peter sharply forward, Peter into the steering wheel and Allison's forehead into the dashboard!

From up the road, Pedro and his men watched with satisfaction as the car took off, leveled out in mid-air, and then plunged nose-first toward the ocean. It seemed to take ages before it struck the waves fifty feet below, but it struck with what seemed to Pedro an especially satisfying crash. The car hesitated on the surface, and then slipped underwater like a submarine in a slow dive.

"Let's get out of here before someone comes," Pedro ordered, once the waves had closed over the roof and the car had disappeared from sight.

Nicolette could see that Mark needed reassurance. She looked at him, not daring to approach at first, as he sat curled up in the corner of their room, crying as she had never before seen him do.

The polished wood floor was wet from his tears. His little face was red and contorted. His teeth bit hard together as he stared down at his small clenched fists, white at the knuckles from frustration at his inability to end their desperate situation. He banged one fist against the other with such force that the resulting smack sounded like bones snapping.

Mark knew they were going to be moved on. Their room had been emptied of all the toys and belongings that had adorned it upon their arrival. The beds had been stripped of their sheets and blankets. All that was left were the clothes they wore. It was obvious that they would be going soon—but where? To what? The photographs that had been taken of them naked worried him. He couldn't understand why they were taken, but he felt that it was wrong.

They were helpless.

And yet, in the midst of his desperation, Mark felt Nicolette's hand lightly caressing his back, reminding him that he was not alone and that someone who loved him was nearby. He turned around and suddenly hugged her so hard that she squealed. He released his tight embrace but kept his loving arms around her as the last few teardrops left dark spots on her light-blue cotton dress.

Within a few minutes, Nicolette felt his arms relax. His body grew heavy. She bent her head back and looked at his face, half buried in her shoulder. He was asleep! She couldn't support him any longer and tried to ease him to the floor, but he was too heavy for her and he plopped down. His head was last to hit the floor, and even though it hit with an audible *bonk*, the force of the blow did not awaken the exhausted boy.

Chapter 29

▼

"She's dead!"

Chavez looked mystified. "What?" he asked in consternation, looking at Pedro's self-satisfied expression.

"*Sí*, Señor, she's *dead!* It was—"

"What do you *mean?*" interrupted Chavez before his henchman could explain.

Pedro was perplexed; he'd expected a large pat on the back for so expeditiously disposing of Allison Cox. But Chavez's strange reaction did not dampen Pedro's enthusiastic explanation. He was proud of his achievement.

"*Estás completamente loco?*" Chavez said when Pedro's revelation had sunk in. "*Have you completely lost your mind?*" Chavez repeated, raising his voice.

"But, Señor, you ordered me to…"

"I did no such a thing!"

"The letter on the plane…you told me to get rid of the Tincopa woman—"

"That meddling *teacher*—yes—but not the *U.S. envoy!* What got *into* your head?"

"I was just killing two birds with one stone…You see…the American and her friend had photos linking me to the Del Solar kids' kidnapping…I had to take them out!"

"And who was this friend of hers?" Chavez asked, mortified, his mind racing to think of a cover-up.

"I don't know, chief—" Pedro lied.

"Well, you'd better fucking well *find out!*" Chavez rose to his feet and spat the words in Pedro's face.

Pedro, who normally took no nonsense from anyone, stepped back.

Chavez turned and stared out the picture window. The view of the country-side around Chiclayo would help calm him.

"Is there *any* chance they got out alive after you left?" Chavez's question was calmly put, but he didn't turn to face Pedro.

"None, sir," Pedro replied with conviction.

"Are you absolutely sure?"

"They were tied together and the man was secured to the steering wheel," Pedro explained, exasperated. "With the speed the car was sinking—where they went down is pretty deep—there's no way they could have freed themselves in time. And the car was like a sieve and would have soon filled up with water. There's no chance they're alive."

Chavez sighed audibly. He knew the coastal road well and pictured the spot where the car had gone over.

"Pedro…you've failed me—*failed* me! I'm disappointed, and I'm *angry!* Do you understand that?"

Pedro was annoyed. He wasn't used to being dressed down; he had shown *initiative* and done Chavez a favor. It took determination to be servile and answer, *"Sí, Señor,"* and much self-control not to simply kill Chavez outright. He bit his tongue—for now.

Chavez was thinking. "You realize the U.S. government will stop at nothing to find out what has happened to this Cox woman? She was probably sent here to get me and my organization. Her disappearance will not go unnoticed. So *you* had better sort this out and make absolutely sure we come out of it lily-white. Because if I have to serve you on a platter to the Americans to save my skin, I'll do it—you'd better believe it!"

Pedro eyed Chavez with malice.

"And don't think about double-crossing me!" Chavez said.

Pedro suddenly felt fear. He moved his left arm slightly to feel that his pistol was still holstered there. He knew what befell those who went against Chavez.

"The best we can do now is make sure it looks like an accident," Chavez continued. "Get a diver to go down there and untie them—and, oh yes, place a couple of empty bottles of booze in the car…give the impression they were drunk and just went off the road. And don't forget to empty the trunk!"

The room fell silent again, Chavez mulling things over, Pedro quietly waiting.

"And as for her friend—there must be some identity papers on him," Chavez finally added. "You said you cleared the stuff from their rooms?"

"Sí, Señor," Pedro replied.

"Thank goodness at least for that! Well, what are you waiting for?" Chavez snapped. "Get to it before someone discovers the wreck!"

In the momentary calm following the deafening impact of the car hitting the ocean, Peter and Allison thought the car would float. It felt buoyant, righted itself, and the water streamed off the windshield. They saw the waves before them smacking the safety glass, but seawater was pouring in like a waterfall through Peter's open window.

The noises were confusing. Peter's ears rang from the violent crash. There was a muted banging sound from behind him, and Allison was shrieking in his ear.

"*Close the window,*" she screamed. "*CLOSE THE DAMNED WINDOW!*"

She clambered over him and started madly rolling up the window. With his left wrist bound to the steering wheel and his right hand to Allison, he could do nothing. The water was halfway up the window and spurting in around the doors, under the dashboard, through the air vents...rising about them. The car was underwater now! The daylight outside was gone, replaced by a murky green-brown mass, growing darker. They were going down...and the ties held them in.

"A knife in my pocket!—the back one!" Peter yelled. "Get the knife!"

Allison twisted and reached around but couldn't force her bound hands into the pocket. Peter arched his back and felt her pull the knife free. She clasped the blade in her teeth, pulled it out, and with both hands sawed at the hard nylon tie binding Peter's wrist to the steering wheel.

"This won't work!" she yelled. "It's not cutting—"

"It *is*—keep going!" Peter shouted in encouragement.

Suddenly, it cut through and the blade sliced into Peter's forearm. He felt nothing, not even the stinging of the saltwater in the cut. He yanked the knife from Allison's hand, hooked the blade under the ties between their wrists and, with one upward motion, jerked the blade through them.

Peter looked at Allison; the unspoken question was clear. *What do we do now?*

"Wait until the car fills up—then break out!" she shouted. Authority had returned to her voice, and Peter followed her lead.

The water was to their chests and rising steadily. The car was dropping, diving. Suddenly there was a crash from behind and the floating suitcases rammed their necks. They turned and saw the back of the rear seat move violently toward them. A pair of black-booted feet appeared, as if struggling to climb out. Peter suddenly realized that *someone in the trunk* had kicked out the back seat!

Peter clambered back, fighting his way past the suitcases, caught hold of the back of the seat and tugged savagely until he had yanked it out. He grabbed the two feet, which immediately kicked him away and then vanished into the depths of the trunk.

Then a woman appeared, her body writhing, her face contorted with fear. Water spluttered out of her mouth. She pushed and pulled herself out of the trunk with such panic that she pushed Peter under into the tangle of water, suitcases, and the women's arms and legs. The water was rising fast now, forcing out the little air that remained. The sickening sea salt was in their mouths.

Romy's long skirt twisted about her legs, but she fought to keep her face in the bubble of air trapped under the ceiling. Allison's face was there, and Peter's, thrust clear to gasp the heavenly substance.

"Out!" Allison shouted. "We've got to get out *now—!*"

The car hit bottom and settled in the soft sand. The abrupt change in motion sent the water over their heads and down their throats. Panic grew to madness as their faces touched the ceiling in search of the elusive air pocket. Only Peter and Allison found it—and it was so small that their faces were scrunched together in order to breathe.

"Get out!" gasped Allison.

"How?" appealed Peter, spluttering water.

"*Smash* the window!"

Before Allison had finished her sentence, Peter had plunged back down into the car. His ears hurting from the water pressure and his eyes blind in the dark water, he groped madly for the window crank. He found it, but it turned easily— too easily! It was not gripping the glass! *God, he needed air…!* He forced his mouth to remain shut against his lungs' instinct to draw in. The palms of his hands desperately followed the window to the top until his fingers found a space—*Yes, a narrow space!* An *inch!* He pushed down but he could get no force…Then it gave. Peter had to breathe…he had to *breathe…!*

He shot back to the ceiling, moving madly from corner to corner, desperately searching for air.

Allison pushed and shoved Romy's inert body out the window and slipped through after her. Once out, she grasped Romy around the waist and, with expert strokes, propelled herself and her burden up to the surface. As she broke through, she drew in the sweet air, and between agonizing breaths, screamed. But the woman beside her did not gasp! Allison must get her to land; she took a life-saving grip and struck out toward shore.

Down in the hellhole, Peter—trapped—was certain he was going to die. He would open his mouth—there was no other way! Dying would be better than this! He was on his back searching for an air pocket. But there was none...

All of a sudden, he inhaled seawater and air, the last tiny pocket—but it was enough, and he made a final dive for the window. But an object blocked it. He struck at it with his fists, desperately pushing it out of the car in front of him. It was the package with the gun! He grabbed it and, as he rose, hung on. *Can I make it?* His strokes became faster, less efficient. He was panicking, but he kept his vise-like grip on the package. Finally, his head burst from the surface. He inhaled and inhaled...and inhaled...pain! *Oh my God!* Automatically, he began treading water.

It took minutes to accustom his eyes to the daylight after the murky depths below. By the time he could distinguish the shoreline and clearly make out the figure on hands and knees there, he had recovered enough to swim toward it.

Dragging himself out of the water onto the sand, Peter found Allison giving mouth-to-mouth resuscitation to the woman.

Perplexed, John Vandervelt replaced the receiver. He had just called the Mira-flores Hotel and been told that Allison had already checked out. And yet she had told him when he had called yesterday that she expected to be in Lima a week. Now, less than twenty-four hours later, she was gone.

Normally, he would have been overjoyed at the prospect of her finishing her business early and returning to Washington. Having been with her again, he real-ized how lost he felt without her.

She had left no forwarding address. Her sudden departure was news even to the local U.S. embassy, which was her contact point. She should have reported in before leaving; it was standard procedure for U.S. government personnel travel-ing in a foreign country. And it was unlike Allison to go it alone when on official business.

The embassy promised to check into her whereabouts but admitted that U.S. official visitors often left without notice when they completed their business early. But John was still worried...

Chapter 30

▼

Romy regained consciousness to find herself lying on her side on sand and violently coughing up seawater. Her lungs felt as if they had collapsed—she simply couldn't draw breath. A sudden blow on the back jolted her and her lungs sucked air again. She groaned, heaved herself up to her knees and, bleary-eyed, looked around. The surf was only a few yards away, and beneath her was the dark and stony sand. The beach was narrow and stretched just a few feet back to the foot of a crumbling sandy rock face that rose steeply behind her.

At her side was a woman with a friendly face. The woman was smiling.

"Are you okay?" Allison asked in Spanish.

Slowly nodding, Romy let out a faint *"Sí."* Her throat hurt terribly. "I think so," she added uncertainly.

It all started to come back to her: the car, the trunk, the water…and the chili!

"They tried to *kill* me!" she blurted out. "The murderers! And they're going to kill the children too…" She broke down and sobbed uncontrollably. "And I can't do anything to stop them…the murderers! Oh! Miguel! Alicia!"

Peter dropped to his knees beside them. He let go of the wet parcel and, in answer to Allison's concerned look, blew out an exhausted, "I'm okay…how about her?"

"I think she'll be fine—at least she's breathing."

"Do we know who she is?"

"No. All she's said is something about 'murderers'—and she mentioned 'children' and a couple of names—"

"Are you American?" Romy asked in English, looking from one to the other.

"I'm American," Allison answered, pleased that the woman spoke English. "My name's Allison. And this is Peter; he's Swiss. Who are you?"

Before answering, Romy looked at them both again, especially Peter, searching for something she couldn't put her finger on. "Romy Tincopa," she finally replied. "I'm from Argentina, but that does not matter…"

The trio fell silent, too exhausted to digest information about one another. They surveyed their surroundings and absorbed the little remaining warmth of the late-afternoon sun. The sun was far in the west. This would be a cold, wet evening.

After a while, Allison asked, "Who tried to kill you?…and why?"

Romy grunted, then said, "It's a complicated story. I don't know exactly who did it—probably Señora Del Solar or Chavez—influential people in Peru—but it's certainly because I went to the police about the children that—"

"Which children?" Peter interrupted.

"Miguel and Alicia," Romy answered, taken aback by his sudden interest. "How can I explain this? You see, they have two children that they adopted, and they're going to send them off somewhere horrible, and I tried to stop it! But it's all lost now! *Mi Dios!*"

Peter was about to charge in with another question when Allison motioned for him to stop.

"Tell us more about these children," Allison calmly asked. "Why are they sending them off to this horrible place—where is it?"

Romy gazed at Allison dubiously. She no longer knew whom she could trust. Allison sensed what she was thinking.

"We're here looking for two children—this man's children," Allison said, laying her hand on Peter's shoulder. "And someone tried to kill us as well. None of us was meant to escape from that car." She looked out to sea. "The man who pushed the car over the precipice kidnapped the children and I think he tried to kill us because we know too much…"

Romy stared at Peter: "*Madre de Dios!* You're Miguel and Alicia's father! I see it in your eyes—they're just like theirs." *This* was what she had seen in Peter when she had first looked at him on the beach. "Oh! Thank the *Lord…!*"

Peter looked at her, stunned.

Romy suddenly started to get up. "We've got to get there quickly—" she said.

"Wait!" Allison cried, grabbing Romy by the arm. "Let's get everything clear—you *know* where Peter's children are? But their names are not Miguel and Alicia. What do they look like?"

Romy described them, first physically and then their mannerisms. She guessed that their ages were five and eight. A light came on in Peter's eyes.

"Does the boy have a small round mark on his forehead—over his right eye?" Peter asked excitedly. "It's about this size," he added, showing Romy a space between his thumb and forefinger. "A scar from chicken pox."

"Yes, he does!" Romy answered excitedly.

Peter extracted from his wet wallet a photograph of his children. His fingers were shaking. "Is this them?" he asked, petrified that the answer might be "no."

"*Sí—Sí!*" Romy replied joyfully. "It's them! Yes, it's them for sure!"

"Oh my God! Let's go! Where are they?" Peter shouted, getting to his feet. "God, they're alive!" he yelled, holding out his arms to the sky.

"Wait!" Allison shouted, and tried to think clearly. "Let's not blow this." She placed a reassuring hand on Romy's arm. "Romy? You must explain to us everything you know, as calmly as you can and in as much detail as possible—and then we'll decide on our next step. Let's not lose sight of the fact that we're up against hardened criminals who'll stop at nothing."

"But she said they're going to send them away!" Peter cried.

"Yes," Allison agreed. "But first we've got to find out where they *are*. While these thugs think we're dead, they'll feel less urgency to move them. For once, the element of surprise is on our side. We can't blow this—we won't get a second chance! Now," Allison said, turning her attention back to Romy, "tell us everything from start to finish, and don't leave out any details—however minor."

In fierce agitation and near panic, Peter listened as Romy told them everything she knew—from the time she started as their tutor through to her visit to the local police. And of the children's attempted escape by sea.

Peter wept with pride at the courage and audacity of his children.

"Yes!" Allison said when she learned that John's lead had been correct. Romy omitted the punishment episode—this father didn't need to hear about that.

Peter told Romy the children's real background.

"I knew it!" Romy uttered.

"So, how do we get to this place—*Pimentel?*" Allison asked, getting down to the business at hand.

"I don't know. Where are we now?" Romy replied.

"Good question!" Allison said. She thought back to the road sign she had seen on their way to the coast. "Perhaps," she said carefully, "we're not too far away. I saw Pimentel on a road sign on our way here—with a place called 'Puerto Eten'?"

"We must be somewhere along the coast south of Pimentel," Romy said. "But did you go through Puerto Eten?"

"No," Allison said.

"Then, we can't be far away," Romy said, encouraged. "We'd better start walking; it'll soon be dusk."

Allison turned to Peter. He was busy tearing apart the wet package that he'd brought ashore. "What are you doing?" she said, "What is that thing?"

"My gun," Peter replied. "We're going to need it! Nobody will get in my way this time."

He pulled the black weapon out of the case, opened the action, closed it, pulled the trigger, and the gun let out a metallic *click!* "Good!" he said. He checked the munitions clip, saw it was full and slammed it into place. He put the extra cartridges into his side pockets, and stuffed bank notes in other pockets wherever he found space.

Romy looked at him aghast; she had never seen such a daunting weapon before, or laid eyes on so much money!

The way Peter was handling the weapon made Allison uneasy; she thought of the murdered detective and his wife in Los Angeles. Suddenly Peter appeared surprisingly capable of violence. Then she remembered the people they were going to be dealing with. Peter's gun gave them the means to protect themselves—and possibly the means to rescue the children. And after that? How would they get away once they got the children? Here they were in a foreign country, with no identification papers, being pursued by gangsters—. She stopped. *One step at a time*, she resolved. But the problem remained on her mind.

Peter stood before them, the gun slung over his shoulder, looking like a resistance fighter posing for a photograph. "I'm ready when you are!" he said.

It was the first time in ages that Allison had seen Peter so eager and determined.

"You can't go like that!" she said. "We'd be picked up immediately. We've got to cover that gun up somehow."

"Here!" Romy said, pulling up the bottom of her long skirt and wriggling out of a petticoat. "This should do!"

Peter wrapped it around the gun so the weapon appeared to be only a harmless bundle.

"Now, let's get going," Allison ordered. "We can get up the cliff over there," she pointed. "There's a trail to the top."

It was a difficult climb, especially for Romy, still weak from her near-drowning. It took them a good half hour to make the ascent.

When they reached the top, Allison looked at her watch. It was nearly six o'clock. "This way?" she asked, pointing north.

"Yes…" said Romy, out of breath.

"Well, we'd better start walking," Allison said.

"Perhaps we could catch a truck or something?" Romy ventured.

"Catch a *truck?*" Peter repeated incredulously.

"I can't walk far—certainly not to Pimentel!" Romy said. "And trucks aren't expensive."

Allison remembered that in remote areas in Peru, travelers used passing trucks as buses. *And in our case,* she thought, *far less conspicuous than traveling on foot.* "Good idea! We'll hail the next one that comes by. But let's not hang around here; Pedro and his friends may come back to gloat over their handiwork."

Only one car came by as they walked. They didn't even hear it until it was already upon them, and it sped past without even slowing down. A full twenty minutes had passed when the distinctive slow groan of an engine heartened them. All three turned and waved their arms until the truck slowed and ground to a stop.

"Where you want to go?" the driver asked in heavily accented Spanish that only Romy understood. Romy did all the talking. The weather-beaten man looked Andean.

"Pimentel," Romy answered. "How much will it cost?"

The driver surveyed them curiously. They were wet but well dressed; their desperate appearance emboldened him. "Fifty dollars," he said without flinching.

Exorbitant! Romy looked to Allison for a decision.

"It's okay," she answered, also realizing that they were being overcharged. But it was pointless wasting time haggling. "But tell him we're in a hurry!"

When Romy relayed the message, a broad smile crept across the driver's tanned face, and he motioned them to climb into the back of the truck.

They would be out in the open, but at least they would not have to enter into conversation with the driver. Peter was the last one to climb up and as he did, the driver patted him on the shoulder and handed him a half-empty bottle. *Chica de Jora*, according to Romy, a spirit distilled from corn—probably homemade, she added. They concluded that either the driver felt guilty about overcharging them, or, more likely, he had determined from their appearance that they needed it.

"I don't care what it is," Allison observed. "I need a drink!" She raised the dirty bottle to her lips, took a mouthful, swished it around to get rid of the salty taste still in her mouth, and then let it trickle down her throat. She squinted and stifled a cough—it was *strong*—then sighed in contentment, and passed the bottle to Romy. "It's not bad," she said, "and it'll do you good."

Romy tentatively took the bottle to her lips. Unaccustomed to alcohol, she convulsed as she swallowed, but soon the warmth spread like a series of explosions throughout her body. "Mmm…" she murmured, then coughed again and, smiling and looking embarrassed, passed the bottle to Peter. Unhesitatingly, he chugged a large mouthful without a murmur and sat back, seemingly in a trance. They no longer felt damp or cold.

They arrived at the outskirts of Pimentel shortly before seven. Although the streets were empty, before reaching the center of town they jumped out and gave the truck driver back his nearly empty bottle, and he, unconcerned, drove off.

Romy led the way down through several streets to the port and finally onto the stony beach, where they stopped below the old rusting ironwork jetty. Romy pointed out the house.

Peter's eyes followed Romy's gaze up beyond the sands and a broad field spotted with pampas grass to the top of a hill, where sat a forbidding house that overlooked the ocean.

"That," she said quietly, "is the children's prison."

Peter was beside himself. "So that's where they've been all this time—I'll kill those people." He wanted to head straight for the house; he couldn't handle the anguish of waiting. Was he, after so long, finally in sight of his dearly loved children? Perhaps he would spot them at a window—or they might catch sight of him and realize their father loved them so much that he had crossed the world to find them.

Or is this the end of a false trail? Peter's mood suddenly changed. After coming this far, if he found that the children had already been moved on to some unknown destination it would break his spirit. He would have little strength left after this; perhaps he would be better joining Martine in the hospital and living drugged out of his senses…But Allison's voice broke into his thoughts.

"You're sure they're still here?" she asked Romy.

"No," she said. "I can't be completely sure, especially after my trip to the police station. They were to be moved only on Wednesday—day after tomorrow. But let's not delay. The children need you," Romy added, looking at Peter.

"And the house is usually most calm after about nine, once everyone has eaten?"

"Yes, the servants that don't live in go home, and the others are cleaning up in the scullery."

"And Don Gonzalo and his wife?"

"They go their separate ways after the pretense of an intimate dinner," Romy explained. "He retires to his study, and she goes to her bedroom, and one rarely sees much of them around the house after that…And it's possible that Don Gonzalo isn't even here; he was away in Lima when I, um…left."

"Maybe we should wait?" Allison suggested.

"No! We've got to go now," Peter broke in. "I haven't come all this way to sit and let them slip away under our noses."

"I understand," Allison said calmly. "But if we attack the house prematurely and fail…no, we wait until dark—which should be about what time, Romy?"

"Around eight-thirty," she said.

"Less than an hour…Peter?"

Peter was leaning against a rusty strut of the jetty, emptily staring up at the house.

"You've got to understand," Allison said, "it would be foolhardy to act before then. We need the cover of darkness—especially to get away afterward…"

Without acknowledging Allison, Peter turned and hit the jetty with the base of his fist in frustration.

"I want to free Mark and Nicolette as much as you do, Peter—or I wouldn't be here," Allison said. "And we can use the time to plan how to get away once we've got the children. I don't suppose you've thought about that, have you?"

Allison looked straight at him. She was trying to divert his thoughts, to get him focused on that stage of the operation.

"I don't know," Peter replied. "Get to Lima…catch a flight home…"

"Without passports? No one will be looking for us? Once we grab the children, they'll know we're alive and won't stand back and wave us through! No, we've got to have some idea where to bolt to when we're through at the house—we won't have the luxury then to argue and decide."

"Well, what ideas have *you* got, Allison?" Peter asked pointedly.

"Absolutely none…but if we start thinking, *maybe* something'll come to us!"

Romy had been listening in silence. "How about the attack on the house—how are we going to do that?" she asked.

"I've already thought about that," Allison said, "and this is how I suggest we go about it." She quickly outlined her plan. Romy added details about the layout, and Peter suggested minor alterations to Allison's plan. He admitted to himself that it was a better plan than he would have concocted. This all suddenly seemed doable. Peter put aside his doubts and came back to the post-rescue escape plan.

"Okay, once we're through with the house, couldn't we hijack a car and drive to the nearest embassy and get protection there?"

Allison nodded. "Yeah, I thought about that too, Peter," she said. "It's a good idea, but I doubt we'd make it that far—the embassies are all in Lima. Also, we'd never get out afterward. The Peruvians would block it—"

"But not the *U.S.* embassy," Romy said, "...they wouldn't dare, not with all the aid your government gives them."

"True, but..." Allison looked at Peter intently. "They wouldn't," she hesitated, "be able to help a *non*-American..." What Allison feared, but didn't want to say in front of Romy or spell out for Peter, was that Peter, a suspected felon, would be deported to the States and held there. "No, we've got to think of somewhere else to go."

They fell silent and waited for the sun to set. That they were tired to the bone and hadn't eaten in many hours was nothing to them; having escaped death and being now so close to the children, they had to go on.

It was past eight before Pedro found a diver who could be trusted—a man dragged out of a bar in Puerto Eten and sobered up. It annoyed Pedro to hang around while strong, bitter coffee was poured into the diver's reluctant mouth. There remained absolutely no doubt in Pedro's mind that everyone had perished in the sunken car; but he was impatient to have it confirmed once and for all. He must satisfy that *stupid* Chavez!

Once sober, the diver protested. "Can't it wait 'til morning?" he asked, his words still slurred.

"No! Get him into the car!" Pedro ordered.

Pedro's men bundled him and his diving gear into the back of the Escalade. The man pulled on his black wetsuit with great difficulty in the confined space of the SUV as it jolted along on the coast road.

The moon, nearly full, aided their climb down to the beach now that night had fallen. The diver put on his fins and air tank and waded out into the shining surf. He swam just below the surface until he reached the place where Pedro said the car had gone down, and then he switched on his powerful dive light and propelled himself to the ocean floor. The depths were dark and cloudy with churned sand, and he could see nothing except the beam of his light. He swore to himself as he methodically combed the bottom.

It seemed to him that he had searched the seabed forever. He checked his pressure gauge to see how much longer before his air supply was gone. Only a few minutes and he must go up and change tanks. He continued his pointless search.

"Oh!" he blurted, nearly spitting out his mouthpiece. He had but an instant to pull himself up to avoid slamming headfirst into the car. He hated working at night, especially on his own. He found everything eerie and likened it to walking through a haunted house. And the car looked particularly ghostly...and knowing what he would find inside made it worse.

He hesitated before beaming his light in, and he swallowed hard—as much as he could underwater. Finally he mustered the courage to look. He shivered when at first he found no bodies. He instinctively turned his head to look behind him, expecting a body to drift up. Momentarily satisfied that none were lurking, he looked back inside through the open window and scrutinized every nook and cranny—there was no one there; just a couple of suitcases. Something shone clear white as his flashlight beam passed over it—a broken nylon tie snagged in a crack in the vinyl cover of the steering wheel. He pulled it free, examined it and tucked it into the net bag attached to his waist. He had been told to cut these off the bodies, but someone had got there first. He looked around again, pulled open the door and hauled himself all the way into the car. There was definitely no one in there. He was to check on the body in the trunk as well. But the back of the rear seat was out, and he saw that there was no body in the trunk either. *Pedro will not be happy...*He wondered how to break the bad news to him. He checked his watch again; it was time to surface.

Pedro, however, was already prepared. While the diver was below, one of Pedro's men had gone to the foot of the bluff to relieve himself and had discovered the remains of the torn-open package behind some rocks. A one hundred dollar bill fluttering in the night breeze had given its position away. Pedro looked at the case. What had it held? He remembered it in the back of the car with the other belongings, and now here it was on the beach! Perhaps it had been ejected from the car during its fall, and its contents had been rifled by a beach bum. But as the diver removed his dripping goggles, the expression on the diver's face said that something was wrong—*terribly* wrong.

"How did they get out? How the fucking hell did they get out?" was all Pedro could say as he paced back and forth staring at the cut nylon tie in his fingers.

His men held back, waiting for Pedro to calm down.

Christ, I'm in deep shit! he said to himself. *Unless...Of course!* That's *where they would go!* He smiled and his eyes flashed wickedly.

Chapter 31

▼

Allison stood in the phone booth, crestfallen. She had taken a risk walking to the center of Pimentel to try to call John Vandervelt in Washington and seek his advice. The problem was, she could recall the number of her telephone credit card to make the call, but she couldn't remember John's number. It was in her cell phone, and that was in the sunken car. She had tried countless variations of what she thought was his number but none of them patched her through to John.

Exasperated and annoyed, Allison slammed down the receiver a final time. Suddenly, she thought about her two boys, and had the urge to call them. She might never hear their voices again; she did at least know her own telephone number.

Allison quickly calculated the time difference. It was past two in the morning in Trélex, and the boys would be at home. She dialed the number, and a sleepy voice she recognized as Steve's answered.

"Who is it?" He sounded annoyed.

"It's me, hon—did I wake you? Sorry but—"

"Well, *duh*, Mom. It's the middle of the night!"

Allison tried to sound normal, but small talk was all she could manage. "What's happening back there? How's school?"

Steve thought his mother was crazy calling at that hour just to see how things were going at school! But he dutifully ran through whatever he could remember. "Brian's dad bought him a 2,000 dollar laptop for school…We went with Mike and his parents to a jazz concert in Montreux…Mrs. Hottinger's expecting a baby—they're in the Bahamas now on vacation…Oh yeah, the math teacher was kicked out of the International School for smoking pot!"

"Where did you say the Hottingers are?" Allison interrupted. "The Bahamas?"
"The Bahamas…Yeah…you know, in the Caribbean—"
"Did Bruno—Mr. Hottinger fly them there?" she asked breathlessly. An idea was forming in her head.

"I suppose so, Mom…He's a pilot isn't he? But don't worry about us; his old mother's staying at their place looking after Irène and keeping an eye on us too. It's good to hear from you, Mom…but it's the middle of the night. When'ya coming home?"

Allison paused. She felt her throat contract. "Soon…I hope," she answered. She was unsure if she would ever get back. "Mr. Hottinger didn't leave you his number in the Bahamas by any chance?"

"Sure did…We got it somewhere…But do you want it now?" Steve asked.

"Yes—urgently—and I can't stay on this phone much longer…" Allison tried not to sound desperate. "Please go and get it for me now—I'll wait…"

An eternity passed before Allison heard her son pick the receiver up again. "I found it, Mom!" He raced through the number, and she asked him to repeat it slowly. He did. Allison tried to memorize it; she didn't have any way to write it down. Finally, an idea struck her. She tore out a wad of pages from the old, already partially dismembered telephone book in the booth. As her son repeated the number a final time, clearly irritated, Allison arranged the page numbers in the same order. She had it. She thanked him, said, "Love you!" and hung up.

She dialed the number and got through to the Nassau Beach Hotel. But Bruno was not in his room. She left a message, consulting her watch carefully, and prayed he would return soon and wait for her next call.

Leaving the message gave her another idea. She called the night-duty number of the Mission in Geneva and left a long voicemail to be forwarded to John Vandervelt in Washington. As succinctly as she could, she told him about Chavez, Pedro, Peter and locating his kids, and finally about the very real danger that she might not return. When she was done, she felt dispirited and exhausted.

The sunset was fading fast behind the old jetty when Allison returned to where she had left Peter and Romy. She was relieved to see that Peter was still sitting on the sea-washed tree trunk and had not launched a solo attack on the house.

Peter and Romy saw her coming and were relieved; they had begun to worry.

Allison didn't say anything about calling Bruno in the Bahamas—the idea seemed too far-fetched. She only shared with them her disappointment at not reaching John, whom she described obliquely as "a friend who might be able to help us."

"It's time to move on the house," she said. It was now eight-forty PM.

Peter motioned to Allison that he wanted a word with her in private. He took her to the water's edge and stood looking out at the ocean and listening to the soothing breaking of the waves. "Allison..." he said. "Allison, I want you to promise me something."

"If I can," she replied.

"I've been thinking while you were gone...It's this." He took a deep breath. "If—if we don't get them back—if we fail—I want you to promise me you'll kill them—"

"*What!*" Allison exclaimed. "Your *children?* You—"

"Listen, Allison. I haven't gone out of my mind," Peter insisted. "But if we can't rescue Mark and Nicolette, then they'd be better off dead—I *want* them back alive. But—for me, for Martine, and for them, it will be better for them to die than to enter the hell of a...well, you know."

Allison didn't know how to answer. Peter was not desperate but very matter-of-fact—and deadly serious.

"If I can't get them out of these bastards' hands, I'm going to kill them—be sure of that," he insisted. "All I want from you, Allison, is that if I fail—if I am unable for any reason to do it, you'll promise to put them out of their misery for me."

Allison's throat went dry. "I—I can't think about doing such a thing, Peter!" she uttered. "Look, we'd better make a move now; it won't come to that—"

"But if it *does*," Peter insisted, taking hold of her arm, "I need your promise as a friend that you'll back me up—think of the children, Mark and Nicolette—what if it were your sons? You'd do it then!"

Allison turned away. It was her turn to stare at the waves. She looked at her watch; it was getting late. "Okay," she sighed. "I'll get them out of their ordeal—one way or another," she added cryptically. "Now, let's get moving and try to get them out alive."

They walked in silence up to the house along the path that—though unknown to them—was the very one Mark and Nicolette had used in their foiled escape attempt two weeks ago.

Pedro scrambled up the cliff cursing. His cell phone hadn't worked down on the beach but it would now that he was back up on the road. He auto-dialed Don Gonzalo's number again. After a few bleeps and clicks he heard a busy signal! "They're on the fucking line! Stupid fools!"

He swore again and ran to the SUV, impatiently beckoning his men to follow. They were standing out of breath at the top of the cliff. They got in without any thought for the diver they'd left on the beach collecting his equipment. The doors slammed, the wheels spun in the dirt, and the Escalade raced off down the road.

Between repeated urgings to the driver to go faster, Pedro kept redialing the number. It was always busy. "Probably that Del Solar bitch chatting to her socialite friends!" he said under his breath.

"*Step* on it, damn you!" Pedro barked.

The back door was locked. Romy rang the buzzer and waited nervously. She was shaking all over. The palms of her hands were sweating, and she felt beads of perspiration forming on her forehead. She wanted to turn and run, but she couldn't. Her worst fear was facing Señora Del Solar; but the señora never deigned to answer the back door in person. Nobody came, and, after a few minutes standing, waiting, Romy feared the worst: the children had already gone and no one was left; then the door opened—"

"Oh! Señorita Tincopa!" The voice sounded surprised, but pleased. It was Carmen, the part-time evening maid—a nice girl who wouldn't have suspected anything bad of anyone. "Come in—are you coming back now? We were told you'd left."

Romy thought quickly; there would be less argument and suspicion if she agreed. "No…I just had to come back to get something." The maid looked puzzled. Romy didn't know that her things had already all been cleared from the house. "It won't take long," Romy added, feigning nonchalance. "Are the master and mistress in?"

"The master's out, but she's in—in the study—on the phone for ages!"

Romy glanced toward the kitchen; she could see that Carmen had been in the middle of cleaning up the dinner things. No one else was there. Romy turned and motioned to Peter and Allison, who emerged from the shadows and came in.

"These are friends of mine who've come to help," Romy explained in answer to the concerned look on Carmen's face. "Oh! Are the children in their room? I want to say hello to them…"

"I suppose so…but they must be asleep by now. I must finish cleaning up," Carmen said, and she returned to the kitchen.

"Thanks," Romy said kindly. "They are still *here!*" she whispered. With Peter and Allison in tow, she proceeded to the center of the house.

"What about the girl?" Allison asked in a whisper.

"She knows not to meddle," Romy said confidently. "She values her job."

In the main hall, Peter cast aside the cloth that covered his gun and readied himself to use it. "Up there?" he asked Romy eagerly.

She nodded, and Peter pushed brusquely past the two women and headed for the staircase.

Apprehensively, Allison and Romy watched Peter sprint up the main stairs two at a time.

He quickly reached the landing. "Where are the other stairs? Which way?" he whispered impatiently down to them.

"To the left!" Romy pointed and hurried upstairs after him.

Allison hesitated, surveying the layout of the house from the entrance hall. Someone was talking—a woman?—in one of the adjacent rooms. But all the doors giving on to the hall were closed and she couldn't judge which room it was. She strained to listen. Then, satisfied that no one had been alerted to their presence, she quietly dashed up the main staircase after the others.

But Señora Del Solar had heard the noise. She politely ended her conversation, and hung up the phone. She got up from the desk and opened the door to the hall. Behind her, the phone rang. Its shrill tones arrested her, and she turned back to answer.

Allison, who had barely disappeared from view in the upstairs hall, also heard the door open and the ringing. She pressed on up the second staircase.

Señora Del Solar picked up the receiver. Pedro was shouting at her, telling her to *Shut up and listen!* She thought, *What impudence!* and nearly hung up on him. *But the urgency in his voice!* she thought.

Seconds passed; she said quietly, "I think they're here already. You'd better get here quickly."

She put down the phone carefully and opened the top right-hand drawer of her husband's desk. Searching toward the back, she felt the cold metal, grasped the revolver, and pulled it out. She checked to see that it was loaded, and retraced her steps to the study door. Señora Del Solar crossed the hall and quietly started up the stairs.

On the top floor, Peter found the door to the children's room locked. Romy looked where the key usually hung, but the hook was empty. Peter immediately threw his shoulder against the door, but the lock held. Peter raised his assault rifle and with clenched teeth repeatedly brought the butt down onto the doorknob. The noise reverberated through the house until the brass doorknob clattered to the floor. The door still held. Peter turned his fury onto the wood around the lock, which crunched and split as he attacked it with frantic blows. He dared not shoot through the lock and risk hitting the children, if they were inside…

"Hurry!" Allison said. "They *must* know we're up here!" To her relief, at that moment, Peter burst through the door.

"They're at the house," Pedro said to the three men with him in the speeding Escalade. "If you bungle this one like you did the car over the cliff…you know what Chavez'll do to you! He wants them all dead—no trace. Is that clear?" Pedro had raised his voice to a shout. The men nodded. "How long?" Pedro demanded.

"Fifteen—maybe even ten minutes, boss," the driver replied.

"Make it five!" Pedro barked. He tapped another number into his cell phone and waited.

"Gimme Rodriguez—quick! This is urgent! Tell him it's Pedro."

Pedro tapped his fingers impatiently. "Where the fuck *is* he?" he said under his breath as they raced on and the phone remained silent.

"Ah, my friend Pedro…" the police lieutenant said at last. "What a pleasure—"

Pedro cut off Rodriguez's fawning voice. "Listen, you slimy son of a bitch—listen carefully! There's a raid going on at Don Gonzalo's house—a man and two women—they're trying to kidnap their kids. Get down there with as many men as you have and block off the town—"

"You mean the whole of Pimentel?" Rodriguez said incredulously.

"Yes—the whole fucking town! These are international agents—I'm dealing with them—got that? All you have to do is make sure nobody gets out. I'm on my way to the house now."

"But…" The policeman hesitated, "I have to clear such a deployment with—"

"No fucking buts about it! Get your ass down there now! We pay you, and don't you forget it! And I want complete discretion—*entiendes,* discretion! Just put a barrier around the town and leave the rest to me. Is that clear?" Pedro shouted into the phone.

"*Sí,* Señor Pedro," the man said. "*Sí, Señor!* I'll get some men out there now."

Pedro hung up without another word; Rodriguez would do his bidding. He huffed impatiently, and the tires squealed as the Escalade devoured the winding country road.

C h a p t e r   32

▼

Peter dropped his gun with a loud clatter on the bedroom's polished wood floor. Allison thought perhaps someone had forced him to drop it and that everything was going wrong.

But Peter fell to his knees, stretched out his arms, and, in a flash, a little girl ran to him and Peter's arms engulfed her. When Allison saw this and recognized the delicate form of Peter's daughter Nicolette, a wave of relief ran through her. "Oh…" Allison uttered, "we *found* her!"

Peter looked up. There was Mark looking incredulous, not knowing what to do. Peter unfurled one arm, stretched forward, grasped Mark and pulled him to his chest.

Allison heard the choking sobs of joy that prevented Peter from pronouncing a single word. The children were weeping!

"Papi…Papi…"

Then—*CRACK!*

Allison jumped and Romy screamed. Allison saw Peter fall and roll onto the floor clutching his stomach, and she saw a small red patch on the back of his shirt.

"Oh *no!*"

Allison turned to see a woman standing at the end of the hall aiming a revolver at them.

"Duck!" she shouted. Marine training made her next move instinctive. In a single motion, she pushed Romy aside and dived toward Peter's gun. Grabbing the assault rifle, she spun on her back, righted herself, and took aim. The barrel erupted and the whole gun shook, the butt stabbing Allison in the shoulder as a stream of bullets tore down the hall and smashed into Señora Del Solar.

No one dared move. Nicolette broke the silence. "*Papi?*" she screamed, leaning over her father's body. Mark moved away from his father. Allison got to her knees and examined Peter while Romy stood over them, stunned. Allison found his pulse. Peter moved. "*Siech...!*" he said, his voice full of pain.

Suddenly, another shot pierced the silence. Allison was on her feet in a flash, assault rifle in hand, her finger on the trigger. But the lamentable sight she saw was not what she expected. Mark was standing over the body of Señora Del Solar with the woman's revolver in hand; he was poised to pump a second round into her head.

"*No! Stop!*" Allison screamed. But it was too late. Mark fired again and another bullet entered her skull, splashing blood onto his arms and face. Allison leapt forward, grabbed the gun away from the boy, and pulled him aside. Mark's cold expression shocked her. She dreaded to think what the woman on the floor must have done to inject such hatred into an eight-year-old boy.

Allison gazed down at her. If she hadn't been dead before, she certainly was now. Allison tucked the revolver in her belt and led Mark by the hand back to where his father lay. Peter was sitting up now, clutching his stomach in obvious pain.

Romy was tearing a clean sheet into bandages. The bullet had hit Peter in the back and exited below his ribs.

A sudden fear came over Allison. "Is Nicolette okay?" Nicolette had been hugging her father. How was it possible the bullet hadn't hit her? Allison quickly examined her and found a slight scratch on the outer side of the girl's right thigh. The bullet had grazed her—nothing more—and Nicolette, concerned only with her father, seemed totally unaware of it. *God, these are some kids!* Allison said to herself. But they were wasting time...

"We've got to get out of here—fast!" Allison cried. "Peter? Can you walk?"

He nodded, biting his lower lip in pain.

"And you two," Allison said in French to Mark and Nicolette, "stick close— we're taking you away from here." But she didn't need to worry; neither child would be pried from their father's side.

While Romy bandaged Peter's wounds, Allison, assault rifle in hand, walked to the top of the stairs to check that no one else was on the way up. She then returned to help Romy get Peter to his feet and down the stairs. In the main entrance hall, they spied Carmen, hiding in the passageway and looking terrified.

"Don't worry!" Romy shouted. "Nobody's going to harm you—"

"Who else is in the house?" Allison said to the maid. The maid opened her mouth but no sound came out. "Are you the only one? Tell me?" Allison's voice was commanding. The maid nodded.

"Good—at last a break in this god-awful mess!"

Nine o'clock in the evening and Pedro wants Pimentel surrounded—he must be out of his mind! Rodriguez complained to himself. "Upstart!" the police lieutenant said aloud.

Except for the man on the desk, Rodriguez was the only one on duty. Where was he going to find enough men to put a blockade around Pimentel? He didn't even have enough cars to put one across every street leading out of the town. *Dammit!*

"But I've got to do something," Rodriguez mused. He knew only too well the consequences of failing to meet one of Pedro's demands. He should, of course, get the chief's okay for such a deployment. But what reason could he give without saying he was in the pay of Chavez? *The whole operation will be over in a couple of hours, probably, and by morning I'll just explain it away as a surprise exercise.* Pleased by his sudden ingenuity, Rodriguez picked up the phone and dialed the first number on a list of home telephone numbers hanging on the wall. "Hey! Marcelo, *qué tal? Bien.* Look—I need you on duty right away!"

"What, now?" the bewildered policeman replied. He had already taken off his uniform and was just sitting down to his evening meal.

"Yes, right away! We've got to block the main roads out of Pimentel to stop some international terrorists escaping from the town—this is important stuff—"

"But…" protested the policeman, trying to think up a good excuse not to go back to work. "…I live out north and I haven't got a police car…it would take me ages to get back and pick one up…"

"Exactly," Rodriguez agreed. "That is why you should go straight to Pimentel in your own car to save time, and, as you're on that side of town, place yourself across the main road to Piura, and stop anyone suspicious. You'll be fine with your uniform on. But it's imperative that you get out there pronto!" Rodriguez placed his finger on the telephone hook to cut off the line and any further protest, glanced at the list on the wall for the next number, and then released the hook. Without wasting a second, he dialed…

Finally, Pedro was within sight of Pimentel. Wondering what was going on, he called the house again and waited impatiently while the phone rang and rang…Pedro was worried—

"*Sí...*" a woman's voice said. But Pedro didn't answer it immediately. It didn't sound like Lucia's. He had heard that voice somewhere before. Could it be one of the servants? No! It was slightly accented...Allison Cox's voice! A smile crept over his face.

"Hello Allison," he said simply. "I have to admire you...escaping from that car and making your way there...all without my assistance." Pedro spoke slowly as his car sped on toward the house. He would fascinate her with his charm and pin her down until he arrived—

"Go to hell Pedro!" Allison said, and slammed down the phone.

Pedro scowled as the line went dead.

Chapter 33

▼

Renée Hottinger pushed the hotel bedroom door open with her back because her arms were full of Bahamian straw bags and other souvenirs she had bought on Bay Street to take back to Geneva. Once she had cleared the open door, she kicked it closed behind her and dumped her purchases on the bed.

Luckily we're going back on a private plane, she mused. *We could never take all this on a regular flight!* She was so busy admiring her huge pile of purchases, she hardly noticed the red message light blinking on the bedside phone.

Renée didn't like telephone messages; they were always for Bruno anyway, usually from the businessmen he had flown out here to the Bahamas. She made a mental note to tell Bruno about it. She had left him in the hotel's business center sending a fax and would meet him in a few minutes in the restaurant for a leisurely evening meal.

Renée went into the bathroom to freshen up. She wanted to look nice for Bruno, and took a bit of time arranging her hair and make-up. Then she realized she was taking too long; it was rare that she could spend all this time with her husband, and she didn't want to keep him waiting. "Hmm…that'll have to do," she said, looking at her reflection and patting her hair one more time. She hurried out and down the hall straight into a waiting elevator.

No sooner had the bedroom door banged shut than a shrill ringing joined the blinking light on the bedside phone.

Allison's heart sank as she listened to the phone ringing unanswered 2,000 miles away. She had just hung up on Pedro, realizing with horror that he was coming after them. The operator at the Nassau Beach hotel finally came back on the line and said, "They're not in—I'll connect you to voicemail."

"Shit!" Allison swore again and slammed down the phone. She was stressed and afraid. Her whole body was shaking. *Get a grip!* Allison admonished herself.

They had to get out of this house and away from here—but to *where?*

As she was leaving the study, something caught her eye—a pink cell phone in its charger on a side-table. It gave her an idea and a glimmer of hope. She snatched it up, sending the base unit tumbling to the floor. She also grabbed a pen and a notepad from the desk and some car keys that were lying there and ran back into the hall.

Peter was where she had left him—sitting on the bottom step of the staircase in obvious agony. The children were clinging to him. There was no sign of Romy or the maid…

Just as Allison was thinking the worst, Romy reappeared from the kitchen, carrying a large, bulging brown paper bag. The maid followed, proffering a white box.

"Here's a first-aid kit," she told Romy, who stuffed it under her arm.

Allison took the maid by the arm. "Is there a car here?" she asked harshly, dangling the keys in front of the maid's face. *"El coche? Dondé el coche?"*

"In the garage—" the maid stammered.

"It's this way!" Romy broke in, pointing to a door. *"Muchas gracias,* Carmen," she said in a softer tone, trying to reassure her with an appreciative smile. "You've done the right thing helping us."

With difficulty, Allison hoisted Peter's arm up over her shoulder and pulled him to his feet. God! He was heavy! And she was exhausted.

"Peter!" she huffed, already out of breath, "you've got to help me…"

"Let's go…" he groaned, wincing as he put more weight on his feet. "I'm sorry I screwed things up—"

"You didn't, Peter," Allison reassured him. "We've got the kids, now let's get out of this damn place."

They shuffled into the spacious garage that adjoined the house and saw the only car that was there: a pearl-white Mercedes sports coupe with its roof down. Allison glanced at the keys in her hand and with relief saw that they bore the Mercedes emblem. "Well, it's not very big, but it'll have to do!"

She eased Peter down in the front passenger seat, and the children scrambled over the sides into the convertible's two small rear seats. Romy placed the bag she was carrying into the small trunk and then clambered over the side and squeezed uncomfortably in beside the children. Without legroom, she sat sideways with her legs on their laps, and the children actually giggled! It brought warmth to Romy's face; she had never seen them happy before. Even Allison smiled, but her attention was soon back on the urgent matter at hand.

"How the hell do we get out of this garage?" she yelled, searching for a switch to operate the electric door.

"Um...quite simple..." Peter answered with difficulty, as he leaned forward and pressed a remote control on the glove compartment. "Open...sesame..." he groaned, and collapsed back into his seat.

The massive garage door slowly opened behind them. Allison dropped into the driver's seat, started the engine, selected reverse on the floor-mounted gearshift and furiously backed the car out into the light of the nearly-full moon. The car spun around on the driveway as she turned hard on the steering wheel. She engaged DRIVE, slammed down the accelerator, and the spinning tires sprayed gravel. The house quickly disappeared behind them as they shot down the driveway and pulled out onto the street.

Allison turned left, heading north. Pedro had to be coming from the coast farther south where he had tried to kill them.

A couple of hundred yards down the road on the right-hand side, she spied an old beach-house. There were no lights, and it stood in an overgrown garden. She pulled off the road and into bushes that hid the car from view.

"What are you doing—why are we stopping?" Peter said with alarm.

"I want to see what's going on behind us—don't worry, Peter. I've got to plan our strategy..." Allison grabbed the assault rifle, entered the bushes, and crouched down with a clear view of the entrance to the house they had just left. She felt her pulse pounding in her temples.

Her thoughts were interrupted by the sound of an approaching engine. But it was coming from behind her, from the direction they had been heading. She had misjudged Pedro. A black limousine sped past and turned into the driveway of the Del Solars' house, illuminated by the still-open garage door. Allison didn't recognize the car as Pedro's, and she hadn't recognized him inside the car as it passed. She got up to return to the Mercedes, but the distant sound of another speeding vehicle stopped her in her tracks. It came from farther away, from the opposite direction—south. She waited, pulse racing. The car's headlights came into view, momentarily blinding her as they swung to turn into Don Gonzalo's house behind the other car. This time, she clearly recognized Pedro's SUV.

Christ! Allison thought. *Who the hell were those first people?*

There was no time to ponder the question now. Allison hastily climbed back into the car and as quietly as possible drove carefully back onto the road and away from the house. They were heading north again, and Allison drove for a mile without headlights. As soon as they were at a safe distance from spying eyes, she switched the headlights on and accelerated hard.

The road was poor and rough, and Peter groaned in pain but gestured for her to keep going. On the outskirts of Pimentel, in the distance they saw an old Volkswagen Beetle parked at the side of the road. As they neared, a man in police uniform stepped out from behind it and motioned for them to stop.

"You'd better get out of the way, buddy!" Allison said against the windy noise of the open car. "We sure aren't stopping now!" She pressed the pedal harder and the sports engine responded instantly.

Marcelo suddenly realized that the car wasn't going to obey him and stop. Perhaps the driver hadn't noticed his signal. Gingerly, he stepped into the center of the road, held out his right arm and waved the flashlight in his left hand...But—

"Get out of my way, sucker!" Allison screamed, gripping the steering wheel as if her life depended on it.

Marcelo leapt back to the side of the road and flattened himself against his old car. He felt the wind from the Mercedes' slipstream pick up the tail of his jacket as it zoomed past.

Why, it's that Del Solar woman—she always drives like a maniac! "You could have killed me—you bitch!" he shouted, shaking his fist in the air. However, it wasn't worth reporting her; she could do what she liked.

After smoking a cigarette to calm himself, Marcelo moved his car into the middle of the road; this might be a more effective strategy for stopping vehicles.

Pedro slapped Carmen viciously across the face; he must make absolutely sure she was telling the truth. He had no time to waste listening to her drawn out and muddled explanation.

The maid screamed as the force of the blow sent her head sideways and nearly knocked her off her feet. *"Por favor!"* she pleaded, holding up her hands to protect herself from the next blow.

Pedro's hand was poised to swat her again. "Where did they go? *Where did they go? Answer me!*"

"I don't know, Señor!—I swear, I don't know!" Carmen was terrified.

Pedro advanced until his face was an inch from hers, and he saw with satisfaction that blood trickled down from the cut at the corner of her mouth. "Where? What direction?"

"They took La Señora's car and drove off—I don't know which direction. I was here—I swear—it all happened so fast...please...!" She collapsed on her knees, sobbing pitifully.

"How long ago did they leave?" Pedro persisted. "Five—ten minutes? How long?"

"Five minutes...no more," the maid answered meekly.

"An American woman and a man?"

"Um...yes..." Carmen added with hesitation.

Pedro grew suspicious. "Were there others? Was the Tincopa woman with them?—*Answer* me!"

"*Sí*, Señor—" Her voice was resigned.

"So Romy Tincopa was with them...Anyone else?" Pedro went on.

"No, just three people."

"And who shot *La Señora?*"

"I don't know—I swear! I was in the kitchen when it all happened," Carmen replied hurriedly, petrified that Pedro would strike her again.

Pedro glanced around the hall and spotted drops of blood on the floor by the door leading to the garage. By the time Peter crossed the hall, the blood had soaked through the improvised bandage and left telltale drops on the parquet floor.

Pedro pulled the maid up by the arm and dragged her across the hall. "Whose blood is this?" he demanded, squeezing her arm until it hurt. "Whose blood?"

"The man's—" Carmen replied in pain.

"What *happened?*" Pedro shouted. "Was he shot?"

"*Sí*...I suppose so—I saw nothing, Señor, other than that he was bleeding..." Carmen sobbed again. "I was in the kitchen working..."

Pedro released her as though she were filth, then mused knowingly. "They got the kids, killed Del Solar...but got hit. That will slow them down..."

A voice bellowed in the hall behind Pedro. "Where are those damn kids?—I paid big money for them! Your boss promised me delivery; I looked upstairs and they're not here!" The man took Pedro by the shoulder to turn him around.

Pedro spun and viciously grabbed the fat, greasy man who had dared lay a hand on him. "Don't put your filthy hands on me!" Pedro shouted into the man's face, tightening his grip on the front of his shirt.

"What...?" the man started to protest.

"And *shut the fuck up!*" Pedro was furious at how Allison Cox had slipped through his fingers again.

The man was astonished. "I am Don Eduardo, and you are just one of Chavez's lackeys—"

"You miserable, puffed up pedophile!" Pedro shot back. "Don't threaten me, or I'll shut you up for good—*is that clear?*" The man's mouth dropped open in shock. "Without me," Pedro said, "you'll never get your precious kids. So just shaddup while I think…"

The man recoiled meekly and looked at the two men he had brought with him in the black limousine to ensure there would be no trouble when he picked up the children. But neither dared mess with Pedro, and both remained where they were.

"*What* are we going to do?" Don Eduardo asked Pedro after a couple of minutes' silence. He tried to sound self-assured.

"We're going to damn well find them, of course, and the people who took them," Pedro replied. "They won't get far—the police are blocking off the town. And if you want to locate your merchandise *quickly*," Pedro added, "you might want to lend us a hand."

"Of course. What do we do?"

"Get your men out checking all the roads—which way did you come in?"

"From Piura."

"And you didn't meet a white Mercedes sports car?"

"No—there was nobody out on the road."

"Hmm…" Pedro mused. "I didn't come across anybody either, and I came from the opposite direction…But they couldn't have gone any other way—at least not until they left the town…" Pedro pulled out his cell phone and called Rodriguez. "We'll soon find out if anyone saw them leaving," he told Don Eduardo.

The only person at the police station was the desk officer who told Pedro that Rodriguez had left for Pimentel. He added that he had received strict instructions from Rodriguez to radio him if anyone called in with a sighting of the international agents. But so far there had been nothing.

"Apparently, they're still in town somewhere," Pedro said, snapping closed his phone. "Get out there with your men and scour every place they might be hiding—remember, the only transport they have is the car, and it's the only one like it in the area."

Don Eduardo puffed himself up with importance again and led his men away.

"What else did they do?" Pedro asked gruffly, turning to Carmen.

"Nothing, Señor—"

"*Nothing!* There must be *something!*" Pedro shouted.

Carmen's eyes opened wide again. "They just left...the woman went to the study," she said, pointing to the open door, "and used the telephone, I think— but that's all, I swear..."

Pedro strode into the study and looked around. *Of course she was in here—I spoke to her on the phone!* Everything appeared normal to him except...He bent down, picked up the pink cell phone charger lying on the floor and searched for the cell phone that would normally have been in it. After a couple of minutes, he yanked the cord out of the wall and went back into the hall.

"Carmen? Did the American woman only answer the phone, or did she also make a phone call?"

"I don't know, Señor, I wasn't there..."

"Where's the cell phone that goes with this?" He held up the charger.

"It should be there, Señor. It's placed there every night for recharging."

Pedro thought hard. *Allison Cox must have called someone; otherwise why was she near the phone when I called? Why did she answer? Was she waiting for someone to call her back? She certainly didn't expect it to be me. All my call did was to get her out of the house more quickly. And she took the cell phone to make the call later. Who is she trying to reach?*

Pedro's own men had come back to the hall after checking the rest of the house. "Nothing, boss," one of them said.

"Okay, let's get out of here and find 'em!"

C h a p t e r   34

▼

It was a calculated risk to stop again so close to Pimentel, but risk was the only resource Allison had in plentiful supply. The roadblock left no doubt that Pedro would soon find out which way they were heading. And now she knew the police were looking for them too—dashing any hope of getting help from the local authorities.

She turned left toward the coast. *Any* direction to confuse their pursuers! But she had no idea where to go, and if they kept traveling aimlessly, it would be only a matter of time before they were picked up. And Peter was in increasing pain. The roar of the wind rushing through the open car muffled his groans. But Allison could tell that he needed to stop.

Odd clumps of trees and bushes stood as dark shadows in the moonlit, arid landscape. Allison found one grove far enough off the road and large enough to hide the car. It wasn't thick enough to completely obscure the gleaming white bodywork, but it would have to do.

Romy helped Allison carry Peter and lay him beneath a tree with his back against the trunk. The children took the red tartan blanket they had found in the back of the car and lovingly placed it over their father, tucking him in as they would have tucked in a favorite stuffed toy. The large brown paper bag that Romy had carried from the house was full of food and drink from Don Gonzalo's pantry. Mark's and Nicolette's eyes opened wide when they saw the cheese and crackers and bananas that Romy offered them. They ate as though starved.

Allison hadn't time to be hungry. With Romy holding a flashlight, she opened the first-aid box and found sterile bandages that had to be better than the sheeting that was holding Peter's wounds closed. There were also painkillers and disinfectant.

"How are you feeling?" Allison asked.

Between coughs that made him grip his side in agony, "It burns less now," he said, "but it aches, and I feel hot and shaky."

As Allison peeled away the bandage that congealed blood had glued to his side, Peter screamed and the children wept and covered their ears. "If only we could get him to a hospital!" Allison said. "Are there any doctors we can trust?"

Romy shook her head in despair: "Nobody," she said.

"We'll just have to do our best on our own then," Allison sighed.

She cleaned and bandaged the wound and made him swallow a couple of painkillers.

Peter looked up at her. His voice husky and weak as he said, "I'm desperately sorry I got you into this, Allison. I'm slowing you down. Leave me! Take the children and go! Mark and Nicolette's lives are what matter. Go! You must do it! Get them back to Martine!" Then he whispered, "Look at them, Allison. Have you ever seen anything so beautiful in your life? I found them, Allison. I found them!"

His eyes closed, and for a moment, Allison thought he was passing away.

She shook him gently, "Peter, wake up!"

His eyelids flickered.

"Peter! Look over there—Mark and Nicolette want you to see what they're doing."

He smiled.

At that moment, the children were mixing handfuls of soil with the contents of one of the large plastic bottles of soft drink and plastering the muddy mess all over the exposed shining parts of the car. Allison had tasked them to do this while she and Romy were attending to Peter's wounds. Although it didn't do a perfect job of camouflaging the car, it did dull the white and lessen the possibility that they would be spotted in their hiding place.

"Keep an eye on them, Peter; I need to work with Romy on our escape plan."

Hovering over a map from the glove compartment, Romy showed Allison that they were not far from *La Panamericana*, a highway running along the seaboard of Peru from Chile in the south to Ecuador in the north. "I think," said Romy, "that we can reach it by driving across the Sechura desert."

"Leave the road?" Allison said.

"We can do it," Romy said. "The desert is hard and flat. The moon is bright and we can drive without lights. The police don't interfere with traffic on *La*

Panamericana. It's the main route for drug traffic, and they take pay-offs. We can make it into Ecuador."

"And without papers at the border of Ecuador?" Allison said.

"Money speaks louder than anything in this part of the world," Romy said. "A bribe will take us across."

Allison smiled inwardly; this schoolteacher was really getting into the mindset of a fugitive! "Yes, but this car sticks out so much—"

"It's quite a busy road, especially with heavy truck traffic," Romy said. "And it only has one lane in each direction, so we'd be less conspicuous there than elsewhere."

"Hmm…" Allison murmured. "And Pedro? He and his hoodlums won't stand idly by and wave us *Bon Voyage!* There's got to be a better way…"

She wandered off, leaving Romy pondering over the map. Allison sat down out of earshot and let out a tired and frustrated groan. She bit her lip as her head slumped down on her chest and tears began weaving their way down her face.

As she searched in her pockets for a handkerchief, her hand came upon the cell phone she had taken from the study. Between the roadblock and worrying about Peter, she had completely forgotten she had it. Allison wiped her tears with the back of her hand and tapped in the Bahamas hotel telephone number. Her heart thumped.

Renée and Bruno had just been served their main course when Renée remembered to tell her husband about the flashing telephone light. Bruno was annoyed; he was on call for his business clients and had to respond to their requests right away. If only his cell phone would work in the Bahamas…

He excused himself abruptly and went into the lobby to find the telephone operator's window.

"You have a message for me—Bruno Hottinger in room 203?" he asked the operator.

"Let me check, suh…" she sang in her Bahamian accent. "Why…yes, suh…There surely is one! Just press 203 on the phone there and you can listen to it."

Bruno punched in the number and a computerized voice told him the message had come at eight twenty-five PM. And now, he thought, it's already past nine! "Damn!"

Suddenly, he heard Allison's urgent voice. Bruno was flabbergasted. *Allison Cox! How did she know I was here?* He listened again, and wondering, returned to the restaurant.

"What did they want?" Renée asked, seeing his mystified expression. "Is everything okay?"

"It was from Allison—you know, Allison up the road back home," Bruno replied. "She wants me to wait for a call from her; says it's urgent—important—an emergency, something like that. I can't understand what it might be."

"Oh, no! I wish I'd picked it up!—I'm really sorry, Bruno…"

"Allison isn't someone who'd call for no reason," Bruno continued, puzzled. "I'd better get up to the room in case she calls again—but you finish your meal, dear. I'll see you upstairs."

"But didn't she leave a number to call back?"

"No," Bruno replied. "And that's not like her…I'm going upstairs."

The call came through just before nine-thirty. Renée had just joined Bruno in the room when the bedside phone rang. "Hello—Bruno Hottinger here…" The line was crackling badly. "Hello…is that you, Allison?"

"Yes!" she screamed. "It's me—oh, I'm so glad I got through to you…we're in a god-awful—" The line went dead. A second later, Bruno heard the crackling again. Renée bent down and listened along with Bruno.

"Allison? Are you there? There's break-up on the line…"

"—es—, yes—can you hear me now? I've moved into the open…"

"Loud and clear," Bruno answered. "That's better—"

"Bruno, we need your help—bad! Peter's been shot. We've got the kids—Mark and Nicolette. But we're stuck out in northern Peru and being pursued by hoods who want to kill us…"

Bruno's jaw dropped.

"Is this a joke?" Renée mouthed.

"I don't think so," Bruno said.

"Bruno?" Allison said, "Are you there?"

"Yes—yes," Bruno said incredulously. "You've found the children? Peter and Martine's?"

"Yes—"

"That's fantastic—*fantastic* news!" Bruno said excitedly. "Where were they—I can't believe it. And what did you say about Peter? Did you say he's been shot?"

"Yes. He's *badly* injured—Bruno, we're in deep shit—we need help getting out of here!"

"You're in Peru? What kind of help?"

"Yeah, way out in a rural area…Bruno, could you find someone who could fly us out of here, no questions asked?"

Bruno exhaled sharply. "Where again?—in northern Peru?"

"We're near a place called Pimentel…there's an airport at Chiclayo—"

"God, Allison, it's not my part of the world—I've never flown there…hmm…" Bruno murmured. "I could call and see if any of my contacts know of someone—are you in a hotel?"

"No—we're out in the open, hiding in a thicket from corrupt police and hoods—gangsters—searching the countryside for us. If we move, we're done for. Please help us, Bruno!"

Bruno and Renée looked at each other in dismay. They'd both heard the pleading voice on the other end of the line.

Renée whispered, "Do you know of anybody—anyone at all down there?"

"No," Bruno replied. His mind was blank. "I could ring around…but it'll take time…" He took his hand off the mouthpiece.

"Allison? Allison—"

"Yes, I'm still here—"

"Can't you get help from the U.S. embassy or consulate? With your government connections…"

"No—they're down in Lima, hundreds of miles away. What we really need, and fast, is someone with a plane or chopper or whatever to lift us out of here…*Please*, Bruno! Try and find someone? We're desperate!"

"Look Allison—you've got to hang in there! This is going to take time—and I can't promise anything—but I'll do what I can. Give me a couple of hours to phone around—and even if I do find someone, it'll cost—"

"We'll *pay*," she shouted. "Just find someone! Quickly!"

"But can you get to that airport…*Chiclayo?*"

"I don't think so…I don't know…Maybe."

"How can I reach you?" Bruno asked. "What's your phone number?"

"Oh God! I don't have a clue! I stole the phone," Allison replied. "And there's…no number on it…"

Bruno looked at Renée and raised his eyebrows in astonishment. *Allison Cox? Stealing?* He thought quickly.

"Allison? Can you note down some numbers?"

"Yes! What?"

"The number of the phone in the plane—I'm on a charter and I might be in the air when you call." He read out two strings of numbers. "The second one's the seven-digit pin code—without it, you won't be put through."

Allison hurriedly scribbled the numbers on the notepad she had taken from Don Gonzalo's study.

The signal was getting weaker. He raised his voice. "Allison? You got that?"

"Yeah, I think so," came the faint reply. "I can phone you directly on the plane?"

"Yes. If you can't reach me here at the hotel, try the plane. Call me in two hours—that'll be about eleven-thirty tonight. What time have you got down there now?"

"About nine-thirty," Allison answered.

"Good!" Bruno said. "At least we're in the same time zone—call me at eleven-thirty and hang in there!"

All Bruno could hear now was a hollow sound—like the sea in a conch shell. He replaced the receiver and went to his laptop on the desk. Anticipating his next move, Renée had already turned it on and called up the world atlas.

"Do you think it'll be in here?" she asked.

"Should be—these aviation maps are pretty comprehensive. Let's see what we can find."

Bruno typed in *Chiclayo*, and a map of Peru appeared with an arrow pointing to a red dot near the top of the country. He zoomed in until a detailed road map occupied the entire screen. "They're down there somewhere," he pointed. "If we can find a local pilot who'll fly them out…" His voice trailed off uncertainly. "I hope they've got an alternative plan, because this is not going to be easy."

It was close to midnight. After three hours of fruitless searching at Chavez's command, Pedro, Lieutenant Rodriguez and Don Eduardo had all assembled at Chavez's house. Chavez made no attempt to conceal his rage as he paced back and forth.

"You're a bunch of *incompetents—fucking incompetents!*" he shouted.

It was unlike Chavez to lose control of himself, and the sight sent shivers down Pedro's spine. Was he more enraged at the death of his mistress or at what might happen if Allison Cox escaped to the United States?

Chavez stopped pacing and turned his ire on Pedro.

"I *warned* you that something like this might happen! You didn't *listen*—you thought I was losing my nerve, my mind! *Didn't you?*"

Pedro watched him coldly and said nothing.

"And you were probably planning to take over from me…you *bastard!* You son of a *bitch! You utterly incompetent, naïve fool!*" Well, let me tell *you!* I'm not done for yet! But *you* will be if you don't find those people *soon!*"

Chavez began to pace again.

"I just cannot understand how you've screwed up! *All* of you! How hard is it to find a few people on the run: two *children*, two *women*, and an *injured man?*

And they're roaming *our* local countryside—an area they don't know—in a car that flashes by like a beacon! Plus they drive right by one of *your* men, Rodriguez, and he ignores them…"

"He thought it was Señora Del Solar—" Rodriguez said.

"I just don't *understand* it…" Chavez shook his head and continued as if the police lieutenant hadn't spoken. "Perhaps I expect too much."

He paused again. Don Eduardo started to say something about money but Chavez cut him off.

"Shut up! You greasy bag of pork fat, you'll get your warm little bodies before long. From now on, *I'm* in charge!"

Chavez walked over to a map that lay open flat on the table. The others followed. "Now, where do we think they are?" he asked no one in particular.

"Hiding somewhere in this area north of Pimentel," Pedro volunteered, circling an area with his finger.

"So, unless someone's hiding them, they'll have to come out of wherever they are sooner or later—and probably sooner, since the man needs medical attention, right?"

The others nodded in agreement.

"But, what if the Americans are helping them?" Don Eduardo ventured.

"Well, if some 'Delta Force' is dropped in to pluck them out, they have little to fear from incompetents like you, and we can safely assume they're already back in the United States. However," Chavez continued, "no one's noticed any strange arrivals in the area. And if help is coming their way from the U.S. embassy in Lima, then they'll either try to take them out by helicopter—and we'd surely notice that—or by plane. Has anyone checked the airport at Chiclayo?" Chavez asked, looking up suddenly. "It's the nearest."

"Of course," Pedro jumped in. "Rodriguez alerted the airport police, and I've sent one of my men there to check—"

"That's not enough!" Chavez retorted. "Close the airport—*Close* it! That'll stop anyone from coming in or going out."

"But," Rodriguez said. "I haven't got the authority—"

"You have now—*mine*," Chavez shot back.

"Get to it!" Pedro ordered Rodriguez.

Looking worried, the lieutenant hurried out of the room.

"And charter companies—has anyone bothered to find out if any private pilots or planes have been contacted or already booked to fly these people out? This might be a better planned operation than we thought!"

"I'll check them all out," Pedro said. "There aren't that many, and they all work out of the airport."

"Yes, but check in Lima and other places as well," Chavez said. "Call them all, even if you have to wake them up!" That possibility dealt with, Chavez continued. "How else could they get away?"

"By road, probably up *La Panamericana* to the border," Pedro noted. "But it's a long drive and they'd soon be spotted—"

"And by sea?" Chavez said.

"The Coast Guard's already been alerted—they haven't got much chance there."

"Well, that seems watertight then," Chavez concluded, slapping his silver pen down on the map. "Now…all you've got to do is pounce on them as soon as they start moving. I'm going to bed, and I'd better hear some good news when I wake up in the morning. Please don't let me down again—I react badly to disappointments."

Chapter 35

▼

The Gulfstream rose majestically into the night sky, leaving behind the Caribbean paradise. Bruno and Renée looked sullen as they sat in the cockpit, their faces weirdly illuminated by the bank of state-of-the-art electronic instruments.

As soon as they had gained enough altitude, Bruno set course for Geneva and what he knew would be eight hours of miserable flying time. It was not that their working vacation had come to an end that disturbed them, but that they could do nothing to help Allison and Peter. Their powerlessness haunted them.

Bruno had called everyone he knew who might have contacts in Latin America, and he had drawn a complete blank. It was frustrating, terribly frustrating. And to add to it, Bruno's boss at Geneva Business Jets had ordered him back to Geneva that night.

"Hey, I'm glad you called, Bruno!" Erik Uhl had said, picking up on Bruno's call to one of the other pilots. "I was just about to call you! No, I don't know anybody down there—look, something urgent's come up. We've got two more high execs who need to join your group in the Bahamas ASAP. So I need you to bring the plane back right away, and then Alain's ready to turn it around and fly it back with them as soon as you're in—"

"But I need to find a charter in Peru—"

"Look, Bruno, I don't give a damn about whatever you're looking for in Peru! Are you okay to fly?"

"Yes, of course—"

"Is the plane fueled and ready to go?"

"Yes…but—"

"Well, get the hell out of there and back here!" In a calmer voice, Uhl added: "This is a big contract for us, Bruno, so please get moving…Once you're in the air, call me on these other questions—okay?"

"Gotcha!" Pedro exclaimed. He stood a yard in front of where Allison lay. She looked up and saw that he was pointing a gun right at her face.

He let out a deep laugh. "So you thought you could outsmart Pedro, eh?" he said. Then he bent down and screeched, "You stupid bitch, *nobody outsmarts Pedro—nobody!*"

Allison let out a scream.

Someone took hold of Allison from behind and put a hand roughly over her mouth—

"Leave me alone!" she tried to scream, but the hand stifled the sound.

"Wake up!" Romy whispered urgently in her ear. She shook Allison hard again. "Wake up—please wake up!" she pleaded. Her voice was grave. "The police are here! You've got to get up!"

Allison opened her eyes and immediately closed them again. Romy slapped her on the cheek. Allison suddenly came to and took in her surroundings. She had been dreaming! She looked around again—it was first light! "Oh!" she exclaimed.

Romy had intended to stay awake last night and keep watch, but she had drifted into a deep sleep soon after watching Allison nod off. She had been pleased to see the American woman get some rest and had meant to awaken her in a couple of hours. But those two hours had become six, and now it was approaching five AM. Romy felt guilty at letting Allison down; obviously Allison hadn't meant to remain in the thicket this long. But now it was done.

"There's a policeman coming!" Romy hissed again.

Allison got to her feet and went to the edge of the thicket. Although dawn hadn't broken yet, it was light enough that she could clearly see the uniformed man making his way toward their hiding place. He was only twenty paces away, intently looking down at the ground and following the tire tracks through a patch of soft damp soil. Everything else around them was as dry as a bone, but they had driven through this small patch of stagnant water!

Allison turned and grabbed the assault rifle. Her movement in the quiet morning air was enough to alert the policeman, who suddenly looked up. He had the advantage of surprise but the disadvantage of being young and inexperienced—and on his own. When he saw Allison facing him, assault rifle in hand, he turned and ran back toward his motorcycle parked at the edge of the road. He wouldn't have had a chance of covering the short distance that separated him from his dark-blue-and-white patrol bike; at that range, any assault rifle could have cut him down. But Allison hesitated; she had never developed the automatic killer instinct that a professional soldier needs.

But if he gets away! Allison aimed and squeezed the trigger. Nothing! She looked down; the ammunition clip was missing. She looked back. There it was where she had removed it from the gun last night to refill it. She must have fallen asleep before reattaching it. She stepped back and with one swift stroke swiped it up and slammed it into place. But as she looked up to aim the second time, she heard the motorcycle's engine roar. It was too late. Her chance of hitting the moving target was too slight; it wasn't worth wasting the ammunition.

If she hadn't been sure what they were to do next, now she was. They had to get away from their hiding place—and without delay!

The fleeing policeman was so petrified of being shot that he rode his bike like a madman for a full five minutes before turning to look back. Satisfied that he was not being pursued, he stopped his machine but kept the engine running and was still shaking as he radioed in his news. He was so agitated that he had to repeat several times before Lieutenant Rodriguez could understand it.

"We've got 'em!" Rodriguez told Pedro with pride. "They're here," he said, drawing a small circle with a marker on the wall map. "Here—with only two ways to go—"

"East, back to where they came from, or west to *La Panamericana*," Pedro jumped in, stealing Rodriguez's conclusion.

"They'll flee west and up to the border," Rodriguez said.

"That's obvious!" Pedro sneered. "Because, if they go east, they'll bump into us—and the Cox woman's no fool."

"Now we catch the rabbits as they bolt from their hole?"

"Yes," Pedro replied with satisfaction. "It's time to go hunting!"

Chapter 36

▼

"What do you mean, he had to fly back to Geneva?" Allison screamed at the hotel operator in the Bahamas. "He can't do that—was that the only message he left?"

"Sorry Ma'am—yes. Got another call…" The phone went dead.

Allison was sick and disheartened. As soon as the police motorcyclist had sped off, she had dialed the hotel number hoping Bruno had found a way to help them. But *this* was devastating!

Using the number he had given her, she tried to reach Bruno on the plane. But after two attempts at punching in the long string of numbers, all she got was a recorded message that the plane was "unattainable." Why had she fallen asleep so early last night and failed to call Bruno at the agreed time!

Cell phone in hand, she stood at the edge of the thicket, paralyzed.

Romy was alarmed at seeing Allison like this, dispirited, her will to fight gone. Romy would try and spur Allison back into action. "Allison! Allison, help me get Peter into the car—I can't do it by myself! They'll be back soon!"

"What's the point?" Allison said dully. "We're going to be caught sooner or later…"

"But we've got to get *out* of here and head for the border—please! Just take an arm…he's getting weaker!"

Allison looked at Peter struggling unsuccessfully to get up. He too had slept well during the night—sedated and with a child nestled in each arm.

Seeing Peter struggle brought Allison back to her senses. She walked over to the car and put down the assault rifle between the front seats. Then, as gently as she could, she helped Romy support Peter and settle him into the front seat.

"Okay then," Allison said, taking charge again. "Everyone in the car." Her voice sounded resigned. She glanced at the two children getting comfortable in the back seat and remembered the promise she had made to Peter out by the jetty. She put her hand to her side to feel the three remaining cartridges that she had saved in her pocket. She had purposely not loaded them into the ammunition clip. Two for the children and a spare for...she stopped thinking about it and got behind the wheel.

As they pulled out into the open, she checked the fuel gauge: less than half a tank. Enough for the time being, but it probably wouldn't get them to the border. *But we'll probably never get that far...*Fighting depression again, she looked over at Peter; he looked sickly. *What a mess!*

They hadn't gone far when the cell phone rang. *Bruno!* Allison thought—or even John...How she needed him now! She'd probably never see him again. She brought the phone to her ear. "Hello?" She didn't bother trying to answer in Spanish.

"Good morning, dear Allison—and please don't hang up! I have an important offer to make to you..."

Pedro's voice. Strangely, its familiarity sounded almost comforting. "Go ahead," she said, staring blankly through the windshield while the air whipped her hair. Her tone was surprisingly businesslike.

"Allison, my dear..." Pedro's voice was soothing. "You must cease this silly chase and give yourself up. You know it's leading us nowhere. We're closing in on you—you must realize that. So stop now, and I'll guarantee you safe passage back to the United States..."

"That's very generous of you, Pedro. All of us?"

"Just you—the others need be no concern of yours."

"But I've made them my concern."

"Allison," Pedro went on, "you sound a little tired and depressed—am I right?" He didn't wait for an answer, and Allison wasn't about to give him one. "Allison, we are two of a kind. I understand you. We don't want this kind of a life. I have been forced into mine because I didn't have the chances you did...I cannot go back, but you can. You have family—two sons, isn't it? Just think of them. Wouldn't it be nice to see them again and put all this behind you?"

Allison was just about to be lulled into saying, "Yes," when she glanced in the rear-view mirror and saw what looked like a police jeep in the far distance. The tranquilizing call had caused her to drop her guard and slow down.

"You're a mean son of a bitch, Pedro—*go to hell!*" Allison snapped the phone shut and threw it to the floor. Grasping the steering wheel with more purpose, she floored the accelerator and the Mercedes surged forward.

The police jeep was no match for the German sports car, and Rodriguez cursed as he saw the Mercedes speed up and recede in the distance. "Where the hell's Pedro?" he spat out, and then cursed his driver for not getting more speed out of the jeep.

Pedro's powerful SUV had a better chance of keeping up with the Mercedes, but he had stopped a couple of miles back to relieve himself at the side of the road. That was when he made the call to Allison.

Pedro was back on the road when Rodriguez radioed to say he had sighted the fugitives.

"Keep going—I'm on my way," Pedro replied. "And radio the cars on *La Pan-americana* to head back this way and cut 'em off."

"Will do," Rodriguez agreed enthusiastically. "There's no way they can escape now!"

"Why doesn't Allison call us? I gave her the number." Bruno shook his head in annoyance.

Even at the refueling stop, Renée had remained in the cockpit in case Allison called. But the on-board phone hadn't rung.

As they neared the end of their flight, Bruno had a flash of genius. "Where's our hotel bill?" he asked Renée excitedly. Perplexed, Renee found it in her travel bag. "Okay, the second page," he said. Renée handed it to him. "Aha!" he cried triumphantly. There, in black and white, was Allison's cell phone number, recorded automatically when she had phoned.

Renée tried the number. But it was busy...

At that precise moment, Allison was wasting time listening to Pedro's hollow offer.

"Keep trying!" Bruno implored.

The conversation with Pedro had had the desired effect. Allison's thoughts turned toward her sons and away from this predicament. *What a waste!* She would never see them again, and they would never know what had befallen their mother. It would be the same for Martine. For the rest of her existence in that mental institution, she would remain ignorant of the effort her husband had made to save their children, and she would never know that her son and daughter were peacefully dead. *Oh God!* she prayed, *Let the truth come out! Let those who love us know what happened!*

Allison had no doubt now that she would do what Peter had asked; she would shoot the two children sitting behind her. Peter had sensed it might end this way. But Allison had not. Her life was about to end in such failure and despondency!

A new noise interrupted her thoughts. Through the rushing air, she heard the cell phone ringing—Pedro again! Damn!—and a drawn-out sound like distant thunder…

Inside her head, her voice pleaded: *Go away! Leave me alone…*

The persistent ringing irritated her. She leaned down to pick up the phone, and the car swayed close to the edge of the road. She flicked it open and stabbed the OFF button twice with her thumb and dropped the instrument back by her feet. The car swerved as she jerked the steering wheel to move it back to the center of the road. Peter eyed her strangely, but said nothing. A moment later the phone started ringing again.

"I'm going to turn that damn phone off for good!" Allison shouted, leaning back down to grab it.

Peter blocked her arm and picked up the phone himself. "No—don't!" he croaked, his voice weakened even by picking up the phone. "I…want to speak to this Pedro fellow before I—Hello, this is Peter Zucker…the father of the children you kidnapped." He took a heavy breath before continuing. "I'm going to kill you…"

The distant thundering had turned into an irregular whine coming from their left. Allison turned to look and saw a plane in the distance above the gray-brown landscape of the Sechura desert.

"Oh shit!" she swore. "They're following us in a plane now! We're done for…*Dammit!* And we're so close to the highway!"

Peter looked up to his left, still holding the cell phone to his ear. His attention suddenly refocused on the earpiece that was spluttering words in Swiss-German.

"Peter! Peter! This is Bruno! Bruno!"

Peter listened again to make sure that his exhausted brain wasn't playing tricks on him.

"Will someone answer? Is anyone there?" This time the voice coming out of the cell phone was in English.

"Bruno—Bruno—" Peter stammered. "Please make it be you…this is Peter…Bruno?"

"*Verdammt!*" Bruno shouted. "Don't you guys ever answer the phone? Where the hell are you?" The pilot turned to his wife in the cockpit. "It's them—we got through!" he told her excitedly.

Peter stretched over in the car and shook Allison's arm. "Allison—Allison, listen!" Peter shouted with all his might. "It's Bruno—"

"It's too late, Bruno. We're in deep shit here!" Allison screamed back. "Look!" She pointed ahead, and Peter saw a police car heading straight for them.

In the distance, Allison could already make out the traffic on the Pan-American. But the oncoming police car was between them and the highway. She saw to her right that the desert bed was flat but littered with stones and boulders. They had little choice. Allison turned the wheel hard right and the low-slung sports car hit bottom as it left the paved road and bounced onto the rougher terrain.

Peter was in agony. He bit his lower lip and held his stomach as the car bounded forward.

The police car also turned off the road, but higher up, and headed straight for them on a collision course.

Allison could see that it was gaining on them; the Mercedes had lost its speed advantage when it left the paved road. Allison made a decision. She took her foot off the accelerator and slammed on the brakes. The Mercedes ground to a halt, its tires crunching on the hard desert surface. She grabbed the assault rifle and leapt out of the car.

"Get down, all of you! *Get down in the car!*" she shouted. She then sprinted toward the oncoming police car before abruptly dropping down on her stomach. She pushed the assault rifle out in front of her and deftly snapped down the short bipod legs. Propping herself on her elbows, Allison aimed at the car bearing down on her.

Peter's heart sank. He defied Allison's command and watched. In the half-light of the early morning, he saw the police car's headlights pick out Allison on the ground. The car was still driving straight at her. Peter was just about to cover his eyes when he heard the tight *putt-putt* of his Swiss army rifle and saw the car's lights shatter and go out. And he saw Allison roll out of its path. The car passed out of control within yards of the Mercedes and crashed into a huge boulder fifty feet away. The explosion rocked the Mercedes, and Peter felt the heat from the fire that engulfed the police car. As he watched, no one emerged from the flaming wreck.

Peter, Romy, and the children were mesmerized by the fireball. When Peter turned to look for Allison, she was walking back toward them. Then, to Peter's horror, he saw two more vehicles bearing down on them—the police jeep and a big black SUV. They were still a distance away but their intention was clear. Despite the pain, Peter waved madly to Allison and pointed.

Allison turned, saw them, and, not wasting a second, threw herself into firing position on the ground. She waited until the vehicles were in range and aimed the first burst of fire at the SUV. It stopped short, and the jeep, following suit, pulled up alongside. Allison stopped firing. She realized with alarm that the ammunition clip was nearly empty.

Allison's throat constricted and her heart pounded. She drew in a deep breath. Why the vehicles had stopped, she couldn't tell. The SUV's two front doors were now open, facing her. If there were men leaning out behind the doors, using them as shields, she was extremely vulnerable.

A minute passed, perhaps two. Allison couldn't tell. She had to be decisive and take the lead. To get more oxygen quickly to her brain, she inhaled and exhaled rapidly like a panting dog. "Your victory is going to damn well cost you!" she mumbled through gritted teeth. She switched the gun from automatic to single fire, took careful aim at the center of the left door, and squeezed the trigger. The shot harmlessly shattered the glass above the door panel. She made a quick correction and fired again. The door jerked slightly. She heard a cry of pain and saw a man collapse sideways to the ground. Her adrenaline mounted. She shifted her focus on the other door and fired. But as she pulled the trigger, a man with an UZI stepped clear, firing from the hip in her direction.

Bullets snapped in the sand all around her. They threw dirt and bits of stone into her face, and she cried out, "My eyes!" They felt red-hot. Wincing, she reopened her eyes, and though her vision was blurred, she saw the man changing clips and poised to shoot again. "The bastard! It's Pedro!" She switched back to full automatic fire and blazed away. She held her finger tightly on the trigger, following him as he dove headfirst into the jeep. The bullets twanged against the steel and blew out one of the jeep's headlights. Allison was about to pitch the stream upward to the windshield when the gun went dead. Her heart skipped a beat. She was out of ammunition.

She quickly drew from her belt the revolver she had taken from Señora Del Solar, and poised to use it in a desperate final defense. The jeep's engine suddenly roared to life. "This is it!" she murmured between clenched teeth.

She held the revolver out in front of her, using both hands to make it rock-steady. As the vehicle started to move toward her, she raised the barrel slightly—she must wait until it was closer. But suddenly the jeep changed direction. Allison was dumbfounded—it was turning! A sharp U-turn...and it sped away leaving the empty SUV and Allison in a cloud of brown dust!

Allison staggered to her feet, unable to believe that they were gone. They could not have known that she'd run out of ammunition. She stumbled back to the Mercedes, her face stinging and eyes watering. She felt sick. She looked at the burning wreckage of the first car and then turned to look again at the abandoned SUV and the body lying beneath the door. She thought of the men she had killed.

It was too much for her.

Supporting herself with one hand on the Mercedes' trunk, she bent over and violently threw up. The retching was followed by choking tears.

Romy was out of the car in an instant, her arm gently around Allison's shoulders. She sensed that Allison needed more and gently pulled her to her bosom as she would comfort a child.

"You've shown so much courage," Romy whispered. "I wish I could help you as you've helped us."

But Romy's words brought little comfort. Her throat burning, Allison said, "We're out of ammunition, and they're going to be back—and better prepared." Allison was sobbing now. "We'll never make it to the border, and I've got no other solution—"

But then a piercing and thunderous sound shook the ground. Everything was vibrating around them. Anguished, they turned and saw an airplane descending, now only a few feet above the ground. As its wheels touched down on the hard desert, the sudden screeching and the terrible whine of the powerful jet engines reversing their thrust shot pain through their ears.

"This is the end—Chavez has come to finish us off…" Allison said.

She squared her shoulders and watched as the jet slowly decelerated and came to a halt at what seemed like a mile away. Then she spied the red tail with a white cross on it—and recognized the Swiss flag.

Peter had raised himself up on the side of the car. He was calling back to her. "Allison, it's Bruno!…He's come to take us home!"

Allison Cox fainted.

Chapter 37

▼

"What—what are you doing?" Pedro shouted, aghast, as he pulled himself up from the floor of the moving jeep. He threw worried glances out the back as the jeep accelerated away from Allison. Pedro stared at Rodriguez in disbelief as the police lieutenant kept driving. "Where the hell are you going?" he screamed.

"To save our skins, that's where!" Rodriguez replied without hesitation.

"Turn this fucking jeep around *now!*" Pedro yelled.

Rodriguez looked at him. Pedro, with his disheveled hair and blazing eyes, looked demented. "You must be kidding!" Rodriguez replied, amazed by Pedro's demand. "You might want to get shot up, but not me—"

"But she was out of ammo—you fool!"

"Oh yeah? That's what I thought too…then she started turning us into a sieve and—" Rodriguez felt a sharp pain and turned his head to see that Pedro had shoved his handgun into the side of his neck. "What the—?"

"Turn around!" Pedro ordered. "*Now!*"

At the same instant the jeep bounced on a boulder. The violent jolt threw Rodriguez into Pedro and knocked the gun off his neck. Although a man of little courage, Rodriguez had enormous pride and for a long time had been forced to swallow Pedro's bullying. And now Pedro dared threaten him with a gun—*the upstart!*

"If you want to go back, then *go fucking back!*" the policeman said bitterly as he let go of the steering wheel and pushed Pedro toward the door.

But Pedro was a superior fighter. Without hesitation, he jammed his pistol into Rodriguez's stomach and pulled the trigger twice. Rodriguez was stunned at the muffled explosions. His vision blurred, his eyes glazed over, and his brain was so occupied by these new sensations that he felt neither Pedro propelling him out of the jeep nor the impact as he struck the ground and rolled.

Pedro lost no time getting behind the wheel and yanking the vehicle around. But the turn was too sharp, and the jeep flipped and rolled again and again, until at last it stood precariously on its side, wheels spinning and engine racing. Ejected as if from a slingshot, Pedro landed heavily on his shoulder and head. In his last flicker of consciousness, staring up at the sky, he glimpsed the silhouette of a plane, beacons flashing at its wingtips, as it passed overhead.

Romy lit a match, extinguished it, and held the smoking matchstick under Allison's nose. At once the irritating, pungent fumes did their job. Allison's head twitched, her eyelids flickered, and she opened her eyes wide.

"What…where am…no…"

Romy heaved Allison's crumpled body up into a sitting position and propped her against the Mercedes. She left Allison looking confused but came back with a paper cup of water and held it to Allison's lips. "Here—drink this," Romy ordered pleasantly.

Allison leaned forward, intending to take just a sip, but was obliged to take two large gulps as Romy tilted the cup, deciding for her. Allison coughed and pushed the cup away. She had been jerked back to consciousness.

Romy handed her a damp cloth, and Allison dabbed her eyes and blood-specked face, then looked around; it all came back to her now…She rose to her feet, her body responding grudgingly, and then paused to let the sudden vertigo pass. She refused but then accepted the peeled banana Romy offered. She felt awful and the banana tasted sickening. Her nose could only smell burning and gunpowder residue. She remembered everything clearly now.

"Oh my God! How long have I been out?" Allison was terrified.

"Just a few seconds," Romy said. "How are you feeling?"

"Like shit!" She looked around and spied the business jet in the distance. "Bruno?" she queried, staring at Peter.

"Yes," he said, "…Bruno the unpredictable. He called on the cell phone and I talked him in…" He winced. "It was like being back in the control tower again!" he added. "And I did it without a radar screen. I haven't lost my touch—they'd be proud of me back at Skyguide…" His voice trailed off.

Allison couldn't tell whether Peter's voice faded due to his reminiscing or to his mounting weakness. But it reminded her that it was urgent to get Peter aboard the plane. She helped him back into his seat.

"I'm fine now," she said, seeing Romy's concern. "Get in quick—we've got a plane to catch!"

Allison turned and smiled reassuringly at Mark and Nicolette, crouched in their seats, trying to understand. That they neither complained nor asked questions made Allison wonder what horrible things they had been through.

It didn't take long to cover the distance to the Gulfstream. It had turned to the left at the end of its landing path and was now pointing toward the Pan-American Highway. The sight of the plane's profile, like a gigantic, elegant bird silhouetted against the yellow-blue dawn, made them stare in wonder. And its T-tail rising high above the still-singing jet engines gave the plane an aura of invincible power.

"God, it's enormous!" Allison shouted. "Nearly the size of a passenger jet!"

"Beautiful sight, eh!" Peter murmured, staring up at the red and white tail that represented the Swiss flag.

As they neared, Bruno was already out of the plane, standing by the nose wheel and looking up at the landing gear. Another figure stood atop the narrow embarkation staircase. It was a woman—and she was *waving* at them.

"It's Renée!" Peter gasped. "Renée…"

Driving up to the fuselage, Allison was impatient to be in the air and out of this hellhole. She got out and ran to the foot of the staircase.

"*Salut!*" she shouted above the deafening sound of the jet engines. Renée's friendly smile warmed Allison's heart. She climbed the staircase and embraced her. "What a relief to see you here—thank you!…Thank you so *very* much!"

"*Ce n'est rien!*" Renée answered, joking that it was no trouble. "How's Peter?"

"In a bad way—he's been shot and needs help," Allison said. "We'd better get him on board right away."

"*Et tu as les enfants…*" Renée added, smiling down at the children in the car.

"They're still in shock, but I think they're okay. Let's get everybody aboard."

Allison clambered down while Bruno was helping Peter out of the car.

"Bruno—Thank God! I thought you were going back to Geneva!" Allison shouted as she gave him a quick hug.

"We were," Bruno said, "but we changed our minds." He smiled. "We Swiss are not as straitlaced as you Americans think!" Bruno looked at Allison's tired and blood-speckled face and added more seriously, "And, by the looks of you all, it is a good thing we came when we did."

When Allison ordered the children into the plane, they shook their heads. "*Allez!*" she said, repeating the order for them to go. Mark pointed at his father, and Allison immediately understood. She motioned for Mark and Nicolette to help their father into the plane, and they obeyed without hesitation. They refused to be separated from him again.

"How did you find us?" Allison asked Bruno as they walked Peter to the plane.

"It was actually quite easy. Peter told me you were by that fire...and he told me—the liar!—that it was quite flat down here." Bruno gave Peter a friendly but gentle punch on the shoulder. "You air-traffic controllers."

"Well, I got you down in one piece, didn't I?" Peter argued, wincing.

"Yes—*just!* But we're not out of the woods yet," Bruno said, looking Allison straight in the eye.

"What do you—"

"Let's get everybody on board first and then we'll discuss it."

Pedro sat up holding his head in his hands. He looked around and anger boiled up inside him. He got to his feet shakily, searched for his pistol, and found it only a few yards away. The UZI was nowhere to be seen, and Pedro would not waste time looking for it. His trusted Tanfoglio was enough; all Allison had left was a revolver.

Pedro searched the horizon. *Where's that plane?* He heard the distant whining of its engines and smiled to himself. *They're still on the ground!*

He went to the upturned jeep and examined it. The engine was still running, the wheels turning in the air. He shut the engine off and set about righting the jeep. Heaving and wedging, he rocked it until it bounced back onto its four wheels.

Pedro's eyes narrowed in hate as he set off once again in pursuit of his quarry.

Chapter 38

▼

Peter lay on the executive divan of the Gulfstream, his face horribly pale, his movements weaker and weaker, his speech slurred. Mark and Nicolette sat across the aisle strapped into their soft leather seats, utterly exhausted. Despite drooping eyelids, they were keeping a concerned eye on their father and a wary eye on the others.

Unnoticed, Romy had gotten off the plane, and was standing down by the Mercedes.

In the cockpit, Allison pulled Bruno aside.

"What do you mean 'we're not out of the woods yet'?" she asked with concern. "We can't waste time sitting here—we've got to take off!"

"I know," Bruno said quietly. "But this plane was built for tarmac and concrete, not rough desert terrain—"

"What are you telling me, Bruno?"

"Okay, quite simply, I have grave doubts about our taking off from this surface."

"You mean the desert?" Allison said.

"Yes..."

"But you got down okay."

"Sure—but it was pretty rough. We damaged the nose-gear—it's leaking hydraulic fluid—and if it has to absorb many more bumps, it'll fold. Then we'll really be stuck. And I doubt I can get enough speed to take off; the ground's way too resistant."

Allison sighed. "Damn!" She thought, glancing back down the cabin to where Peter lay. "But we've got to get off—can't we just give it a try?"

Bruno pondered. "Not a chance, I'm afraid." He sounded resigned. "Unless you know of salt flats or smoother terrain near here—we could taxi to that."

Allison brightened. "How about a road?" she said. "The Pan-American Highway's just over there!"

"I thought about that—I wanted to come in on it, but it was too full of traffic."

"Well, we'll have to damn well clear it!" Allison said decisively. They hadn't a minute to lose; on the ground they were sitting ducks for Pedro, who, she knew, would soon be back. "Bruno—you taxi this thing to the highway," she said, pointing. "I'll go ahead in the car and see what I can do to get you a break in the traffic. Then you take off—no hesitating! You understand?"

"Okay," Bruno said. "But I'll need a substantial break, we're heavy on fuel—"

"How long—a couple hundred yards?" Allison asked, impatiently.

"No, more like two thousand—"

"What! That's—that's over a *mile!*" Allison's face fell.

"I'm sorry," Bruno said. "But this is a business jet. We need a clear 6,000 feet or we won't get into the air!"

"Just get this thing to the highway…" With that, Allison ran down the plane's stairs and to the car. Romy was standing there like a chauffeur waiting for a VIP to disembark, and Allison wondered why.

Romy knew why. She had been on board, getting the children strapped in and making Peter comfortable, and no one had paid any attention to her. That was all right with Romy; she *preferred* it that way, but now, hesitating between saying good-bye to the children and watching from a distance, she had withdrawn. That the children were safely back with their father and friends made her happy. That she had played a role in helping them get there was compensation enough. It would be easier if she just melted away.

Now, resolutely standing beside the car, hair blowing as she faced into the desert wind, she watched Allison approach.

"You'd better get inside—quick!" Allison shouted in Spanish.

"I'm not going," Romy answered. "I can't."

Stunned, Allison said, "You *must!* You *can't* stay here! Why do you *want* to stay?"

"This continent is my home, and it's best that I remain here."

"But Pedro and Chavez…"

"I don't intend to stay in Peru," Romy said. "I'll take the car and drive north across the border and try my luck there."

Romy looked a little sad, but there was enough conviction in her voice that Allison sensed she wasn't going to change her mind. She wanted to ask why an educated and cultivated woman like her wanted to end up as an itinerant refugee-teacher, but there was no time now for that.

"If that's your decision, all I can do is wish you good luck," Allison said. "But you've still got a few minutes to change your mind." Allison looked up at the plane, reminding her of the urgency of getting off the ground.

"Get in the car," Allison shouted.

Romy obeyed, and as her car door closed, the Mercedes tore off, away from the plane.

"We've got to stop the traffic on the highway," Allison said.

"What!" Romy looked aghast.

"The plane can't take off here—it needs the road as a runway!"

"But how are you going to stop the heavy traffic?" Romy asked.

"I don't know yet, but I've got to do it if we're going to get out of here."

At the edge of the highway, Allison stopped the car. Glancing over her shoulder, she saw the Gulfstream taxiing huge and heavy in their tracks.

She looked back at the road in desperation. "How the *hell* am I going to do this?" she shouted above the noise of the massive transcontinental trucks speeding by.

Perplexed, Romy said nothing, but she gripped the door handle as the car was buffeted every few seconds by the wake of the passing trucks.

As the Gulfstream lumbered closer, Allison noticed the traffic slowing as drivers stared. *Drug traffickers probably use desert landing strips to make pick-ups and drop-offs,* she thought. The local population was no doubt wary of armed drug-runners, and this gave her an idea.

Allison took the three remaining cartridges out of her pocket and looked at them for a split second before jamming them into the clip. She switched the weapon to single-fire and waited for a break in the traffic. It came when the next approaching truck was still several hundred yards away.

Allison ran the sports car out onto the road, blocked the southbound lane of the two-lane highway, and got out. She walked a few paces toward the truck, fast approaching from the north, and stood erect, legs apart and the rifle across her chest. As the truck got nearer, she raised her right hand firmly to signal the driver to stop. The whine of the Gulfstream pulling up at the side of the road drowned out the fearful squealing of brakes. But when only a few yards from her, the cab of the semi-trailer suddenly veered to the side, and a cloud of black smoke belched out of the rooftop exhaust as the vehicle suddenly accelerated again. It drew across into the oncoming lane, roaring past the barrier and away from trouble in a swirl of dust.

This raised Allison's hackles. The mere sight of her in dusty clothes, holding a weapon, obviously wasn't going to be enough. As the next truck approached, she gritted her teeth and leveled the gun to her shoulder. It wasn't even going to slow down! Without hesitation, she put a well-aimed shot straight through the center of the truck's windshield. The Marines had taught her that overt force was the best way to demonstrate intent. It worked, and the truck ground to a halt. Allison didn't lower her sights until it was clear the driver was going to remain there, stopped in the southbound lane. Vehicles coming from the opposite direction sped past, not daring to slow down to stare at this disheveled, wild-eyed woman holding a truck to heel under her gun.

Bruno and Renée watched incredulously from the cockpit where they had a panoramic view of the highway. This was Allison Cox in a new light! It brought home the true desperation of the situation.

Trucks pulled up one after the other behind the first, the drivers leaning out to see what was causing the holdup. Several climbed down and started toward the front of the line.

"She's going to need help!" Bruno told his wife. "Don't touch anything—I'll be right back."

Renée watched with her heart in her throat as Bruno disappeared back into the plane. When he opened the door to deploy the stairs, the roar was deafening. Then she saw him emerge from under the plane and walk toward Allison, who by now was gesturing dramatically as she talked to the driver of the first truck.

Bruno was approaching her from behind.

As Bruno neared, he shouted, "Allison—it's me—Bruno—I'm behind you!"

"Get back in the plane," she shouted, turning her head but keeping her eyes on the driver.

"You need help!" Bruno shouted back in French. "Other drivers are coming up…"

Allison stepped to one side and gazed at the line of trucks. "Oh, Jesus…!"

"Here take this!" she said, passing the rifle to Bruno. "Hold them back while I deal with traffic from the south—you know how to use it?"

"Sure—I'm Swiss, remember!" Bruno said, smiling.

"There're only two shots left!" she warned him. "Use them wisely!"

"*D'accord!*" Bruno acknowledged, looking businesslike. "A good pilot's always cool under pressure!" He held the gun with confidence as he had been trained to do.

Allison pulled the revolver from her belt and turned to the road coming from the south.

In the safety of the cockpit, Renée put her hand over her mouth. "Oh, *cheri!* Be careful."

More drivers approached, and Bruno fired a warning shot that ricocheted off the tarmac four trucks away. It stopped the drivers in their tracks. *Allison, hurry! I can't buy you much more time!*

As Allison headed for the Mercedes, she looked south where a line of northbound vehicles had stopped at a safe distance from the roadblock. The sound of the gunshot reminded her how little time she had. Allison got into the Mercedes and ordered Romy out.

Alone in the car, Allison looked down at the odometer and set the trip-counter to zero. It was in kilometers—1.6 kilometers would be a mile, and she needed a little more than that. She started the engine and started driving south. She pulled up level with the first stopped vehicle, a small pickup truck, and pointed her revolver at the driver's head.

"Drive on past that roadblock—without stopping!" she shouted in Spanish, her voice as blunt and mean as she could make it.

The driver hesitated.

"*Te vaya!*" she screamed, waving the revolver and pointing to where Bruno stood. "It's none of your business—go! Past those trucks—keep going north and don't stop!"

The pickup took off and Allison drove to the next vehicle where the truck driver saw her gun waving him to go. He wasted no time and followed the pickup. With three more waiting trucks waved on and proceeding north, the road was now clear, and Allison accelerated hard. She looked down at the trip-counter—0.7 kilometers—and kept going. A truck appeared on the horizon, and Allison floored the accelerator.

The car crept up to 150 kilometers an hour—nearly one hundred miles an hour—and though Allison felt a frightening sensation of speed, the trip-counter numbers turned with agonizing slowness: 1.2...1.3...1.4. When she was nearly to the oncoming truck, she decided to let it go past and hoped Bruno could deal with it. Another was approaching—a tanker of sorts. She checked the distance: one-point-six—she needed more. There were other trucks behind it. She began to panic—she could not stop them all.

When the tanker was about fifty yards away, Allison braked hard and swerved the Mercedes across the road. She got out and aimed the revolver squarely at the slowing tanker. When it was in range, she put a shot into the front grill and waited, poised to fire again or leap out of the way. The driver pulled up just yards from where she stood, peering angrily through the steam rising from the pierced radiator. Before he could think of doing anything to retaliate, Allison ran to the cab, hoisted herself up by the door mirror, pointed the gun, and ordered him out.

He obeyed grudgingly.

"What are you carrying?" she shouted, as she jumped back down to the ground.

"Cooking oil," the driver answered with an angry sneer. "What are you going to do? Sell it at the side of the road? Fucking hijacker!"

"No, this!" Allison replied. She shot into the side of the gigantic tank above and then into the fuel tank below. A spark from the metal-jacketed bullet as it tore through the steel fuel tank ignited the vapor inside and the resulting explosion nearly blew Allison and the driver off their feet. The fire spread rapidly in the leaking cooking oil.

"I'm sorry!" Allison shouted to the bewildered driver as she ran back and jumped into the car. She gunned the engine, did a tire-squealing turn, and raced at full speed back to the first roadblock. Allison looked in the rear view mirror; the road was still clear except for the blazing tanker. *That should block the traffic for a while,* she thought.

The Mercedes quickly covered the mile back to where Bruno stood holding the group of drivers at bay. But they were closing in and forming a semicircle around him.

"I'm back!" she shouted.

"What now?"

"Give me the gun and get the plane onto the road—you've got a mile—just!"

Allison took the assault rifle in one hand and the revolver in the other. The revolver was empty now, and, she assumed, the rifle as well. But the truckers didn't know that.

After a long moment of playing visual cat-and-mouse with them, she saw their attention move to something behind her. The ear-piercing crescendo and the sudden intense heat pressing into her back told her that they were watching the Gulfstream pull onto the road and turn, ready for takeoff. Allison backed away to where Romy stood.

"Are you coming with us or not?" Allison screamed through the noise. "It's now or never!"

"No, I'm staying—it's best for everyone. This is where I belong. Good luck and Godspeed!"

"Take the car *now* and start driving while you can!" Allison shouted. "And thanks for everything—now *go!*"

"Que le vaya bien!" Romy said. She wished Allison well, and, after one last desperate hug, got into the Mercedes and drove away past the stopped trucks.

Seeing the car escaping, the truckers started to advance.

Allison shot a glance over her shoulder; from the door of the plane, Renée was urgently beckoning her to come. Allison aimed the assault rifle above the trucker's heads and pulled the trigger. Nothing happened. She dropped both weapons and turned and ran with all her might. The plane was already moving. The truck drivers had also broken into a run after her, but Allison was fast. She quickly caught up with the plane, threw herself at the stairs and clambered on board. Renée pulled up the stairway and shouted down the intercom to Bruno. Bruno shoved the throttle forward, and with a sudden roar and fiery blast from the rear-mounted engines, the plane shot forward, forcing them back into their seats and taking their breath away.

Outside, the drivers gave up the chase, shielded their eardrums and watched helplessly as the plane thundered away down the highway.

Although many Peruvians disliked close ties with the U.S., the Peruvian government saw that its economy needed the preferential trade terms America offered friendly countries in the Western Hemisphere. Therefore, when the U.S. embassy in Lima asked the Peruvian authorities for help in locating one of its nationals, they quickly complied. A request was promptly sent to local police departments around the country—without, of course, mentioning the U.S. government by name.

The U.S. embassy itself was given only the bare bones, just the necessary information. There was no mention in the TOP SECRET cable from Washington that a ranking FBI official was behind the request.

John Vandervelt wouldn't normally have been worried about Allison's disappearance; there was no reason why her official mission to track down the source of the *baby-parts* stories would lead her into any particular danger. And she was not the kind of person to place herself unnecessarily in harm's way. But her voicemail forwarded from the Mission in Geneva worried him. So he initiated the request for information and specified the area around Pimentel.

The faxed request was given to the police chief in Chiclayo, since Lieutenant Rodriguez was nowhere to be found. Seeing the reference to Pimentel—which was right in the middle of his jurisdiction—the chief realized that he would have to file a status report quickly. He called in all available police officers to check and see whether this American woman, Allison Cox, was in the area. But then he saw Rodriguez's message about last night's impromptu police exercise to find "international terrorists."

"That upstart!" the police chief exclaimed angrily. "What the *hell* was he thinking!"

He immediately ordered everybody back to headquarters.

The recall order came blasting out of the jeep's radio. "Shit!" Pedro swore. He had counted on a couple of patrol cars to back him up.

"I'll do it myself then!" he muttered. "They're all so fucking inept and stupid anyway…"

No doubt this plane was the help that Allison had been waiting for all along. *Damned Americans!* It had never occurred to him that she might be waiting for a plane to come to *her*; he had assumed she would rendezvous with one at an airport, not out here in the Sechura desert.

Pedro had reached the highway south of the burning tanker and was driving toward it past the line of vehicles that had been forced to stop.

"I'll get around this line and surprise that damn plane!"

Allison entered the cockpit and crouched behind the co-pilot's seat where Renée sat. Everything seemed eerily noiseless inside the plane, but her ears were still ringing from the jet engines' tearing whine. And her heart was thumping madly.

Bruno didn't move a hair to acknowledge her presence or remind her to sit down and buckle up. As the plane picked up speed, he was totally absorbed in controlling the mass of power at his fingertips; he had to keep the Gulfstream's nose dead center on a very narrow road.

To Allison, everything appeared smaller from the cockpit, except for the burning tanker. That was getting larger incredibly fast.

Beads of perspiration rolled down the sides of Bruno's ill-shaven face. He glanced down at the airspeed indicator: fifty knots. According to the computerized calculations of the plane's flight management system, they would have to accelerate to 152 knots before they could lift off safely. The plane was still heavy with fuel; he kicked himself for not dumping some of it before landing.

But the early morning desert air temperature was low; this would give the engines extra thrust and the wings added lift.

The electronic dial crept up: eighty-five, eighty-six, eighty-seven knots…

Bruno concentrated hard. His knuckles were white from his tight grip on the control yoke, and he hardly dared breathe. The burning tanker grew horribly close. He would wait until the very last second before pulling the nose up. This was a one-time take-off—there was no possibility of aborting and starting again. If he hit the flaming tanker, with the fuel they carried, they would turn into an instant fireball…

The airspeed indicator was rising more quickly now as their momentum multiplied the acceleration: 135—138—141 knots…

They were thundering along and everything seemed possible now…but suddenly Renée and Allison gasped as they saw an open-top jeep pull out from behind the tanker and head toward them on a collision course.

From its single remaining headlight, Allison recognized it as the police jeep she had fired on. And there were tiny flashes coming from the driver's hand—he was *shooting* at them!

Instinctively, Bruno pulled back on the controls, and the plane responded. Its nose lifted upward just in time to avoid colliding with the jeep that disappeared out of sight below them. At the sudden lifting of the nose, the Gulfstream's tail scraped the ground, causing a fierce reverberation through the plane. Almost simultaneously, as the Jeep shot under the plane, the wing's trailing edge clipped its windshield off.

Pedro ducked, but the 600-mph exhaust speed of the engines at full thrust smashed into his back like a thunderbolt, crushing his spine and ripping his head from his body.

Pedro's maniacal final attempt to prevent his enemies from getting away hadn't stood a chance.

Inside the thundering plane, no one even breathed while Bruno held the control yoke back and implored the plane to "Climb—for Christ's sake, *Climb!*" He was on the verge of a stall and even the plane's advanced avionics couldn't help him now. The outcome of this insanity was now in the hands of a greater force.

Sudden darkness blanked out the light as the plane plunged into the wall of black smoke billowing from the inferno below. He waited in dread for the undercarriage to strike the burning tanker and send the plane tumbling to the ground, rolling and flying in pieces across the desert floor.

The wait seemed eternal. But as suddenly as it had left, light flooded into the cabin again, and the thunderous engine roar continued unabated. It was sweeter now, without the rumbling from the undercarriage. The highway stretched out in front of them—but it was below them and getting smaller. They were in the air and climbing fast.

Romy stopped the Mercedes and looked back at the Gulfstream soaring into the clear morning sky until it appeared no bigger than a small bird. Her eyes stung with tears of joy that they had made it, but they were also tears of grief; she would never see Miguel and Alicia again. If only Romy could know that after she had left the plane, Nicolette had looked around. "Mark," she had said, her voice very small, "where did the nice teacher go?"

Romy waited until the plane was not even a speck against the blue; then started the car again and continued her journey northward. This episode in her life was over.

Chapter 39

▼

"I never *ever* want to do that again," Bruno said grimly when he was sure the Gulfstream was climbing. He retracted the landing gear and flaps, and leaned back in his seat as the plane rose through 1,000 feet. "Whew!" he caught his breath. "That was too damn close!"

"I just want to scrub the last twenty-four hours from my mind!" Allison said as she got up from the floor.

Renée placed a comforting hand on Bruno's thigh. "You're a great pilot, Bruno. Nobody else could have done that."

Bruno said nothing and just blew out another breath of air. Then he turned his head slowly toward Renée, and with a cheeky smile said, "You've always wondered why I'm so tired and stressed after work, well…"

"Liar!" she laughed. Then getting up, she said, "I'm going back to make sure everyone else is all right—there's certainly nothing wrong with you!"

Bruno turned to Allison. "Okay, where to now?"

Allison hadn't had time to think about the next step. She took a deep breath and then exhaled. "Home," she said, "back to Geneva."

"Sounds good to me!" Bruno agreed. "But Peter needs medical attention—we're talking ten-plus hours in the air before reaching Geneva…"

"I'll go back and check on him," Allison said. "But you're saying we can just fly straight back to Geneva?"

"Sure…we've got enough fuel," Bruno verified his calculation with the flight management system.

"But haven't you got to file a flight plan or something like that?" Allison queried.

"Normally, yes. But if we'd done that with the Peruvian authorities before we left—"

"Yes, I know…" Allison said, smiling. "But what about other planes in the air corridors…and over-flying other countries?"

"At almost 50,000 feet, we don't have to worry about commercial air traffic—we'll be way above them. With us barreling along at just under the speed of sound, by the time anyone realizes we're in their airspace, we won't be in it anymore. And once we're over the Atlantic—there's no air traffic control out there—we'll be on our own until European radar picks us up, and then we're home."

"But if we need to stop because of Peter?" Allison asked.

"Then we'll put down somewhere—the best place would be the U.S.—Florida maybe. But we're still talking a few hours. And then we could be stuck there for a while because of the problem with the nose gear. It could collapse on the next landing—"

"The U.S. is out of the question." Allison was categorical. "Keep it to yourself, Bruno, but Peter got into trouble with the law back there, and he's liable to be arrested and the kids put into foster care…" Allison exhaled. "Let me go back and check on him—in the meantime, head for Geneva."

"Roger," Bruno said, releasing one hand from the controls to pick up an aviation chart.

Allison walked unsteadily down the sloping floor of the still-climbing plane back into the passenger cabin.

Renée was already there. Everyone was thirsty and hungry, and Renée, trying to forget that horrendous take-off, was busy in the galley.

It was the same day in Geneva, but six hours ahead of the western coast of Peru. After an exhausting morning attending to patients in the Belvoir clinic, Claude Dubois was about to leave for lunch. He was looking forward to his daily walk down to the *Café Fleuri*, where he would enjoy a bowl of the *soupe du jour* and a hunk of crusty fresh bread. He needed a break from the intense atmosphere of the clinic before his afternoon appointments.

The intercom buzzed…

"What is it?" Dubois asked irritably, looking up at the wall clock.

The nurse in the outer office hated these moods of his. "There's a call for you from—"

"Tell them I'm out to lunch and that I'll call back."

"I told him that you were about to go out…but the man's very insistent."

"Did you say I was still here?"

"Well—"

"Who is it?"

"It's a Monsieur Zucker—about his wife…"

"Zucker?" *The man disappears for weeks and then calls me when I'm going out to lunch!* "Oh…put him through."

"Are you Doctor Dubois?" the voice at the other end of the crackly line asked. "The one who's caring for Martine Zucker?"

"Yes—"

"I'm going to connect you to Peter Zucker—but let me explain something first. This call's coming to you from a plane over the Atlantic, so if the line breaks up now and then, don't hang up!"

"What *is* this?" Dubois interrupted. "Who are you?" He was getting more irritated.

"Look, Dubois, if you listen, you'll find out." Bruno raised his voice to match the doctor's unpleasantness. "I'm the pilot, and I have Peter Zucker on the plane with me. He's badly injured and needs urgently to talk to his wife, Martine. So please put us through to her."

"This is most irregular…I'll make an exception and talk to him myself, but I can't allow him to talk to his wife. She's in a highly delicate condition and I cannot allow her to get excited or upset—"

"Listen, Dubois!" Bruno shouted down the mouthpiece of his headset. "Don't give me the runaround. I'm extremely tired, and I've got neither the time nor the patience to argue with you. I've just evacuated Peter Zucker from Peru where he found his children. While rescuing them, he got shot in the stomach. They're now here in the plane with me, and we're flying over the Atlantic as fast as we can to get back to Geneva. Peter's still conscious, but I don't know for how long. And the reason his wife is in your damn clinic is because her kids disappeared. The least you can do is let Peter speak to his wife and give her the good news!"

"But—"

"And I swear to God that if you keep stonewalling me, I'll land this goddamn plane in the parking lot of your clinic and—"

"Please don't get excited!" Dubois said. "This *is* great news about the children. I'll have to check the patient—she might be asleep or under sedation. I'll call you back—that's the most I can offer."

"No, I'll call you back in…um…forty-five minutes—that'll be one forty-five your time in Geneva. So please be there!"

"Okay," Dubois agreed and placed the receiver in its cradle. He leaned back in his chair and considered what to do. The case of Martine Zucker was unique and required a unique solution. But whether this call—if it were real—would help, Dubois couldn't tell. The only thing he knew was that he had three-quarters of an hour to decide.

Dubois leaned forward and pulled up Martine Zucker's file on his computer screen. As he methodically read through the copious notes, all thoughts of steaming soup vanished from his mind.

"So, do you think he'll get Martine?" Allison asked Bruno. She had been listening to the conversation through the co-pilot's headset. "Peter's counting on it—he begged me to set it up…"

"I hope so," Bruno replied. "I tried to put the fear of God into him. But he must also see the sense of it, especially if what Peter said about him being a good man is true."

"We'll find out, I suppose, in forty-five minutes…"

Bruno had used his notebook computer to search a CD of Swiss phone numbers for the Belvoir Clinic.

"Could I check your CD for a few numbers?" Allison asked.

"Sure, go ahead," Bruno replied, sitting back and relaxing in his seat while the autopilot shot them through the upper atmosphere at 0.8 Mach.

It didn't take Allison long to locate the numbers she needed. Bruno showed her how to use the cockpit phone and smiled as he listened in. When she had finished, he looked over at her in amazement.

"I always wondered how you press guys work…"

"It ain't over 'til it's over," Allison said.

Chapter 40

▼

In the clinic in Geneva, Martine was crouched over the phone, and her golden hair obscured most of her gray face. Her slender body, clothed in the white clinic nightgown, was curved like a crescent moon, for she no longer possessed the will to sit up straight. Dubois wondered whether she still remembered what a telephone was for. He felt a great foreboding that he had made the wrong decision. But then, nothing else had worked. Why not try?

He had taken a professional risk in going ahead with the call without consulting his colleagues, but he knew what they would have said. They all would have advised him to be cautious, and the head of the clinic might even have refused...but Dubois wanted to give it a chance and had tried to prepare Martine. He had told her only a little, and doubted she would have understood much more.

Some 4,000 miles away and 50,000 feet up, with great difficulty, Peter pushed himself up on one elbow to grasp the telephone handset that Renée had pulled from its wall socket above his head. Mark and Nicolette sat on the edge of the divan—happy to be near their father. Peter had explained their mother's condition to them, in simple but accurate terms. Mark and Nicolette had obviously been forced to grow up during the six months since their kidnapping, and they took his explanation stoically.

"We'll help her get better," Mark had said, and at his side, Nicolette had nodded her agreement.

Peter felt such relief that he momentarily forgot the waves of pain racking his body. For the first time in months, he had peace of mind and hope for the future. But this couldn't quell a sadness that he didn't want to think about.

Dubois was monitoring the call and recognized Peter Zucker's voice as it came on the line. The doctor looked anxiously at Martine. She didn't budge.

Peter summoned his remaining strength and repeated her name: "Martine, my love...Martine? It's me...Peter..."

Peter looked imploringly at the other faces in the cabin for support.

In the cockpit, Bruno held his breath as he, too, listened in. The silence at the other end was sheer torture...

Peter's eyes moistened as he repeated his wife's name, this time nearly inaudibly. "Martine? This is Peter—your husband..." He took a deep, agonizing breath. "I have the children—Mark and Nicolette are here...Please say something? I beg you..."

The enduring silence was too much for Peter. His face contorted as he tried to hold back tears of grief and distress. Mark put a comforting hand on his shoulder and looked down at the floor. Nicolette started sobbing.

Dubois stepped over to take the phone away from Martine; the experiment obviously wasn't working. He would end it now to prevent her from sliding even further back into despair and desolation—

She seized his arm with a forceful grip that surprised him and thrust him away. The movement cleared her hair from her face, and Dubois saw the intensity of her concentration on the sound coming out of the phone. He stepped back and picked up the monitoring earpiece again.

"*Mammi*...it's me—Mark!" the boyish voice said matter-of-factly, as if he were calling from a friend's house where he had gone to play. He had taken the phone from his father's sagging arm. "Will you be at the airport? I've missed you a lot."

Martine's short fingernails slipped on the hard plastic of the phone as she pulled it closer to her face. "Marky...? Marky...oh, Marky..." was all she said. She looked up at Dubois. "It's Marky..." A look of wonderment was on her face.

The doctor broke the pocket clip on his pen in nervous anticipation. She had shown a sign of recognition. He smiled down at her, nodding to tell her that it was okay to keep listening.

"Marky..." Martine repeated into the mouthpiece. "Why didn't you come home? Niki didn't come home either...the naughty girl..."

"She's here as well!" Peter blurted into the handset that he had excitedly taken from his son. "Martine?" he asked again, desperate for some sort of recognition that she had heard him. "Martine? Please listen—they're coming back home...I've found them, Mark and Nicolette, and they are alive and well! Martine?"

Dubois waited with bated breath. He suddenly felt very close to this family. "Peter...you went back...Peter...I'm tired now—"

"Please don't go!" Peter pleaded, gripping the handset tighter and ignoring the pain the effort produced in his side. He paused to catch his breath. His breathing was more labored now. "Martine, my love—Martine! I'm bringing them home...I went and found them..." He winced. "The children are coming back to you...but I'm not going to make it."

Allison and Renée exchanged shocked looks.

"It's up to you now—you've got to take over," Peter persisted. "You've got to get well and look after Mark and Nicolette—they need you! Please help me—I'm not going to make it..."

Peter's voice trailed off as his head fell back on the divan. His face was awash with sweat and tears. His irregular breathing rattled in his chest. The children tried to comfort him, but they didn't know what to do. Such was Peter's pain and distress that he did not hear the last words Martine spoke into the phone. "Looking forward to seeing you again, Peter..."

Dubois watched as Martine put down the receiver and stared at the wall. She looked exhausted. He motioned to the nurses to take her back to her room.

Peter gasped and his head fell immobile to one side. Allison and Renée searched frantically for his pulse. Neither could find it. Allison put her ear to Peter's chest and listened desperately for his heart. A chill went through her. She felt for his breath—there was none...She shoved a cushion under his neck and bent his head back to straighten his windpipe and put her mouth to his to breathe for him. Renée found an oxygen canister and placed the clear plastic mask over Peter's face while Allison folded her hands and repeatedly threw her full weight down onto Peter's chest to pump his heart. After a few frantic minutes, they realized it was no use. Allison fell back against the seat on the other side of the aisle and wept.

"What's happening?" Mark shouted out in French. "What's happening to *Papi?*" The boy looked terrified as he glanced rapidly from his father to Allison and to Renée. No one replied. Mark looked around again, and saw the sadness in Renée's eyes and the distress on Allison's face. Tears welled up in his eyes and rolled down his cheeks. "He can't be dead...It's not fair!"

Nicolette stared helplessly, not understanding her brother's agonized expression. But she realized that something bad had happened to her father. "*Papi?*" she whimpered. "*Papi...*"

Renée took the children aside and tried to comfort them. They stared at their father and wept silently.

Allison made her way to the cockpit and told Bruno.

"Oh no…" was all Bruno could say. He left the plane on autopilot and followed Allison back into the cabin. After checking Peter for himself, he covered the body with a blanket and walked over to the galley, where he searched through a cupboard until he found a first-aid kit. He rifled through it and pulled out a bottle of Benadryl. He measured a small amount into two paper cups and handed them to Mark and Nicolette. "Drink this—it will help you sleep," he explained kindly.

Allison sat down with Mark and Nicolette, took each one by the hand and looked lovingly into their blank, tear-streaked young faces. "Your father was the bravest man I have ever met," she said quietly.

Their mouths twitched and their eyes pleaded for more.

"Your parents never gave up thinking about you from the time you were stolen from them at Snapdragon," Allison said, looking from one to the other. "Your mother was ill with worry—she loves you so much. You'll be seeing her again soon—very soon."

At that, Nicolette's eyes brightened and she gave a little bounce. Mark put his arm around her.

"Your father, he loved you so much that he moved heaven and earth to find you. He took you from that horrible house and got you here. You're safe now. And he's safely up in heaven looking down at you—as he will be for the rest of your lives—happy that you're being brave as well."

Mark nodded and then yawned. Despite her efforts to stay awake, Nicolette's eyes were closing. Seeing that the sedative was taking effect, Allison reclined the seats to help them sleep, and then slumped back into her own seat and watched them drift off.

Bruno sat for a while with his arm around Renée, waiting patiently until she had wept out her grief. Outwardly stoic, Bruno was shattered too. All he had done had not been enough. It was too late now for Peter—but not for Peter's children.

He got up and walked purposefully back to the cockpit.

Chapter 41

▼

Gary Long speed-dialed the press officer at Geneva International Airport. Long, the Associated Press bureau chief in Geneva, had just hung up the phone with Allison Cox and his adrenaline was surging. He had a news veteran's nose for a good story, and he smelled one here.

"Bonsoir, Bureau de Presse," answered Pierre Schneider.

"Hey Pierre, this is Gary. What arrangements have you made for tonight?"

"What are you talking about?"

"Allison Cox of the U.S. Mission phoned and said there's a Gulfstream landing this evening that we need to cover." Gary knew Allison well and respected her as a reliable source. She had promised him a "good story" if he came out to the airport, but she had remained cryptic on the details.

"Oh really?" Schneider said, clearly annoyed that he was learning this from a journalist and not from Allison herself. *Those U.S. Mission people think the world stops for them...*"What time is it supposed to land?"

"Nine-thirty."

"Did *she* give you any other details?" Schneider asked sarcastically.

"No. Just that it would be worth my while and to spread the word—it sounds as if this is the first you've heard about it."

"It is—"

"Well, you'd better start making arrangements, because most of the Geneva press corps is going to be out there soon!"

Schneider glanced at his watch. It was already ten past eight, and camera crews would soon be arriving for the lengthy security checks. He scoured the big plasma screen on the wall showing the remaining arrivals and departures that evening. *Satellite 40 looks the easiest…*

"Come out to Satellite 40 at nine—we'll have everything set up there." Schneider sighed. His wife was going to kill him—it was their anniversary.

"Thanks." Long hung up and immediately dialed the press center's loud-speaker. He heard his own voice bellowing through the halls and back to him through the wall speaker in his office: "Satellite 40 at nine, Sat 40 at nine for the landing."

Schneider also wasted no time. He called routing and told them to close Satellite 40 to passenger traffic and reroute the remaining flights that evening to other gates. He then dialed security to tell them to isolate the satellite for a press event. It was easy to do since the round, glassed-in cluster of departure gates was separate from the main terminal and only accessible by means of a single underground walkway. Lastly, he called his wife and gave her the news…

Maria Romero—the Geneva correspondent for *El Crónico* who had written the original *baby-parts* story and had tried to match wits with Allison Cox—found that her plans for the evening had been ruined as well. She'd locked her office and was on her way out to her car when she'd received a call on her cell phone from Allison. Maria, assuming that Allison no longer worked in Geneva, was taken aback by her call from the plane. "Be at the airport tonight—there'll be a couple of great stories about Peru for *El Crónico*," Allison had told her. Maria wasn't interested until she found out that every other journalist from the press center was planning to cover the plane's arrival.

Serge Kaufmann was the third person to get a call from Allison. He was the chief Geneva correspondent of the Swiss news agency, *ATS*, and a trusted friend of Allison's. She let him in on the secret of what would be happening at the airport, and Serge agreed to tell the Swiss TV correspondents that it would be worth their while to cover the arrival.

Half an hour before the plane's scheduled landing, Satellite 40 was full of reporters. An expectant buzz filled the air as they milled about carrying notepads, tape recorders, and cameras, trying to find out from each other what was going on. It was exactly as Allison had hoped.

Outside, at the edge of the runway, two yellow airport fire engines were waiting, their foam cannons at the ready. They had heard from air traffic control that the Gulfstream might be landing without a nose-wheel. An airport ambulance was also standing nearby.

The stark neon lighting inside the building made it hard for the journalists to see what was happening out in the dark. For security reasons, they would not be permitted to venture out onto the tarmac until a few minutes before the plane's arrival. Few would have wanted to go out anyway, given the icy wind off the Jura Mountains that was slicing across the runway.

So no one except the two airport security officers standing guard outside the satellite noticed the white minivan with the Belvoir Clinic markings quietly drive up and stop nearby. A third officer accompanied the vehicle, showing that it had permission to be there.

Everyone inside and outside the satellite waited in anticipation.

At nine forty-two, the air traffic control tower gave Bruno permission to land. At the same moment, emergency services received the get-ready signal. And Schneider appeared in the satellite to announce to the throng of reporters, "It's going to land in two minutes."

The glass doors opened, and reporters rushed out onto the concrete taxiing area. They searched the sky for the plane. "There it is!" one hollered, pointing to colored specks of blinking light far in the distance.

Every reporter's eyes locked onto the lights as they approached. Puffs of warm breath proved how cold it was on this February evening. The TV crews wiped their camera lenses with demisting cloths before focusing on the Gulfstream as it came into view above the end of the runway. The cameras were rolling as the plane made what seemed to be an almost perfect touchdown. They followed the flashing metal bird as it decelerated, its nose still in the air. In the darkness, they couldn't see that the nose gear wasn't down.

Bruno had tried to deploy the gear, but the hydraulic system had failed; he had no choice but to land on the main undercarriage wheels and try to keep the plane's nose from coming violently down. But he knew that before the plane came to a halt, the nose would hit the runway. And it would be frightening, especially from where he sat. The cockpit would be only feet above the high-speed abrading of the shiny aluminum fuselage by the concrete runway. For that reason, he had banished Renée and Allison from the cockpit and insisted they sit in the relative safety of the passenger cabin.

As the nose finally dipped and struck, a stream of fiery sparks cascaded through the darkness.

"Shit, this is awesome," the Swiss TV cameraman murmured in wonderment.

It was not a pretty picture for Bruno. He had lost directional control of the plane, and amid the screeching that pierced his eardrums, he had to focus on bringing the plane to a halt before it slued madly out of control and caught fire.

The tearing of metal against concrete seemed to last forever, but finally Bruno felt his seat-harness dig deeply into his shoulders as the reverse-thrust took effect and the Gulfstream ground to an ungainly stop in the grass at the side of the runway.

Jets of foam from the fire engine cannons blasted the cockpit and obscured Bruno's view. He exhaled deeply, finally able to let exhaustion engulf him. Before getting up, he patted the controls. *Thank you for bringing us back safely.*

The Gulfstream sat with its nose crimped flat on the ground and its T-tail high in the air. Its two days of valiant service had come to an ignoble but honorable end.

Serge Kaufmann immediately filed a report over his cell phone to the *ATS* desk, and the Swiss TV cameraman called his producer to recommend that the live feed break into the ten o'clock news.

The first story Allison had told Serge to watch for, *Swiss rescue flight lands in Geneva without nose-wheel,* had come through as promised. Now, he waited eagerly for the next one.

As soon as Bruno cut the engines, Allison, Renée, and the children evacuated the plane, but remained nearby with blankets over their shoulders. Allison gazed around at the terminal lights and savored the fresh, icy cold mountain air again.

The Belvoir Clinic minivan pulled up next to them. Allison introduced herself to Dr. Dubois and started to explain the situation to him. But a violent banging from inside the minivan interrupted her—it was Martine trying to get out! Dubois signaled *OK* to the male nurse, and, as soon as the door was unlocked, Martine bolted out. She had spied the children and ran to them, clutching them both in an embrace that Mark and Nicolette would remember forever. She wept tears of joy while Mark and Nicolette shouted *"Mammi! Mammi! Mammi!"*

"We'd better get them away from here," Allison suggested to Dubois. "The press is out there…"

She quickly briefed the doctor on Peter's fate and left it to him as to when and how to break the news to Martine.

Bruno stepped over. "Renée and I can make arrangements to have the body taken to a funeral home," he offered.

"Thank you so much, Bruno—for everything." She hugged him briefly, then turned her gaze toward the platform. "And now, I've got to get to work."

Allison quickly covered the fifty yards to the assembled reporters, took a deep breath, and stepped boldly up to the microphone that was set up on a stand in front of a crowd-control barrier. She felt stale and slightly ill, and assumed she looked deathly pale in the harsh light of the TV cameras. But she had to succeed with this press conference. She smiled confidently and stepped into her professional role.

"Hi, everybody!" she said as cheerfully as she could. "Thanks for coming out here this evening—I see you're all better dressed for this climate than I am!" She pulled the blanket tighter around her shoulders.

"What's happening out there, Allison?" one reporter asked.

"It's a bit complicated, so let me first tell you what I have to say, and then I'll take questions. You probably all recall that the U.S. government was recently shocked and deeply hurt by a series of fallacious articles that appeared in the Peruvian press, notably *El Crónico*, on 'baby-parts.' We have repeatedly denied the allegations that America is purchasing—or has ever purchased—organs, members, or other parts of Latin American babies or children for use in transplants. Because these stories *didn't* go away, my government sent me to Peru to look into them. And as a result of my investigations, I can announce to you here tonight my findings that the articles are completely baseless and untrue—"

"What proof do you have?" Maria Romero shouted with disdain.

"I have irrefutable proof that these stories are a complete fabrication," Allison shot back. "Their sole purpose was to discredit the United States people and government..."

Allison glanced down and saw with satisfaction that a reporter was scribbling the key words "irrefutable proof" and "complete fabrication." Others were doing the same, and she then knew that her message would be picked up in all the stories written that night.

"Why did they do it—write the articles, I mean?" another voice asked.

"Thank you—a good question," Allison said graciously. "I was coming to that. The articles were written to divert attention away from a lucrative child-trafficking ring that was operating in Peru. The United States was helping Peru look into this, a matter of special concern because the ring was suspected of being behind some cases of missing American children. I can only assume that the traffickers thought attack was the best form of defense, and that launching a campaign accusing the United States of involvement in something even more horrendous—baby-parts—would draw attention away from their ring. Well, let me tell you, it hasn't worked."

"Where's all this proof then?" Maria sneered. "You can't expect us to simply take your word for it!"

"I have proof—I have documented proof that I will be submitting to my government. It contains sensitive information that, unfortunately, I cannot share with you until my government has examined it. But I have it—"

"I don't believe her!" Maria snapped.

This gave Allison the opening she needed.

"I also have *physical* proof in the form of two Swiss children who were kidnapped in the United States last summer by the ring, and whom we rescued and brought back on the plane this evening." Allison's voice was firm. "They just got off the plane and were reunited with their mother—some of you probably saw them at the foot of the plane a few minutes ago, and those of you with cameras and zoom lenses, I'm sure, captured the event…"

From what Allison could judge through the blaze of lights and from the mounting murmuring, the reporters were excited by what she was giving them.

Serge Kaufmann's powerful baritone voice suddenly rose above the throng. "Let me get this straight, please, Allison. You're saying that you rescued two Swiss children who were kidnapped and held for six months…in other words, that the U.S. government went into Peru and plucked them out?"

"Yes and no, Serge," Allison replied. "Yes, we rescued two children who had been kidnapped. No, the United States did not undertake a…let's say, 'commando-type raid' into Peru to rescue these children. Peru is a sovereign state and a friend of the United States, and we wouldn't interfere in that way in a country's internal affairs. We'd use diplomatic means first—as we have been doing to inform Peru of child-trafficking activities on its soil. These activities were organized by criminal rings that Peru has been attempting to clamp down on. And it's one of these criminal organizations that was obviously feeling the heat and thought up the *baby-parts* media attack against the United States as a smokescreen…"

The reporters seemed transfixed by Allison's words. She continued without missing a beat.

"…I found out when I was in Peru that the owner of *El Crónico*, a certain Luis Chavez, was behind the *baby-parts* stories. He was also involved in the trafficking of children. He was the one who organized the kidnapping of Mark and Nicolette Zucker, who, as I've just said, were reunited with their mother a moment ago. And that's how I became involved in helping rescue the children."

"So, you did go into Peru in order to pull out the children?"

"No, that was *not* the reason I went to Peru. While I was there to talk to *El Crónico*, by chance I met up with the children's father, Peter Zucker, who had taken it upon himself to find his children when official searches proved fruitless. We soon realized that the same person was behind both activities—that is, the *baby-parts* issue and his kids' abduction."

"Can we speak to Zucker—the father?" another reporter asked.

Allison hesitated before answering. Thinking she was hedging, the crowd of reporters began muttering. With a tightness in her throat, she then said, "I'm afraid Peter Zucker can't speak to you because, in rescuing his children, he lost his life—he was shot while freeing them from a Chavez-controlled house and died in the plane on the way home."

A hush fell over the crowd.

Allison's voice became more solemn: "Peter Zucker was a courageous man who deeply loved his family and would not accept that his children had disappeared forever. He set himself the goal of tracking them down and went to enormous lengths to find them—eventually making the ultimate sacrifice to save them from a truly horrible fate. Personally, and as an employee of the U.S. government and the American people, I was honored to know Peter, and am happy to have been able to provide him with the little bit of help that I did. It's a tragedy that it cost him his life, but all along, he was prepared to make that sacrifice to get his children back. He's a real hero of our time."

To Allison's relief, the lights suddenly left her. Attention had moved to the plane. She turned around and saw Peter's body, covered by a sheet, being wheeled on a gurney to a waiting airport ambulance. When the ambulance had driven off, the camera lights turned back to Allison.

Now was the moment, she thought, to help Bruno. Allison knew he believed he would lose his job for having made the detour to Peru, not to mention for having damaged his employer's prize plane. She hoped Bruno's boss would be watching the live television coverage and would see the value of the free international publicity she was about to give him.

"I want to thank Geneva Business Jets for generously diverting one of its planes to transport us out of Peru, and especially its pilot, Bruno Hottinger, without whose skill we would not be standing here tonight. He's a great pilot, as you saw by the way he landed here tonight."

Again, nobody said anything, and a short silence followed. Allison prayed it was a signal that the press conference was over. But Maria Romero was not giving up.

"Did the Peruvian authorities help you with the rescue of the children?" she asked.

Allison had anticipated this question and had prepared an answer.

"Yes," Allison lied. "There's no way we could have left Peru without the authorities' approval. Of course I can't go into the operational details." While not truthful, this answer was politically expedient. The Peruvians, if they had known what was going on, probably would have helped, and this left the door open for their help in the future.

"So, the Peruvian government had nothing to do with the actual kidnapping or the *baby-parts* lies?" Gary Long asked.

"No, none whatsoever," Allison said confidently. "It is the criminal organization led by Luis Chavez, who is also the owner of *El Crónico*, that is the guilty party and bears all the blame."

Allison suddenly felt totally exhausted.

"I'm feeling tired and cold, brr..." Allison wrapped her arms around herself for warmth. "So thank you for coming out here—"

"One last quick one?" Serge asked.

"Sure, but it has to be the last..."

"Is what you've been telling us exclusive or have you already given this information to the U.S. media—by phone from the plane, for example?" This was a sore point with Geneva-based journalists; often, they were second in line to receive information—behind their colleagues in New York and Washington.

"No Serge, it's all yours—for once, I've given you an exclusive story here in Geneva. So, you'd better get going and file it," she added with a weary smile.

As Allison stepped down, Schneider handed her his cell phone. "It's a Mr. John Vandervelt for you." Suddenly, Allison no longer felt cold and weary.

The veins in Ambassador Helm's temples looked as if they would burst. The staff at the ambassador's official residence had never seen him so angry—or coarse—before. "The little bitch!" he roared as he sat looking at the television screen. "How dare she! I'm the only one allowed to represent U.S. interests in Geneva!"

Not only was Allison stealing what he considered *his* limelight in the *baby-parts* affair—after all, it was *his* prerogative to make the kind of announcement *she* was making—it was also clear to him now why so few reporters had turned up to hear his greatly touted policy speech on human rights that evening at the UN. They were all out at the airport! And he had planned to talk about *baby-parts* in his speech as well.

"Shit—shit—shit!"

Allison had upstaged him. It was a tremendous blow to his pride, and the erosion of his public image would last for the rest of his tenure as U.S. ambassador to the United Nations in Geneva.

Allison's timing had been coincidental, or nearly so. When she had originally called Gary Long from the Gulfstream to set up the airport press conference, Allison had asked him, "Is there any other news event that could conflict with our arrival?"

"No, nothing major—except, of course, your ambassador's speech at the Palais this evening on human rights. His staff has really been twisting our arms to cover it."

"Oh, really...?" Allison was remembering the way Helm had last treated her. "Don't worry about that. Trust me, Gary, you'll get a real news story out of what I'm going to say—an exclusive that nothing else'll beat!"

"If you say so, Allison."

Epilogue

▼

Peter Zucker was buried in the small cemetery of Trélex, half a mile from his house. The cemetery was situated at the edge of the village and had an unobstructed view of Lake Geneva and the white Mont Blanc peak beyond. He was laid to rest there instead of in his hometown of Zug, in northern Switzerland, so that he would remain close to his wife and children.

As Martine watched the coffin being lowered into the earth in this idyllic setting, she thought she heard Peter's voice again: *"…it's up to you now—you've got to take over…"* She looked to see if anyone else standing around the newly dug grave had heard it. But no, it was for her ears alone. Peter's voice had cut through to her very soul and broken up the clouds that had fogged her mind for so long, so that now, she saw the world in a bright, new light. The shroud that had enveloped her for the last half-year had suddenly lifted.

From that point on, her recovery was steady. Martine moved back into her house shortly afterward. She needed around-the-clock supervision at first, which, along with a professional nurse, Bruno and Renée were happy to provide. Witnessing Martine's steady progress made Peter's sacrifice seem worthwhile. It was what Peter had sought for so long.

A month later, Allison and her sons moved back to Washington, where she learned that as a result of her findings, Luis Chavez's business assets in the United States had been frozen, and that if he set foot in the country, he would be arrested. What Allison didn't know was that Don Gonzalo, guilt-ridden for his part in the whole sordid business, had, while seated at his desk in his now grimly vacant house, put a bullet through his brain.

The Peruvian government was quick to publicly state its abhorrence of child-trafficking activities on its soil and vowed to root out the criminal organizations involved. It also took it upon itself to discreetly hush up the shootouts surrounding the children's rescue and their escape from the Pan-American Highway. All leaks were explained away as a settling of scores between rival drug-running gangs.

Romy read about the children's safe return to Switzerland in an old copy of the *International Herald Tribune* that she found in the private English school in Ecuador where she worked. It was a relief to know that they were safe and well, but the news brought with it a pang of longing.

As the Swiss winter turned into spring and the gray clouds parted to reveal the clear blue sky over Lake Geneva, people came out of their apartments and houses into the sun's warmth to walk with their children by the side of the lake.

The cloud that had hung over the Route du Soleil in Trélex since the children's disappearance began to lift as well. Mark and Nicolette went back to the village school and found their friends, who knew not to ask where they had been. The swing-set in the garden that had stood lonely and unused for so long began to squeak again as its rusty pins complained at the movement. Incredibly, the children bounced back into their former life, playing the same games with their friends as before that fateful vacation—except for one. They drew back at the mention of hide-and-seek, a thing that puzzled their playmates.

For both Mark and Nicolette, the recollection that remained most vivid in their minds was of the last time they had played that game, at Snapdragon's outdoor café. They had run into a clump of bushes to hide and play a trick on *Papi* and *Mammi* who were away getting food. But that day, they themselves had been surprised by a frightening man with a moustache who had sprayed their innocent, shocked little faces with a horrible smelling aerosol.

THE END

About The Author

Robin Newmann's international experience and heritage inspire his writing. Born in England to a Belgian mother and British father, Robin often traveled during his childhood to other European countries to visit family and friends. His wanderlust and ability to speak several languages led him to a career in journalism in the international cities of Brussels and Geneva, and later to a position as spokesman for an international organization.

Robin's work brought him into contact with people of diverse cultures and took him to many places around the world. During long plane rides, he was always relieved to have a fast-paced novel to pass the time, and he decided to draw on his experiences to write such books himself. *Kidnapped Hope* is his first novel.

Robin met his wife, an American journalist, in Geneva. They have two children who spent their formative years in Switzerland. Robin and his family now live in a town on the California coast near San Francisco.

978-0-595-39277
0-595-39277-6

Printed in the United States
60791LVS00003B/154-207